COWBOY Trouble

JOANNE KENNEDY

Cover design by Randee Ladden
Cover images © ImageSource/Getty Images; Karl Weatherly/Corbis; RiverNorthPhotography/iStockphoto.com

Published by Sourcebooks Casablanca, an imprint of Sourcebooks, Inc.
P.O. Box 4410, Naperville, Illinois 60567-4410
(630) 961-3900
FAX: (630) 961-2168
www.sourcebooks.com

Printed in Canada.
WC 10 9 8 7 6 5 4 3 2

To my parents,
Don and Betty Smyth.
It wasn't always easy to be my parents,
but it's always been a blessing to be your daughter.
I was born lucky.

Chapter 1

A CHICKEN WILL NEVER BREAK YOUR HEART.

Not that you can't love a chicken. There are some people in this world who can love just about anything.

But a chicken will never love you back. When you look deep into their beady little eyes, there's not a lot of warmth there—just an avarice for worms and bugs and, if it's a rooster, a lot of suppressed anger and sexual frustration. They don't return your affection in any way.

Expectations, relationship-wise, are right at rock bottom.

That's why Libby Brown decided to start a chicken farm. She wanted some company, and she wanted a farm, but she didn't want to go getting attached to things like she had in the past.

She'd been obsessed with farms since she was a kid. It all started with her Fisher Price Farmer Joe Play Set: a plastic barn, some toy animals, and a pair of round-headed baby dolls clutching pitchforks like some simple-minded version of American Gothic.

A Fisher Price life was the life for her.

Take Atlanta—just give her that countryside.

Libby had her pickup half unloaded when her new neighbor showed up. She didn't see him coming, so he got a prime view of her posterior as she bent over

the tailgate, wrestling with the last of her chrome dinette chairs. The chair was entangled in the electric cord from the toaster, so he got a prime introduction to her vocabulary too.

"Howdy," he said.

Howdy? She turned to face him and stifled a snort.

Halloween was three months away, but this guy was ready with his cowboy costume. Surely no one actually wore chaps in real life, even in Wyoming. His boots looked like the real thing, though; they were worn and dirty as if they'd kicked around God-knows-what in the old corral, and his gray felt Stetson was all dented, like a horse had stepped on it. A square, stubbled chin gave his face a masculine cast, but there was something soft about his mouth that added a hint of vulnerability.

She hopped down from the tailgate. From her perch on the truck, he'd looked like the Marlboro Man on a rough day, but now that they were on the same level, she could see he was kind of cute—like a young Clint Eastwood with a little touch of Elvis.

"Howdy," he said again. He actually tipped his hat and she almost laughed for the first time in a month.

"I'm Luke Rawlins, from down the road," he continued. The man obviously had no idea how absurd he looked, decked out like a slightly used version of Hopalong Cassidy. "Thought maybe you'd need some help moving in. And I brought you a casserole—Chicken Artichoke Supreme. It's my specialty." He held out a massive ceramic dish with the pride of a caveman returning from the hunt. "Or maybe you could use a hand getting that chair broke to ride."

Great. She had the bastard son of John Wayne and

Martha Stewart for a neighbor. And he thought he was funny.

Worse yet, he thought she was funny.

"Thanks." She took the casserole. "I'm Libby Brown. Are you from that farm with the big barn?"

"Farm? I'm not from any farm." Narrowing his eyes, he slouched against the truck and folded his arms. "You're not from around here, are you?"

"What makes you say that?"

"You calling my ranch a farm, that's what." A blade of wheatgrass bobbed from one corner of his mouth as he looked her up and down with masculine arrogance. "There's no such thing as a farm in Wyoming," he said.

"Well, what do you call this, then?" Libby gestured toward the sun-baked outbuildings that tilted drunkenly around her own personal patch of prairie.

"A ranch."

"That's not what I call it. I call it 'Lackaduck Farm.'" She pointed to the faded letters arched over the barn's wide double doors. "That's what the people before me called it too. It's even painted on the barn."

"Yeah, well, they weren't from around here either. They were New Yorkers and got smacked on the bottom and sent home by Mother Nature. Thought they'd retire out here on some cheap real estate and be gentleman farmers. They didn't realize there's a reason the real estate's cheap. It's tough living." He looked her in the eye, no doubt judging her unfit for a life only real men could endure. "You think you're up to it?"

"As a matter of fact, I am." Libby hoped she sounded

a lot more confident than she felt. "This is what I've always wanted, and I'm going to make it work."

She didn't mention the fact that she had to make it work. She didn't have anything else. No career—not even much of a job. And no boyfriend. Not even a dog.

The dog died in September, right before the boyfriend ran off. Lucky couldn't help it, but Bill Cooperman could have stuck around if he'd only tried. He just had a wandering eye, and it finally wandered off for good with a hotshot editor from the *Atlanta Journal-Constitution*. The hotshot editor was also Libby's boss, so she basically lost everything in the space of about six weeks. All she had left was a broken heart, a cherry red pickup, and the contents of her desk in a battered cardboard box.

Since her professional and romantic aspirations were a bust, she'd sold her one-bedroom condo in downtown Atlanta and literally bought the farm. She was now the proud owner of thirty-five acres of sagebrush and a quaint clapboard farmhouse in Lackaduck, Wyoming. At the moment, tumbleweeds were her primary crop and grasshoppers her only livestock, but the place was as far from Atlanta as she could get, and she figured a fresh coat of paint and a flock of free-range chickens would make it her dream home—one utterly unlike the one she'd left behind. So far, Wyoming was like another planet, and that was fine with her.

"I'm definitely going to make this work," she repeated, as much to herself as to her new neighbor.

The cowboy reached over the truck's battered tailgate for the dinette chair, which freed itself from the toaster cord the minute he touched it.

"Guess you'll be glad to get some help then."

He swung the chair over his shoulder and headed for the house.

Libby sighed. She had her pride, but she wasn't about to turn her bad back on an able-bodied man who was willing to tote furniture for her. Beggars can't be choosers, and Luke Rawlins wasn't really such a bad choice, anyway. She wasn't in the market for his brand of talent, but it sure was fun to watch him move furniture. Those chaps, with their swaying leather fringe, must have been designed by the early cowboys to highlight a man's best assets.

Luke set the chair in the kitchen, then traipsed back out and scanned the contents of the truck bed. He'd been worried when they sold the Lackaduck place, but the new neighbor seemed all right. More than all right. When he'd first seen her, tussling with her furniture in the back of the pickup, he'd thought love might have finally come to Lackaduck. Then he'd realized all he could see was her backside and decided it was probably just lust.

Besides, her sofa was definitely a deal breaker.

It was enormous. And hideous. Once they wrestled the dang thing inside, it dominated the homestead's tiny front room like some evil crouching monster. Carved cherubs on each corner lofted a complicated scrollwork banner in their pudgy fists. They were probably supposed to be cute, but Luke thought they looked like evil leering babies, preparing to strangle unsuspecting sofa sitters with their long wooden ribbon. He made a silent vow to stay as far away from that piece of furniture as he could.

"Careful," Libby said as they swung it into place. "It's an antique."

"Antique?" He did his best not to sound judgmental.

She tipped her lightly freckled nose in the air and flashed him a hard look. "French Victorian Baroque Provincial," she said. "That's what the dealer said."

French, he could believe. And Victorian, and all that. But mostly, the thing was plain ugly. It seemed like a city girl should have better taste—especially one who was obviously educated. There were at least fourteen boxes of books in the bed of the truck. It took him a good twenty minutes to haul them all into the house and stack them in the front hall.

"You a schoolmarm, or what?" He set down the last box and parked his Stetson on the newel post.

"I'm a journalist. I have to read a lot." She picked up his hat and tipped it onto her head for a half-second, then whipped it off and plopped it back on the banister.

"A journalist? Well, good luck finding a job around here," Luke said. "We've only got one newspaper, and it's barely surviving, because there isn't any news at all." He picked up the hat and set it back on her head, adjusting it to a rakish angle. "Don't take that off," he said. "It suits you."

"No thanks." She took it off and shook her springy brown curls back into freeform disarray, and he had to agree the wild, untamed look suited her way better than the hat.

"So I guess my new job will be a challenge," she said.

Oops. He'd stepped in it, as usual. Said precisely the wrong thing. "You're going to work for the *Lackaduck Holler*?"

"That's the plan."

He couldn't think of any response to that. *The Holler* was the most pathetic excuse for a newspaper he'd ever seen. The most exciting headline of the past six months had been the one about Chet Hostetler's freak heifer. That one had made the wire services—popped up in papers coast to coast, and all over the Internet. It was pretty sad when your hometown's only claim to fame was a two-headed cow.

But Libby didn't need to know that. Judging from that sofa, she was accustomed to something a little more cosmopolitan than Lackaduck had to offer. Once she figured out that one day in Lackaduck was pretty much like the next, she'd probably move on, and that was a shame. Interesting women were in short supply in this town.

It was time to turn on the charm. He gave her a grin that had melted the hearts of half a dozen rodeo queens, then turned and scanned the tiny hallway, stacked high with book boxes. "Well, I bet you're a real smart lady."

She shot him a scowl. "You know, I can tell you're not John Wayne. When you're not thinking about it, you drop that hayseed accent and talk almost like a normal human being."

Yikes. Most women fell all over him when he channeled the Duke, but this one was a mite on the prickly side.

"Yeah, well." He slumped back against the post. "Most of the women I meet from back East are pretty hot for the cowboy type."

"Not me," she said. "No cowboys for me. No boys of any kind at the moment. I'm on my own and staying that way. Got it?"

"Got it." Luke straightened up and gave her a pitying look. "So are you gay or heartbroke?"

She looked up at him, her brown eyes taking on a teary sheen, and for one terrifying moment he thought she was going to cry. He glanced over at the door, planning an escape route, but she just blinked a couple times, then stiffened her back and straightened her shoulders. Somehow, that was even harder to take than tears.

"None of your business," she said. A lock of that crazy hair flopped over her forehead and dangled over one eye. He reached over and flipped it into place.

"Sorry," he said. "Forget I asked." Her hair was surprisingly soft, with none of that sticky spray stuff all the local girls used. Of course, the locals knew about the Wyoming wind. Those thirty-mile-an-hour gusts would tangle Libby's hair in a hurry. She'd end up looking like she'd just gotten out of bed.

His bed.

Now where had *that* come from? He brushed her hair back again, savoring its softness, surprised when she didn't swat him away. Maybe he hadn't blown it yet. Maybe she liked him.

"Sorry. It's just that you're awful pretty to be out here on your own," he said. "It doesn't seem right." He spun one corkscrew curl 'round his finger, then let it spring back into place. "What are you running away from?"

Libby could feel her face flushing at Luke's touch—and her backbone stiffening against temptation. Despite a tragic case of hat-hair, something in his green eyes was

turning her insides to warm, wobbly Jell-O, and she had to rein in a sudden urge to spill her whole life story.

"Nothing," she said. "I'm not running away. I'm running toward."

"Toward what?"

"This, I guess."

He glanced around the shabby hallway. "This?"

Libby followed his gaze and winced. The house had obviously stood empty for months. Cobwebs spanned every corner, and it needed a good coat of paint and a lot of scrubbing. It hardly looked like anybody's dream home, but it was hers.

All hers.

"Yeah, this." She squared her shoulders. "I might have to fix it up a little, but it's what I've always wanted. And anyway, even if I was running away—and I'm not—but if I was, at least I'm moving. Getting somewhere." She set her hands on her hips. "How long have you been at that ranch of yours?"

"All my life," Luke said. "I got lucky. I was born right where I belonged."

He was lounging against the newel post, his pose casual and relaxed, the ridiculous cowboy duds looking perfectly natural on his angular frame. The thighs and inseams of his jeans were worn almost white from riding, and his eyes were framed by faint crow's feet, etched by the Wyoming sun. He was right, Libby thought. He belonged here. He was a cowboy, pure and simple.

She hadn't had any idea such a thing still existed. It was like moving to Austria and finding your neighbors decked out in lederhosen.

"You are lucky," she admitted. "Sometimes I'm not sure where I belong. Maybe I have to build a place myself. Start from scratch." Hoisting a box in her arms, she struggled to set it on top of the stack he'd started against the wall.

"Whoa there," he said. Libby had a feeling that corny cowboy line had tamed more women than horses, but she was relieved when he leaned over and helped her slide the box into place.

"So are you going to live out here all by yourself?" he asked. "No boyfriend? No dog?"

She looked up, startled by the realization the guy was a total stranger. For all she knew, he was the latest heir to Ted Bundy. She looked down at his hands, square and strong and calloused from work, and imagined them clenched into fists. Then she studied his face, searching his eyes for some sign of sociopathic mania, but it was tough to get past that smile and come to any rational conclusion.

"I've got a dog," she lied. "I just didn't bring him yet."

"Well, good. I hope he's a big one for protection."

"Oh, yeah, he's a big one, all right." She searched her mind for a really good name—one that would discourage even the most depraved serial killer. "Nobody messes with Ivan."

"The Terrible?"

She nodded. "Right."

"Well, I guess you'll be okay then." He tipped the hat back on and started toward the door, then turned. "Be careful, though. A gal went missing from around here a while back."

She thought of Ted Bundy again and her stomach flipped over. "What do you mean, she went missing?"

"She disappeared." Luke's easy smile was gone. "They think she might have been abducted—maybe even murdered, but they never figured out what happened."

Libby sat down on a box of books and tried to ignore the *Jaws* music thudding through her subconscious. "They never found her?"

"Nope. The sheriff just about lost his mind over it. Now it seems like he's given up." He slapped a streak of dirt off his jeans. "It's been almost three years."

"So somewhere in this town is a kidnapper, or a murderer. It could be anybody." She shook her head. "And you say there isn't any news. Good thing you're not a journalist."

"Well, it was a long time ago. And it was probably a transient, or a tourist. Somebody passing through."

"Wow." She traced a line across the dusty hardwood floor with the toe of her sneaker. "I'll bet I could figure it out."

"You?" He looked doubtfully at her torn jeans and ratty sweatshirt, and she realized she wasn't exactly dressed like a superhero.

"Yeah, me." She sat up a little straighter. "I covered crime stories for the *Atlanta Journal-Constitution*. My boyfriend—ex-boyfriend, I mean—was a police detective." She cleared her throat. Despite Bill's betrayal, her voice still went all husky every time she tried to talk about him. "He was a jerk too, but he was good at his job, and he taught me a lot. I don't mean to brag, but I'll bet I know more about tracking down killers than your average small-town sheriff."

Luke shrugged. "Our sheriff doesn't know much about anything. He's kind of a good ol' boy."

Libby pictured a Boss Hogg type, narrow in the mind and big in the belly. "Guess this place really is perfect, then." She stood and tore the tape off one of the boxes. It was full of reference books: *Games Criminals Play*, *Why They Kill*, *Crime Scene Investigation*. "*The Holler* hired me to write features and local political stuff, but what I really like to do is crime stories." She waved a forensic textbook in the air. "Maybe this case just needs some city smarts."

Luke reached into the box and pulled out a copy of *Profiling Today*. "Looks like you know what you're talking about," he said, flipping through the pages. "Maybe you could find Della."

"Was that her name?"

He nodded. "I could give you some background if you want. We could get together sometime."

The *Jaws* music was starting up in Libby's head again. Either this guy really was a Bundy brother, or he was dangerous in some other way. She looked at the laugh lines around his eyes and the dimple that flashed when he smiled and decided he probably wasn't a Bundy.

"I'd like to hear more about it," she said. She wasn't about to bounce into a rebound relationship, no matter how fetching that dimple was, but she wanted to know more. Besides, she thought she might enjoy another look at the fine Wyoming scenery—as presented by Wrangler.

Luke brushed the dust off his hands. "Tomorrow?"

"Sure. I'll be home all day." Libby gestured vaguely toward the boxes stacked in the hallway, then waved toward the dilapidated outbuildings. "I've got plenty to do."

"Great." He adjusted the brim of his hat and glanced back at her from the doorway. "Make sure you let that dog of yours know I'm coming, though. Wouldn't want to cross old Ivan."

Chapter 2

WHEN HE PULLED UP THE NEXT DAY IN HIS BATTERED old Mazda, Luke barely caught a glimpse of Libby before she ducked into her chicken house.

She was probably trying to hide. Pockmarked with rust and hail damage, his car looked like a junkyard reject. She probably thought the Clampetts had come to call.

He shut down the engine, then struggled to extricate his long legs from under the car's steering wheel. When he finally turned his attention to Libby, stifling his laugh was like trying to swallow a toad.

Despite the hot summer weather, she wore baggy overalls under a long-sleeved shirt, with gloves on her hands and a bandanna tied across her face as if she was on her way to hold up the First National. Her hair was tucked up under a *Charlie's Angels* baseball cap and safety glasses protected her eyes. The whole ensemble was dusted with a light coating of fiberglass, asbestos, and fossilized chicken poop.

"What the heck are you doing?" he asked.

"Cleaning out the chicken coop." She took off the hat and shook her hair loose, then yanked the bandanna away from her nose and mouth and gestured toward the ramshackle shed behind her. The building—if you could call it that—obviously hadn't seen a chicken in decades. The boards were warped, with rusty nails

protruding in all directions, and the ceiling had fallen in, letting old insulation blanket the floorboards like a deep spring snowfall.

"I think the insulation has asbestos in it," she said. "So I figured I'd better cover up."

She shrugged off the shirt and flailed her arms in a futile effort to brush the dust from her overalls. With all that guano and an assortment of feathers sticking to her outfit, she looked like an enormous incontinent chicken preparing for takeoff. Luke stifled a grin.

"What did you think I was doing?" she asked. "Getting ready for the fancy dress ball?" She struck a pose, one hand on her hip, the other behind her head. "I can go as a hazmat worker."

"Well, okay," he said. He was pretty sure she was joking, but he wasn't taking any chances. He knew better than to question what a woman chose to wear. "I'm glad you're ready to go," he said. "I thought I'd take you out on the town."

"I'm kidding." Libby slapped at the dirt on her overalls and one strap slid off her shoulder, revealing a barely-there tank top silkscreened with the legend "NSFW: Not Suitable for Work." Luke felt a slow smile spreading across his face.

"Besides," she said, "I've got too much to do."

"Come on, Cinderella, give it a break." He reached out and flipped the strap back into place, then stepped back, squelching the zing of pleasure that zipped through his fingers at the heat of her bare skin. "You won't even have to clean up much. I was just going to take you to the Roundup."

"The Roundup?"

"The Roundup Bar. It's out on Hat Trick Road, just past the grain elevator. It's got a good jukebox, fine brews on tap—even shuffleboard."

"Shuffleboard?"

"Well, I wasn't sure the jukebox would be enough to lure you away from Lackaduck Farm," he said. "I didn't know what might work for you. You're not like the other girls." He smiled. "You get excited about farming."

"But not shuffleboard."

"Well, let's go in and you can clean up to go." He started toward the house, then paused. "Or should I stay out here? Is Ivan in there?"

"Ivan?" Libby gave him a blank look, as if she'd completely forgotten she had a dog. "Oh, Ivan," she finally said. "My dog. Right. He's… um… you're right, you'd better stay out here."

"Okay. Hurry up, though. It's Two-for-One Happy Hour."

"What should I wear?"

Luke assessed her ensemble from top to bottom, grinning. "Well, you should definitely stick with that top," he said.

He watched a faint flush rise from underneath the overalls, coloring her chest and cheeks. Nice. He'd have to embarrass her more often.

"Just tidy up a little," he advised. "It's hardly a formal place, but you'll scare them walking in like that. And besides, you're shedding." He reached out and brushed an ancient downy feather from her arm.

"Are we taking that?" She gestured toward his car.

He folded his arms across his chest and clenched his jaw. The car was a piece of crap, but no one else was allowed to say so.

"Yes," he said. "We are."

"I thought cowboys drove pickup trucks."

She was right—they did. But it was going to be a while before his Dodge was back in action.

"Rolled it. Don't ask." He hung his head and eyed her hopefully from under his white straw Stetson. He'd dressed for Roundup success in a brightly striped shirt—a clean one—and even pressed his Wranglers.

She looked him up and down, and he thought her eyes lingered a little on the clean shirt.

"Okay," she said. "I'll go. Give me a minute to change."

They say you should never get into a car with a strange man. Luke Rawlins wasn't all that strange. In fact, he seemed like a nice, normal guy. Still, Libby never should have gotten into that car. There was no doubt the man was a genuine Wyoming cowboy, but he drove like a New Yorker.

"No wonder you rolled your truck," she chided as he squealed around a curve.

"That was the squirrel's fault. Little buggers need to stay out of the road." Luke swatted the turn signal lever and slammed on the brakes, careening into the bar's parking lot with a dramatic spray of gravel.

Once she saw the parking lot, Libby realized his crazy driving was probably a form of manly overcompensation for his wimpy little car. Massive four-wheelers dominated the scene, looming over the tiny Mazda like a flock of eagles surrounding a half-plucked chicken. She realized she'd probably look just as out of place once

they got inside. She'd changed into a short denim skirt and piled her hair on top of her head in a trendy up-do that hopefully concealed her hat-hair, but the Roundup looked like an abandoned barn.

Maybe she should have stuck with the overalls.

The place looked like a barn on the inside too. Rough-hewn beams and rustic log furnishings gave it a big dose of manly cowboy atmosphere, but what really stood out was the taxidermy. A tattered duck was frozen in flight over the pool table, while a snarling cougar prowled the rafters over restrooms designated "Bulls" and "Heifers." Various animal heads peered from the rough, wood-paneled walls, including a bug-eyed pronghorn and a massive moose head decorated with multicolored Christmas lights and a cigar. Perched behind the counter was a perky little rabbit sporting tiny horns.

Stepping into the dark saloon from the bright Western sunshine, it was hard to see the men seated at the bar. Libby squinted to make out a row of cowboy hats and baseball caps above frosty mugs clutched in calloused hands. One fellow had an artistic depiction of a chainsaw tattooed on his biceps. Another sported a P.E.T.A. cap: "People Eating Tasty Animals." An attractive dark-haired woman presided over the beer taps.

"Hey, Luke. Long time, no see," she said.

"Hey, Crystal." Luke guided Libby up to the bar with one warm hand resting gently on the small of her back, radiating a subtle but palpable heat to all the most sensitive parts of her anatomy. "This is my new neighbor, Libby Brown. She bought the old Lackaduck ranch," he said. "Libby, this is Crystal Hayes. She knows everybody

and everything in Lackaduck. You want information, just stop by the Roundup."

Crystal nodded a brisk hello. "Nice to meetcha." She turned and gestured toward the bar. "These guys are the Mikes. That's Big Mike, Mean Mike, and Crazy Mike. The guy at the end is the sheriff."

The sheriff stood to shake hands, and Libby threw Luke a dirty look. This guy was no Bubba. He was tall, at least six-five, and looked like a California surfer, with blond hair and pale blue eyes set in an angular face bronzed by the Wyoming sun. Luke was nice to look at, but where Luke was spare and wiry, this guy was solid muscle, with Gold's Gym biceps and broad shoulders that tapered down to narrow hips. The whole package was wrapped in a brown sheriff's uniform, topped off by a shiny, star-shaped badge that reminded her of a bow on a really nice birthday present. If looks counted for anything, Lackaduck's sheriff would catch every criminal in the county.

"Cash McIntyre," he said. "Nice to meet you."

Libby looked up into his eyes and smiled. She was almost six feet tall, and men big enough to make her feel delicate and feminine were few and far between.

"Libby Brown," she mumbled. Staring slack-jawed at the badge on his chest, she searched her mind for something intelligent to say. "Yeah," she finally said. "Nice."

"How 'bout a drink, hon?" Crystal interrupted.

Libby came back to earth as the bartender slapped a cardboard coaster in front of an empty barstool beside Luke.

"What's on tap?" Libby dropped the sheriff's hand

and turned away so she couldn't see him anymore. It was the only way she could regain consciousness.

"Coors, Coors Light, Bud, Bud Light," Crystal rattled off.

"Coors," Libby said. She laid a five on the bar.

"Let me." Cash pulled a wad of cash out of his pocket and started counting out bills.

"No. Me," Luke said. His eyes narrowed into a Dirty Harry squint and he drew his wallet like a gunfighter. He and Cash traded a look, and Cash went back to his seat. Libby didn't want any fistfights starting, but it sure felt good to be popular.

"How 'bout you, Luke?" Crystal asked. She flashed a warning glare at both men. It was clear she didn't tolerate fights in her barroom.

"I'll have a Smirnoff Ice."

Libby turned to him in disbelief. "You can't order one of those sissy drinks in a place like this!"

Every head swiveled toward Luke. No doubt he'd been branded a pansy forever in the minds of his drinking buddies.

Wait 'til they saw what he was driving.

"Coors for me too, then. Light," Luke decided.

Libby snorted.

"What—is light beer for sissies too?"

She was glad he was still smiling after her clumsy teasing and the encounter with the sheriff. She gave Luke five points for being good-natured. Trouble was, Cash got ten points just for standing up.

"Yup," said a deep voice from further down the bar. "Light beer's for sissies, all right."

"Big Mike, don't you make trouble," Crystal said.

"Some folks just don't want to get a beer gut like yours. Luke's watching his girlish figure."

"Thanks, Crystal." Luke turned to Libby and winked. "I'm trying to convince Libby, here, that I'm a Western tough guy, and you call me girlish."

"Aw, she knows better," Crystal said. "She's seen your driving, right?"

"I sure have." Libby shuddered. "He drives like an Easterner."

"You from back East, hon?" asked one of the Mikes.

"Atlanta," Libby said. "I was a crime reporter for the *Journal-Constitution.*" She'd been on the crime beat for less than a year, but she'd covered some major stories—stories of murder, greed, and robbery. In Lackaduck, she'd be covering stories about cows, horses, and the Future Farmers of America. Maybe she'd get lucky and somebody would rob a liquor store or something.

She eyed the sheriff hopefully. Maybe he'd give her the inside track on that missing girl.

The sheriff slid his beer down the bar, edging a little closer to the new arrival.

"Crime reporting? Back East? That must have kept you busy." He couldn't picture this woman surviving in a city like Atlanta. She wasn't small—more what you might call statuesque—but surely those long legs and all that crazy hair drew the wrong kind of attention on the street.

"I can't imagine living back East," he said, thinking out loud. "All the crime, the gangs… I could never live there."

"That's why I'm here." The woman surveyed the bar like she was soaking up the Wild West atmosphere. Cash grinned. Eastern girls who liked that Western stuff always went for the sheriff. They thought he was like Matt Dillon, or something.

Actually, he was a lot like Matt Dillon. But this girl was no Miss Kitty, all fluttery and feminine. She was her own woman, he could tell. Independent. Fiery.

Hot.

Too bad she was with Luke.

"I'm trying to forget about the city and become a real Westerner, like Luke," she said, resting one hand on the rancher's arm. "He's teaching me to think like a cowboy."

Cash snorted. That was the only problem with women from away. They actually thought cowboys were romantic. Though how mucking stalls and tormenting baby cows with hot irons was attractive, Cash could never figure out.

"Cowboys think?" he asked.

Luke shot him another nasty look while Crazy Mike's falsetto voice piped up from down the bar.

"He'll just teach you how to think like a sissy."

The guy sounded like a cross between Mike Tyson and a Bee Gee, but Cash knew that gentle voice was deceiving. Mike was a big guy, almost as big as Cash himself, and he wasn't quite right in the head. It was a dangerous combination.

"Cut it out, Mike." Cash rose to his full height, setting one hand casually on his hip, near the butt of his gun. "You want to be rude, go somewhere else."

Mike ducked his head and hunched his shoulders, cowed. Cash nodded, satisfied, and sat down again, turning his attention back to Libby.

"This Mike thing is confusing," she said to Luke. "It's a good thing your name isn't Mike. I wouldn't know who to go home with."

"You can go home with me, honey," Big Mike said.

Cash narrowed his eyes. She wasn't trying to stir things up, but the woman was like a firecracker with a short fuse, and the whole place could explode any minute. Cash believed in stopping that kind of trouble before it had a chance to start. So far, his tactics had worked. Lackaduck was practically crime free.

Except for Della McCarthy.

He pushed Lackaduck's only unsolved mystery out of his head. He didn't like to think about Della. He'd much rather think about this new girl. He'd make sure nothing happened to her, that was for sure.

Starting now.

"Knock it off," he said to Big Mike, rising from his barstool.

His icy tone hushed the whole bar. He hitched up his belt, then noticed that Libby was watching. She quickly lifted her gaze to his face, but it was too late—he'd caught her looking a lot lower. He swallowed a smile and gave her a stern look, pretending he hadn't noticed her wandering eyes.

"Don't let these guys give you a hard time," he said. "I'm out of here, but Crystal, you'll call me if anybody gives her trouble, right?"

"For God's sake, Cash." Crystal laughed. "Don't get your knickers in a knot. This isn't the OK Corral. Just your friends and neighbors hoisting a few beers."

"Can't be too careful," Cash said.

He was surprised Crystal didn't know better. She'd been the Roundup's bartender for almost ten years, and

she'd broken up her share of fights. Cash had a lot of respect for her, but sometimes she didn't get a handle on things until it was too late. He leaned over the bar to talk to her, lowering his voice.

"We don't see her kind around here too often." He thumbed toward the line of men at the bar. "Hard telling how they'll react."

"What 'kind' am I?" Libby asked. She cocked her head and smiled, letting that crazy mass of curls shift to dangle around her face.

Cash grinned back. "My kind, I hope." He pulled a business card out of his shirt pocket and handed it to her. "Call me if you have any trouble." He stepped closer and lowered his voice. "Or even if you don't."

She met his eyes and he felt a sudden spark shoot between them, hot and bright, but now wasn't the time to act on it. Turning, he strode out, letting the saloon doors slap behind him like a slow, fading drumroll.

Chapter 3

LUKE WATCHED THE DOORS THUMP OUT THEIR SLOW tattoo and grimaced.

"What a load of self-satisfied horseshit that guy is," he said.

Libby turned to him and laughed a little too brightly. She seemed like a fairly sensible person, but obviously the sheriff's tough guy act was giving her heart palpitations. Luke had seen it before—the magic spell Cash's bronze star seemed to cast over otherwise intelligent women.

"Yeah. That was a little much." Her eyes darted around the room, obviously searching for a distraction. She pointed to the tiny horned creature behind the bar. "So what kind of rabbit is that?"

"That's not a rabbit, miss. That's a jackalope," said one of the Mikes.

"A what?"

"A jackalope."

Luke grinned. Libby obviously didn't know any more about Western wildlife than she did about sheriffs. Well, she'd learn—but he didn't have to make it easy. A little hazing wouldn't do her any harm. Besides, it was almost obligatory to give Eastern greenhorns a hard time.

He turned toward her, raising his eyebrows, all innocence. "Haven't you ever seen one? They're pretty rare—endangered, even—but you see them once in a

while, out on the plains. And I bet you've heard them singing at night."

"They sing?"

"Only at night," he said. "Like coyotes, only prettier."

"I never saw one before." She eyed the creature speculatively, as if pondering its suitability as a pet, and Luke stifled a chuckle.

"He's pretty cute," she said. "But isn't it illegal to have an endangered species mounted and stuffed like that? I mean, aren't they protected?"

"That's made from one of Crazy Mike's jackalopes," said Big Mike. "He's got a whole bunch of 'em out back of his place, in that old shed."

"You mean he breeds them?" Libby leaned over the bar for a better look at the little animal and the guys exchanged grins behind her back. "I might be interested in buying a couple of those. Are they hard to breed?"

Crazy Mike piped out a goofy high-pitched giggle. "Not too tough. The hard part's making the jackrabbit stand still for the antelope!"

The bar erupted in laughter while Libby blushed. She was being a good sport, but suddenly Luke felt like a heel for leading her on. "It's a rabbit, see?" he explained. "With antelope horns stuck on it."

The rest of the men were high-fiving, rejoicing in the success of the setup. "It's a good thing you don't have one of Mike's dancing muskrats up there," Big Mike said.

"Dancing muskrats?" Libby looked skeptical. At least she wasn't totally gullible.

"Yeah," Crazy Mike said. "They look real cute, dancing. I stand 'em up, you know, with their little arms out, and put dolly tutus on 'em. With sparkles. And little tiaras."

"If she saw one of those, she'd be out by the creek on Christmas Eve wondering when *The Nutcracker* was going to start," Big Mike said.

The men whooped with laughter. Libby squeezed out a good-natured chuckle, but it sounded more like a death rattle. All this probably wasn't helping her credibility as a journalist. Luke changed the subject to bail her out.

"So I was telling Libby about that missing girl," he said. "Since she's a journalist, she's pretty interested."

"Della McCarthy," said Crystal. Her voice cracked on the last syllable. She always got broken up about Della. "She was just seventeen years old. Maybe eighteen. Still tried to get a drink out of me, though." She smiled sadly and shook her head.

"Crystal was the last one to see her alive," piped Crazy Mike.

"I was the last one to see her at all," said Crystal. "They never found her, dead or alive." Her hand quivered as she poured another beer for one of the Mikes.

"What happened to her?" Libby asked.

"That's the question." Crystal set the beer in front of Big Mike and shook her head. "Nobody knows. Only thing we know is nobody's seen her since she left here. It's sad." She pulled a white rag out of her back pocket and wiped up a glass ring. "Now she's officially a missing person. Probably got her picture on a milk carton somewhere. Nobody knows if she got herself killed somehow or just ran off."

Libby's shoulders slumped. "Just ran off," she muttered. She stared off across the bar, her eyes glistening as if she could see some painful episode from her past etched in the smoky air. Luke touched her shoulder

and she twitched toward him as if he'd woken her from a dream.

"Hey," he said. "You okay?"

"Fine." Libby tossed her curls and pasted on a smile, but her eyes still shone. She was a pro when it came to playing the brave little buckaroo, but Luke wondered again what she was running away from.

"Come on," he said, easing off his stool. "Let's put a quarter in the jukebox. A little country twang'll cheer you right up." He scanned the title list, running through the litany of lost love and heartbreak. "Just don't listen to the lyrics, okay?"

An hour later, Luke pulled the Mazda to a halt in Libby's driveway. With the silvery moonlight washing over his face, he looked like the hero of some old-time Western movie, ready to rescue the prairie-skirted dame in distress. He was cute, she thought. Really cute. She felt like a seventh-grader on her first date—all excited, but scared to death too.

When he stepped halfway out of the car, looking hopeful, she panicked.

"Better stay in the car." She hopped out and slammed her door, then trotted around to his side of the car. "Ivan's grouchy at night."

"Funny he's not barking," Luke mused, glancing at the house.

"Oh, he's a sneak-attack kind of dog," she said. "Everything's quiet and then whammo! Gotcha!" She clapped her hands and Luke jumped. He glanced around nervously and pulled his leg back into the car.

"Well," he said, looking down at his lap. "See ya."

"Okay." Libby skipped up onto the porch and gave him a vague little wave. "'Night. Thanks."

She watched Luke's taillights fade as he careened out of the driveway, tires spewing dust and gravel. If she hadn't seen his crazy driving before, she'd have thought he was mad.

She flicked a switch and the fluorescent light over the sink shimmered as it hummed to life, saturating the kitchen with harsh white light. The place looked so empty and stark she almost regretted letting Luke go.

Almost.

She should really get a dog, she thought. A dog would welcome her when she got home. A dog would always be glad to see her.

At least until it died, or ran off.

Kicking off her shoes, she sat down at the table and flipped her laptop open, chafing at the slow dial-up service that was her only choice out here in the boondocks. Googling "Della McCarthy" brought up a site featuring the missing girl's picture.

"Have You Seen This Girl?" a banner shouted over a studio photo of an attractive teenager. Her dark hair curled around her face in unruly tendrils, and her eyes stared straight at the camera. She wasn't smiling; she looked calm and serious, as if she was thinking about the future. A short biography preceded a plea for her return, written by her mother.

"If you have seen our daughter, please call us. If you know where she is, please call us. Help us find her and all is forgiven. Please end this agony of not knowing."

At the bottom of the page, a banner read: "Della: Forever Loved."

Libby studied Della's picture, noting the firm set of her jaw, the glint of humor in her eyes. Was she a runaway, hiding in some small town, shacked up with some itinerant rodeo rider? Not likely. The girl in the photograph had the same solid, confident look Luke did—the look of someone who belonged, who'd found their place in the world. Someone like that wouldn't run away.

She wouldn't need to.

Libby stood and stretched, then grabbed a beer from the refrigerator and wandered out onto the porch, stepping cautiously across the splintery boards in her bare feet. Leaning against the rickety railing, she gazed out across the prairie.

No lights. No cars. No people.

She remembered the view from her apartment balcony in Atlanta—the once-genteel tenements falling into disrepair; the all-night diner feeding the city's lost souls and ladies of the evening; the dive bar issuing its endless stream of stumbling drunks. The city's nonstop soundtrack of honking car horns and random shouts had been annoying, but at least it was human. Out here, all she could hear was the insistent screeching of some unknown insect and a whisper of wind rattling the sagebrush.

If someone had kidnapped Della, she could be anywhere out there—buried in a shallow grave, or held prisoner in some abandoned outbuilding. Heck, the same thing could happen to Libby herself. Hardly anyone knew where she was, and if she disappeared, the locals would just figure she'd moved on. It was

strange to feel you could be lifted out of the world, murdered or abducted, and no one would even notice you were gone.

She shivered and wished again she'd let Luke stay, or at least kissed him, touched him, made some human connection before she'd let him go.

Chapter 4

Why on earth had she told Luke Rawlins she had a dog?

The question woke Libby at sunrise, bringing with it the chilling realization that her neighbor was going to think she was some kind of psycho fibber if the fabled Ivan didn't put in an appearance at their next meeting. The only solution was to get herself a dog, and she'd sworn off dogs, men, and anything else that could break her heart.

It was chickens or nothing.

Still, it was awfully quiet around here. She thrashed her way out of the covers and stared at the sea of sage-strewn prairie that filled the bedroom window, remembering her morbid musings from the night before. The dawn sky was solid silver, empty and expressionless, and not a single light winked in the distance.

She was very, very alone.

She shook off her self-pity and got busy, spending the morning scrubbing her kitchen cabinets and arranging her mismatched dinnerware on the paper-lined shelves. The busywork let her mind wander freely, and it kept wandering down the driveway after her handsome neighbor. She wondered if he'd been disappointed last night when she didn't invite him in.

She wondered what his house was like, and whether he was awake yet.

She wondered what he looked like naked.

She'd better get that dog, she decided. Losing Bill had left a great big hole in her heart, and if she didn't find herself some puppy love, she'd end up filling it with her friendly neighborhood cowboy. She'd have to kiss her self-esteem good-bye if her firm resolution to stick to the single life lasted all of a day and a half.

The Lackaduck animal shelter was filled with lonesome souls who had lost their happy homes. Some of them peed on the carpet. Others barked too much. There was a leg humper, a cat chaser, a habitual runaway, and a boyfriend biter. Glenda Parsons, the shelter manager, was eager to introduce Libby to every one of them.

"What exactly are you looking for?" she asked, resting a red-booted foot on a stepstool. Her blond hair, stick-straight and dry from the Wyoming wind, was tied back in a bandanna, and slim-fit Wranglers hugged her angular hips. "Did you have a particular breed in mind?"

Libby shrugged. "Not really," she said. "Something for protection."

Glenda pointed out a few likely prospects—a German shepherd with an endearing floppy ear, a husky with a white-tipped wagging tail, and a massive black Lab mix who looked like he should be guarding the gates of hell until he gazed up at you with his appealing brown eyes and begged you to love him.

They were all like that.

"These are too nice," Libby said. "I'm not looking for a pet. Just a guard dog. Long as it's got four legs and a sharp set of teeth, I'm good."

Glenda gave her a sharp look. "They're dogs," she said. "They're nice. Sounds like you're looking for an alligator."

Libby laughed. "That would probably be about right."

"Let me guess." Glenda squinted up at Libby's face. "Did you lose a pet recently?"

Libby nodded and swallowed, remembering Lucky.

Glenda laid a hand on Libby's arm and looked into her eyes with heartfelt sincerity. "Don't be scared," she said. "Sure, it's tough when they head off to that big doggie park in the sky. But you've got to get back on and ride the horse what throw'd you, you know?"

"I've got to… what?"

Glenda sighed. "You know. When a bronc throws a rodeo rider, he has to climb back on again. Conquer his fear. That's what you need to do—open yourself up to love."

"Wow," Libby said. "You should be one of those life coaches."

"Right. Sure. But it's not about me." Glenda made an impatient little gesture, shooing Libby down the aisle. "Now get out there and find yourself a soul mate. You'll know the right one when you see him. Just follow your instincts."

Libby walked past cage after cage, struggling to resist the pleading eyes besieging her from every side. Every dog there deserved a home, but none of them produced the spark of recognition she was looking for. Not one was her lover from a past life, or the reincarnation of her great-uncle George. They all looked her in the eye, but none of them looked any deeper than that.

Except Penny.

"Some idiot dropped this one off on our doorstep a month ago," Glenda said. "Her and four puppies." She sighed. "Poor thing bred true. See those ears?"

They were hard to miss. The dog's head was dwarfed by what appeared to be a pair of enormous triangular radar dishes.

"Jack Russells aren't supposed to have stand-up ears," Glenda explained. "They're supposed to flip forward."

Libby ran her hands over her hair, smoothing down the renegade cowlick that always stuck up at the crown.

"And look at her tail. It should be straight, or docked—not curly like that. And the puppies look just like her. The breeder couldn't sell 'em, so they dumped the whole lot on us."

Libby looked closer. Penny was pure white, with a perfect brown circle over each eye. She was sitting up in a classic begging stance, paws clasped, head cocked, studying Libby with an intensity that was different from the other dogs. She swiveled her ears and Libby wondered if the dog could hear her heart thumping out the bassline to some corny country love song.

Of course she could. Heck, she could probably hear Russian satellite transmissions with those ears.

"I can get her out for you," Glenda said.

"No, that's okay." Libby sighed. "I really wanted a big dog."

Penny wavered unsteadily on her haunches, but her eyes never left Libby's face.

"Jack Russells think they're big," Glenda said. "And they make great watchdogs."

"Come on, that's not a dog. That's an overgrown

lab rat." Libby struggled to break eye contact with the ridiculous animal so she could move on.

She failed.

"You'd be surprised what Jack Russells can do." As Glenda spoke, she opened the kennel door. Penny sat back on her haunches for a half-second, then launched herself upward like a miniature torpedo. Next thing Libby knew, she was drowning in dog slurp.

"Oh my gosh. She loves you!" Glenda laughed as Penny hooked her paws over Libby's shoulders and continued her onslaught of affection. "She's not usually like that. She's really laid back. She just really, really likes you."

Libby grasped Penny around her middle and gently extricated her from her face. The dog's stubby legs pedaled the air frantically. "Really?"

"Really." The shelter manager nodded somberly. "She's kind of stand-offish."

Libby looked down as Penny gave up pedaling and settled quietly into her arms. The dog gazed into her eyes adoringly, and Libby's heart thumped its way to a pulsating crescendo, drowning out whatever sense she had left.

She was lost.

Penny was hers.

Minutes later, she was signing papers and ponying up sixty dollars, promising to spay her new dog, and swearing to have and to hold, forever and always.

"Now I need just a few more signatures." Glenda slid a stack of forms across the counter.

Libby had heard how tough it was to get an animal out of most shelters. She was prepared for a brutal

interrogation on every aspect of her life, but Glenda was jumping through administrative hoops like a saluki in an agility trial.

"You'll love Penny. She's such a sweet dog," she said. "Yeah, she's got a lot of energy, but you live in the country. She'll love it there. Room to run, that's what these dogs need. Room to run."

Penny needed room to run, all right. The living room, the bedroom, and most of the kitchen. After ten minutes of non-stop action, Libby was worried her new pet would wear a racetrack into the carpet.

They'd finished the twenty-seventh round of an endlessly repetitive game of fetch when Penny pricked up her ears and stalked stiff-legged toward the door, a low growl emanating from her tiny chest. Straining her ears, Libby heard a car door slam.

Footsteps crossed the porch. Loud footsteps. It had to be a man. The fur on Penny's back lifted into a makeshift Mohawk and the growl turned into a snarl.

That was helpful. Libby's so-called guard dog was scaring the crap out of her. The dog, and the fact that she was living miles from any other human habitation with no more protection than an animal the size of a housecat.

Knuckles rapped hard on the door.

"Libby? It's me. Luke."

Libby felt relief flood every cell of her body, then looked down at Penny and froze. There was no way she could explain how Ivan the Terrible had become Penny the Terribly Cute. Scooping the dog up in one

hand, she chucked the animal into the pantry, slammed the door, and rearranged her panicked face into a welcoming smile.

Chapter 5

Luke grinned as Libby swung the door open. She smiled back, but it was a pasted-on grin that never quite made it to her eyes.

"Luke," she said. Her voice was flat. He tried not to take it personally.

"Hi. I brought you something." He handed her the folder he'd brought and stood back with his arms folded to watch her reaction. "A present," he said.

She flipped through the contents, which were Xeroxed and filed neatly in chronological order. The headlines flashed by: "Wyoming Teen Missing, Feared Dead." "Search Continues for Wyoming Teen." "Teen's Parents Suspect Foul Play."

"Wow," she said. "Thanks." This time the smile seemed genuine, and she stepped back to let him in.

"See? You're definitely not like other girls," he said, stepping inside. "You get excited about farming and murder." He eased a little closer and caught the fresh scent of new-mown hay coming from her hair. She must have been working outside. Either that, or she used some sweet-scented girly shampoo.

Taking off his Stetson, he spun it in his hands and glanced around the front room. She'd cleaned the place up, hung some pictures on the wall. It looked better—almost homey, despite the evil sofa lurking in the far corner.

He was still fooling with his hat, trying to come up with some polite conversation, when a loud crash sounded from the pantry.

He spun to face the sound. "What was that?"

"Uh… rats," Libby said.

"Yikes." He cringed. The vermin had to be huge to make a racket like that. "That's awful."

"You have no idea," she said, but a smile tweaked the corners of her mouth. Well, at least she wasn't afraid of animals, like some women.

Not even rats.

A high-pitched whine pierced the air, followed by a volley of yapping barks that clearly emanated from the supposedly rat-infested pantry.

"That's a rat?" He lifted a doubting eyebrow.

"I, um, I put Ivan in there. To catch them," she said.

There was another crash, then a series of loud thumps. It sounded like all her canned goods were cascading to the floor. Another series of yaps pierced the air.

"He sure doesn't sound big," Luke said. "He sounds like a poodle."

"Oh, he's no poodle," Libby said. "Definitely not a poodle."

Luke's curiosity was piqued. He couldn't picture those yapper-dog yelps coming from anything bigger than a shih tzu. "Maybe you'd better let him out."

"No way." She shook her head. "Not with you here. He bites first, asks questions later."

She turned away and flipped through the folder, pausing on a photo from the Cheyenne paper. It showed the sheriff leaning against his cruiser, talking to some other guy. *"Sheriff Cash McIntyre leads the search for*

missing teen Della McCarthy," said the caption. Libby looked at the picture a little longer than the rest, then paged forward, then back again. Her tongue darted out and wetted her lips. She finally tore herself away from the photo and glanced up at Luke. He caught a flash of something like guilt in her eyes.

A frantic flurry of scrabbling hit the pantry door. It sounded like it might be a rat, but then it let out one of those half-assed barks.

"What kind of dog is he again?" Luke asked.

"Not sure," Libby said. "Some bullmastiff, maybe a little mountain lion." She cleared her throat and waved the folder at him. "These pictures are great. I mean, these articles."

Luke smiled weakly. "Yeah," he said. "I can tell it's all about the articles."

Libby flipped through the folder, trying to concentrate on the headlines. She could feel Luke watching her, his gaze pleasant but penetrating. He hadn't shaved for a day or two.

Stubble suited him.

"So," he said. "Farming, murder—what else gets you excited?"

She started to say "stubble," then thought better of it and shrugged.

"Maybe rat traps?" he asked. "You've got a real problem there."

He was right. But the problem wasn't rats. The problem was that she was a psycho fibber, and she couldn't seem to stop. She kept digging her grave of lies deeper

and deeper, and it was past time to find a way out.

Maybe she could convince Luke that Penny was a rat. The little dog looked kind of like a rat, and was about the same size. Then she could act really surprised and say Ivan must have disappeared somehow. She could tell him the pantry was the new door to Narnia.

Or she could just change the subject.

She pulled the first article out of the folder and scanned it. Someone had written "*Cheyenne Eagle Tribune*" and a date at the top in neat block printing. The article was a short one—probably the first official notice of Della's disappearance. The next page was from the same paper, a day later. The research involved in putting together a collection like this would take the skills and dedication of an experienced journalist—or the single-minded obsession of a bona fide nutcase.

Libby knew Luke was no journalist. All of a sudden, he was starting to look like a Bundy brother again—tall, dark, and dangerously handsome, with an intense gaze that made her a touch uneasy. She thought of the serial killer characteristics she'd learned from one of her criminology books and realized she didn't know much about his childhood or home life.

"So," she said casually. "How's your mother?"

"Oh, she's driving me nuts today, like usual. She took all the curtains down and put 'em in the refrigerator. Thought she was washing them. I got that bit straightened out, but who knows what I'm going home to."

"You, um, live with her?"

He nodded and she glanced at his ring finger. Bingo. Single and living with his mother at the age of... well, he was definitely over thirty. And his mother was

obviously insane. The screeching violins from *Psycho* started sawing away in her head.

She cleared her throat. "Have you been, um, collecting these articles long?"

"All morning," he said. "At the library."

"Oh," she said. "The library." She hacked out a phony little laugh. There was no way someone could put together a collection like this in a single day. Or a single week. No, this was a long-term project.

"Wow," she said. "Thanks."

Luke nodded. "I promised you background on the case, remember? And I always keep my promises."

Libby eyed the folder again. Maybe it wasn't so extraordinary. Maybe he was just a good researcher. A hard worker.

She hoped so.

Because it had been a long time since she'd met a man who kept his promises. It would be a darn shame if the guy turned out to be a serial killer.

Libby couldn't sleep.

That wasn't unusual. Her old job at a big-city newspaper came with a wide range of anxieties, and sleepless nights were part of the package. This time was different, though. She was in a new place, with new sounds: the house creaking, the jackalopes singing…

Wait a minute. There were no such things as jackalopes.

She got up to investigate. It didn't take her long to figure out where the bloodcurdling howls were coming from. Penny crouched by the front door, nose raised

high, keening. Libby had taken her to bed, letting her curl up near her feet, but the dog had paced all night, clicking her toenails up and down the hardwood floor until Libby finally let her out of the bedroom.

"What's wrong, baby?"

Penny answered with a deep moan that spiraled into yet another howl. Jackalopes had nothing on this baby.

"Are you hurt? Are you lonesome?"

Trotting to the front door, she tossed her head back for another howl.

"You need to go out?" Libby opened the door. Stars blanketed the sky, casting a faint silver glow over the crooked outbuildings that made up her little empire. Penny stared out at the night-shrouded farm, her tail tucked between her legs, then curled up on the doormat and moaned. Then she moaned again.

It was a long night.

By the time it was over, Libby was convinced her new dog was deathly ill. No amount of stress or loneliness could account for this kind of misery.

It was definitely time for an introduction to Lackaduck's one and only veterinarian.

Pale and doughy with a gap-toothed jack-o'-lantern grin, Ron Stangerson was hardly God's gift to women—but somehow, he'd missed that memo. After a brief speech proclaiming his eligibility as a bachelor, the vet flexed his biceps to show Libby the muscles he'd developed over the years yanking calves from reluctant Hereford mothers, and began recounting his many adventures in the bovine birth canal.

"Yep, that heifer squeezed my arm until my fingers went numb, but I just reached in there and grabbed that sucker by the nose. The trick is to get your fingers up their nostrils, so you can pull 'em round and drag 'em out frontwards. It's hard work, but I'm the man for it." Suddenly, he doubled over and grimaced. Libby thought he'd been taken ill until she realized he was contorting himself into a bodybuilder's stance to display the muscles obscured beneath his pallid flesh.

She faked admiration to placate his ego, then turned the conversation to Penny's problems and described the dog's nocturnal agony. Stangerson looked down at the sad little pup that lay in her arms with a "take me now, Lord" expression on her furry face and nodded.

"It's separation anxiety," he said.

"But we're hardly ever separated. She follows me everywhere. This morning she tried to get in the shower with me. How can she have separation anxiety?"

"It's not separation from you she has a problem with. She came from the shelter, right?"

Libby nodded, setting Penny on the stainless steel table.

"Had a litter of pups not too long ago, didn't she?"

Libby was impressed. To her eye, Penny had shed her baby weight in record time, but evidently Ron could still spot the effects of her recent pregnancy.

"Yeah." She sighed, holding Penny steady on the slippery table. "They said she had four of them."

"Well, that's your trouble right there," Ron said. "She's missing her young 'uns. And you don't have any other dogs, right? You're living out there all by yourself."

"Right," Libby said. She was tempted to resurrect the myth of Ivan the Terrible, but she told herself she was

being paranoid. Then Ron stroked Penny's head and his fingers brushed against hers, pausing a beat too long. She felt a jolt of alarm and jerked her hand back.

"Just making sure there's no physical cause," Ron said, continuing to run his hands over the dog's body. Libby relaxed as he examined Penny's eyes and teeth, convinced she'd misread his touch.

"Yep, she's a healthy pup. I'd say it's just a severe case of empty nest syndrome," he concluded.

"Will she get over it?" Libby stifled a yawn. "I sure can't go through another night like that."

"She'll probably forget eventually. But it'll take a while. I'll give you some sedatives that'll help her out." Ron stroked Penny's head and made soft, consoling noises. In return, the dog jumped up and threw her front paws over his shoulders, making a concerted effort to stick her tongue up his nose as she showered him with smooches.

"Wow. They said at the shelter she was a little standoffish. She sure does like you though—in spite of that bit with the thermometer."

"I have a way with critters," he boasted. A leer creased his face. "Especially the female kind."

Her skin crawled, and her estimate of Penny's intuition about human nature took a dramatic nosedive and crashed to the ground. The guy was a creep.

She wished she hadn't admitted to living alone.

"How nice for you," she said. "Bill me, would you?" She snapped on Penny's leash and beat a rapid retreat out the door to her pickup.

She needed to go home and wash her hands.

~

Libby spent the rest of the day tidying up the house—shelving books, washing windows, and creating a cozy, homey nest for Penny and herself out of the skimpy leavings of her previous life. At the end of the day, the little farmhouse gleamed with cleanliness. She was starting to feel like she'd come close to creating a real home, and Penny fit right in. Libby took her outside and threw a stick over and over, hoping to get the dog tired enough to sleep through the night.

It didn't work. After another night of Penny's histrionics, somewhat abated by one of Ron's Doggy Downers, Libby couldn't get to the shelter fast enough. Glenda was sympathetic when she explained her plight.

"I was afraid of that," she said. "I almost suggested right off the bat you get more than one. But it's so hard to train multiple dogs."

"I know. But she's losing her mind. What'll I do? It's bad enough dealing with one Jack Russell. I can't take on a whole herd."

"Why not just foster them?"

"Foster?"

"Yeah, just take care of the puppies until we find homes for them. That way, they'll go one by one and she'll be more secure at your place by the time they're gone."

It seemed like a good idea at the time.

"You'll keep looking for homes for them, right?"

"Oh, yeah, and they're such a popular breed right now, what with Eddie on TV and all. We'll find homes for them. Honest."

Libby should have paid attention when the *Psycho* violins resumed their rhythmic screeching inside her

head, but she ignored them. Deep down, she wanted those puppies. Sure, she'd sworn off every kind of pet but chickens, but resolutions were made to be broken. A squadron of feisty puppies would take her mind off her troubles, and she couldn't wait to see Penny's reaction when she brought home her bundles of joy.

The bundles of joy made themselves right at home. Against Libby's better judgment, she named them all, but she gave them dumb names so she wouldn't get attached to them. The noisiest one she called Rooster. The fast one, who chased everything that moved, was called Rabbit. Then there was Rotgut, who had trouble at first keeping anything down. It was probably the excitement of seeing his mom again. The last one she called Roto-Rooter, since he opted for a drink from the toilet with so much enthusiasm he fell in.

Penny didn't care what they called them; she was just glad to see them. After a long spell of crazy running and barking and squirming all over each other, the whole family settled down to rest, panting happily in a patch of sunlight on the lawn. Penny licked each pup from its oversized ears to its adorably curly tail, as if making sure they were all intact, and then settled down to make up for the sleep she'd lost.

Chapter 6

Libby still blushed when she thought about the jackalope episode, but at least it had given her inspiration for a story. Taxidermy was obviously big business in Wyoming, and a craftsman whose signature product was tutu-clad muskrats surely had something interesting to say. Sure, Crazy Mike seemed a little nuts—he hadn't earned his nickname for nothing—but lots of creative people were flat-out bonkers. Look at Salvador Dalí. Jackson Pollock.

Crazy Mike Cresswell might turn out to be just as interesting.

Of course, he also might turn out to be a psycho killer whose fascination with cutting up dead animals was just a step along the way to slashing up curly-haired journalists who asked too many questions. That's why Libby was bringing Luke for backup.

The rancher said he was her closest neighbor, but the sign for the Rawlins Ranch pointed down a long road to nowhere. As far as she could see, the rocky two-track wound into the distant mountains and disappeared into the haze. It was flanked by a wide expanse of prairie on each side, the sagebrush and yucca plants caged by strings of barbed wire stapled to random sticks and boards of every imaginable size and shape. The makeshift fence posts leaned this way and that, nary a one standing straight.

The fence didn't bode well for the ranch to follow. Maybe Luke lived in a tent. Or a lean-to in the mountains, constructed of more crazy wood scraps. In any case, she was going to find out.

Her intrepid Ranger bopped along the road, conquering puddles and potholes with spring-loaded stoicism. A few pronghorn antelope gleamed white against the brown prairie, and at one point a turkey hen skittered clumsily across the road in front of the truck. The road curved as the land lifted, rising into foothills that shielded the flat from the mountain winds. Tucked under a ridge in the distance was Luke's house.

It wasn't a tent.

It was Home, with a capital *H*—a white clapboard farmhouse, neatly kept and newly painted, with dark green shutters and trim. A covered porch stretched the length of the front, its support posts hung with brimming baskets of impatiens in alternating red and white.

Libby was struck by a spasm of doubt as she parked the truck. She'd thought it would be fun to see her new neighbor in his natural surroundings, unedited and unprepared. That's why she hadn't called or waited for an invitation. But now she was a little nervous.

What if he was naked?

She hopped out of the truck and headed for the house. She could deal with naked. She'd had plenty of practice lately in her ridiculously randy dreams. Apparently, her single status had revved up her libido to the point where she was dreaming about sex acts that had never even occurred to her when she'd had a boyfriend. She wasn't sure you could even *do* the things she was dreaming about, but she was pretty sure Luke would be willing to try.

Then there were the morning after dreams, where the two of them cooked a hearty breakfast together and then stood side by side at the sink, doing the dishes. She washed and he dried. For some bizarre reason, that was even more satisfying than the sex scenes.

So it would be okay if Luke was naked. What she was really worried about was that he'd reveal some kind of redneck alter ego dressed in tightie-whities and a wife-beater.

On the porch, a tiny gray-haired lady was swaying to and fro in a wooden porch swing, pumping her short legs like a toddler on the playground. As Libby approached, the woman tipped herself onto the gray-painted floorboards and set her hands on her hips.

"It's about time you got here," she called out.

"I know. I'm sorry," Libby stammered as she mounted the steps. The woman was right. She'd been a bad neighbor. Luke had come to welcome her on her very first day, and she'd never made the effort to stop by and introduce herself to his parents. They were older. She should show more respect.

"Did you bring your scissors?" the woman asked.

Libby paused. Scissors. Was there some sort of weird Western tradition involving scissors she wasn't aware of? Had Luke said something about scissors?

She didn't think so.

"No," she said. "I'm sorry."

The woman sighed. "Well, you can use mine. They're in there on the counter." She gestured vaguely toward the kitchen. Libby looked from her to the door, confused. "Well, go, girl." The woman waved toward the door again. "Get 'em."

Libby let herself in and looked around. The kitchen was cozy and old-fashioned, with yellow checked wallpaper and cupboards painted in shiny white enamel. It looked homey and very clean—just the way a farm kitchen should.

There was a pair of scissors on the counter near the stove. They were sewing scissors, antiques, embossed to resemble a long-legged stork with sharp, tapering blades for a beak. Libby picked them up and returned to the porch, wondering what she was supposed to do next.

The woman she assumed was Luke's mother leaned forward on the porch swing and fluffed her hair. "I want it a little shorter on the sides," she said. "And let's try bangs this time. I've always wanted to try bangs." She closed her eyes and smiled, her chin raised expectantly.

"You want me to cut your hair?" Libby asked.

"That's what you came for, right?" The woman nodded briskly. "There's no reason for me to go all the way downtown when I've got you right here."

Libby held the scissors suspended in midair by the woman's right ear, wondering what to do. She didn't want to be rude. But she didn't want to mess with Luke's mother's hair, either. The last time she'd cut anyone's hair, it was her own. She'd been ten, and she'd decided she wanted to look like Jennifer Aniston. She'd ended up looking more like Captain Kangaroo.

"Hey. Put those scissors down," a male voice behind her said in a steely monotone. "Real slow. No sudden moves."

It didn't sound like Luke. Libby set the scissors on the porch railing and turned slowly, hands in the air. An

elderly man was standing in the doorway, resting the barrel of a revolver on the top rail of an aluminum walker.

"Now, back up," he said. "Keep those hands where I can see 'em."

Luke heard his father's voice, loud and commanding, booming from the front porch. He looked up from his newspaper. "Dad?" he said. "What's up?"

"There's some woman on the porch threatening your mother with the sewing scissors," his dad said. "I got her covered, but you better get out here."

"What…" Luke stepped out onto the porch and his eyes widened in horror. Libby Brown was standing next to his mother's porch swing, her hands in the air. Her eyes widened too, and he felt a brief spasm of embarrassment. He'd given rein to his inner redneck this morning and was putting it on display by wandering around the house with no shirt on. Just jeans—seriously, nothing else—and he suddenly realized they were hanging dangerously low on his hips. One false move and they'd be down around his ankles. He yanked them up by the belt loops and crossed his arms over his chest. Not that he had anything to be ashamed of. He might not have the bulk of a bodybuilder, but years of ranch work had left him lean, muscled, and tan. And judging from Libby's expression, she appreciated that body type. Even at gunpoint.

"Dad, that's Libby," he said. "Our new neighbor. Put the gun down."

"She was threatening your mother," his father said. Luke was relieved to see his dad's hand relax, letting

the gun barrel point down at the floorboards instead of at Libby's heart. "With the scissors."

"She wanted me to cut her hair," Libby said. "She asked for bangs. I was just trying to help."

"Oh, Mom." Luke knelt down beside his mother and took her hand. "That's Libby. The new neighbor I told you about. She's not Stephanie."

"Definitely not," Libby said. "Who's Stephanie?"

"My sister," he said. "She's a hairdresser in Rock Springs."

"Oh," Libby said. "Your mom..."

He nodded. Nobody needed to say Alzheimer's. It was pretty obvious.

Libby glanced over at the man with the gun. "And your dad..."

"Oh, I'm fine," Luke's dad said. "Sorry about the gun. I just get a little protective where Ella's concerned. And it sure looked like you were about to skewer her in the eyeball with those scissors."

"Um, so this is my dad," Luke said, flashing Libby an apologetic smile. "Dad, this is Libby. She bought the old Lackaduck ranch."

"Nice to meet you," Libby said. Luke was impressed. She'd recovered her manners pretty fast, considering his dad was still holding the gun. At least he wasn't pointing it right at her vitals anymore. His own right foot, however, was in imminent danger.

"So what's up?" Luke asked.

"I was wondering if you'd meet me at the Roundup later," Libby said. "I'm interviewing Crazy Mike. I'm a little nervous, and he's a friend of yours, right?"

"Mike Cresswell? Oh, yeah," Luke said. "We're old friends."

"Sorry I showed up unannounced," she said, watching his father shuffle back into the house.

"Don't be. I'm glad you got to meet my folks." Luke stood and left his mother's side to take Libby's elbow. He urged her down the porch steps as his mother serenely resumed her rocking. "Sorry about Mom," he whispered. "She has a few scenarios that seem to repeat themselves on some kind of memory tape-loop. Having my sister cut her hair is one of them."

"It's okay," Libby said when they reached her truck. "I felt bad I couldn't do it for her." There was an awkward silence while she bit her lower lip, glanced at the house, then back up at Luke.

"Did your dad have an accident?" she finally asked.

"He was in Nam," Luke said. "Brought home a bunch of shrapnel."

"So, wow," Libby said. "You must have to do all the work around the place yourself." She took in the flowers in their hanging baskets and the porch swing padded with patchwork pillows. "It's pretty," she said. "You do a good job."

She seemed surprised, like the whole thing was some kind of revelation. She'd probably thought he was some mama's boy, living in his parent's basement watching *Star Trek* reruns or something.

Good thing he'd gotten that straightened out. For all he knew, she'd thought he was keeping Della McCarthy prisoner in a pit somewhere.

Chapter 7

Crazy Mike was already settled at a table when Libby and Luke walked into the Roundup, and his choice of lunchtime companions confirmed Libby's suspicions that the guy was, well—crazy. A stuffed and mounted muskrat, decked out as promised in a pink tutu, pirouetted daintily on the chair beside him. On the table, a group of bullfrogs shouldered bats and lifted tiny baseball mitts as if to catch a storm of fly balls. They were dressed, too, in tiny pinstriped Yankees uniforms.

"This is Sadie," he said, when he noticed Libby's eyes fixed on the muskrat. "I brought her to show to Crystal. The frogs too. Sadie's a looker, huh?"

"She sure is," Libby said, wondering just what his relationship was with these creatures. Seeing him seated at the table in the company of half a dozen dead animals made her realize just how peculiar the man was. Sure, the animals were mounted with incredible skill—but they were still dead.

She was glad she'd brought Luke.

So was Mike. "Luke," he said, his face splitting into a broad grin. "Hey, how are ya, buddy?"

"I'm good." The two of them performed a complicated handshake, moving through half a dozen different grips and ending with a high five. "So you're a big deal now," Luke said. "Libby wants to do a story on you."

"A story? On me? Like what would I do? Can I be the good guy? The one that rescues the girl?"

"Not that kind of story, Mike," Libby cautioned.

"Yeah, I could save the day—you know, like I was a superhero or something. Or I could be a detective. Like in Mickey Spillane. I like those stories, Libby. Let's do that. With dames and stuff." His hands clenched and unclenched with excitement.

She hated to burst his bubble. "No, Mike, you don't have to be any of those things. I want to do a story about *you.* You and your work."

"Me?" His bushy eyebrows disappeared into his hairline.

"Yeah. You're an interesting guy, Mike. An artist, making all those little creatures."

"I guess so," he said slowly, furrowing his brow. "I never thought of it like that."

"We'll put your picture on the front page too," she told him. "I could come to your workshop tomorrow and take some pictures."

"No." He ducked his head, hunching his heavy shoulders.

"No?"

Mike stood abruptly. His voice was flat. The excitement was gone as quickly as it had built up.

"No," he repeated. "My workshop's not nice. Nobody wants to see it."

Libby sighed. *That's a man for you,* she thought. He just didn't want to have to clean.

"But Mike, I should take your picture there. In your natural surroundings."

"This is my natural surrounding." He patted the table. "The Roundup. Take my picture here."

"But I need to see where you work, Mike. Can't I come to your workshop?"

"No. Do it here."

She gave up. She'd lose the story altogether if she kept insisting on a visit. Maybe it was just as well. She was a little nervous about being alone with Mike and his tools.

"Okay," she said. "We'll do it here."

Happy again, Mike beamed as Libby fished a notepad out of her bag. "I'll answer all your questions," he said. He folded his hands and lowered his brow in concentration like he was preparing for a CIA interrogation. "Ask me anything."

"Okay." She cleared her throat. "So, first, I wondered how you decide what to do with a given animal." She gestured toward the muskrat. "Like Sadie. How did you decide to make her a dancer?" She nibbled the end of her pencil while Mike pondered the question with all the seriousness of a Supreme Court nominee at a confirmation hearing.

"I just knew she was a dancer," he finally said. "I saw it in her eyes, you know?"

"Before or after you shot her?"

Luke snorted, stifling a laugh, and Libby winced. She hadn't meant to put it that bluntly, but it didn't seem to bother Mike. In fact, he seemed very much at ease. Maybe it was Luke, or maybe these creatures were his true friends. That would be sad, but hey, some of the folks she'd interviewed in Atlanta didn't even have dead animals for friends.

Of course, they were mostly drug runners, thieves, and politicians, but still…

"I decide after," Mike said. "I look at them, you know, and they tell me stuff. They, like, talk to me. Not

like people. Not with words. I have to do the voices, but they tell me what to say."

Libby glanced over at Luke. He nodded encouragement, so she plunged onward.

"What do you mean, you have to do the voices?" she asked.

"Like this." Mike picked up a frog and made it dance back and forth on the table. "There's no crying in baseball!" the frog said in an eerie imitation of Tom Hanks.

"That's the team manager in *A League of Their Own*," Luke said.

"Right." Mike grinned. "So I knew he had to be a ball player." He frowned, looking down at the frogs. "That movie had Madonna in it, but I couldn't find a Madonna frog."

"Okay." For once, Libby didn't have a follow-up question ready. Not one she wanted to ask, anyway. She wasn't sure what qualifications defined a "Madonna frog," and she didn't want to find out. She tapped her pen on the tablet, thinking.

"Do you always hunt the animals yourself?" she finally asked.

"No, not always," he said. "Some animals I can't get around here. Like the armadillos." Mike bent over and began rummaging in a burlap sack under the table. "This one's in an attack pose." He pulled out an armadillo dressed in white silk boxing trunks. It was sitting up on its heels, claws extended, a snarl twisting its leathery face.

"Yikes," Luke said.

"Yeah." Mike grimaced. "People always want the attack pose so it looks like they're tough—like they had to kill a really vicious animal. Really, most animals when

you kill them they're running away. But nobody wants them mounted like that."

"Why do you put clothes on them?" Libby asked. "Why not mount them more realistically—like they are in nature?"

"This *is* like they are," Mike insisted. "I show their *true* natures. Like if they were people. Animals don't have many opportunities, you know. A muskrat like Sadie, there's no chance she'd ever get to be a dancer. Not in real life. But that's who she is. And the frogs—well, they probably don't know anything about baseball, but they're team players, you can bet."

"Really?" Libby looked at the tiny frogs, forever frozen halfway through a double play.

"Yeah. You ever hear them singing at night? All together, like a chorus. Once I did a church choir. They wore long white robes."

Weird as it was, Libby was starting to like Mike's image of the natural world.

"See, they all have the *potential* to be more than they are," Mike said. "I just let their true natures show."

Libby figured that would be her headline: "Local Taxidermist Shows Animals' True Natures." She delved a bit deeper into that angle, then dug out her Nikon and got some promising shots of the artist with his creations.

She was a little concerned about how the photos would look on the front page of the local paper. After all, a man embracing a tutu-clad muskrat seemed more suited to a supermarket tabloid than the *Lackaduck Holler*. Still, it would attract attention.

Maybe the *Holler* would sell a few extra papers this week.

Chapter 8

LUKE NODDED WHEN CRYSTAL STOPPED BY THE TABLE and tilted her coffeepot, but Mike shook his head and stood up. "Gotta go to the little bull's room," he said, ducking his head. Libby stifled a smile as he shambled off to the men's room.

"Thanks," Libby said to Luke. "I'm glad you were here. I think it helped make him more comfortable."

"We've been friends a long time," Luke said. "Mike's a good guy."

"A little odd, though," Libby said. "No wonder they call him Crazy Mike."

Luke grimaced. Sure, Mike was a little eccentric, but that was no reason to call him names. He'd hoped Libby would be a little more enlightened than that—a little kinder. "Don't call him that," he said. "You'd be odd too if you had to live his life."

"I'm sorry." She looked genuinely contrite, and Luke forgave her in an instant. She'd probably heard the guy labeled so many times, she hadn't even thought about the cruelty of it. "You're right. I shouldn't say that."

"It's okay. Everybody else does." Luke sighed. "Half the town laughs at him, and the other half's afraid of him. When he was a kid—well, it was awful. Everybody made fun of him."

"Kids can be cruel," Libby said.

"More than cruel." He sipped his coffee, watching her over the rim of the steaming mug. "I'm glad you're doing this story. You won't make him look stupid, will you? Or weird?"

"Not at all," she said. "The way I see it, he's an artist. I mean, his quotes might put some people off, but I'll try to put them in context."

"Good." He nodded. People's reactions to Mike were sort of a test for him, and she'd recovered from her initial fumble to run for the end zone. "Maybe all those people who made fun of him as a kid will see that he's somebody after all."

Libby's gaze softened. "You were his protector, weren't you?"

Luke shrugged, remembering the fistfights his skinny twelve-year-old self had endured for Mike. His playground status had suffered for the friendship, but it had been worth it. No one was more loyal, or made him feel better about himself.

"He needed someone to protect him, that's all," he said. "He still does." He pushed back his chair. "I have to go," he said. "Dad needs some stuff at the drugstore."

Libby watched Luke thread his way through the chairs and tables to the saloon doors. He was going to pick up stuff for his dad. It seemed like he was always helping someone. Who would've thought she'd meet such a nice guy her first day here?

Too bad she wasn't looking for a cowboy to call her own.

Because she wasn't, she reminded herself. The last

thing she needed in her life was more boy trouble. She'd had enough heartache with Bill to last a lifetime—and she had a feeling cowboy trouble would be even worse.

Mostly because of the chaps. Luke didn't wear them all the time, but when he did, they seemed to draw her eye inexorably to parts of his anatomy she really shouldn't be thinking about.

She moved to a stool at the bar and ran her fingers through her hair while she started outlining her story. Meanwhile, Crystal presided over the late lunch crowd, along with a ratty-looking individual Libby assumed was the chef. He was thin and waifish, with the bright eyes of a young man in a face worn out by hard living. Greasy handprints decorated a ragged white apron that proclaimed, "Kiss Me, I'm the Cook."

She wasn't tempted.

There were only a few people scattered among the tables, and most of them were drinking, not eating, despite the early hour. A man in a business suit was sipping a martini in the corner, and a couple of grungy biker types were washing down burgers with copious quantities of beer.

Crystal was rinsing glasses at the bar sink. "You two make a good couple," she said. "You and Luke."

Libby frowned. "We're not a couple. We're friends."

"Oh." Crystal lined up the glasses on a rack to dry. "It's just that I've seen you two together a lot."

"Twice," Libby said.

Crystal smiled. "Around here, that makes you practically married."

Great. In elementary school, Libby's best friend had

been convinced you got pregnant by holding hands with a boy. And here in Lackaduck, people thought you were headed for the altar if you just looked at each other a couple times. By that standard, she'd been a polygamist back in Atlanta.

Until Bill came along. Somehow, he'd convinced her she didn't need anyone but him. She'd gradually gotten absorbed into his world, losing contact with her friends, and since her parents were gone, he hadn't just left her when he took up with her boss.

He'd left her *alone*.

But she was finding her way back into the world, becoming part of this small community, making friends again—including Crystal. "So what's for lunch?" she asked.

"David'll tell you." The bartender grabbed the chef's arm and hauled him to the bar. "Hey, David, here's somebody I want you to meet. Libby, this is David. Makes the best buffalo burgers in Wyoming. And on top of that, he's the best handyman in town. He can fix anything."

"Then he's just the man I need. I've got a chicken coop that needs a lot of work—roof repairs, that kind of thing. Is that the kind of stuff you do?"

"Sure," David said. "I'm off Monday."

"That would work great. How 'bout noonish?"

He clicked his heels and dashed off a hasty imitation of a military salute. "I'm your man," he said. Libby still didn't want to kiss him, and she definitely didn't want him to be her man, but she was warming up to the guy.

"So what's the chef's special?" she asked.

David grinned as he rolled the entire menu off his tongue. "Buffalo burgers, Buffalo Cheeseburgers, Bacon Buffalo burgers, Bleu Buffalo Burgers, Bar-B-Q

Buffalo Burgers, and Biggie Buffalo burgers. Any kind of cheese, toppings of your choice—all the veggies, five kinds of cheese, you name it."

"I'll have the Bleu Buffalo Burger, please, with mushrooms and bacon."

He hustled through the swinging doors behind the bar. A joyous solo rendition of "Sugar Magnolia" floated from the kitchen, accompanied by the banging of pots and pans.

"Saw my baby down by the river…"

Crystal swabbed the counter in time with the song. "David's our mascot as well as the cook. He's part of the place, and he does make a mean buffalo burger."

"He looks a little… well…"

"A little rough? Yeah, he still looks like a druggie, doesn't he? But he kicked all his bad habits years ago. Now he needs to trade his 'Narcotics Anonymous' T-shirt for one that says 'Workaholics Anonymous.' You'll see. He'll have that chicken coop of yours fixed up in no time."

"How the heck do you get to be a drug addict in Lackaduck?" Libby asked. "Aren't we kind of off the beaten path?"

"Not for methamphetamines. Wyoming, Nebraska, the Dakotas—they're loaded with meth labs. It seems like Cash finds a new one every month." The saloon doors swung open and she looked up. "Don't you, Sheriff?"

Libby jerked her head around to see Cash posed in the doorway like the hero of some cheesy Western, his gun-belt draped low, the star gleaming on his chest. She wasn't worried about drug dealers now, not with him around. She wasn't worried about terrorists or mountain lions either.

All she had to worry about was Cash sitting down

beside her. Because then the whole town would figure they were doing the nasty on a nightly basis. And judging from the way the sheriff was looking at her, he wouldn't mind making that bit of gossip a reality.

~

Cash settled down beside Libby at the bar. She seemed flustered, fooling with her silverware, pretending to look for something in her purse—anything to avoid looking at him. If he didn't know better, he'd think she'd committed some crime and had a guilty conscience.

But no, Libby was innocent. She just didn't want him to know how she felt about him.

She lifted her eyes to his and he felt something inside him twist with anticipation. The lady gave as good as she got. He felt like she was seeing into his soul.

Or at least into his libido.

"So is that true?" she asked.

Cash tried to remember what they were talking about. Then he remembered they hadn't been talking. The look they'd shared had said everything that needed to be said as far as he was concerned, but women liked to talk.

"Is what true?"

"That you find a lot of meth labs."

"Sure do," Cash said. "Seems like every time I shut one down, two take its place."

Libby looked down at her silverware again. She'd probably expected Lackaduck to be a regular Mayberry, with cozy small-town values and no crime more significant than the occasional jaywalker. But those places didn't exist anymore—not even out here on the plains. Still, he didn't want to scare her. He'd better replace

the rock he'd rolled aside before she changed her mind about settling here.

"It's not really that bad," he said. "Mostly Lackaduck is pretty clean-cut."

"Sure," she said. She didn't sound convinced.

"Anyway, what are you up to?" He pointed to Libby's notepad. "Working on a story?"

"I just interviewed Mike Cresswell," she said.

"Crazy Mike?"

"Mike Cresswell," she said again. She looked annoyed.

It figured. She was probably one of those liberal do-gooders, seeing the world through a haze of good intentions. People like that didn't understand that you needed to be careful around people like Crazy Mike.

"Oh," Cash said. "Sorry. But everybody calls him that."

"That doesn't make it right," she said.

The men's room door swung open and Mike shuffled out. "There he is," Libby said. She gave Mike a welcoming smile, but he took one look at Cash and moved to a table across the room.

"Oh," Libby said. "He was sitting with me before. I guess..."

"I guess he's not comfortable sitting with the sheriff," Cash said. "That ought to tell you something right there." He lowered his voice. "Be careful, Libby."

"Careful? Of Mike? I thought he was kind of sweet," she said.

"Not really." Cash squared his shoulders, hoping she wouldn't take his warning the wrong way. He wasn't prejudiced against the handicapped or anything. He just

knew what Mike was capable of. "He can get a little obsessive about women. Don't let yourself be alone with him. And be careful around Luke Rawlins too."

The doors swung open and a gray-haired woman entered and settled in at a table by the jukebox.

"Luke?" Libby asked. "What do you mean? Why should I be careful around Luke?"

"Never mind." Cash stood abruptly and hiked up his belt. "Got to get back to work."

Libby opened her mouth to ask Cash again what he meant about Luke, but he was gone before she could blink. She wondered what he knew about her neighbor. She'd gotten over that Bundy brother thing, but maybe she should be a little more careful.

"Guess the sheriff was in a big hurry," she said to Crystal as the barkeep grabbed a menu for the latest customer.

"Cash takes his job pretty serious." Crystal scooped up a place setting and rolled it into a napkin. "We don't have to worry much with Sheriff McIntyre on the job."

"I suppose not," Libby said, "but between the meth labs and that murder they were talking about last night, Lackaduck's looking a little less rosy to me."

"Murder?" Crystal fastened a strip of paper around the napkin and turned her back, hunching her shoulders. "There was no murder."

"You know, the Della McCarthy thing," Libby reminded her.

Crystal whirled to face her, shaking the napkin-wrapped flatware. "We don't know she was murdered," she hissed through clenched teeth. She slammed the

place setting in front of Libby. "She's probably fine. Just fine," she stammered. "Maybe she met somebody. A man, you know? Maybe she's shacking up somewhere, like Big Mike said." Crystal gave the gleaming bar sink a final swipe. "I'm sure she's fine."

"She's not! She is *not!*"

Libby spun her barstool around as Mike stood abruptly, knocking his chair over backwards onto the floor. "She's not shacking up," he shouted. "She's dead! She's *dead!*"

Crystal set one hand on the phone and reached beneath the bar with the other. Libby wondered what she had under there—a baseball bat, maybe, or even a gun. "Stop it, Mike," she said. "You know you can't raise your voice in here. You settle down, or I'll call the sheriff. You settle down right *now.*"

The big man bowed his head and pulled his chair up off the floor, then dabbed at the table with a cocktail napkin where his beer had spilled. "She's not alive. She's not well," he mumbled as he shambled out of the bar.

Crystal's hands trembled as she grabbed a handful of silverware, then dropped it with a clatter. Libby had never seen her so upset.

"Oh my gosh, Mrs. M., I'm so sorry," Crystal said to the gray-haired woman. "So sorry."

"It's okay, Crystal," the woman said. She approached the bar and stood beside Libby. She was tall, with silver hair swept back in tidy waves from her forehead. She looked tired and sad, but she carried herself with dignity.

"We all know that man's—well, he's not right in the head. In fact, I've always wondered… oh, we've all wondered, right?"

Crystal nodded.

The woman's hands quivered as she gripped her purse in front of her, but she managed to give Libby a polite nod. "I'm Mary McCarthy," she said. "I was—I *am*—Della's mother."

Libby felt like she'd been punched in the stomach. "Oh, God. I'm sorry," she stammered. "So sorry. I—I shouldn't have brought it up. I had no idea Mike would act like that. It's just I—I'm a reporter, and I can't help asking..."

"It's all right," Mary repeated. She leaned over and patted Libby's hand. "I'm glad to have someone take an interest. Sometimes it seems like the whole world's forgotten my baby girl."

"Nobody here's forgotten her," Crystal said.

"Not Mr. Cresswell, obviously," Mary said.

"You really can't pay attention to what he says," Crystal said, her voice pleading. "He's crazy. You know that."

"I know," Mary said. "It's hard to hear, but I've gotten used to blocking things out. Sometimes I think I'm just in denial, but I can't help hoping you're right, and she's out there somewhere."

"Cash will find her," Libby said. "And he was just here. It's too bad you missed him."

"No, it's not," Mary said. "He left when he saw me come in, and I don't blame him. He's got nothing to say." She sighed. "The sheriff has a whole town to protect. He can't be running around at my beck and call, and I know it."

I could run around at your beck and call, Libby thought guiltily. She remembered the flush of pleasure she'd felt when she learned there was a possible murder

case to solve in Lackaduck. She'd been glad there was a tragedy. Glad there was a young girl missing. She was turning into one of those tabloid types, glorying in other people's pain. She looked at Mary's haunted eyes and wondered how she'd strayed so far from the heart of what journalism was all about.

She was supposed to be helping people.

"Do you have any new ideas?" Libby asked. "Were there any leads Cash didn't follow up on?"

"Yes, but I can't be down here to do anything about them. My husband—he had a stroke about a year ago, and I have to stay with him. He doesn't remember much. Sometimes he doesn't even seem to know who I am." Mary looked away, pretending to adjust her makeup, but Libby suspected she was dashing away a tear. "He remembers Della, though. He asks for her all the time. He complains she never comes to see him. It about breaks my heart."

Libby looked down at the table, tracing the curves of the wood grain with one finger. She'd been feeling sorry for herself for weeks, moping about her petty problems. So her boyfriend left her. So her dog died. Big deal. This woman was mourning her daughter while she cared for a husband who no longer recognized her.

"So did you say you were a reporter?" Mary asked.

Libby nodded. "I work for the *Lackaduck Holler* now, but I did some crime reporting in Atlanta. Investigative work."

"Well, maybe you could do some investigating for me."

Libby felt a jolt of excitement, then a wave of shame realizing she was still using Mary's tragedy to boost her career. Looking at the woman's flushed, expectant face,

she decided it probably didn't matter. All Mary wanted was a reason to hope—a faint possibility that her daughter might be found.

"I could try," Libby said. "I'd be glad to try."

Chapter 9

"So what brought Della to Lackaduck in the first place?" Libby asked, patting the chair beside her.

"She stopped here on her way to visit the university." Mary sat down and nodded a thank-you as Crystal set a heaping chopped salad in front of her and slid a teetering plate of burger and fries Libby's way. "She was headed there in the fall, and she loved this town. She'd shown her horses at Lackaduck Days every year since she turned fourteen. The last couple years, she spent the whole summer here, working for a veterinarian."

"A veterinarian? It wasn't Ron Stangerson, was it?"

"Yes. At the Lackaduck Animal Clinic."

Libby wondered. Could the Ronster have taken his flirting too far with a girl that young? Surely he had more sense than that. Then she remembered her last appointment and realized he didn't have any sense at all.

She noted Ron's name under "Suspects" in her mental file cabinet, just behind Mike's, then glanced up as the saloon doors flapped open. A tall figure silhouetted against the daylight stepped into the bar and resolved itself into her friendly neighborhood cowboy.

At least she thought he was friendly. But Cash's comment was nibbling at her subconscious, eating away at her newfound trust, hinting at something sinister going on under that well-worn cowboy hat.

He sure didn't look sinister. He looked—well, he looked *good.* And he sure acted like an honest-to-God good guy. But judging from Libby's previous romantic escapades, she was no judge of character. For some reason, her taste in men tended toward lying, cheating scumbags. And judging from the spasms of lust that ricocheted through her nether parts whenever Luke walked into a room, he was probably the lyingest, cheatingest scumbag around.

"Hey," he said. "I finished my errands. Am I too late for lunch?" He nodded toward Mrs. McCarthy. "Ma'am," he said. He tipped his hat off and clasped it to his chest, nervous and polite as a cowhand come to Sunday dinner at the big house. "May I join you?"

Libby fooled with her fork. Mrs. McCarthy was smiling knowingly, no doubt thinking she was watching a romance develop. Crystal had been thinking the same thing. So was everybody else in town, including Luke himself.

This had to stop.

"I'm kind of in the middle of something here," Libby said. "Sorry."

"It's all right," Mary began, but Libby shook her head slightly and the woman hushed.

Luke glanced at Mary, then at Libby. He was wearing the same charming, hopeful expression that had lured Libby to the Roundup with him the week before, and sent her off in search of him this morning. She kept her face impassive and waited for him to get a clue.

"Oh," he said. "Sorry." He set his hat back on his head and turned to leave. When he reached the door, he looked over his shoulder and smiled hesitantly. "I'm not

stalking you or anything, you know. I just thought—oh, never mind."

Libby shrugged and picked up a fork, rubbing an imaginary speck of dirt off the tines.

"See you around then," Luke mumbled. The doors flipped back and forth a few times behind him, and she squelched an unwelcome stab of regret. Mary winked at her.

"He likes you," she said with a playful lilt in her voice. "And he's cute. If I were your age… well."

"I'm just not looking for that right now," Libby said firmly, as much to convince herself as to inform Mary. "I'm actually doing him a favor. My last relationship didn't end well. It'll be a long time before I can trust anybody."

Mary leaned forward, her expression earnest. "You'll get over it." She patted Libby's hand and looked toward the window, watching Luke cross the parking lot. "Our country boys are a lot more trustworthy than your city types, you know."

"I hope so." Libby sighed. "They're sure better looking." She pushed the image of Luke's hopeful smile out of her mind. "Let's get back to Della." She squirted a dab of ketchup onto her plate and dipped a fry in it. "She was into horses?"

Mary nodded. "She had a Paso Fino stallion—a real winner. We bought him just before—well, just before she came here this last time."

"Paso Finos? Out here? Aren't they from Peru or something?"

Mary nodded. "They're actually very versatile. That's what Della said, anyway." She sighed. "He was expensive, but we figured as long as Della was at the

stable, she wasn't likely to get involved with drugs or boys. Skydancer kept her safe." She cleared her throat to keep from choking on the irony. "At least, that's what we thought."

Libby nodded and picked at her fries, giving Mary a chance to recover her equilibrium. The woman pushed her salad around the plate, but she didn't eat a bite.

"Della was meeting some friends here," she finally continued. "That's how we found out she was missing." She stared across the room, as if reliving the day her daughter disappeared. "Brandy—she came up here from Cheyenne—called us right away when Della didn't show up. And then Larissa, their friend from Billings, came down later. She and Brandy hunted all over town for Della."

"Was Della's car here?"

"They never found it. That's the one thing that gives me hope. How could the car disappear without Della driving it?"

"Maybe a carjacking gone wrong?"

"Trust me, nobody would steal that car." Mary's laugh was shaky. "It was a little tiny thing, a Geo Metro, all beat up."

"I'll need to talk to her friends," Libby mused. "Brandy, was it? And Larissa?"

"I can get you their numbers. But let me tell you my three suspects."

"Shoot," Libby said.

Mary held up one finger. "The first one's that Crazy Mike, of course," she said, then tilted her head toward the kitchen. "The second one's the chef."

"Because of his record?"

"That, and he just gives me the creeps. Always smiling, after all he's been through. It's not natural."

Libby pictured the chef in his apron, his eyes sparkling as he dashed off the entrees.

"Okay," she said. "But I doubt he's involved. In my experience, most drug addicts, recovered or otherwise, don't have the energy to commit crimes of passion unless someone's standing between them and a fix. It doesn't sound like Della was involved with anything like that—was she?"

Mary drew back as if insulted, then thought better of it and relaxed. "I know you have to ask that, but no. She was a good girl."

"I figured that," Libby said. "So who else?"

Mary raised another finger. "That vet. The man's a creep."

"I've met him, and I know what you mean. I didn't realize Della worked for him. That's interesting."

Mary looked at her watch and pushed her chair back. "I've got to get home. The visiting nurse leaves at five, and it's a three-hour drive at least. Can you follow up on some of what I've told you?"

"I can. Give me your number, and I'll give you mine. Maybe you could call me with the numbers for Della's friends."

They scrawled their numbers on bar napkins, then stood and hugged awkwardly.

"Let me get lunch," Libby said, rummaging in her satchel.

"Now, Libby, that's the least I can do," Mary protested. "You're taking all this time to help. I'm certainly paying for your lunch."

"All right. But I'll get the tip." Libby felt around for her change purse. She always kept a few small bills in there for just this kind of occasion. Now where was it? She began emptying her bag onto the table—wallet, makeup bag, gum… no change purse. This was embarrassing.

"I'm sorry, Mary, I've lost my change purse somehow." She opened her wallet and grimaced. "All I have is a twenty."

"Well, I don't see why you should pay anyway." Mary handed Crystal her own twenty and waved away the change. "Worth every penny, Crystal."

Libby followed Mary out to the parking lot and watched her clatter off in an old Ford pickup that had obviously seen better days. She wondered what the woman's life was like, with her daughter gone and a sick husband, and shook her head.

"Aww, don't say no, honey," a voice behind her said. "Not 'til you know what we got to offer."

She turned and saw the two bikers from the bar leaning against a black pickup truck. They were both thoroughly upholstered in black leather, and the truck, loaded with add-on chrome, was perched so high on its oversized tires that it looked like it might tip over right there in the parking lot.

"I don't think you have anything I want," Libby said brusquely, and stalked over to her truck. She glanced around the parking lot, wishing the sheriff hadn't left.

"But we got a real treat for you, baby," the man said. He gyrated his hips and gestured obscenely.

His friend grinned, revealing the few crooked teeth he had left in his gums. "We got paid," he said gleefully. "We got a whole case of Coors and a real nice room at

the Super 8. You could come on back with us. We could have us a real fun party, honey."

"I don't think so," Libby said. She swung up into the pickup and slammed the door, hitting the locks the minute it closed.

"Come on!" the first guy shouted. He ran to the side of the pickup and tried to boost himself into the bed. Libby started the truck and slammed it into reverse.

He fell and staggered away.

"Bitch!" he shouted, struggling to stand. Libby heard something hit the back window and looked back to see his gap-toothed friend selecting another missile from a handful of rocks. She gunned it and got out of there.

Lackaduck's idyllic small-town atmosphere was fading fast.

Chapter 10

Luke spent most of the next day in the north pasture after an ornery steer broke through the fence and led the herd over a mess of barbed wire to mill around in County Road 12, bawling their dismay at being lost and having their legs cut up. He and Tango herded them back to pasture easily enough, but it took half the day to repair the fence and patch up the bovine cuts and scrapes.

Just as he finished up and mounted Tango to head for home, he spotted a plume of dust billowing down the dirt road that connected his ranch to Libby's place. She had company.

No concern of his.

Or was it? She was his neighbor, she was a woman, and she was all alone out there. Cowboy chivalry demanded that he check it out—right? He cocked his wrist and checked his watch. He had time. He could stop by Lackaduck Farm and still make it to his appointment in Laramie later.

He urged his horse into a trot and headed for the road, squinting to make out the vehicle at the head of the dust cloud. It looked like a UPS truck. She'd probably ordered something for that sparsely furnished house of hers. With any luck, it'd be a slipcover for that hideous sofa. Tapping Tango with his heels, he relaxed into the rhythm of the quarter horse's fluid lope. Libby probably didn't need protection from the UPS guy, but he needed a distraction.

He slowed Tango to a walk when he hit the driveway. No sense letting his new neighbor think he was bored enough to chase after every vehicle that cruised the road—even though there were days when that was true. Ranching was a long series of dull, eventless days, punctuated by non-stop panic when a storm struck or calving time hit. There was either too much to do, or not enough.

Today was a not-enough day.

Something small and white skittered in front of Tango's hooves when he turned into Libby's driveway, and the horse shied to one side. The creature looked kind of like a chicken, only skinnier. It dove into the sagebrush and disappeared before Luke could get a really good look at it. Could chickens move that fast? Maybe it was some kind of racing poultry.

He calmed the horse and trotted him up to the house, turning him into a small fenced area beside the barn.

"Wha'dja get?" He jogged up the front steps as the delivery man pulled away. "Anything good?"

Libby lofted a large white box in the air. Frantic peeping blasted from the air holes poked in the side, and something was skittering around inside, scrabbling against the cardboard.

"Chickens," she said.

"More? You already have some, right? I saw one on the way up. It scared the crap out of Tango."

"Oh, that's not mine. That's Wild Thing. She belonged to the previous owners, but I guess they couldn't catch her when they left. So she's gone native." She grinned. "She pretty much scares the crap out of me too."

Libby flipped the screen door open, propping it with her foot while she jockeyed the big box inside.

A high-pitched yelp greeted her, and Luke braced himself for his first encounter with the terrible Ivan.

But what rocketed out of the living room definitely wasn't Ivan, though it was terrible in its own way. It was a seething mass of brown and white, leaping and spinning like a breaking wave around Libby's heels.

"What the…" He backed against the wall. The creatures broke off tormenting Libby and surged toward him. They were dogs, all right—little yapper dogs. If there was any bullmastiff in these guys' DNA, it had been completely obliterated by some wimpier strain. Like lab rat, maybe, or hamster.

"What the heck are these?" He bent down and picked one up. It was obviously just a puppy, white with brown patches. It looked up at him and let loose a tiny belch, then slurped him on the lips.

Libby scooped up the biggest dog and held it to her chest. "Umm, this is Penny. And the rest of them are her babies. I'm fostering them for the shelter. Look out. That's Rotgut. He throws up a lot."

Luke hastily returned the puppy to the floor and wiped his mouth with the back of his hand. "What does Ivan think of them?"

Libby collapsed onto the sofa as if surrendering more than the truth. Looking up from under her lashes, she seemed to be going for some effort at female supplication. It obviously didn't come easy.

"There is no Ivan," she said. "I lied because I thought you were a serial killer."

Luke fell onto the sofa beside her, laughing. The momma dog leapt onto his chest, joining in with a toothy grin, and he ruffled her fur. "So Ivan is… is…"

"Totally made up. I couldn't help it," she protested. "There you were, telling me how dangerous it was to be alone, and all of a sudden I realized it might be you that was dangerous. For all I knew you were Ted Bundy's kid brother."

Luke quieted, wiping his eyes. "I get it, and I'm sorry. I can see why you'd be nervous."

And he could. Hadn't he felt a spark of alarm when he'd seen the truck heading for her place? He couldn't imagine how she felt, out here all alone and unprotected. Although judging from her demeanor, it took more than a few days on her own to get her spooked. He laid his hand over hers. "I just can't believe it," he said, shaking his head. "I come up here expecting Ivan the Terrible, and instead you've got these ridiculous little animals that hop like bunny rabbits. What the heck are they, anyway?"

"Jack Russell terriers. And only the mother is mine. I'm just fostering her puppies until we find homes for them." She leaned forward, her eyes aglow with sudden enthusiasm. "Do you want one? Jack Russell terriers are really popular. Remember Eddie on *Frasier*? He was a Jack Russell."

"No, thanks. Jack Russell *terrors* is more like it." He watched the puppies, who had resumed their antics and were hopping desperately around the table in an effort to reach the box of peeping chicks. "Hey, aren't those the ones Glenda was taking around town?"

"What do you mean?"

"I think it was last week. She had 'em in a basket, all dressed up with ribbons and bows, looking real cute. Tried to palm one off on just about everybody."

"Everybody?"

"Yeah, pretty much. But she couldn't find anybody fool enough to take 'em. I mean, anybody, um, kind enough. You know. Like you."

"Yeah, like me," Libby said. "Stupid. Oh, great."

"Don't worry. They'll be good pets," he said. "If you like your pets kind of... active. It's just that they're not much good for ranch work or anything. And aren't you afraid they'll eat your chickens?"

"You're right," she said. She looked down as if she'd just noticed his hand on hers and jerked away like he'd burned her. "I'd better keep an eye on my peeps."

"Peeps?"

"It's a technical term." She hopped up and grabbed a pair of scissors from a mug on the counter. Carefully slitting the tape on the box, she lifted the lid. "Aren't they cute, though? And this is just the start. I've got a whole bunch more coming in about a month."

She snagged a skittering ball of fluff and lifted it gently from the box, looking into its beady little eyes before she set it in a larger wooden box she'd set up with a lightbulb mounted in one corner to provide heat. Luke stood to watch as she transferred the others. The babies staggered toward the warmth, climbing over each other's backs to get close to the bulb, cheeping loudly and unceasingly.

The sound drove the puppies crazy. They took turns jumping up and down, struggling to get a look inside the madly peeping box. It looked like they were riding invisible pogo sticks.

Luke picked up a chicken and held it at eye level, feeling the bony, fragile body warm in his hand. Its peeping

increased to a crescendo as it struggled, kicking its legs. He cupped his hand around it and it finally settled down, its shrieking dwindling to a gentler, rhythmic peep. He held it close to his face and gently stroked the soft down with one finger.

"Big feet for little birds," he commented.

"They're white Orpingtons," Libby said. "They get pretty big. They're the one breed I could find that seemed hardy enough to survive the winters here."

"So you know about that."

He'd wondered if this city girl realized what she was in for. Tourists often opted to settle in Wyoming, lured by the wide-open spaces and endless skies, but they rarely lasted more than a year or two. Once they realized that all that space just gave the biting winter wind more room to work up speed, they planted "For Sale" signs and headed back where they came from.

"Yeah," Libby said. "I'm going to run electric out to the chicken house for heat and warm water. They should be okay."

"Orpingtons," he mused. "Sounds like some aristocratic British breed."

"You're right. The original Orpingtons were black, and came from County Kent in England. The first examples in this country were shown at Madison Square Garden in 1895."

"You really know your chickens, don't you?"

"Yes, I do. My chickens are very important to me."

"You're an odd duck, Libby. Very odd." He set the chick gently into the box and watched it rush into the fray, clambering over its fellows to reach the warm bulb. "So do we get eggs or meat out of these guys? They

don't look like much now." He'd be the first to admit baby chicks were cute when they were fluffy and yellow, but a few of these guys were starting to enter the awkward age. Occasional feathers were spiking through the fluff, creating flamboyant Einsteinian hairdos that made them look like tiny homeless men awakened from a long, cold night on the streets.

"That's what's great about Orpingtons," Libby said. "They're good for both. They'll start laying at four or five months. When they get older—well, we don't want to talk about that." She lowered her voice. "Not where they can hear us."

"How do you know these are girls?"

"Don't ask. I could demonstrate, but do you really want to get that intimate with a chicken?"

"Not with a chicken." He looked straight into her eyes, and her expression was suddenly wary.

Wary, but hardly hostile.

Stepping closer, he swept an errant lock of hair gently behind her shoulder. "This is going to be a serious poultry farm, isn't it?" He wondered if she could tell from his tone that he was serious about something far more interesting than chicken farming. He was starting to really like this woman. Like her, want her, and respect her—all at once. It was a new experience for him.

"Poultry *ranch*," she insisted, oblivious to the undercurrents flowing through the conversation. "And I prefer to call it a *herd*."

"That's not correct chicken terminology, is it?" he asked. "I thought it was flock."

"Not out here in Wyoming, where the men are men

and the sheep are scared. Here in the West, we call it a herd." She set her hands on her hips and lowered her brows in a schoolmarm squint. "Repeat after me: Libby runs seventy-five head of chickens on her poultry ranch."

"Sure." He laughed. "You're really getting the hang of Western living, aren't you?"

"You bet, cowboy." She cocked a hip and grinned, the pose spunky and somehow seductive. Maybe she was catching on to those undercurrents after all.

"I guess this makes you a chicken wrangler, doesn't it?"

"It sure does." She tossed her hair. "I'm a top hand."

He scanned her from her bare feet to her ragged cutoffs, then moved his gaze up to the skimpy tank top that peaked over her breasts.

"You certainly are," he agreed. "But we need to outfit you accordingly. Chaps, I think. And a cowboy hat." His eyes worked their way back down her body, taking their time and pausing to linger on every curve. "Nothing else," he said softly.

Libby could feel her body warming under Luke's gaze, her breasts straining against the thin fabric as if they were determined to announce just how scanty the top really was. She reached up to tug at the neckline, and one of the spaghetti straps slid down her shoulder, exposing a delicate swatch of pale skin.

Maybe a man really could undress you with his eyes.

She was starting to hope so. The heat of his gaze, and the not-so-subtle hints scattered through his

conversation, had awakened an answering warmth in the pit of her stomach—or maybe a little lower.

He reached out, and for a moment she thought he was going to dislodge the other strap, but he gently pushed the fallen one back into place. His hand lingered on her bare shoulder, sending a heating flush down her back, then moved to the nape of her neck. His fingers gathered a handful of curls as he bent to kiss her.

Their lips touched, softly at first, but she let out a little moan—in pleasure or protest, she wasn't sure which—and his lips grew instantly harder and hotter. He swept one arm around her waist and pulled her close, pressing her body to his. When his tongue found hers, a flush of warmth flooded her veins and turned her muscles to mush. Her knees gave way and he cupped the seat of her shorts.

Suddenly, all her barriers collapsed like Troy under siege and she knew what she wanted, what she needed, and it was Luke—his lips, his tongue, his hands. She wanted him to taste her, touch her, run his hands over her, kiss every inch of her body. Twice. Maybe three times.

What she didn't want was a dog jumping onto the table and knocking the box of chickens onto the floor.

But that's what she got.

"Grab the puppies!" She jerked out of Luke's arms and grabbed Rooster and Rotgut by their collars. "Penny, stay!"

The dog stayed, but just barely, trembling while the chicks skittered around on the kitchen floor, peeping in panic. Penny wanted those chicks so badly she could barely control herself.

Libby knew just how she felt.

Luke grabbed the other two puppies and looked to Libby for instructions as they squirmed in his arms.

"The pantry," she said.

They pitched the puppies in, then slammed the door and fell against it side by side, panting.

"You're a good man in a crisis," she said.

"I know. You should thank me." Luke lifted one eyebrow and she felt her body warming again, softening, readying for his touch.

"You're right," she said.

He turned and faced her, smiling expectantly, his eyes half-closed.

"Thank you," she said. She dropped to the floor and scuttled after the nearest chick. "Now can you help me pick up the chickens?"

"That wasn't exactly what I had in mind," Luke said, but he knelt and helped her herd the chicks, who had gathered in a peeping mass under the kitchen table, back into their box. Their hands touched as they steered the last fluffy renegade home, and Luke gave her a hopeful glance, but Libby pulled away and pretended absorption in the chickens.

"Hey," he said.

Libby kept her attention firmly on the chickens. "Mm-hm?"

"I was wondering…"

She was wondering too. She was wondering what the hell she was thinking, letting a man she barely knew kiss her like that. And she didn't really want to know what Luke was wondering. Maybe he wanted to know if she'd kiss him again. Maybe he wanted to adjourn to

the bedroom and finish what they'd started. She wanted that too, but she wasn't going to give in to the primal urges coursing through her nether parts. She'd come to her senses.

Sort of.

Maybe.

Chapter 11

Luke cleared his throat. "I was wondering if you wanted to go for a drive. I need to go to Laramie, and I thought you might like to come."

A drive. He wanted to go for a drive. Libby felt the heat leave her body in a rush. Suddenly she was cool, calm, collected, and horrified by her total lack of self-control.

She knew she should say no. She didn't want her life complicated by romance, even if said romance came with red-hot, soul-stirring kisses and sex to match. And she wasn't sure she could sit beside Luke in his truck for an entire hour without giving in to the temptation to reach over and fondle whatever part of him was closest.

But she really wanted to go, and she could rationalize just about anything. She reminded herself that Della McCarthy had been headed for the college too. Maybe she could pick up the missing girl's trail there. See if she'd enrolled in any classes.

But she needed to make sure he understood that the kiss was a mistake. A freak accident. Something that would never be repeated. She ignored the stab of regret that pierced her chest and nodded.

"I'd like to go along," she said. "But I think we need to talk first."

"Oh, no." Luke backed away as if she'd suggested they take him over to the veterinary clinic for neutering. "It's okay. We don't need to talk."

"But..."

He lifted one hand in a "stop" gesture and continued to backpedal until he slammed into the wall. "I'm sorry, okay? I was way out of line. I shouldn't have kissed you. I just—I just got kind of—well—excited. Sorry. I'll behave, I promise." He raised two fingers. "Scout's honor."

Libby tried to breathe a sigh of relief, but what came out was a shuddering heave of unfulfilled lust. Didn't he like kissing her? Didn't he want to try again?

Apparently not.

She didn't want to either, but she was never one to turn down a challenge. The mere fact that Luke didn't want to kiss her made her want to seduce him into stuttering oblivion.

Maybe she needed to dress for success. Chaps, he'd said, and a hat. Nothing else. She visualized the outfit.

Yeah. That would probably get her kissed—and then some. She tried to remember where the nearest Western wear store was.

"Libby?" he said.

She gave herself a mental slap. She didn't want Luke to kiss her. Not at all. She was glad he'd promised to behave. Glad.

"Okay," she said. "But you have to drive slow. I have a family now." She gestured toward the dogs. "I wasn't sure I'd survive that trip to the Roundup."

"I'll drive like an old, old man, I promise. Thirty miles an hour."

"Works for me. You mind if I take Penny? She needs to get used to leaving the puppies. We can put them in the barn." Libby figured Penny would make a good

chaperone. She could hold the dog in her lap and stroke her soft ears instead of petting the driver.

"Penny? The ferocious watchdog?" Luke's eyes gleamed with humor. "Won't she attack me?"

"Oh, just forget that. I didn't know you. I thought it was safer to let you think I had a big mean dog. Just in case you started hanging around the place, or something."

Luke grinned. "Or something."

"Right." Libby looked down at Penny, who was still trembling from her thrilling encounter with the chickens. Libby was shaking too, but it had nothing to do with chickens.

"She's actually a pretty good guard dog," Luke said. "She didn't bite me. She just sicced a herd of vicious chickens on me."

"You were lucky to survive." Libby smiled and found herself looking straight into those green eyes again. Something thrilled through her that felt a lot like the kiss—hot, hard, and hungry. She steeled herself against it, but it ricocheted around inside her for a while before she managed to tamp it down.

Obviously, Luke's driving wasn't the only thing that was dangerous.

Between Lackaduck and Laramie, the interstate weaves like a wide gray ribbon through an undulating landscape of golden hills and dark ravines. Occasional antelope break the monotony, and the long stretches of sage-strewn pastureland are mottled with black and brown cattle. There are few trees, and the mountains are just a misty outline on the horizon. The sheer vastness of

the prairie always made Luke want to gallop through the sagebrush on a palomino, singing some corny Gene Autry song about big skies and no fences.

He'd gotten the truck fixed since he rolled it—sort of. The cab was still dented and battered, and the bed and one door were a different color than the rest of the truck, but that only added to the authentic cowboy look. The metallic rattle that clattered from somewhere behind the dash was an authentic cowboy sound, too, along with the clanging of the tailgate every time they hit a pothole.

He reached toward Libby and she sucked in a quick breath, glancing toward him with wide eyes. Good. She was still feeling it too. There was definitely something between them—something inevitable. But she was skittish as those hyper little chicks, and it would take time to gentle her down.

He watched her relax as his hand stopped at the radio dial. Spinning it past the static, he settled on a scratchy rendition of a Lawrence Welk tune, complete with oompah backup.

"You a big polka fan?" Libby asked.

"You have to be if you live in Lackaduck. It's the only station we get."

"Great," she said sarcastically.

"It's not so bad," Luke responded. "Ike Rasmussen runs it out of his basement. What Ike likes is what you get. And Ike likes polkas. It grows on you after a while."

Just out of Lackaduck they turned onto Latigo Road. Latigo wound through a long stretch of rural Wyoming, passing dwellings that ranged from upscale log homes to broken-down trailers. Lots of people lived out there because they loved the beauty of the wide-open spaces,

but just as many chose it for its total lack of zoning regulations. You could have as many rusted-out cars as you wanted in your front yard. And when the siding started to peel off your trailer and the screen door hung crooked, you didn't have to fix it. There was something slapdash and casual about rural living that Luke loved, even if the aesthetics weren't always great.

The university offered even less in the way of architectural interest. They passed a series of dull concrete dorms, each crouching on a yellowed lawn scorched by summer drought. Whatever the quality of its faculty, the place was a long way from the Ivy League in atmosphere. Any ivy planted there would undoubtedly wither and die.

Young minds, however, thrived—or so the university brochures would have people believe. Luke, whose mind wasn't really all that young anymore, was signing up for MBA courses in the fall.

"A cowboy with an MBA?" Libby cocked her head and studied Luke, whose long legs bracketed the truck's steering wheel. "You barely fit in a truck. How are you going to squeeze yourself behind a desk?"

He wondered about that himself sometimes, but it was a sad necessity. "These days, you have to be a businessman to run a ranch," he explained. "Knowing stock science isn't enough anymore."

"What are you taking?"

"Corporate law, accounting, and an ag course to round it out," he replied. "Oh, and organic chemistry."

"Organic chemistry? You're doomed, cowboy," she said. "Organic chemistry has kicked finer asses than yours."

Luke laughed. "That's what they said about calculus,

and I got through that all right. I'm smarter than I look, you know."

She smirked. "Thank God for that!"

"Okay, I deserved that. Walked right into it."

Libby giggled and held her hand out the window, letting the air whoosh through her fingers. Luke smiled and watched her out of the corner of his eye. She was starting to relax. Starting to fit in. Wyoming was going to be good for her.

And she was going to be good for him.

If you look up "Dragon Lady" in the dictionary, you'll find a picture of Alice Wilson. Squatting toad-like behind the admissions desk, she spent her days breathing fire on the hapless students who needed her services. Libby was fortunate enough to be mistaken for a parent, so the woman made a valiant effort to be pleasant.

"How can I help you?" she asked with a ghastly simper that set her jowls to wobbling. She slipped a pair of cat's-eye glasses onto the bridge of her hawkish nose and peered at Libby myopically.

"I'm here to inquire about a student," Libby said with feigned confidence.

"And the student is?"

"Della McCarthy."

"Social?"

"Yes, I believe she was fairly social."

Enunciating her words as one would for a small child, the dragon lady leaned forward and said, "So-shell Seck-yoo-ritty Num-ber?"

Libby gulped. "Can't you just look her up by last name?"

The dragon lady removed the glasses and fixed her with a baleful glare. "The system *requires* a social security number."

"I don't know it," Libby admitted.

"Are you a relation?"

"N-no," Libby stammered. "I'm a friend. A good friend."

Mrs. Wilson pushed her keyboard aside with pudgy, bejeweled talons. "Student information is *confidential*."

"I just need to know if she's registered here as a student."

"*Strictly* confidential," the woman repeated.

Libby was up against it, and for once she couldn't think of a good lie. Much as she hated to enlist this woman as her ally, she'd have to do it.

"Look, Mrs. Wilson, I really need to know. It's very important. I'll keep the information in the strictest confidence."

"*Nothing*," said Mrs. Wilson, "is more important that *student confidentiality*."

Libby grimaced. She was going to have to bring out the big guns. She leaned across the table and looked the dragon lady in the eye.

"What if I told you it was about *murder*?" she whispered.

Mrs. Wilson reared back in her chair, chins wobbling. "Murder?"

"Yes." Libby plopped down in the orange plastic chair in front of the desk and folded her hands into an attitude of supplication. "Della's missing, and I think she may have been murdered. But the police won't listen. They think she's a runaway or something. If I can prove

she registered here as a student, maybe even put down a deposit on her tuition, they'll see she was planning for the future. Maybe then they'll take me seriously. You've got to help me, Mrs. Wilson."

It worked. The dragon lady was hers. Pulling the keyboard into position, Mrs. Wilson tapped the keys with scarlet-painted claws.

"M-C or M-A-C?" she asked.

"M-C, I think."

She shot Libby a doubtful look—how good is a friend who can't even spell your last name?—but tapped the name into the computer.

"Della, you said?"

"Yes, D-E-L-L-A."

A look of satisfaction crossed Mrs. Wilson's broad face. "Your hunch is correct, my dear. Miss McCarthy did indeed pay a sizeable portion of her tuition up front."

"Can you tell if she ever showed up for classes?"

The excitement was almost too much for Mrs. Wilson. Practically panting, she stabbed at a few more keys.

"Never. She didn't even come to orientation."

Libby stood. "Mrs. Wilson, I can't thank you enough," she said earnestly. "You won't regret this. If you see in the paper that this young girl's killer has been discovered, you'll know you helped bring him to justice."

Pursing her fleshy lips, Libby's new friend squirmed with pleasure. "All in a day's work, my dear. All in a day's work."

Chapter 12

All the way home, Luke kept his hands on the wheel and his eyes on the road, but he could feel the memory of that kiss simmering in the sun-warmed air of the truck cab. Penny snoozed in Libby's lap while they discussed the university and their ranching ambitions—or, in Libby's case, her farming ambitions. By the time they pulled up at her place, she'd told him all about how she'd played with some Farmer Joe toy as a kid, dreaming of the day she'd have a big red barn of her own.

It was cute, really. And he had to admire her for doing everything she could to make that childhood dream come true. He'd always wanted to be a rancher, but he'd been born into his dream. She was starting from scratch, all by herself. Not many women he knew would have the guts.

He eased up the driveway and pulled to a stop as Wild Thing scampered across the yard and dodged behind the barn. She was truly the ugliest chicken he'd ever seen—scrawny, with mean little eyes and a bunch of feathers missing on her neck so she looked like a flightless white vulture.

"Wonder what she was up to?" he mused.

"I don't know," Libby said. "I get the impression she pokes around when I'm gone. I found beak-marks in the front door once, like she'd been trying to peck her way in, and sometimes there's chicken poop on the doorstep. I think she's plotting a takeover."

Luke laughed and they lapsed into silence while he tried to figure out how to say good-bye. He had no idea where they stood relationship-wise at this point. She'd discouraged his advances after their Roundup date, but then delivered a scorching kiss in her kitchen this morning. Between the kiss and today's conversation, he felt like they really knew each other now—but did that entitle him to another kiss? Or maybe something more?

It was worse than those word problems they threw at you in fourth grade math. Here he was at point A, and he had no idea how to get to point B. Or C. Or D, which was where he really wanted to be. And he had no idea how long it would take them to get there. He could go from zero to sixty in half a second when it came to relationships, but women usually didn't have that kind of horsepower.

"Well," he said, and cleared his throat. He turned to look at her, trying to read her expression. Then something caught his eye out the window behind her and suddenly, point B was the last thing on his mind.

"Oh, no." He yanked open the driver's side door and jumped out of the truck. "Don't get out. Just stay right there."

Libby turned and let out a little scream of horror. Her red pickup tilted unsteadily in front of the house on four slashed tires. Someone had scrawled "EVIL BITCH" in deep scratches on the driver's side door, and the hood was dented as though someone had stomped across it in steel-toed boots. The windows were smeared with something that looked suspiciously like dog poop—at least, Luke hoped it was from a dog.

Her truck. Her precious truck. She'd told him how all her friends in Atlanta had driven sensible city cars, Hondas and Toyotas, but she'd bought the shiny red Ranger because it looked like something Farmer Joe would drive—like a Fisher Price version of a pickup truck.

Now it was practically destroyed. Luke loped back to the car and opened her door. She was crying. He stepped back, squelching the urge to run, trying desperately to think of some comforting phrase that would stem the flood.

"My truck," she said, her voice quavering. She took a deep, shuddering breath. "Who would do that? Who hates me that much?" She caught a sob in her throat, then almost fell out of her seat and into his arms.

"That guy?" Luke asked, patting her shoulder. "That old boyfriend? Would he..."

"He doesn't care enough about me to bother," she said. Her tone was matter-of-fact, but Luke could sense an undertone of deep sorrow. "It has to be someone from here." She was still leaning on him, mumbling into his shoulder, and he wrapped his arms around her and held her tight.

"Who would do this to you?" Luke was stunned to realize he was shaking—but with rage, not passion. "Because I'll kill them," he said. "I'll *kill* them. Jesus, Libby." He gripped her shoulders and pushed her away, holding her at arm's length and looking into her eyes. "Who would do this?"

"There were a couple of toughs in the parking lot at the bar yesterday," she said. Her nose was red, her eyes bleary and swollen. She looked terrible, but for some reason that only made him want to hug her harder. "They tried to pick me up. Nasty looking guys, said they were staying at the Super 8."

"What did they look like?" He tried to slow his breathing, but a glance at the truck set his mind spinning with rage again. He'd been right to worry about Libby out here on her own. Some kind of ugliness had come to his peaceful neighborhood, and it was threatening the woman he—

Liked. He really liked her.

He'd just never liked a woman enough to go all dizzy over her like this. He felt like he'd fallen off a horse—like he was sitting dazed on the ground, wondering what had happened and watching his old life run away like a spooked stallion.

Weird thing was, he wasn't sorry to see that stallion go. But he'd feel a lot better if he could find whoever did this to Libby's truck and beat the crap out of him.

"They looked like bikers," she said. "But don't worry, Luke. I'll call the sheriff." She pulled Cash's card out of her purse, and he remembered the sheriff handing it to her at the bar. "It's his job. Don't get yourself in trouble."

He snorted, eyeing the card. "The sheriff. The sheriff won't do anything." He scanned the side of her ruined truck. "But I guess you'll have to call him. You'll need a police report for insurance." He turned away. "I can't do that for you."

He scuffed one booted toe in the dirt, wishing for the first time that he was something more than a rancher.

Wishing he had a shiny badge of his own.

~

Libby flipped her phone open and dialed the number on Cash's card. Maybe the sheriff would come over and sweep her up and put her back together again.

Not that Luke wasn't doing a good job. He was there, he was supportive, and he was a strong shoulder to cry on—but he wasn't wearing a star. Right now, she needed a superhero, and Cash was the closest thing Lackaduck had to offer. The guy was a little full of himself—heck, he was a *lot* full of himself—but when she pictured him swooping down in a cape and tights, handcuffing the bad guys and hauling them off to the pokey, the tights looked pretty good.

Luke was scuffing the toe of one boot in the dusty driveway and faking absorption in the distant mountains as if he knew his own superhero status was on the wane. Libby turned away when Cash answered, cupping one hand around the phone.

"Libby," the sheriff said. "I was just thinking about you." His tone was silky and self-assured, and she wondered what exactly he'd been thinking. She was tempted to ask, but she had to tell him about her truck.

"Evil Bitch?" he said when she'd finished. "You make some enemies around here or something?"

"I guess so." She told him about the two roughnecks in the parking lot. "Luke said they were probably from the pipeline, or maybe the railroad."

"Probably." His tone sharpened. "Is Luke there with you?"

"Uh-huh," she said.

"Have him make sure there's nobody around, okay? Tell him to check the barn and the house."

"Okay." Libby glanced over at Luke. He was walking around the truck now, and as she watched, he stroked the long side of the "B" in "Bitch" with one finger. She made a cutting motion with her free hand. "You need

to come out and dust for fingerprints, right? Check for tire tracks?"

"Sorry. I can't," Cash said. "I'm actually in the middle of a traffic stop. And then I have to answer a call at the Loaf 'n' Jug. Shoplifter in custody, and I'd better get out there before the salesclerk takes the law into his own hands and beats the crap out of a teenager for heisting a pack of gum." He chuckled. "The thrilling life of a lawman, right?"

"So you'll come out later?"

He sighed. "Look, Libby, I'm the only law west of the Lackaduck River these days. I just don't have the resources to collect evidence for something like that. The best thing you can do is stop down at the station and fill out a report. Meanwhile, I'll keep my eyes peeled for those guys."

"Okay." The sinking feeling in her gut made Libby realize how much she'd been looking forward to her rescue. Some superhero. "So you're not going to do anything then."

Luke rolled his eyes.

"Sorry, Libby," Cash said. "I can't."

"Okay." She crumpled up his business card and started to toss it in the dirt, then thought better of it and shoved it back in her pocket. She didn't want to be a litterbug. "Whatever."

She clicked the phone shut. Some sheriff. Here she was, with a truckload of property damage staring her in the face along with some pretty clear threats to her safety, and he was too busy at the Loaf 'n' Jug to do anything about it.

She wondered if there really was a shoplifter. He was probably just stocking up on doughnuts.

Luke put his arm around her shoulders and gave her a sympathetic squeeze. She wished she could stop shaking. She wished the fear would go away.

She was afraid of the bikers, and she was afraid of being so isolated in a town full of crazy taxidermists, missing teenagers, and feral chickens—but most of all, she was afraid of Luke. Because if she had to deal with a few more episodes like this, she was liable to trade her treasured independence for the safety of having a man around the house.

Chapter 13

Out on the prairie, nighttime was quiet time. There was no traffic noise, no hum from passersby, just the breeze tickling the sagebrush and a few night birds calling. The silence should have been calming, but after the day's experiences, it just made Libby uneasy. And to make matters worse, her canine companions were convinced it was their doggy duty to alert her every time a blade of grass moved. She'd started the evening jumping at every sound they made, but after a while she'd realized their barks were meaningless. They yapped and growled at the wind, at random squirrels, and even at birds flying by.

But when they all leapt to their feet in unison and ran to the front hall, she knew something was out there. Over the cacophony of barks and growls, she heard a tapping, then a full-out pounding against her flimsy front door.

Her first impulse was to dive under the bed, but she wasn't about to let a couple of ignorant barflies scare her. If she was going to live on her own, she'd have to toughen up. She shrugged into her bathrobe and rummaged through her purse for her mace canister. She'd walked the dark streets of Atlanta many times with it concealed in her fist, cocked and ready. Now she was arming herself in her own home.

So much for the serenity of country living.

She grabbed her cell phone too, and beeped over to "last dialed." That put the sheriff's number up on the screen, a finger punch away. Surely he'd tear himself away from Lackaduck's mean streets if he heard her being murdered in real time.

She paused in the hall and tried to steady her breathing. It was probably just Luke. He must have forgotten something. But the dogs knew Luke, and yet they were shying at the door, growling low in their throats, then bursting into hysterical tirades of barking.

She suddenly wished she'd taken his advice and gotten a bigger dog.

Putting her eye to a gap in the curtains that shielded the hallway's tiny window, she squinted. She couldn't see all of her visitor, but it definitely wasn't Luke. It wasn't the jerks from the parking lot, either. This guy was a lot taller, and quite a bit wider, too. Dirty jeans sagged in the seat, and the hair on his arms was reddish and thick. A tattoo of a chainsaw peeked out from under a ragged sleeve. It was Mike.

Crazy Mike.

Libby told herself she'd get some better locks as soon as she could. Standing there with just a rickety old doorknob between her and a mentally unstable taxidermist was a bad feeling. If this was a slasher movie, he'd be coming to kill her so he could stuff her and keep her forever. Would he mount her in the attack pose?

He'd have to. Because if Luke was wrong about Mike's gentle nature, she wasn't going down without a fight.

"What do you want?" she shouted through the closed door.

"I want you to stop asking questions, that's what!" Mike shouted in his weirdly high-pitched voice.

"Questions?" She wondered how she'd offended him. Was this about Della?

"Just stay out of it. Just mind your own beeswax," he reiterated.

"I'm sorry, Mike, I don't know what you're talking about." Libby tried to keep her voice level. "I'm not in anybody's *beeswax* but my own."

"Good. Stay there. Or you'll be sorry."

She recoiled as her visitor peered in the window, his face inches from her own. His hair was dirty, with flakes of paint or worse flecking the curls, and his clothes were filthy and ill-fitting. He looked like he'd come from a hard day's drinking, and his eyes had a strange, unfocused look.

"I can tell you, you'll be really sorry," he repeated. "Sorry you ever even knew she existed."

"Who, Mike? What are you talking about?"

"You know who I'm talking about. Della. Pretty Della. You stop asking all those questions about her, or you'll be sorry." Turning abruptly, he trudged down the steps and headed for a beat-up Ford Fairlane parked halfway up the lawn. "Really sorry, real, real sorry," he mumbled as he jerked open the driver's side door.

Libby watched him spin the car around, flinging divots of turf in his wake. Her already pathetic lawn bore an arched scar where he'd pulled out. She opened the door and stepped outside as he careened down the driveway, the old car weaving from side to side. The dogs shot past her and hightailed it down the driveway, barking madly, their courage restored now that the enemy was leaving the scene.

"Penny, Rotgut, Rooster!" She called the dogs off and they reluctantly returned. Her hands were shaking as she grabbed her phone and hit "send."

"Cash? It's Libby again."

"Hey. Good to hear from you." His tone was surprised and kind of flirtatious. "You've been on my mind all night."

"Really? Well, I've evidently been on Crazy Mike's mind too." She swallowed. Whatever Luke said, the nickname fit. "He came out here and threatened me."

"You're kidding. Mike never goes anywhere. Home, the bar—that's it. What the hell did he want?"

"He said I should stop asking questions. About that girl—Della McCarthy. He said I'd be sorry I ever heard she existed."

There was a pause on the other end of the line.

"You've been asking questions about Della?"

"Yeah—just a few." Libby was embarrassed to be caught second-guessing Cash's investigative skills. He was the sheriff, after all. He probably didn't like civilians meddling in his business.

But she wasn't a civilian. She was a reporter. And besides, she was working for Della's mother. Just because she wasn't getting paid didn't mean it wasn't official.

"Where are you now?" Cash asked. There was a new urgency in his tone.

"I'm home. In my kitchen. Why?"

"Where's Mike? Is he gone?"

"Yeah, he took off down the driveway in his beat-up old car. Took half my lawn with him."

"Libby, if he comes back, don't open the door." His tone was suddenly urgent. "Don't talk to him, don't

let him know you're there. Hide if you have to. I'll be right over."

"Cash, what's up? Is he dangerous? Has he hurt somebody before?"

"He may have killed somebody before. He may have killed Della. Just sit tight. I'll be right over, and we'll make out a report."

"I'll be here. In the closet, probably." Libby sank down on a kitchen chair, her knees shaking. "Geez, Cash. Do you think he'll come back? Why do you think he did it? Was he involved with Della somehow?"

"He gave you one good piece of advice, hon: stop asking questions. I'll explain everything when I get there."

Libby hung up the phone and ran through the house, checking the feeble locks on her windows and doors. She wondered if she should turn on every light in the place so she could see Crazy Mike coming, or shut them all off so he couldn't see in. She finally compromised by leaving a light on in the kitchen and sitting in the dark bedroom at the other end of the house.

The dogs weren't much help. For one thing, the puppies weren't much bigger than kittens, and not nearly as vicious. Their mom was a big 'fraidy cat too. She plastered herself against Libby's leg, shivering and whimpering at every sound. The only way she was helping was by making Libby feel brave by comparison, and self-esteem wasn't her biggest problem at the moment.

Her biggest problem was deciding whether to bolt for the basement if a car pulled in the driveway. She wondered how she'd tell if it was Crazy Mike coming to finish her off, or Cash coming to rescue her.

Chapter 14

Cash made the most of his entrance, reeling into Libby's drive with sirens screaming, a cloud of dust billowing behind the cruiser. The porch light flickered to life, and the front door opened as he approached. Libby leaned against the jamb, watching him. He put a little extra lawman swagger in his walk so she'd feel safe. Protected.

"You okay, hon?" A herd of little yapper dogs leapt behind her like a herd of crazed rabbits, barking their heads off, then scrabbled their paws on the linoleum in their haste to run and hide as he approached.

Libby blushed, and no wonder. She was hardly dressed for male visitors. He'd hoped she might be wearing some kind of lingerie, or at least a lacy robe—but the single life apparently hadn't done much for her nighttime fashion sense. She was dressed in an outfit that could only be described as jammies. Granny jammies.

And she had bunny slippers on her feet. Pink ones, with googly eyes.

Still, she looked kind of cute. He reached out and touched her arm. "You okay?"

"I'm fine," she said, but her voice was shaking. She drew away, folding her arms. Probably resisting the urge to touch him back. "It's just too much. First my truck, now this."

Cash pulled out a chair at the head of the kitchen table and sat down, pulling a pencil and a memo pad from his pocket. "Tell me as much as you can about what Mike said. It could be important."

Libby perched on the edge of the chair next to him and tried to explain the events of the past hour. Her story was a little convoluted, but then her memory was probably scrambled by fear. She didn't seem to have any trouble remembering what Crazy Mike had said, though. Those words were probably etched on her brain.

"He said I'd be sorry if I didn't stop asking questions—that I should mind my own business," she said.

Cash jotted down the phrase. "Did he say what he'd do?"

"Not specifically. But I don't think I'll be asking any more questions around Crazy Mike." She blew out a long breath. "So what's the story, Sheriff?"

Cash tucked the notebook back in his pocket. "There's no story, really. We haven't got anything on him, except that he talked about Della a lot after she disappeared. Asking everybody where she was, what happened to her." He sat back, bouncing the eraser end of the pencil on the table. "A lot of people think he had something to do with her disappearance."

"Do you?"

"Yeah, I hate to say it, but I do." He looked away from her expectant face and the pencil tapped faster. "A lot of people think Crazy Mike is harmless. He grew up around here, and if you knew him as a kid, it's hard to see him hurting anybody." Leaning forward as if to emphasize his point, he returned his

gaze to Libby's face and let the pencil rest. "But he was never quite right."

"What do you mean?"

"There's no impulse control," he said. "For instance, he had this little dog a while back. Looked a lot like these critters you've got." He motioned toward the dogs, who were bobbing and weaving in the doorway. The siren had freaked them out, so it was one step forward and two steps back as they edged their way into the room. Cash's gesture sent the puppies back a few feet, but Penny skittered across the floor and jumped into Libby's lap. "It went with him everywhere, and he was really attached to it—always carrying it around, wouldn't let anybody touch it. It was always 'mine, mine.' About a month after Della disappeared, the dog did too. A few days later I found it out back of his place in the woods." He pushed back from the table and shoved the pencil into his pocket. "Its neck was broken."

"Oh, no. You think he killed it?"

"Yeah. He loved that little dog, but he was so possessive about it. He probably squeezed it too tight, or got mad when it tried to do its own thing or something." He shifted in his chair and cleared his throat. "And the possessive thing he had with the dog? He was that way about Della, too—following her, talking about her, hanging around the place she was staying. His coming out here makes me think you're on his mind in the same way. That's not good, Libby. Not good at all."

"He really is crazy," she murmured.

"He sure is," Cash said. "But he's right on one thing." He gave her a hard look. "You should stop asking questions."

"You're probably right," she said, straightening the fringe on a place mat as if it was the most important task in the world. "It's just—I'm a reporter, Cash. I know there's more to Lackaduck than Grange meetings and quilting bees." She abandoned the place mat and looked up at Cash, setting her jaw. "Asking questions is my job."

"I know that. But I don't think you'll make any friends if you put Della's case in the paper again. It's something this town would like to forget."

"Della's mom doesn't want us to forget, Cash."

"I know that. And I haven't forgotten. Far from it." His voice dropped into a gentler tone. "Libby, I'm doing the best I can. I haven't forgotten Mrs. McCarthy's little girl, and I haven't given up on finding her. Can you tell her that for me?"

"I will." She got up. "I'm sure it'll make her feel better. Would you like a cup of coffee, Sheriff?"

"Well, we're about done here."

"I'd just as soon you stick around a while."

He couldn't blame her. She'd had a bad scare, and was probably just realizing how foolish it was for a woman to settle out here on her own. No wonder she liked having a man in the house—especially a man with a badge and a gun.

"I wouldn't mind coffee. I've got a long night ahead."

Libby picked up a bag with a Starbucks label and dumped some beans in an electric grinder. She sure was a city girl. Most folks just kept a can of Folgers on the counter, but she had to grind hers fresh. It was kind of nice, though. Smelled great. Homey.

Over the roar of the machine, she asked, "So how long have you been the sheriff?"

"About four years."

"What did you do before that?"

"I sold insurance for a while and ran some cattle on the side, but a year or so ago I got into horses full time. Picked up a really good stallion and bred some real winners. I mostly ran for sheriff 'cause nobody else would step up and take care of things."

"It seems to suit you."

"It does." He adjusted his belt and settled back in his chair. "So what goes on between you and our friend Luke?"

Libby measured the pulverized beans into the coffeemaker and hit the start button.

"Nothing special." She turned to face him. "What was it you were saying about him the other night?" She tried to remember his words, but all she could recall was that he'd made it sound like Luke was dangerous. "You said I should be careful around him."

He shrugged. "Oh, nothing."

"Nothing?" It hadn't sounded like "nothing" the other night. It had sounded like a warning.

"It's just that I thought you had something going with him," Cash said.

"Well, I don't. I mean, I got in a car with him once." Her tone took on a sharp edge. "Apparently, around here, that makes us a couple." She watched the cocoa-colored liquid drip into the pitcher. "Anyway, why is it so important? Is there something wrong with him? Or are people here really that hard up for gossip? Dang. I've never seen a grown man so interested in soap opera stuff."

"I'm not interested in soap opera stuff."

"Could've fooled me." She set two mugs on the table, along with a quart of milk and a hideous sugar bowl shaped like a chicken.

"I'm interested in you," he said.

Yikes, Libby thought. That silky tone on the telephone wasn't just reflexive flirting; Cash really was interested in her. Amazing. She had as much self-esteem as the next girl, but he was possibly the best-looking man she'd ever seen, and his charisma level was off the charts.

So why wasn't she excited?

Maybe because he was *so* good looking, *so* weirdly magnetic. Every time she looked at him, her brain short-circuited, but when he touched her, the thrill she felt was ten percent attraction and ninety percent fear.

And he touched her way too much.

"I'm not looking for a relationship, Cash," she said.

"Okay," he said. "Sorry. I kind of figured that, but it was worth a try. Hopefully we can still be friends?"

"Oh, sure," she said.

"I like to keep a good rapport going with the press," he said. "I need to be able to trust you, and in return, I can give you information that'll help your stories."

Libby didn't really need a course in Journalism 101 from the sheriff, but she was glad he recognized the need for give-and-take between law enforcement and the media. Even if the media happened to be a two-bit local rag that carried more stories on calf roping than crime.

"Listen, I'm not happy you're digging up the Della

McCarthy thing, but if you're determined to do it, we should talk," he said. "Maybe we could meet some evening this week."

"Sure," she said, relieved. Cash didn't seem like the kind of guy who took rejection well, so she was glad he was still willing to cooperate.

"How about Friday? We could meet at Chez Joe's, downtown. They serve food like Mom used to make—meatloaf, homemade mac and cheese, that kind of thing. It's actually pretty good."

She wasn't sure a small-town sheriff was a great judge of culinary quality, but she was partial to meatloaf.

"Sounds good," she said. "But won't everyone think we're on a date?"

"They'll think we're on a date if I so much as look at you," he said. "But what matters is you and I both know it's a meeting. A business meeting."

"Okay," she said. Luke would probably draw the wrong conclusion, but that might be a good thing. Maybe then he'd stop coming around.

That was what she wanted, right?

"I'll pick you up at six." He downed the last of his coffee and pushed his chair back. "Well, I'd better get back to town."

"Wait a minute," she said. "Don't pick me up. I can meet you there."

"In your truck?" He lifted one eyebrow, and she groaned. She wasn't going to drive the Bitchmobile any more than she had to.

"Okay. Good point." She stood to see him out and suddenly remembered her outfit. Ducking her head, she flushed. The sheriff must be desperate. How could he

possibly have lust in his heart for a woman dressed in bunny slippers and flannel jammies? She looked like a Care Bear.

It was embarrassing. She'd have to redeem herself—show him her Barbie doll side Friday night. She turned away and pretended to be busy washing out the mugs while Cash stood in the doorway, shuffling his feet as if he was reluctant to leave.

"See you Friday, then. And call if Mike comes back. If you hear anything, or get scared, just call."

"I'll be okay," she said. "I've got the watchdogs here." The dogs had snuck back into the room, but they were still suspicious of Cash. They skulked around the baseboards like guilty hyenas.

Cash bent and held a hand out to Penny, who was holing up under a chair. She yipped and peed on the floor.

"Yeah, they'll help," he said. "They'll take on Crazy Mike. Call me, Libby. Don't hesitate."

Chapter 15

When Luke pulled into her driveway the next day, Libby was framed by the open barn doors, tugging an oversized hay bale across the floor. There was a towering mountain of golden bales in the center of the barn, and she was apparently trying to clear the space by stacking them against the wall. A disheveled ponytail was collapsing around her ears in damp, spiraling tendrils, and her legs, revealed by a pair of skimpy denim cut-offs, were laced with scrapes and cuts. Rust stains from the baling wire crisscrossed her fingers.

As Luke approached, she braced herself and gave the bale a final heave, then watched in dismay as the wire snapped and the hay scattered across the floor. She collapsed onto the few bales she'd managed to move and slumped her shoulders.

"I miss my two-bedroom condo," she mumbled, hanging her head. He could see flecks of hay speckling the back of her neck, where a fine sheen of sweat proved she'd been at this a while. "I miss my concrete patio and my hanging petunias. I miss being clean." She stared at the unmoving mountain of hay stacked dead-center in front of the barn's big sliding doors. "I never thought I'd say this, but I even miss having a man around the house to help with the heavy stuff."

"Well, I can't take you back to Atlanta," Luke said. "But I could get you clean. We could go take a shower.

I'll soap, you rinse." He grinned to show he was kidding, but it sounded like a pretty good idea. He remembered the strap falling from her shoulder the day before, the flash of untanned skin it had revealed, and imagined her shucking out of her shirt, peeling those cutoffs off her long, tanned legs, stepping into the water and letting it run over her skin, making it glisten and shine. He wanted to touch her again, trace that tan line with his finger, follow it across her skin, see where it led.

She was looking at him like she knew what he was thinking, her eyes narrowed. Her sense of humor had evidently spilled out with the bale of hay.

"Or I could be the man," he said.

She flashed him a warning glare, and he winced.

"Just for now. Here." He jogged up and grabbed a hay bale, effortlessly pitching it her way. "I'll toss, you stack."

Libby laced her fingers through the wire circling the hay bale and pulled.

"Oof." She collapsed backward onto the bales again and rested her back against the wall.

"Sorry," she said. "Break time. I'm really out of shape."

Luke reached down and took her hands, pulling her to her feet with so much energy she stumbled against him. "You'll get there," he said, freeing one of her hands and twirling her around like a jitterbug champ. "Look at all you've accomplished already."

"I need help," she said, grabbing his other hand to steady herself. "Thanks for showing up."

"Why don't you just call the sheriff?" The words came out flat and sarcastic. He couldn't help it. "I bet he'd help, since you two are dating and all."

They stood toe-to-toe, so Libby had to look him in the eye. "We're not dating," she said. "It's a meeting. He came out because Mike was here and—well, Mike scared me, and then Cash and I got to talking, and we decided we should get together." She blushed. "I mean, not *together* together. Just, um, together. A meeting."

Luke narrowed his eyes. "What was that about Mike? About you being scared?"

Libby told him about Mike's unexpected visit—the pounding on her door, the threats.

"Wow." He pulled away so he could see her face. "That's—that's crazy."

"Guess that's why they call him—well, you know." She wrapped her fingers around the wire on another bale of hay. "How'd you hear about my meeting with the sheriff, anyway?"

"Ran into him downtown," Luke said. "He couldn't wait to tell me."

"That's probably because he was nervous about it," Libby said. "He apparently thought there was something going on between us."

"And there isn't?"

"I guess he misinterpreted our friendship." Libby hoisted the bale to chest height, then overbalanced and stumbled backward. She would have fallen if he hadn't caught her from behind.

He pulled her close and set his lips to the curve of her ear. "It's easy to get confused," he whispered. The fresh scent of hay wafted from her hair like fine perfume as she dropped the bale and closed her eyes, leaning back against him.

"I'm a little mixed up myself," he whispered. He

brushed the nape of her neck with his lips, then executed another complicated dance move so she was facing him, wrapped in his arms, their bodies tight together, his lips on hers. It wasn't the hot, hard kiss of the day before; this was gentle, exploring, almost pleading, a last-chance kiss designed to wipe the sheriff from her mind, and he thrilled to feel her answering with unexpected passion.

While his lips distracted her, his hands took a long, leisurely tour of her body, stroking her shoulders and moving down in a long, caressing arc that traced the outline of her breasts before moving on to savor the tuck of her waist and the swell of her hips. The kiss deepened as his hands dipped low and pulled her body into his, and he felt a spark shoot up between his hips and spread like a slow, smoldering flame.

"You're the best friend I ever had," he murmured. His lips left her mouth and moved down her throat and across her jawline, pausing in the angle under her ear for a fluttering kiss that set her trembling. He licked his way across her collarbone, then flicked his tongue in the hollow at the base of her neck. His thumbs moved up her ribs as his fingertips brushed her sides, stroking and caressing until his hands rested just below her breasts.

She sighed and fell against him, lifting her lips to his to rekindle the kiss.

They stumbled across the barn in an impromptu waltz until the two of them collapsed into the hay bales as if one lucky shot had dropped them both. They landed face to face, but Luke miscalculated and left enough distance between them to weaken the force field that had pulled them together.

"Luke," she gasped, pulling away. "Luke." She

brought one hand to her lips and stared at him. He gave her a dreamy smile, his eyes half-closed.

"Mmm?" He felt like he'd just been awakened from a sweet and very satisfying dream.

"We can't do this," she said.

"Yeah, we can." He was still smiling. "In fact, we're really good at it."

"We are." She sat up and rubbed her hand over her lips as if she could erase the whole incident. He should have been offended, but it only made him smile. There was no erasing that kiss. It had burned into both of them like a branding iron.

"That's the problem," she said. "We *are* good at it."

"Doesn't feel like a problem to me," he said. "It feels great." He reached up and tucked a stray lock of hair behind her ear. He loved fixing her hair. It let him hit that hoodoo spot just under her jaw. Every time he touched it, she wound up falling into his arms as if he'd pushed her "on" button.

This time, he'd almost turned her up to high. But there was apparently some kind of automatic shut-off that kicked in when she got overheated.

She stood up, clasping her arms around her waist and hunching her shoulders as if guarding herself from a blow. "I'm single, Luke," she said. "Single and staying that way."

"Have you told Cash that?" he asked. "Because I think he's got other plans."

She turned away. "I told you," she said. "It's just a meeting. It's not like he and I could ever—I mean, we're not soul mates or anything."

He felt a surge of triumph. "But you and I are." It

wasn't a question. He knew it was true, and evidently, she did too. She just wasn't ready to admit it.

"No," she said. "No. It's just—I like you. We're friends. Let's not ruin it."

"Ruin it?" He grinned. "That didn't ruin anything."

"Except my plans," she said. "My life." She dropped down beside him. "Luke, I have a vision of how I want my life to be. And this doesn't fit into the picture." She sighed. "I'm really sorry. I shouldn't have led you on."

"Oh, you didn't have to lead me," he said. "I would have found the way there all by myself." He leaned back, resting on his elbows. Considering she'd just told him he was ruining her life, he felt pretty good about this conversation. In fact, despite her words, he was pretty sure he'd get a chance to ruin it some more.

Hopefully soon.

"I'm sorry," she said again. "I'm just not ready for this." She picked up a scrap of baling wire and twisted it into a tight spiral. "I don't like being alone, but I can't trust anybody. I mean, my boyfriend ran off with my boss, Luke. He'd sit there after work with me and listen to me complain about her, and all the time he was sleeping with her."

Luke reached over and rubbed her back gently, up and down. He kept it friendly, soothing, almost brotherly, with none of the heat of his earlier caresses.

She leaned into his touch and sighed. "There's nothing between me and the sheriff, Luke. Honestly. Nothing."

"It doesn't matter," he said. "Because you're right. You two aren't exactly meant for each other. He's just practice." He grinned. "Not that you need any. Anyway, I'll still be here when you figure out there's not much

more to the guy than the badge and the uniform." He sat back down beside her. "I'll always be here."

"Don't waste your time," she said. "I'm damaged goods, Luke. I'm no good for anybody."

"You'll heal," he said. "I'll help."

Chapter 16

Friday night came too fast. Libby had barely recovered from her encounter with Luke, and besides, the chicken coop renovations had left her nose sunburned and her hands blistered, and the dry Wyoming wind had leached every ounce of moisture out of her hair and skin. She hadn't noticed her creeping transformation into a rough-skinned, straw-haired frontier woman until she stood in front of the mirror and confronted her new, countrified self.

Once she'd soaked up the entire inventory of the Clinique beauty bar, she pondered the contents of her closet. It wasn't a date. She didn't have to look good. But she definitely wanted to erase the Care Bear image that was probably burned into the sheriff's brain from the other night.

A professional look would be best. She'd always had trouble with the Barbie-doll look anyway. When you're nearly six feet tall to start with, high heels and sophisticated fashions lead to one question from the onlookers: lovely, statuesque woman—or drag queen?

After changing her clothes three times, she finally chose a navy pencil skirt and a fitted white shirt. She looked straight-laced and dull, like an FBI agent or an accountant. Maybe that would help Cash take her seriously.

She was slipping into a pair of low-heeled pumps when he tapped on the door.

The sheriff cleaned up nicely. Western etiquette apparently viewed clean, pressed jeans as formal wear, and Cash had paired his with a white oxford shirt and a light straw Stetson. He looked like a country singing star—pure cowboy heartthrob with a touch of sophistication. The only problem was his boots. They were tan Tony Lamas, but they looked really beat up, like they'd been run through a wood chipper.

"What happened to your shoes?" she asked.

"I'm not sure," he said. "I got attacked by some kind of animal when I got out of the truck."

"One of the dogs?"

"No, something else." He brushed the front of his shirt and a white feather drifted to the ground. "I think it was a Chupacabra. Sharp beak, big claws—it's not another one of your pets, is it?"

"Oh, no." Libby stifled a smile. "That was Wild Thing. She was here when I moved in."

"What the hell is she?"

"A chicken."

"No way." He shuddered.

"I think she might be part pterodactyl," Libby said.

"Well, I managed to save these." He pulled a bouquet of daisies out from behind his back. A caution light flashed in Libby's mind.

"Oh, Cash," she said. "You shouldn't have."

She meant it. This was a meeting, not a date. No way should he have brought her flowers. Still, she couldn't exactly leave them to die on the doorstep. Reluctantly, she turned and pulled a vase out of the cupboard.

"You look great." Cash's voice was low and husky.

Maybe he had a cold.

"Thanks." She fumbled around with the flowers as if it required the soul of an artist to jam a bunch of daisies into a vase. Actually, it did require a fair amount of concentration, because her hands were shaking in fluttery counterpoint to the vibrations emanating from the sheriff. She missed the vase twice, then tried again, wondering if Cash was pumping out pheromones on purpose.

Taking a deep breath, she glanced up at him, and the intensity of his stare almost knocked her down. She returned her attention to the daisies, dodging a double dose of testosterone. She was starting to regret the way the fitted skirt clung to her hips.

She grabbed her purse and spun around, almost knocking the vase off the table. "Ready when you are," she said, then blushed. "I mean, ready to go. To go eat. I'm hungry. For—for food."

What was it about this guy that made her IQ drop fifty points every time he walked into the room? Maybe it was the way he was looking at her—like he was the big bad wolf and she was one of those tasty pink pigs.

"What about your dogs?" he asked.

"They're out in the barn. We still have little accidents now and then, so I don't let them stay in the house when I'm out."

Cash laughed. "Is that what those are called? Little accidents?"

"Hey, between Crazy Mike's yelling and your siren blaring, they were totally traumatized that night. Penny's really well housebroken, normally. She was just upset."

"Maybe later you can introduce us properly. I hate for them to be scared of me."

"They'll get over it." It sounded like Cash was angling for an invitation to come back to the house after dinner. No way, she resolved. Maybe she was overreacting, but she was pretty sure he wasn't really all that interested in making friends with her dogs. Or in discussing the Della McCarthy case.

No, Cash was interested in something else entirely.

The waitress at Joe's didn't strike Libby as your typical Wyoming teen. Perky and bright, she sported spiky black hair liberally streaked with hot pink. It was razored short except for a high crest down the center and a long hank of pink hanging asymmetrically over her forehead.

"Hi. Welcome to Joe's Place! I mean, Chez Joe. I'm Josie and I'll be your server!" the waitress chirped. She might have the hair of a rock star, but her personality was pure Betty Boop. "What are you drinkin' tonight, hon?"

"Coke, please," Libby said.

Cash opened his menu. "I'll have a Scotch and water."

"Oh. Wait." Libby knew she should stick to soda, but the mere mention of booze made her feel like a thirst-crazed Bedouin sighting an oasis. Cash had slanted a dozen meaningful glances her way en route to the diner, most of them directed at her thighs, which were possibly a touch too exposed by her skirt. Her nerves were jangling, and her heart was dancing a funky two-step in her throat. Professionalism be damned. Some sedation was definitely in order.

"Make mine a vodka tonic, then, and scratch the Coke."

"Right-O, hon. Vodka tonic."

Libby smoothed her skirt over her thighs while Cash

glanced warily around the room. He stared hard at a well-dressed man in a corner booth, then returned his attention to her, evidently satisfied that the guy wasn't currently starring on any FBI wanted posters.

Libby wondered if he ever took a night off from being the sheriff. He probably kept his gun handy on the nightstand even when he slept.

She wondered what Luke had on his nightstand. Probably a cowboy lamp, or some other tacky boyhood memento. Living with his parents, he probably slept in his old room. Maybe he even had cowboy sheets, with bucking horses on them. The thought made her smile.

"Penny for your thoughts."

Libby blinked, searching her mind for something to say, but her throat went dry as she bent to study the menu, letting her hair fall across her face to hide her sudden shyness. She wasn't about to tell Cash she'd been thinking about Luke's bedroom.

Luke's bedroom. Did he sleep with boxers on? Or briefs?

Maybe he slept naked. She pictured his sleeping face, his lashes dark against his cheek, his lips slightly parted. Then she pictured the rest of him.

"Libby?"

"Nothing." She squinted at the menu. "Just trying to decide. It's… interesting."

Joe's might have been a small-town diner serving country food, but the chef obviously had higher aspirations. The meatloaf she'd looked forward to all day was billed as "Loaf de Meat: ground beef succulently seasoned with a medley of herbs and spices, baked, sliced, and served with rich mushroom gravy." "Pureed

Pommes" and "Bacon-Laced Beans Vert" were recommended as "accompaniments."

Libby glanced over the top of her menu and caught Cash watching her so intently it was as if he'd reached across the table and stroked her skin. "I—I think I'll have the Loaf de Meat," she stammered. "Meatloaf. You know."

"I'm going for the Macarrroni et Frrromage myself," Cash announced. He rolled his r's like Maurice Chevalier, and was glad to see Libby laugh, letting her posture relax. She seemed tense, for some reason. Distracted. The woman was wound tight as a bedspring.

Keep it light, he told himself. He had a tendency to move too fast with women, and he wasn't blowing it this time. He'd keep up this meeting façade, pretend this outing wasn't the prelude to a hot and heavy relationship, and she'd come around sooner or later.

Maybe if they talked about ordinary, everyday things, it would distract him from the overwhelming lust that punched him in the gut every time the woman moved a finger. It had been a long time since anyone affected him like that. And last time, it hadn't ended well. He shoved the memory out of his mind.

"So what are you working on these days?" he asked. "Any stories I can help you with?"

Libby nodded and cleared her throat. "Like I said, I'm checking into the Della McCarthy thing. Wondering if there are any angles you haven't looked into yet, or any new evidence."

"Nope," he said. "Nothing new."

There. That should put a stop to that nonsense. The

Della McCarthy incident was over, and the community needed to forget—not have some hotshot out-of-town journalist reopen old wounds.

"What else you working on?"

She shrugged. "Nothing you can really help with," she said. "I'm here to talk about Della."

"Well, I'm here to talk about just about anything else," he said. "Sorry if we had a misunderstanding. What's coming up in the paper next week? Maybe I can help with that."

"I doubt it," she said. "I'm doing a piece on Ralph Kittredge and his mutton-busting rodeo clinic this week. He's got fifteen four-to-six-year-olds getting ready for Lackaduck Days. I went out to see them in action this afternoon."

"That must have been a sight."

"Yeah. It sure was."

All this polite conversation seemed senseless, like the dull beginning of a spicy movie. Cash wanted to skip over it and get on to the good stuff, but he forced himself to listen as she babbled on.

"Apparently Ralph goes to a lot of trouble to find sheep that have never been touched by human hands," Libby continued. Cash sorted through his thoughts, casting aside the off-topic erotic ones that insisted on floating to the top, and wondered if she could tell that innocuous words like "touch" and "hands" were taking on new meanings in his fevered brain.

"They're totally wild," Libby continued. "He says it makes for better training for the kids. By the time they hit the rodeo, they're ready for anything."

Wild, Cash thought. *Totally wild.*

Ready for anything.

Silence settled over them again, and Libby glanced away nervously whenever he met her eyes.

"Have you decided on your entrees?" Josie set their drinks on the table and cocked her head, memo pad at the ready.

"Yeah, I'll have the Macaroni et Fromage, and my date here will have the Loaf de Meat," Cash said.

"Pureed pommes de terre with that, or Pommes Frites?" Josie looked at Libby expectantly.

"Pardon?"

"Mashed potatoes or fries?" the waitress whispered.

"Oh! Pureed pommes, please. And the Beans Vert. That's green beans, right?"

"Right. With bacon. Sheriff?"

"The usual for me, Josie."

"Thanks, Sheriff. Tomatoes Estewed and Petit Peas, then."

She flicked her pad into the pocket of her frilly apron and headed for the kitchen.

"One meatloaf with mashed and beans, one mac 'n' cheese with 'maters and peas, Joe."

"Josie! How many times I gotta tell you!" came a roar from the kitchen. "Use the proppa names for the dishes, girl! You want the customers to think we serve *ordinary* food here?"

"Sorry, Joe."

Cash chuckled. "Joe decided a couple years ago that nobody was showing enough respect for his culinary artistry. Decided French names were the key to success for all those big-city restaurants, so he changed the menu. Not the food; just the menu."

"I'm not sure it adds any respect for the food, but it's sure entertaining."

"Don't say that to Joe. He takes a lot of pride in his Frenchified cuisine."

The conversation flagged once their meals arrived. Cash was a lifetime member of the Clean Plate Club, and he took that responsibility seriously. Still, he could feel the energy of their jokes and conversation fading away as they finished their meals and stared at each other.

He finally broke the silence.

"You should come to the rodeo next month. I'm in it."

"You're busting broncs?"

"Nope. Bobcat Square Dancing. Luke, too."

Libby shuddered as if she thought he and Luke were actually going to be out there do-si-doing. "Square dancing?"

"With Bobcats. You know, those mini-bulldozers. I have one I use around the ranch. So does Luke. We worked out an act with a couple of other guys where we run them in formation. They spin in unison, then we move in and lift the scoops, then back up, spin again… it's sort of like synchronized driving."

"I'll come," Libby said. "Maybe it'll make a good story."

"Maybe." He felt a resurgence of the tension that had stretched between them when they were alone together in her kitchen—the tight knot in his stomach, the consciousness of her body under that tight little skirt—and he gave himself a mental slap. Things were moving a little fast. Too fast. He needed to make sure this was a woman he could trust.

Not like the last one.

~

An awkward silence stretched between them again. Libby was seething inside, and not with lust. Cash had lured her here under false pretenses, implying he had information about Della, then turned the whole thing into a date.

She tried to keep the conversation innocuous, talking about sheep, the rodeo, anything to avoid those long, awkward silences. The guy had a weird testosterone aura that simmered with sexual innuendo, and every time she shut up, she worried he'd lunge across the laminated table and take her right there in the red vinyl booth. She was relieved when they finished off their meals and rose to go.

"So," Cash said. "You ready to introduce me to those crazy little dogs?"

They stepped outside and the tension between them tightened to the breaking point. No way was she letting him con his way back into her house. Bad enough she had to get in the truck with him. She tugged at her skirt again, wishing she'd worn pants, or maybe a gunny sack.

"Sorry. I, ah, have to work tomorrow."

"On Saturday?"

"Got an interview."

The moon cast deep blue shadows over the dilapidated vehicles scattered around the parking lot. Cash opened the truck door for Libby and took her elbow. He started to boost her into the cab, then tugged her off balance. Stumbling off the running board, she slammed into his chest and he clutched her biceps, pinning her against the side of the truck. His breath was coming in

ragged gasps as he lowered his face to hers. She twisted her head away as a beam of light slashed across them.

"Oops. Sorry." Josie was standing in a shaft of light cast by the diner's open kitchen door, a cigarette poised at her lips. "Smoke break. Did I interrupt something?" She giggled.

"Josie," Cash pulled away and released Libby. She scrambled into the truck. "Dammit, I really wish you'd quit smoking." He stalked around to the driver's side and leaned against the door for a moment while Libby climbed in and fastened her seat belt. She struggled to catch her breath, wishing she hadn't let him drive, wishing her farm was within walking distance, wishing she was anywhere but there in Cash's truck.

"Cash, I wasn't ready for that," she said, while the sheriff settled in behind the wheel. She was pressed against the far door, clutching the door handle. "I told you, I'm not looking for a relationship. This was supposed to be a meeting, not a date."

He scanned her outfit, his gaze resting pointedly on her breasts and legs. "Could have fooled me." He jammed the clutch to the floor and turned the key. "That's a hell of an outfit to wear to a meeting. But whatever you say. Sorry if I jumped the gun."

Maybe he was right. She'd told herself she was dressing professionally, but her skirt was too short, and her blouse stretched over her breasts in a way that could be interpreted as provocative. She should have known better.

The rest of the drive to her house passed in silence,

Cash glancing her way occasionally as if trying to read her thoughts. When he pulled into her driveway, he threw the truck into park and shifted in his seat, angling toward her. She opened her door and the dome light flashed on as she slid to the ground.

"You sure you don't want me to come in?" he asked. "I could check around, make sure those guys didn't come back."

"I'm sure, Cash."

"All right." He smiled, but the expression didn't reach his eyes. "All work and no play's no good, you know. Why don't you come over to my place sometime? I could cook something. Show you my horses."

She hopped out of the truck and slammed the door—a little too hard. Maybe that would give him the message.

"No, thanks," she said. "But I'm sure I'll see you around."

Chapter 17

Luke was starting to think Libby had a secret penchant for playing dress-up like a four-year-old. Not long ago, he'd found her working on the chicken coop dressed like some kind of freaky rural astronaut. Today, she was dressed as a Halloween hobo.

Maybe she'd come up with something really good one of these days. A Vegas showgirl outfit, or one of those French maid get-ups.

She was kneeling in the weed-choked flower beds by the front door when he pulled up, elbow-deep in dirt, yanking up Creeping Jenny by the handful. He wondered if the woman ever did anything civilized, like sip tea or paint her nails. Probably not. But he was pretty sure she wouldn't squeal every time she saw horseshit, either. She seemed to be taking to ranch life just fine.

She must have locked the puppies in the barn, because she'd let the chicks out of their brood box and they were clustered around her, scratching and pecking at the turned-up dirt just like real, grown-up chickens. They seemed ridiculously tame. He wondered how she'd get anything done once she had her full quotient of poultry following her around like a feathered entourage.

He pulled the truck to a stop and watched her work. The wires trailing from her ears to her shirt pocket, along with the rhythmic bobbing of her head, indicated she was listening to an iPod. A bandanna covered her

hair, and she wore ragged denim shorts and a T-shirt tied up under her breasts to expose a long stretch of flat belly. It all might have worked for him if her face hadn't been streaked with dirt where she'd wiped the considerable sweat from her brow. Her knees were dirty too. She looked kind of cute, though. And when she turned to face him, she looked really, really pissed off.

"Hello?" She stamped a mud-caked foot and scowled. The chicks rushed peeping and squawking into their box.

"A phone call, maybe?" she said. "Like, are you decent and can I come over?"

"Oh, come on, Libby." Her temper only added to her charm. He liked his women spunky. "That would spoil the fun. Whatcha doin'?"

"Finding my way to China via dandelion root," she grouched. "I'm almost there."

"Well, knock off for a beer, babe. I brought you a present." The grin widened. He couldn't wait for her to see what he'd brought.

Couldn't wait.

Libby looked over at the truck and her face went dead white. Luke couldn't blame her. The being lounging in the bed of his pickup could only be described as a behemoth.

"That's Ivan," Luke announced. "Ivan the Truly Terrible."

The beast in the truck lolled its enormous head over the side, grinning. It was just a dog, really—but what a dog. It was a dog like the Terminator is a human being. Like Rambo is a soldier. Like Pat Robertson is religious.

It was a Beast, with a capital "B." And Luke knew it was just what Libby needed.

"Is it yours?" Her voice was an incredulous squeak.

"No way, hon. He's all yours!"

"No," she said. "Absolutely not. I've got too much dog already. The Terrors are all the dog I need. They're wearing me out, and eating me out of house and home."

"Yeah, and if your house gets broken into, they'll show the burglar where you keep the silver so he'll stay and play ball. They're nice critters, Libby, but they're next to useless as protection."

The Beast stood calmly in the truck bed, gently swaying from side to side as he wagged his enormous tail. A fine line of spittle trailed from one side of his mouth. His tongue lolled out the other side.

"What kind of dog *is* that?"

Luke shrugged. "I got him at the shelter. Near as I can tell, he's a mixed breed—half grizzly bear, half pony." He flourished his hands toward the truck like a sideshow barker. "And all yours!"

"No, Luke. No way. I can't handle a dog that big."

"He's easy to handle. Watch. Ivan, come."

Ivan vaulted over the side of the truck and came to what could only be described as a screeching halt at Luke's side. Lowering his enormous bottom into a ponderous "sit," the beast grinned up into Luke's face with an adoring, slobbery smile. He had moves like a fine-tuned cutting horse—and was about the same size.

"Good boy. Down. Stay." Luke gave Libby a triumphant smile as the dog prostrated himself on the lawn. "Can we come in?"

She looked at the dog, then up at Luke.

"You can come in," she said. "But not the dog."

"Okay. He's down. He's staying. Let's go in the house, and you'll see he's no trouble at all."

The screen door slammed as Libby opened the fridge and pulled out two beers. Luke folded himself into one of her tiny dinette chairs.

"You need this dog, Libby."

He had to convince her. He couldn't relax knowing she was all alone out here. He couldn't be here every night to protect her from the cretins at the bar who'd vandalized her truck, or from the loopy antics of his old friend Mike.

Not yet.

She obviously wasn't ready for any kind of permanent arrangement. In fact, if he kept showing up unannounced, she might think she needed the dog to protect herself from him—especially since she was so dead-set on staying single. But no worries. He'd kept the dog around the ranch for a day or two, running it through a few obedience exercises. It was putty in his hands.

If only he had that kind of skill with women.

"Come on, Libby," he said. "You need this dog."

She set her jaw and glared at him. This was a woman who didn't like being told what she needed. But he could match her for stubbornness any day of the week. He generally got his way when it mattered to him—and this did. She was in danger out here, and the dog would keep her safe.

"I'm fine, Luke, and it's not your job to look after me," she said. "I look after myself just fine."

"Libby, you've been here two weeks. In that time, you've had to call the sheriff twice—once because somebody vandalized your truck, and once because Mike was out here threatening you. It's not safe out here

for a woman alone." He leaned toward her, willing her to give in. "You need this dog."

Libby splayed her hands. "I can't, Luke. I've got the Terrors, and they'll bark if anyone gets close. That's good enough for me. Too good, actually. I've got more dog than I need already."

"Yeah, well, one big one'll be a whole lot more effective than all those little guys. What are you going to do—hide in the chicken coop if those bikers come gunning for you?"

"No," she said. "I'll hide in the cellar."

"Look at him." Luke gestured out the kitchen window. "He's just what you need."

Ivan was still lying on the lawn, his eyes fixed on the door. Anyone would have to admit he was a handsome animal. There was some Labrador retriever in there, and maybe some German shepherd, along with something very large. If grizzly bears could breed with dogs, that would have been Libby's first guess. The dog's color only added to the mystery—he was a deep, rich red, with four white feet and a white mark on his chest that looked, appropriately, like a question mark. His ears gave no clue to his breed; one hung down in a neat triangle, while the other cocked out from his head at a crazy angle that made him look like the Flying Nun on a bender.

It was the ears that finally got to her. The ears, and the big soulful eyes.

"He's your dog, Luke," she said, weakly.

"Okay. But he lives here."

"Deal."

Libby sighed. Her simple, uncomplicated life was taking on a Grand Central Station kind of feeling. But after Crazy Mike's visit, knowing Ivan was on the job would be a comfort. Maybe she'd get some sleep.

Apparently, Luke had the same idea, because he left as soon as he finished his beer. She locked the door behind him and turned out the porch light. There was a soft whine, and the sound of a big paw scratching at the front door.

"What?" she said, opening the door. Ivan trotted past her and through the kitchen, then laid down in front of her bedroom door, dignified and immovable as a library lion. "All right," she said. "You can stay."

Penny was perched on the bed, her ears laid back, her teeth bared at her new housemate.

"It's okay, girl," Libby said. "I might have let him in the house, but I'm not going to let him sleep in the bed or anything. He's just here for protection."

She glanced out the window, where Luke's headlights were disappearing at the end of the driveway.

"And that goes for the dog, too."

Chapter 18

LIBBY HAD ALMOST FORGOTTEN HER APPOINTMENT WITH David to fix the chicken house, but he arrived Monday at noon as promised, pedaling an old balloon-tire bicycle.

"Puppies! Lookit all the puppies!" he exclaimed. Before Libby could say a word, he was prostrate in the grass, letting the Terrors jump all over him and lick his face. He giggled enthusiastically as the puppies played.

"I'm looking for homes for some of these critters, if you're interested," Libby said. "Looks like you're just the guy to take on a couple of the Terrors yourself."

David extricated himself from the mound of puppies and stood up, brushing dog hair off his jeans. He was wearing a T-shirt that read "Kiss Me, I'm Irish."

The man was obsessed.

"Sorry. Can't," he said. "I live up over the Roundup, so pets are a health code violation." He shook himself, as if shedding his doggie persona and becoming human again. "But let's get down to business, chicken lady. Show me the task at hand, and I'll amaze you with my manly prowess with hammer and nails. Or whatever."

Libby smiled. "Manly prowess is just what this job needs. That needs to be transformed into a state-of-the-art chicken house ASAP. Think you can do it?" She gestured toward the would-be chicken house, which currently looked more like a random stack of lumber.

A feathered head poked out from between two crooked boards and let out a squawk that sounded like Wolverine's claws tearing up a blackboard.

"Holy shit," David said. "What is that?"

"That's Wild Thing," Libby said. "Just stand real still. She'll go away."

"They're not all like that, are they?" David whispered. "Cause if they are, you might want to go for a maximum security facility here."

"No, she's pretty unique."

Wild Thing squeezed between the boards and stalked across the lawn, casting evil glares in David's direction. She'd somehow lost most of her tail feathers, and her comb was crooked.

"Looks like she got in a fight with a coyote or something," David said.

"Yeah. Scary thing is, she probably won," Libby said.

David shuddered and returned his attention to the shed. "Looks like we'll need some two-by-fours to square things up, and asphalt shingles for the roof."

"Just make me a list of the supplies you need. I'll go over to Ace and pick them up. What do you charge for this kind of thing?"

"How about ten bucks an hour?"

"Sounds more than fair to me. "

He glanced around the yard. "Where are the other chickens?"

"They're in the barn. Be real careful the puppies don't get in there. They'd love to *play* with them."

"I'll be careful." He whistled an off-tune rendition of "Ripple" as he strode off toward the chicken coop, and the puppies fell all over themselves tumbling after him.

Ivan, lying stoically on the porch, simply watched him with wary eyes.

By late afternoon, the shed was well on its way to being transformed into the chicken house of her dreams, and Libby was having a hard time thinking of David as a suspect. It was almost impossible not to like a guy who worked that hard. He'd patched the roof, fastened chicken wire over all the windows, whitewashed the inside walls, and even built a miniature doorway in one side with a chicken-sized ramp leading up to it. He'd also insisted Libby pick up paint so he could slap a coat of white latex onto the sunbaked boards.

"After that, I'll work on the fence. We'll make sure those chickens stay right where they belong, and these guys stay out." He nodded toward the puppies, who had spent all day assisting him in his labors and now lay about the grass, speckled with whitewash and thoroughly exhausted. Apparently Jack Russells had two speeds—high and off. When they quit, they quit hard.

"Can I help paint?" Libby asked. "I'll pay you the same."

"Sure. You'd better change, though. Put something over your hair. I paint messy."

It was a clear, hot day, with a cloudless sky so blue it looked like a painted backdrop. Grasshoppers clicked in the dry weeds as David and Libby slapped white paint on the parched gray clapboards. They worked in companionable silence for a while before she got up the nerve to get nosey.

"So did you grow up here in Lackaduck?" she asked.

"I did." He leaned back to assess his efforts, then bent to refill his brush. "My dad was the bank manager

at First National. My mom died when I was little, so I was on my own a lot. Dad thought he'd make up for his twelve-hour workdays by being extra strict when he was home. That didn't sit too well with me, so I took off when I was fifteen." He laughed. "I was a teenage runaway."

"Where did you go?"

"All over," he said, his painting rhythm picking up. "Me and my friends slept in the woods and hopped trains to get from town to town. It was cool—the best time of my life. Except for now." He grinned. "Now's good. You know Josie?"

"From the diner?"

David nodded. "We're going to get married."

"Really? That's great." She could see the two of them together, a perfect match. "When?"

"Probably about a year after I talk her into dating me," he said. "I'm getting close."

"Good for you," Libby said—but she wasn't sure she meant it. Was the guy a stalker? He didn't seem like the type. Judging by the light in his eyes, he was in love with the girl, and Libby suspected Josie could do a lot worse. Still, it was a red flag.

"So what made you come home and settle down?" she asked, shifting back to the topic at hand.

"I crashed and burned." David carefully captured a drip with his brush. "At first, me and my friends just smoked a lot of dope, but then we got into meth. I OD'd when I was seventeen and got sent home to Daddy."

"He must have been relieved to get you back."

"Not really. Having a son in detox wasn't good for his reputation as a businessman. He sent me off to various

schools and recovery centers, but I couldn't stay clean. Finally, I ended up in prison."

Libby dipped her brush in the paint, then wiped it on the rim of the can. "How long were you in jail?"

"Six years."

His voice had gone flat, and the good-natured sparkle faded from his eyes. One of the puppies toddled over to him and fell at his feet, rolling over for a belly rub. He set his brush down and obliged, his customary smile returning.

"So, you see?" he said. "You're helping an ex-con become a useful member of society."

Libby watched him out of the corner of her eye while she painted. David seemed like a nice guy, but he'd had a rough life.

"So did you know that girl that disappeared? Della McCarthy?"

"I just met her a couple times. And I was at the Roundup that night she—you know. That last night."

Libby nodded. "What was she like?" She set her brush down and took a break so she could watch David's body language as he responded to her questions.

"Adorable." David started on the window frame, tilting his brush to avoid smearing the panes. "She had on tight jeans—the kind all the young things wear, you know, real low on the hips—and a low-cut top, too. She was so tiny, such a little girl, but the way she was dressed—you could tell—I mean, she obviously was no kid." His hand was unsteady as he edged around the glass.

"Did you talk to her?"

"Not much. I mean, she was a friend of Josie's, but she was way out of my league." His shoulders slumped.

"With my criminal record and all, I know better than to talk to girls like that."

Libby wondered just how much that bothered David. "So what happened that night?"

David chuckled. "She came into the bar and hoisted her little self onto a barstool and tried to order a Cosmopolitan, like some sophisticated lady. Crystal asked her for ID and she said she'd lost it. Made a big show of going through her purse, looking. Then Cash got up, did his big tough-guy thing, and tried to scare her. Asked her did she know the penalty for underage drinking, and did her parents know where she was."

"What did she say to that?"

"She just laughed, like she thought he was kidding. Then she ordered a root beer and some nachos, and sat there at the bar sipping through a straw like a kid at a soda fountain. Man, she was cute, Libby."

"Did anybody pay a lot of attention to her?"

"Well, Cash, of course. You'd have thought he was her dad. Seemed like he was really mad she was there. And Crazy Mike. He just kept staring at her the way he does."

"Anyone else talk to her?" Libby reached for her brush and rejoined the painting effort, working her way around the door frame.

"There were two other guys there, guys I didn't know. Pipeline workers, probably. They come through all the time, don't stay real long. They looked like bikers. One of them drank too much, tried to hit on Della, but Cash warned him off."

Libby froze, her brush in the air, as David continued.

"They left right after Cash settled their hash. Nobody in the place took very kindly to their hitting

on Della—she was so young. They took off in a black Dodge pickup. Pretty wild looking. Lots of chrome."

It sounded like the two bikers from the Roundup parking lot. She knew from experience that they didn't take it too well when a woman said no.

"Maybe they waited down the road and followed her."

"No. That was me." David smoothed a final brush-stroke onto the window frame and turned to face Libby. "I followed her back to the hotel and then I killed her."

Chapter 19

LIBBY JUMPED TO HER FEET, NEARLY OVERTURNING THE paint can. Instinctively, she held her dripping paintbrush in front of her, pointing it at David like a weapon. It dripped latex into the spreading white pool in the grass. Her hand jerked, spattering paint everywhere and leaving a white streak across David's shirt. "What do you mean?" she stammered. "What…"

David laughed. "I'm kidding. But isn't that what you were looking for? I know I'm a suspect, Libby. I live upstairs at the saloon, remember? The place is as full of holes as Swiss cheese. I heard every word you and Mrs. McCarthy said."

"Shoot." Libby remembered what Mary had said about David. He was on the suspect list, and he knew it. "I'm sorry." She set the paintbrush down and sat beside it on the lawn.

"That's okay," he said with a philosophical shrug. "She said she suspected me because I seem so happy, despite my past. That's sort of a compliment." He dipped his brush in the paint again and continued his work. "Shows how far I've come."

"I don't suspect you, David." Libby yanked a handful of crabgrass out of the lawn and tossed it aside.

"I know. You don't think a drug addict has enough energy to commit that kind of crime." She winced. He really had heard everything. "But now that you've seen

me at work, I'm afraid you'll change your mind," he continued with mock seriousness. "After all, it's taken a fair amount of energy to transform this broken-down old shed into a shining example of henhouse architecture."

Libby laughed as David slapped a last stroke of paint up by the eaves of the chicken house, and stood back.

"There. Beautiful," he said. "There's just one problem, Libby."

"What?" she asked. "It looks great."

"Yeah, but now all your other buildings look like crap. You're going to have to let me paint them too."

"You know, that's not a bad idea." He was right; the rest of the place looked awful by comparison. "Come back tomorrow afternoon, if you want. I'll pick up more paint. I have some stuff to do tomorrow, though, so I won't be able to help you."

"That's okay. What are you working on?"

"I need to write up Friday's Grange meeting, and then I'm interviewing Gloria Stanhouse. She's been crocheting doilies for the troops overseas."

"Yeah, she's covered every surface in Lackaduck with those things, so the troops are the only market she's got left. Bet those antimacassars really dress up a Humvee."

Libby laughed. "Anyway, the shed looks great. See you tomorrow."

"You bet! With bells on." He did a brief shuffling jig, clicking his heels like a crazed leprechaun, then climbed onto his bike and set off down the driveway. Penny scrambled to her feet and watched him go.

"Say 'bye,' Penny," Libby said. "'Bye' to your new friend."

~

By the next day, Libby was a little concerned about Penny and Ivan. It was only natural for a mother to be protective of her young, but the way the twelve-pound terrier bossed the big lug worried her. She'd snarl and lunge for his throat at the slightest provocation, despite the fact that the puppies had played a rousing game of king o' the mountain on his recumbent body without even waking him up.

Ivan had to be ten times Penny's size, and Libby was worried that sooner or later, he'd tire of the bullying. But as she watched him lie patiently on the hearth rug with a puppy worrying each ear, she realized he wasn't a threat—to anyone. Hopefully, would-be burglars wouldn't realize that her fearsome attack dog had the soft, squishy heart of a bunny rabbit.

In any case, a new dog provided a great excuse to revisit the veterinarian. After their first encounter, she'd hoped to steer clear of the Ronster, but she'd noticed a festering cut on one of Ivan's pads. Besides, the vet was the second suspect on Mary's list.

When they arrived at the small frame building that held the vet's office, Ivan leapt to the ground obediently and padded in by Libby's side. Ron was sitting in the waiting room, thumbing through a well-worn copy of *Cosmo*.

"Ms. Brown! Always a pleasure." He shoved the magazine under a pile of stock journals and rose to greet her. "And this is..." He drew back a little. Libby was gratified to see that even a seasoned veterinarian, accustomed to cattle and horses, was shocked by the size of her new companion.

"This is Ivan," she said. "The Terrible."

"Ah." Ron knelt and extended a cautious hand toward Ivan. "Hello, old boy. Nice to meet you."

Ivan rumbled a low growl.

"Ivan!" Libby tried to sound shocked, but the dog thumped his tail as if she'd praised him. Hopefully Ron wasn't equally attuned to her true feelings. "I got him as a gift," she said. "He seems fairly gentle, but he's protective."

"Well, that's good," Ron said. "A pretty lady like you, out there on her own in the middle of nowhere—you need a good watchdog. Now I think he'd like me a lot better if you came over here and let me give you a little hug. Just so he sees we're friends, you know."

Libby glowered. "I don't think so. Don't you veterinarians have ways of handling dogs like this?"

"Yes, of course." His light tone changed abruptly. "They're called tranquilizers, but I'd rather not resort to that. Just come over here and shake hands, at least."

Libby obliged, and was rewarded with a limp, fishy handshake that felt like the last good-bye of a catch-and-release trout. She responded with a brief but firm pump of his pudgy hand. "Ivan, come," she commanded.

Ivan trotted over and sat at their feet. To Libby's chagrin, he allowed the Ronster to caress his crooked ears. "That's better, old pal," Ron cooed. "We'll be friends now. We have so much in common, old boy. I can tell you like Ms. Brown a lot too. We'll both look out for her, out there on that lonesome ranch, won't we?"

That was twice now that Ron had mentioned Libby's isolated homestead. The guy gave her the creeps.

"Ivan provides all the looking after I need, thanks,"

she told him. She led the dog into the examining room. "I wondered if you could look at this cut on his foot." She lifted Ivan's back leg and gestured toward the wound. It was red and swollen.

Ron bent to examine it. "Infected," he said. "Probably stepped on a cactus or something." He probed the pad with his fingers. Ivan panted and gave Libby a pleading look, but made no move to stop the examination. "I'll give him a shot of antibiotics and some pills for you to take home."

He turned and began sorting through a cabinet stocked with bottles of clear liquid. Libby thought about the drugs and medicines available to animal doctors and shuddered. It would be easy enough for the Ronster to subdue a victim if his libido got the better of him.

"You said you use tranquilizers on animals sometimes. Would those be given in a shot, or do you have oral medications—you know, something you could put in a drink or some food?" She congratulated herself on the smooth segue into her investigation.

"Normally, we'd give a shot before an operation or a complex procedure. But if we had a big guy like this, and we really couldn't handle him, we'd put some medicine in a treat, and get it in him that way."

"How long would that keep him unconscious?" she asked.

"Depends on the dosage," Ron said. He rummaged in a drawer and came out with a huge hypodermic. Upending a vial from the cabinet, he shoved the needle into the stopper and drew back the plunger. Libby could feel her breakfast getting restless.

She couldn't help watching as he handled the needle

with casual skill. Her breakfast flipped over again while she turned her questions over in her mind, trying to find a delicate way to pursue her inquiries. If Ron was really a homicidal maniac, she didn't want to arouse his suspicions.

Not while he had a needle in his hand.

"You see horses too, right?" she asked. "I'm thinking about getting a horse." Lying was okay, she decided, in the service of an investigation. Journalistic ethics could be complicated. "I can't decide what breed to get, though. I want something fancy. I was wondering if you've ever had any experiences with exotic breeds."

"Women." Ron clucked his tongue as he gave Ivan a final pat on the head and stood up, leaning against the counter with his arms crossed over his chest. "You ladies always want the pretty ponies. You know, you'd be best off with a quarter horse around here. They have a much more stable temperament than your exotic breeds. Arabians, Thoroughbreds—they're pretty but too high-strung. An inexperienced rider's liable to get hurt."

"I can ride," Libby said. Actually, her total riding experience consisted of two weeks of barrel-racing lessons at a summer camp when she was twelve. Being a competitive kid, she'd been determined to get around those barrels in record time, so she leaned her pony so far into the turns that she spent more time on the ground than in the saddle. But Ron didn't need to know that.

"I used to barrel race," she said.

"Then you should know about quarter horses," he said, puzzled. "Nobody would rodeo on anything else.

Why would you want some crazy over-bred animal when there are so many good quarter horses around here?"

"I want a gaited horse," she said, thinking fast. "I get, um, I get saddle sore."

"Hmmm." Ron looked her up and down with a knowing leer. "I see. You're looking for a smooth ride, aren't you, honey? We don't want you to hurt that pretty little..."

A low growl from Ivan surprised them both.

"Easy, big guy," Ron said. "Easy. I didn't mean anything by that."

"Of course not." Libby bent down to stroke Ivan's head. "We're talking about horses here."

Ron laughed nervously. "Right. Can't imagine what set him off."

"Anyway, I heard about this one breed. Paso Finos, they're called. Do you know anything about them?"

"Sure. I've worked with just about every kind of horse you could name. Including one of the finest Pasos you'll ever see. Skydancer." He drew the name out as if he could taste it.

"Skydancer? Nice name." Libby tried to sound casual as her heart bounced gleefully around her rib cage at the mention of Della's horse. She was good at this investigative stuff. Really good.

"Beautiful animal. Competed at Lackaduck Days a couple years ago. By far the finest horse on the grounds. A dark bay, with just one white marking on his left haunch—kind of odd, looked like a map of Texas."

"Isn't that a flaw?"

"Color doesn't matter much, and the animal's conformation was so good nobody really cared. Beautiful little

lady owned him, too. I got to know her when I treated him for a pretty serious problem. Saved his life, probably."

"What was wrong with him?"

"Pulled a tendon." Ron's definition of life-threatening conditions probably included stubbed toes and hangnails, too. "The young lady was very grateful." A lecherous grin creased his face. Libby knew he was thinking about Della, and looked away to hide her distaste.

"We got very close, if you know what I mean," Ron continued. "She stayed on to help out here at the clinic. Had a real gentle touch."

"How do you know?" Libby offered what she hoped was a conspiratorial leer, but she must have gone too far.

"Oh, not from experience," he said quickly. "Too young for me. Wouldn't have minded a bit if she'd been older, though." He smirked again. "I wish she was still around to give me a hand, you know?"

Libby shuddered. "Yeah, you need a lot of help."

Ron didn't notice the sarcasm in her tone. "She ran off, though. Disappeared. The sheriff was investigating it like she was murdered or something. I think they ought to check with some of those cowboys. She's probably making the rounds on the rodeo circuit. Seemed to have a soft spot for those dumb bronc busters."

"I'll bet her mother doesn't believe that," Libby said sharply. It was hard to listen to this loser talking about Della as if she was some kind of slut.

"Well, she threw herself at one of my customers so hard he called me and complained. Guess he had a hard time resisting Little Miss Jailbait and found her to be a bit of a distraction. I could sure sympathize with him." He gave Libby a sly wink, and she flinched. Poor Della.

It must have been a constant battle for her. The men around here obviously weren't able to overlook her attractiveness and let her do her job.

"Are you done with my dog?" Libby didn't wait for an answer but snapped on Ivan's leash and headed out the door. Ivan looked back and growled again as they left.

"You come back anytime, now," Ron called after them. "You don't have to bring that dog, either. You just come and see me, you know? Just for fun."

Chapter 20

Luke was lunging a yearling in the round pen when the colt shied and reared, pulling the line taut. Following its rolling-eyed stare, Luke saw a slight, dark-haired figure dashing up the drive on a battered old bicycle.

It was David. Maybe the Roundup was on fire or something. Something was sure wrong. David was usually a laid-back guy, and he was pedaling so hard the bike heeled right and left with every stroke of the pedals.

"Luke." David jerked the bike to a stop and hopped off, letting it tumble onto the grass outside the pen. The colt shied again at the clatter of the falling bike, tossing its head. Luke released it and it fled to the far side of the pen.

"Sorry." David bent at the waist, his hands on his knees, gasping for breath. "Libby. Her…"

Luke grabbed David's arm and hauled him to his pickup. The two of them jumped in, and Luke had the engine revved and the truck moving before the winded chef could get out another word.

"I knew something was wrong the minute I opened the door," David finally said. "He was drooling like crazy, foaming at the mouth. He just wouldn't stop…"

"What? Who*?* Who was foaming at the mouth?" Luke pressed the accelerator to the floor and the truck jolted down the drive, loose tailgate clanging at every pothole. "Did he attack Libby? Is she okay?"

"Did he…?" David laughed. "No, man, she wasn't attacked. It was one of the puppies. It's sick. Throwing up. Libby's not even home, man."

"Oh." Luke slowed the truck to a rational pace and glanced over at David. "What were you doing over there, anyway?" He was trying to sound calm, but he was almost as alarmed at David visiting Libby as he had been at the idea of a crazed madman attacking her. Not that David would hurt her. But maybe she liked the undernourished hippie type more than she liked tall, handsome cowboys.

"I'm doing some handyman stuff for her," David said. "Working on the outbuildings."

"Oh." Luke nodded, hoping David hadn't noticed the panic that had crossed his face. "I figured that."

"So she had the dogs in the chicken house so I could play with 'em, you know," David said. "And the others all came barreling out, but Rooster—well, I think it was Rooster, but I still can't tell them apart—was just sitting in the corner, kind of hunched over. I went in and picked him up and that's when I saw he was sick. I left a message on Libby's cell, but I couldn't get hold of her, so I hightailed it over to your place. Thought maybe you could give us a ride to the vet."

Luke nodded, then rolled down his window. He knew David had been part of the Great Unwashed at one point in his life, but you'd have thought a cook would be more conscious of stuff like body odor. The guy smelled awful. He pulled to a stop at the end of the driveway, then started to turn toward Lackaduck.

"Vet's that way," David said, pointing to the left.

"But we have to get the puppy."

"No. I got him," David said. He undid the top button of his shirt and a tiny, miserable face peeked out.

No wonder the guy smelled. Luke was pretty sure the dog had thrown up inside David's shirt.

"I didn't want to waste any time," David said. The little dog heaved and gasped, then gagged hard.

"Um, could you put him back in there?" Luke asked. "My truck…"

David grimaced and shoved the dog back into his shirt. "Like nobody's ever puked in this truck before," he said, scanning the truck's worn, stained upholstery. "You've had this thing since high school, right?"

"Yeah, well, it's been a while since anything like that happened," Luke said. "And I'd like to let it be a little longer."

Luke swung into the vet's driveway, parking beside another pickup. It looked awfully familiar. Especially the insult scratched into the side and the drooling monster hanging his head over the side of the bed.

"Libby," he said.

She rolled down the window and his heart lurched, spun, and fell down at the sight of her. How could anyone call this woman an "evil bitch?" She looked more like an angel with her big brown eyes and tilted up nose. Those curls were like a rusty halo framing her face. He wanted to…

"What's up?" she asked.

Luke stared at her a minute, slack-jawed, then jerked back to reality. "Rooster's sick," he said. "David found him. Come on."

"What happened?" She jumped out of the truck and clapped her hand over her mouth as David hauled the retching puppy out of his shirt. "Oh no."

The three of them ran inside. Ron took one look at the dog and hustled them into an examining room. He was immediately in professional mode, his attention focused on his patient for a change, instead of the nearest female.

"Can you think of anything around your place your dogs might have gotten into?" he asked. "Poison? Insecticide? Antifreeze?"

"No. I don't think so," she said. "I cleaned out the barn and tossed a bunch of old packages of rat poison and roach bait. Still, they were there, so someone might have used some inside the barn." She started to shake. "I should have been more careful. Oh my God, I should have checked more carefully once I found the packages."

Ron shook his head. "This guy had to have ingested a lot of poison to get this sick. And why would he be sick and all the others okay? You're not letting them run, are you? If he bothered the neighbors, they might have fed him something."

"I don't have any neighbors. Except Luke—and he wouldn't hurt them. Besides, they're usually in the barn all day when I'm gone. Today I left them in the chicken house so David could play with them when he came to paint."

"There must be something in the chicken house," Luke said.

"No. It's clean. I scrubbed it all out," she said. "It's probably the cleanest place on the whole farm, actually. The chickens have better living conditions than I do." The puppy gagged again, and Libby moaned. "I can't believe this is happening. Is he going to be okay?" She was trying to keep her cool, but tears welled up in her eyes. "This is Rooster. He's the feisty one. Please, is he going to be okay?"

"I can't say for sure," Ron said. "He's vomited a lot, so there's probably not much poison left in his system, whatever it was. I'm going to give him a sedative and pump his stomach to make sure we get the rest out. The rate he's going, he'll damage himself vomiting this violently. We'll run some tests then, figure out what it was. Meanwhile, I'll give him some intravenous fluids to prevent dehydration."

"He'll have to stay here, then?"

Ron nodded. "Best thing you can do is go home and keep an eye on the rest of them. If you see any signs of sickness—retching, or listlessness, any drooling, anything at all unusual—get them in here fast. I'm surprised it's only one of them that's sick." He picked up the puppy gently. "I'll go get started. You'd better go home."

"Call me, will you, Ron? Let me know if there's any change?"

"Of course."

The pressure had been building up, and now Libby lost it. Luke put his arm around her and coaxed her from the room. Sobbing, she let him hold her a little tighter.

"He'll be okay, Libby." He patted her shoulder. "Remember, he's the feisty one."

When they got home, the rest of the dogs were doing fine. Penny was kind of mopey when she figured out they hadn't brought Rooster back with them, but she perked up when Luke started mixing up the dog food while Libby smothered the puppies with kisses and handed out treats. David prostrated himself on the floor for the dogs' entertainment, and they tumbled over him, showering his face with wet puppy kisses. No one was drooling or retching.

The three of them sat on the floor to watch the puppies devour their food.

"Makes me hungry just watching them," David said, glancing at his watch. "I need to get home." He levered himself to his feet. "Glad everything's okay.

"Only because of you," Libby said. "It's a good thing you were here."

David shrugged, embarrassed by the praise. "I'll be back tomorrow. Finish the job."

He swung out the door and Luke stood, then reached down and pulled Libby to her feet. For a moment she was very aware of the kitchen's silence, broken only by the buzz of the light over the sink and the munching of the puppies at their dish. Luke looked down at their joined hands. "I was wondering," he said.

Uh-oh.

"Why are you looking at me like that?"

Libby blushed. "Like what?"

"Like you're worried I'm going to kiss you or something."

Libby looked down at the floor. "Because—I don't know."

Luke brought his other hand up and tipped her chin, looking into her eyes. "If you're going to worry anyway..."

"Oh, no." Libby backed away.

Luke turned away. "Sorry." He looked genuinely hurt and she felt a rush of regret. "Saving it for the sheriff?"

"No," she said, trying for a light tone. "Just saving it."

"For later?" Luke looked hopeful.

She shook her head.

"Speaking of later, that's what I was wondering. Do you want to have dinner?"

She remembered her awkward meal with Cash and shook her head. She wasn't about to repeat that mistake—not even with Luke. Of course, if Luke pushed her up against the truck and tried to kiss her…

"No," she said. "I'd better not."

"My mom wanted to know, and I forgot to ask. She made meatloaf just for you, 'cause I told her you liked it. I was supposed to call if you couldn't come."

"Well…"

"Good." He nodded, as if she'd come to a firm decision and wasn't standing there dithering. "Do you want to just ride with me? I'll bring you back later."

"Nope. I'll follow you in the Bitchmobile," she said. After Cash, she'd sworn off riding shotgun. "I'll just park it where your mom won't see it. Wouldn't want her to know what an evil bitch I am."

~

Luke's mother had everything ready, all right. The table was neatly set, plates and flatware all in their customary positions according to Emily Post—but Emily might not have approved of the menu. Each plate held a pair of clean white Jockey briefs, neatly folded and decorated with two cherry tomatoes and a sprig of parsley. In the center of the table, a salad bowl held rolled socks, along with a pair of tongs for easy serving.

"Urp," Libby said. She tried to suppress the giggle that was rising in her chest and slid her gaze toward Luke. He took the non-traditional dinner right in stride.

"Mom," he said. "You did laundry."

His mother, standing by the counter, nodded and smiled.

"But it's dinnertime," he said gently. He started to gather the plates from the table. "I'm in the mood for meatloaf," he said. "We had underwear last night."

"Oh." His mom looked uncertain, wringing her hands. "Did I do something dumb again?"

"Mum, it's not dumb," Luke said. He leaned down and kissed her on the cheek. "You're never dumb. But we only have underwear for dinner on Wednesdays."

"These little salad doohickeys are nice, though," Libby said quickly. "They'll look great with the meatloaf." Luke flashed her a grateful smile.

"Oh, the meatloaf!" Ella trotted over to the stove and opened the oven door to release a billow of gray-black smoke. "I must have forgotten."

Luke took his mother's arm and pulled her gently away from the oven. Spotting a pair of potholders on the counter, Libby used them to lift the loaf pan from the stove.

"This looks good," she said. "I like it crispy. Can I have an end piece?" She looked down at the dish in her hands and blanched. She'd pretend it was Cajun meatloaf—blackened.

To her relief, Luke took charge of the meatloaf, sawing off the burned bits and laying a neat slice from the center on each plate. Eagerly, his mother placed the tomatoes and parsley beside each slice, cocking her head as she gauged the correct arrangement for each bit of garnish.

Luke's dad said a quick and quiet grace, and they lit into their food. Libby was worried about keeping the conversation going, but Luke's mom had evidently mistaken her for the beleaguered heroine on one of the network soap operas, and peppered her with questions

about her evil twin, her billion-dollar fashion empire, and her husband's secret life as head of another household across town.

"I'm done with all that now," Libby said, waving one hand. "I divorced the bastard. Killed off the twin, too."

"Oh, I was hoping you'd do that!" Mrs. Rawlins seemed delighted with the solution. "They had it coming. I always said so."

Libby regaled her with grisly details of the twin murder while Luke and his father looked on, bemused.

"So now I'm on the run," Libby said. "You won't tell anyone I was here, will you?"

Luke's mom made a zipping gesture across her mouth and threw away an imaginary key. "Your secret's safe with me." She stacked her husband's plate on her own and pushed back her chair. Rising shakily to her feet, she carried the dishes to the counter. Luke's dad followed his wife with his eyes, tracking her across the kitchen like a wary watchdog. He'd pushed his chair back from the table when she stood, and he was obviously poised and ready in case she wandered into danger.

It was nice, Libby thought. He let her do what she wanted—just looked out for her while she did it. Some men would have let her illness limit her life, but Luke's dad just stood guard, alert and ready. She looked around the kitchen, at the golden light casting a warm halo over the table, at the homespun rag rugs scattered on the floor, at Luke, pushing back his chair to help his mother. It looked like home—but more important, it *felt* like it.

"Let me help." She stacked her plate and Luke's together, along with a serving dish, and carried the clattering pile to the sink.

"Well, aren't you smart," Luke's mom said. "Helping like that." She patted Libby on the head like a child.

"Looks like you went from business tycoon to eight-year-old in sixty seconds," Luke teased as Libby returned to the table for another load. "How'd that happen?"

She shrugged. "Hey, after that good dinner, I'll be whoever your mom wants me to be."

Deafness obviously wasn't one of Mrs. Rawlins's issues. She turned from the sink with a hopeful smile. "Daughter-in-law?"

Libby stammered, glancing from her smile to Luke's.

"Not yet, Mom," he said.

"Oh, son." His mother sighed and turned to Libby. "You just keep on being nice to him," she said. "He'll come around."

Libby opened her mouth to explain, but all that came out was a sickly croaking sound.

"I know," Mrs. Rawlins said. "I get mad at him too." She plugged the drain and cranked the faucet all the way to hot, then squirted in a dollop of dish soap. Libby leaned over and surreptitiously adjusted the temperature down from third-degree burn.

"Look. Bubbles." Luke's mother was squeezing the Palmolive bottle, wafting tiny multicolored bubbles into the air. "Pop!" she said, poking one with her finger. She grinned at Libby. "Go on. Pop one. It feels good."

Libby poked one drifting sphere out of existence, then another, and the two of them giggled as they performed an impromptu dance in front of the sink, bursting every bubble with index fingers raised disco-style.

"You two," Luke said, shaking his head in mock disgust. "Like a couple of kids."

"I always wanted to be a young mom," his mother said, and the giggles started again. Somehow they managed to get the dishes rinsed and slotted into the dishwasher, Libby furtively rearranging Mrs. Rawlins's haphazard placement as they worked.

As they finished, she glanced over at Luke and realized there was a new source of third-degree burns in the room. He was watching her with an intensity that just about smoked her shirt off. Catching her eye, he smiled, warming the look an extra ten degrees.

"I should go," Libby said. She turned to Luke's mother, then to his father. "Thanks so much for having me. I had a great time."

She glanced out the window. Night was falling, and the world had gone gray and white except for the warm yellow halo thrown by the lights from the house. She glanced around the kitchen, wishing she could stay.

Luke's place was so warm, so homey. Her own place, off across the plains, seemed sadly empty by comparison. Sure, it was full of dogs and chickens, and she'd added a lot of personal touches that made it her own—but home wasn't pets, or furniture, or pictures on the wall.

Home was people.

Luke walked Libby out the door, glancing back at his parents sitting at the kitchen table. It had been a good night, a really nice dinner. Lately, those had been more and more rare. The ranch felt empty, somehow, since his mother's memories had flown the coop and she was no longer the guiding force of the household.

But with Libby there, it felt like home again—warm

and happy and safe. And she seemed to enjoy herself, too. He'd never seen her smile so much. Maybe she was ready to stop running away. Maybe she'd finally found what she'd been running toward.

Maybe it was him.

He hoped so. He'd had women for dinner before. They'd been… kind. He'd been relieved when they pretended not to notice his mother's brain blips—but Libby had joined right in with the lunacy and somehow made it seem normal. No, better than normal. She'd managed to remind him that his mom was still her sprightly self—that her spirit and good nature still illuminated the whole house.

"Thanks," he said as he walked her out to her truck.

She gave him a puzzled look. "No, thank *you*," she said. "I had a great time."

"I had a better one," he said. "You… you fit right in."

"Thanks."

They grinned inanely at each other for a beat too long, frozen in the halo of the porch light. One of the moths flitting around the bulb looped downward, hitting Libby's cheek. She flinched and Luke brought a hand to her face, brushing away the powder from the moth's wing.

"They're bad this year," he murmured. "The moths." He stroked her cheek again, slower this time. She looked up at him, lips parted, so tempting she had to be trying.

She might as well beg for a kiss out loud as look at him like that.

He bent to touch her lips just as she hiked herself up on her toes, and they met in the middle with more force than either had intended. The crush of her lips on his sent lust raging through him like flames on a fuse,

burning up his inhibitions, smoking out the feelings he'd been struggling to smother at the dinner table. Out here in the dark, he felt bold and reckless and hungry. He wrapped his arms around her and pulled her close, feeling the length of her body press into his with what felt like a need equal to his own.

Was he right? Was she feeling it too? He pulled away, just for an instant, and searched her eyes. He found what he was looking for: heat and passion, and a gaze focused on something deep inside him.

Deep inside. Other women never looked that far. They saw his clothes, his house, his horses, and they figured he was a cowboy. Then they saw his truck and decided he wasn't quite the cowboy they were looking for. But Libby seemed to look past the hat and the boots and even the truck to the real him—and that forged a connection between them that went way beyond mere attraction.

Way beyond.

He kissed her again, softer this time, holding back to give her all the eloquence he could muster, showing her how gentle he could be, how tender his feelings were for her. He wrapped his arms around her, pulling her close. He loved touching her, holding her. He wanted to let his hands wander and explore, stroke her skin, quicken her breath, but it wasn't about that anymore. It was about something more—something far deeper than the sexual spark they'd shared in the barn.

It was about holding her close. Keeping her safe.

Libby moaned and wrapped her arms around Luke's neck. She'd wanted this since she'd caught him looking

at her in the kitchen with that hard, hot look in his eyes. She trusted Luke as much as she could trust anyone, but in that moment, despite the cozy domestic surroundings, he'd seemed dangerous—and she'd decided a little danger might be a good thing.

She'd spent the rest of the night sneaking surreptitious glances at the way his denim jacket stretched across his shoulders, the way his thighs flexed under his jeans when he rose from the chair. By the time he walked her out the door, she felt flushed and hot, nervous as a high-strung mare. She wanted Luke to kiss her for real. She wanted his hands on her body, his tongue in her mouth, his… everything.

And she'd almost gotten what she wanted—but now he'd gone all careful on her. He was holding her like he was afraid she'd break, his hands clasped carefully around her waist while his tongue teased and danced in her mouth, driving her crazy, making her desperate for more, harder, deeper. She pressed her body against him, needing the pressure of his chest against her breasts, the warmth of his skin against hers.

He made a hoarse, strangled sound as his hands moved down and cupped her denim-clad butt, pressing her close so she could feel what she was doing to him. He was definitely dangerous now.

His lips left hers and she felt the scrape of his five o'clock shadow on her cheek. His warm breath teased her ear as he blew out a shaky breath. Ducking his head, he pressed his forehead against hers and looked into her eyes.

"I want to go home with you. I know I can't, I know it's too soon, but I want to."

She nodded, her heart skipping and fluttering, her breath coming in gasps. "I know."

"I know you're not sure, and I know you're not looking for this. But if you don't want something to happen, you might not want to kiss me like that."

She nodded, biting her lower lip.

"Do you want something to happen?"

She did. She wanted everything to happen, all at once, right there on the porch—but she didn't want to deal with the consequences of a night with Luke. She wasn't ready to risk her heart.

Not yet.

She looked up at him, her lower lip trembling, and tried to answer, but no sound came out.

"I know." He pulled her into him so her head tucked under his chin. "I know." He rocked from side to side and she settled into him, closing her eyes, breathing in his scent.

He gave her a final squeeze and pulled away. "You sure you'll be okay tonight? All alone over there?" He took off his jacket and draped it around her shoulders.

"I'll be fine," she said. "I have Ivan."

He nodded. "You do," he said. "And just so you know, you have me too."

Chapter 21

Libby woke gradually, keeping her eyes closed against the faint glow of morning lighting her bedroom. She'd dreamed of Luke all night, and now her senses were filled with the scent of him. His jacket was coarse against her skin, a button pressing into her neck.

Had she done more than dream?

She jerked upright and scrambled to the side of the bed. Looking back, she saw his jacket draped over her pillow. She glanced around the room, nervous, as if someone might have seen her sleeping with his jacket clutched close like a child's teddy bear.

No wonder she'd had such sweet dreams.

Dreams would have to wait, though. And so would Luke.

Delicious as that kiss had been, she'd regained her senses now that he was a safe distance away. His presence seemed to go to her head, making her forget who she was—*how* she was. She picked the wrong men. Always. And she was probably doing it again.

As her sleep-induced fog cleared—or was it Luke-induced?—she remembered Rooster and made a quick call to the vet clinic. Twenty minutes and a quick shower later, she was in the pickup and on her way to collect her remarkably resilient puppy.

"He's a tough little guy," Ron said. "Seems to have made a full recovery."

He wasn't kidding. Apparently, Rooster's brush with death had given him a new joie de vivre. By evening, he'd bitten Rotgut's ear, eaten most of a fuzzy pink bunny slipper, and rolled in something so revoltingly fragrant that even his own mother wouldn't get near him. He'd also given new meaning to the phrase "the dog ate my homework" by gnawing the yellow legal pad to shreds, destroying Libby's notes for two pending stories.

By five o'clock, Libby didn't feel the least bit guilty shutting him and the rest of the puppies in the barn and heading out on a reconnaissance mission. Her direct questioning of suspects hadn't gotten her anywhere, so it was time to get sneaky. She remembered Mike's reluctance to let her visit his workshop and decided to check it out without an invitation. If the guy really was a psycho serial killer, he'd probably have trophies hidden in there.

She hoped her suspicions were wrong. She didn't really want to find a mason jar full of disembodied ears, or a box of moldering fingers.

Cruising past the Roundup, she checked attendance. Sure enough, Mike's white Ford Fairlane was one of the cars in the lineup outside the bar. Cash's black Explorer was there too, along with a lot of other trucks she didn't recognize. Crystal said Crazy Mike usually stayed at the bar until almost closing time, so Libby had plenty of time to play secret agent.

She cruised down County Road 47, which was barely a road at all—just a gravel-strewn trail that sloped down into a narrow valley where the Lackaduck River wound through a crooked row of half-starved cottonwoods. After driving back and forth half a dozen times, she

finally discovered a short break in the tangle of trees that proved to be the entrance to Mike's driveway.

She bounced down the dirt two-track, weeds scraping the bottom and sides of her Ranger as she maneuvered carefully around jagged rocks and treacherous potholes. Rounding a curve, she splashed through some standing water and a view of the house rose up ahead.

The house looked utterly abandoned, its clapboards gray and warped. It was clear someone had cared about the place at one time, but what was once a flower garden sported only a few shabby blooms, and the carefully placed shrubbery had run amok in the front and side yards. An enormous dying cottonwood loomed over the house, one thick branch arched across the roof like a heavily muscled arm poised to strike.

Libby turned around and headed back to a turnout she'd spotted just before the driveway. She could leave the pickup there, then trek back to the house. If Mike came home early for some reason, she didn't want him to find her truck parked out front.

Hopping out of the Ranger, she almost slid down a steep bank at the edge of the turnout. The marshy ground at the bottom was scattered with rusted cans, old tires, and broken bottles. She spotted a broken rack of antlers nearby, and what looked like a cat skeleton further down. Shuddering, she headed back up the crooked driveway, listening to the crickets trilling in the night air. Dead leaves rustled as nocturnal creatures scurried about their secret business in the woods.

When she reached the house, she thrashed through the tangle of shrubbery to the backyard. Mike's workshop was a small log building about twice the size of her

chicken house, with a rough wooden door that creaked in protest as she swung it open. Pawing the wall, she found a light switch and flicked it on.

Scores of glassy eyes glinted in the harsh fluorescent light, each pair set in the mounted corpse of a dead animal. There were mule deer heads of every conceivable age and condition, bug-eyed pronghorns, and assorted birds, along with a few of Mike's novelty projects—a prairie dog jazz band, a frog wearing an oversized sombrero, and a grinning armadillo drinking a beer. Diagrams of animals in various stages of dissection were tacked up beside a yellowed calendar that proclaimed the virtues of the New Method Fur Dressing Company. The month of July featured a photograph of a blonde woman grinning with predatory pride as she held up the lifeless head of a deer. The seventeenth, a Thursday, was circled with a red crayon heart.

A tarnished metal tray on the counter held glass eyeballs of every imaginable color and size. Sharp knives and scalpels lay beside a cordless power drill, along with several dusty brown glass bottles bearing yellowing labels with grisly skulls-and-crossbones stamped over faded print. A cheap revolving office chair in front of the counter was draped with a shaggy animal skin that was stained and spotted with blood and bile.

Libby knelt on the floor to explore the rusty file cabinets that supported the counter. The first drawer held pictures of animals, hundreds of them, cut from magazines and filed neatly in alphabetical order. The second held eight-track tapes of country music—the Statler Brothers, Tammy Wynette, and Conway Twitty. No doubt Crazy Mike spent his evenings cutting up small animals,

grooving to the tunes of the Grand Ole Opry. The next drawer was Mike's junk drawer, and was filled with a mad jumble of string, rubber bands, and paper clips.

Libby lifted her head, listening. Had she heard a noise outside? The crunch of gravel, maybe, or a twig snapping? She sat motionless, straining her ears, but all she heard was the trickle of the distant river and a bird calling in the distance.

She let out the breath she'd been holding and opened the last drawer. It was obviously the treasure chest of this overgrown child, filled with keepsakes and mementoes. Libby sifted through its contents, digging through oddly shaped rocks, a robin's egg blown hollow, creased snapshots of a man and woman in fifties dress—typical souvenirs of a quiet life in Lackaduck. Digging deeper, she found some more disturbing items. There was a plastic hairbrush with a few strands of long blond hair caught in its bristles. A leather change purse, blue with gold clasps, was empty except for a shiny penny.

She dug a little deeper, then caught her breath and jerked her hand back as if she'd hit a hot coal. Her own change purse was in there, right beneath a bottle of Paris Pink nail polish. She pulled it out, her hands shaking, and opened it. Several crisp dollar bills still nested among the nickels and dimes. Mike hadn't taken the money, so why did he want her change purse? She remembered Cash's words. "*He's kind of obsessive. I'm afraid he's shifted his focus onto you.*"

Her head spun and she felt weak. Seeing her lost purse mingling with Mike's other treasures made his collection of souvenirs take on a new and threatening aura. She returned it to the drawer and stared at it, dazed. She

almost didn't hear the gravel crunching in the driveway over the ringing in her ears, but headlights sweeping across the wall jolted her back to reality. She jumped up, scanning the windows and doors, looking for an exit. Tonight, of all nights, Crazy Mike had decided to lay off the booze.

She slammed the drawer shut and bolted through a side door, yanking it closed behind her. Ducking behind the shrubbery, she dropped to her hands and knees and scurried to the back of the cabin. She turned and peeked around the corner just as Crazy Mike stepped out of his car. He was carrying two large jackrabbits by their floppy ears. Their long hind legs dragged the ground, making four shallow trails in the dirt. He looked like an enormous toddler traipsing off to bed with his favorite toys.

Libby crouched below a window, barely breathing, her heart pounding. The shrubs around the shack were infested with thistles and other prickly things that were stabbing her back and scratching her bare legs. She could hear Mike's heavy tread on the floorboards inside, then a muffled thump that made her figure he'd set the rabbits on the work table. "Good boys," he said softly in his high, piping voice. Good boys? Was somebody with him? Libby knew he was alone. He had to be talking to the rabbits.

No wonder they called him crazy. Luke could protest all he wanted. This guy was nuts.

"Let's see what we can do now," he murmured. "Come here, little bunny. Let's see your pretty face."

Libby couldn't resist a peek. After all, he had the lights on, and it was dark outside. He couldn't see her. She poked her head above the windowsill.

Mike was seated in the office chair at his worktable. One bunny lay prostrate like a forgotten plaything at the edge of the table. The other was cradled in his arms.

"Nice little bunny. Nice boy," Mike murmured, touching a shiny scalpel to the rabbit's throat. Reflexively, Libby's hand rose to her own neck, shielding it in a protective gesture.

"Nice bunny," he said again.

In one smooth motion, he sliced the rabbit's flesh in a neat line from chin to groin. Sweeping the animal onto the table, he slid his hands into its belly and scooped a handful of glistening entrails into a waiting bucket. "There we go. We don't need that anymore, no, we don't."

As Libby watched in reluctant fascination, Mike proceeded to separate the rabbit from its skin. When he was done, the slick underside of the rabbit's epidermis glistened in the bright fluorescent light.

He turned to the second rabbit, continuing to mutter as he worked. "Good boy, good bunny. That's a pretty, pretty boy. You're going to be a pretty bunny. You get to be a jackalope, yes, you do." He finished the second rabbit, then turned the two animal skins fur-side up.

Carefully, Mike draped the bloody heads over his hands like puppets and brought the two dead noses together in a grotesque kiss. "Hello, pretty bunny," he made the first rabbit say. "Hello, darling," the second rabbit said, cocking its eyeless head. "I love you, pretty bunny."

The rabbit on the left took exception to this. "You don't love me! I don't love you back—not at all. You're weird. Nobody could love you, ever, you weirdo!"

"You kissed me," the first rabbit protested. "I kissed you, and you kissed me back."

"I was just being nice," said the second rabbit. "I was just being polite. I didn't want to hurt your feelings."

"No, you love me. I felt it when you kissed me. I know you love me. You have to! You have to! I love you, and you love me!"

Mike contorted his arm so that one rabbit turned its back on the other. "You're a weirdo. I'm telling my friends. I'm warning them to stop being nice to you. I'm telling everybody."

"No!" Mike was shouting now. His face was contorted in an agonized grimace. He was taking this whole rabbit scenario way too seriously. "You're *my* pretty bunny. *Mine*!"

Still shrouding his hand with the animal's drooping head, Mike reached for the scalpel he'd set aside. Now the angry rabbit appeared to be brandishing a large knife. Suddenly, it lunged for its companion, the knife stabbing through the thin rabbit skin and into Mike's hand.

"Oooooow! Ow-wooo!," Mike howled, dropping the rabbits and clutching his hand. Blood dribbled from a deep cut on the fleshy base of his thumb. He stood and spun around, trampling the rabbits underfoot. "You stupid! You stupid! You weirdo!"

He sat again, white-faced, and bent over his bleeding hand. Tears started from his eyes as he dabbed at the blood with a dirty rag.

"You weirdo," he muttered. "Nobody could love you. You stupid freak. Everybody knows. Everybody."

Chapter 22

Libby was hyperventilating when she got back to the truck. She'd scrambled out of the shrubbery and run for the woods while Mike was distracted by his self-inflicted wound. Thrashing through the underbrush, she'd made a wide circle around the house and found her way back to her pickup.

It was a good thing the sheriff was bending his elbow at the bar, because she surely would have gotten a ticket if he'd seen her speeding home. She pulled into the driveway and slouched behind the wheel in relief, grateful to be back at her happy homestead.

The porch light was on and the house was glowing like a Thomas Kinkaid painting. Ivan was doing a fair impression of long-gone road kill on the front step. A puppy, resting its front legs on the big dog's massive shoulders, pricked up its ears and barked a thin, high-pitched yap of welcome. Luke stepped out onto the porch, puppies gamboling about his feet, as Libby threw the pickup into park.

The place looked like the picture for the definition of "home" in some very poetically illustrated dictionary. Libby thought back to freshman year and worked out an Art Appreciation 101 analysis of the scene. It was the lighting, she decided, that made it so appealing. Or maybe the composition. The color. The puppies.

No, it wasn't any of those things.

It was the man.

Much as she hated to admit it, the idea of Luke waiting for her, welcoming her, gave coming home a whole new shine.

She stepped out of the truck, suddenly conscious of her appearance. Her bare arms were scraped and scratched in a dozen places, and her hair was festooned with twigs and shreds of leaves. She'd torn her jeans in her last mad scramble through the woods, and her face was probably streaked with dirt. She decided to act casual.

"Hey, Luke," she said smoothly. "Whatcha doin'?"

"I called to see how Rooster was doing, and you didn't answer. I was picturing you writhing in agony on the kitchen floor, poisoned by some unseen hand. So I came over. The door was open, and these guys seemed glad to see me. I hope you don't mind." He bent and picked up Rooster. "They seem to be doing fine. Even this guy."

"Ron says it might have been arsenic," Libby said, pushing past him into the house. "He's running tests."

She glanced over at the sofa and blanched. She'd been working all day, and everything else had literally fallen by the wayside, including a few articles of clothing. The bright T-shirt she'd traded for a darker secret-agent model was tossed carelessly across the sofa, along with a pair of running shorts and a white cotton bra she'd replaced with a sexier number that seemed more appropriate for her Bond Girl expedition.

She shoved the bra under a throw pillow, then turned her attention to her messy kitchen. She'd left a pile of dishes from the day before by the sink, but Luke had evidently pitched in to help. The sink was heaped with

soap bubbles and a few plates were slotted into the drying rack.

"You didn't have to do that," she said, hustling over to the counter. "I was going to get to it eventually." She plunged her hands into the soapy water and fished out another plate. Cranking the hot water on full blast, she rinsed it and set it in the rack.

"Tell you what," Luke said. "You wash, I'll dry."

She remembered her morning-after dreams and felt a little swoony, then kicked herself back into gear and got busy with the suds. Luke stood beside her, towel at the ready. His shirt smelled deliciously like old leather and horses, and his skin was scented with some kind of sweet-smelling aftershave that was clearly designed to make women lose their minds and tear off their clothes.

"I hope you don't mind that I came over," he said as Libby handed him a salad bowl. His fingers brushed hers, and she felt a thrill zip down to her toes. "I know it's butting in, but you were upset yesterday and I wanted to make sure Rooster was okay. And you." He gave her a tender sideways glance. "I wanted to make sure you were okay too."

"It's fine, Luke," she said. "I'm fine." Her voice came out huskier than she intended, and she had to clear her throat.

He dried the last of the salad bowls as Libby fished around in the dishwater for the wine glasses. She felt a sharp stab of pain and jerked her hand out of the water, holding up a piece of broken stemware. A glittering shard of glass was embedded in the palm of her hand.

"Oh, no." Luke shifted the faucet lever to cold and guided her palm under the numbing stream of water,

cradling her hand in his as he gently eased the glass out of the cut. "Hold it up," he said, lifting her hand to his chest. "Above your heart."

He tore a paper towel off the roll with one hand and gently blotted the water and blood away, then bent and kissed the wound. Libby felt dizzy all of a sudden, and it wasn't from loss of blood.

"You okay?" Luke pressed the towel into her palm and they stood there, face to face, their hands clasped together, their eyes meeting over her injured hand.

"I'm so sorry. It's my fault," he said. "I shouldn't have put the glassware in with the bowls."

"It's okay," Libby said. "They were cheap wineglasses. Wal-Mart." The light over the sink seemed to flicker and dim as she watched her blood bloom red on the paper towel. "I need to sit down," she said. She was pathetic, and she knew it. The cut wasn't even an inch long.

"Sorry," she said as he led her to the sofa. "It's nothing, really. You shouldn't have to take care of me." She tried to laugh, but it came out a little weak. No one should have to take care of her. She could take care of herself.

Why did she keep forgetting that lately?

"I don't mind," he said. He pulled her hand to his lips and kissed it again as they sank onto the cushions. "I'll take care of you any time. Because I do. Care, I mean. I care about..."

His eyes searched hers, probing for even the smallest shred of encouragement. Libby shook off her weakness and willed herself not to respond, concentrating on the clock on the wall, the teapot on the stove—anything but Luke.

"The puppies," he finished lamely, looking down and adjusting the throw rug with the toe of his boot. "I

really care about the puppies, I guess." He set her hand down on her thigh and cupped her fingers around the wad of paper towel. "Just hang on to that a while," he said. "Squeeze. It's almost stopped bleeding." He rose, looking uncertain. "I should go."

"Wait. Help me put a Band-Aid on it." Libby got up and opened a drawer next to the sink, pulling out a box of Curads and a tube of antiseptic ointment. "I'll need one of these big ones, I think."

She sat down at the table and struggled with the ingenious sterile wrapping, tearing it to pieces in an effort to extract the bandage with her one uninjured hand.

"Here. Let me." He sat down next to her at the head of the table and she handed him the package. Squinting with concentration, he fished the plastic strip from the mangled wrapper and peeled the paper back from the adhesive, his big workingman's hands surprisingly agile. "Hold out your hand."

He opened the antiseptic and carefully dabbed the soothing ointment on the wound. Libby squirmed in her chair.

"Sorry," he said.

"You're not hurting me," she murmured. "It feels good."

"Oh, that's nothing," he said, lifting his eyes from her hand. "This'll feel way better."

He pulled her toward him, cupping the back of her head, and kissed her. The Band-Aid fluttered to the floor along with all her resolutions as they savored each other for a long, luscious moment. Running his fingers gently up her arm, he caressed her cuts and scrapes, making her quiver inside.

She'd forgotten all about her wound by the time he stroked his hand through her hair a second time and pulled out a handful of leaves and twigs.

"What were you doing?" he asked.

"Investigating," she said.

"Investigating?" He pulled a heart-shaped leaf from behind her ear and held it to the light. "Let me guess," he said. "You've been spying on Mike Cresswell."

"How did you know?"

"Hydrangea," he said, indicating the leaf. "Mike's mom used to grow them, and Mike would give these leaves to the girls he liked. See? Shaped like a heart." His smile faded. "Besides, everybody wants to blame Mike for the Della McCarthy thing, so I figured you'd end up there sooner or later."

"Pretty sharp, Sherlock," she said. She got up and opened the fridge, grabbing a couple of longnecks and taking them over to the table. Luke twisted off the top of his, then did the same for hers and slid it in front of her.

"So what did you find out?"

She hesitated. "I know you think he's harmless, Luke, but it was sort of scary. He's got all kinds of dead animals in there, and diagrams, and eyeballs and stuff. And he plays with them, like puppets. He made two jackrabbits talk to each other, and Luke, it was really creepy. It was like he was reenacting something from his past."

"Like what?"

"Like being rejected by a girl. And killing her. He made the rabbits kiss, and then the one called the other a stupid weirdo, and then it stabbed him with a knife, but it went right through and Mike was all bloody and he was crying.

And Luke, he's got my change purse. And a lot of other stuff, all girlie stuff, in a drawer in his desk. And..."

"Slow down!" Luke said. "What's this about a knife?"

She explained the scene with the two rabbits, and Mike's self-inflicted injury. "He was crazy, Luke. It's like he went off the deep end, right there in front of me."

"And where were you while this was going on?"

She looked away, pretending to study the designs in the wallpaper. "Outside the window. In the bushes. Peeking in."

Luke started to laugh, then caught himself and tried to scowl.

"What were you thinking, Libby? What if he'd seen you?"

"It was dark out, and he had all the lights on. He couldn't see me. And besides, it was worth the risk. Luke, I'm sure now that Mike killed Della. He must have come on to her, like the rabbit, and she rejected him and he lost it. It's like he played out the whole scene, right in front of me."

"Whoa. Wait a minute." Luke looked really serious now. "Look, I grew up with Mike. And he's a little crazy, it's true, but he'd never hurt anybody. He's harmless, Libby. I hate to hear people say bad things about him. He wouldn't hurt a fly."

"But he cuts up dead animals for fun, Luke! That's one of the sure signs of a serial killer. And how do you explain the scene with the rabbits and the knife?"

"Easy." Luke looked smug. "I can tell you exactly what that was all about. And it wasn't about Della."

"What do you mean?"

He sat back and folded his arms. "When we were in high school, there was this girl, Sara Segal. She was

the town flirt—a real runaround Sue. She came on to all the boys, including Mike. He was always following her around, with his big puppy eyes, adoring her. And she encouraged it, touching him, giving him little hugs and stuff. One time she went too far, and Mike hugged her back. Big time. She freaked out, Libby. Called him stupid, called him a weirdo."

"Just like the rabbits?"

"Just exactly like the rabbits. Word for word. She told everybody about it. All her girlfriends were laughing at Mike, and he knew it. It really hurt him, Libby. Obviously, it still does."

"So you don't think it was about Della?" Libby's prize theory was falling to pieces.

"No, it was about Sara. Sara the slut. And she's still alive, trust me. Mike didn't kill her, even though she just about killed him, hurting his feelings like that. She hurt everybody she could. I guess it made her feel strong or something."

"Sounds like you had your own go-round with Sara the Slut."

"Yeah. I was young, and she was hot. We had a couple good times in the back of my pickup, and then she moved on. She always did."

"The back of your pickup?"

"Yeah—we have a kind of Lover's Lane here in Lackaduck, you know. Dirt road down by the river, with a pullout where the trees thin out and the moon shines through." He winked. "I'll show you sometime."

He looked sideways at her, his lashes shrouding his green eyes. A picture popped up on her mental movie screen: the two of them in the bed of his pickup, stretched

out on a blanket under the stars, crickets chirping in the summer night…

She shut down the projector and looked away. "No need," she said lightly. "I can find it on my own."

"With the sheriff?"

"No, I intend to stay out of the back of his pickup," she said, laughing. "I'll try to keep that particular relationship a little more civilized."

He was still smiling. "Let me know when you want to leave civilization behind, Libby." He ran his fingers up her arm again, and her insides turned to pudding. He was so hot, so *male,* and he was right there, right now, right when she needed him. He was always there when she needed him. Always. She could feel all her resolutions taking wing like startled sparrows.

"I think you need to let loose a little, Libby. I think it's been a while, and you need a little wild time." His hand moved up her arm and swept the side of her breast. She shivered, and he must have noticed because he did it again. She couldn't help herself. She leaned forward and kissed him, gently at first, then harder.

"I warned you," he said softly. "If you don't want something to happen…"

Her hands reached out and caressed his hair, pulling him closer. She felt her heart skipping and stuttering, her resolve collapsing. She wanted something to happen. Wanted it desperately. Wanted it *now.*

If the dogs hadn't chosen that moment to explode off the porch, barking maniacally, she would have gotten it, too.

Chapter 23

"DAMN." LUKE SLUMPED INTO A CHAIR, CRADLING HIS head in his hands as gravel crunched in the driveway. The pups rocketed past him and swirled around Libby, yapping frantically.

"What is it, doggies? What's up?" she asked, opening the door. "It's the sheriff. Wonder what he wants?"

"Same thing I do," Luke grumbled. "Probably not going to get it, though. Not with those mangy curs around."

"I thought you cared deeply about my puppies."

"Is that what you call them?" Luke didn't even try to look her in the eye. He focused a bit lower, then savored the blush that spread up from her chest to color her cheeks. "They're nice puppies." He glanced out the door to see Cash stepping out of his truck. "I'd better go," he said.

"No." Libby grabbed his arm. "Stay."

"Sit? Stay?" Luke fell back into his chair, and Libby darted over to whisper in his ear.

"I don't want to be alone with him," she hissed.

That was good news. Luke raised one eyebrow. "I thought you liked him."

"I told you, I don't. Not like that."

"I don't know. You seem a little… *susceptible* tonight."

She laughed nervously. "You could say that."

"I'd rather prove it," he said softly, reaching up to touch her hair.

She turned away as the sheriff stepped up on the porch, his boots thumping the boards.

"Hey, Cash," Libby said.

"Heard you had an incident out here," Cash said, hitching up his belt and adjusting his holster, where a heavy revolver rested on his hip. He was in uniform tonight. Luke wondered if he was on duty, or if he wore the whole getup to bed, like a kid with cowboy pajamas.

"Stangerson ran some tests," the sheriff continued. "He gave me a call. Said he sent a sample of the stomach contents off to the state labs for confirmation." He was playing the part of the gruff lawman to the hilt. It was probably awkward for him, Luke thought, dealing with Libby on a professional basis after their date.

Luke sure hoped so.

"Is this an official visit, then?" Libby asked.

"It is," Cash said.

Libby had started to rise from her chair, but she sat back down. "No beer for you then."

"Nothing else, either," Luke chimed in.

"What? Oh, hi, Luke." Cash grimaced and shook Luke's hand. "I heard you found the sick canine."

"The puppy. Yes." Luke's mouth tightened as he swallowed a smirk. "Actually, David found it."

"David. David? What was he doing here?" Cash swung around to face Libby, scowling.

"He's doing some work on my outbuildings," she said. "Painting, stuff like that."

The sheriff bit his lip. "Libby, do you know anything about that guy? He's an unsavory character."

"I know. You told me before," she said. "But he seems all right to me."

"Come on, Cash," Luke said. "You know the guy's cleaned up his act."

"Yeah," Cash admitted. "He hasn't been in trouble since he got out of the correctional facility. He was a mess, though. Hard to believe he can stay away from the stuff for long."

Luke decided to leave that battle for another day. "Anyway, he found the puppy." He explained the circumstances as Cash took rapid notes on a small notepad, then turned to Libby.

"Any idea who might have it in for your dogs? Or for you?"

"No, I thought he just got into something," she said. "Rat poison or something."

"That's not what Ron told me," Cash responded. "He says the dog was poisoned. Deliberately. Somebody fed him a nice juicy burger, laced with some kind of poison. Possibly arsenic."

Libby sat down hard, anger and fear crossing her features in quick succession, followed by puzzlement. Burgers, in her mind, would always be associated with David now. But he would never hurt the puppies. Would he?

"Who would do that?" she asked.

"Who has it in for you, Libby?" Cash asked again. He cleared his throat. "Let me clarify that. Who was at your front door the other day, shouting threats at you?"

Luke frowned. "Mike, right?"

"That's right, Luke. Crazy Mike." The sheriff pointed a finger dramatically in Luke's direction. "You hit the nail on the head."

"He might be right, Luke," Libby chimed in. "Mike said I'd be sorry. Maybe he poisoned Rooster as a warning."

Luke leaned back in his chair, tilting it up on its back legs and rocking to ease his agitation. "I told you, Libby," he said. "Mike wouldn't do that. He loves animals."

Cash snorted. "Yeah, loves 'em to death. Like that little dog he had. Like all the animals he cuts up and mounts."

"We don't know for sure what happened to that dog," Luke said, drawing his brows low over his eyes. "And taxidermy is his job."

"Mighty strange job for a so-called 'nice guy,'" Cash said. "I'm thinking I ought to pick him up for questioning. See if I can't get a warrant for his workshop. Check it out."

"Hey." Now it was Luke's turn to point an accusing finger at Cash. "You know you don't have probable cause to go harassing a handicapped guy." He glanced over at Libby. "I've got press connections," he said. "You try to railroad Mike into something, it'll be all over the paper."

Cash looked at Libby too, obviously wondering who she'd support. Judging from her expression as she glanced from one to the other, she didn't know the answer to that one herself.

Luke knew he'd gone a long way toward easing her mind about Mike. The interview had helped too. You had to like the guy once you heard his guileless account of his weird artistic vision, and his obvious fondness, however misguided, for his subjects.

But Mike had blown it with that crazy visit, and Cash had one distinct advantage: his badge. He was labeled as the good guy, sworn to serve and protect. As far as Luke could see, Cash mostly served and protected his

own image, but Libby didn't know him well enough yet to see how far the man's ego outweighed his duty as a lawman. She was looking down at her lap now, lacing and unlacing her fingers as she decided what to do. When she looked back up, it was Luke whose gaze she met, but her expression told him he'd lost this round.

"He's dangerous, Luke," she said. "I know he's your friend, but he's dangerous."

Luke blew out a long breath and brought the chair's front legs abruptly to the floor. "I understand how you feel, Libby," he said. "Mike was drunk the other night, and he scared you. He probably doesn't even remember what he did, but if I talk to him, he'll apologize. He really will, and he'll mean it."

She nodded, but her eyes were filled with doubt.

"Think about it," he continued. "If he wanted to hurt you, do you think that door would stop him?" He gestured toward her flimsy locks. "Do you think he couldn't have gotten in here?" He scooted the chair toward her. "Think about the guy's life, Libby. He's so alone. His parents are dead. The most companionship he gets is at the bar, where they call him names and treat him like a child."

"But he gets these obsessions..." Cash began.

"On women. Right." Luke turned to Cash and threw up his hands. "Of course he does. He's a man the same as you and me, right?" He propped his elbows on his knees and rested his chin on his clasped hands, looking up at Libby, begging her to see things through Mike's eyes. "Men get—well, frustrated, Libby. I mean, I don't always act like I should, and don't think I'm not trying to behave. Think how it is for Mike." He turned to the

sheriff. "He has the same needs as you and me, Cash. And he's never acted on them. Never."

"That's what you think," Cash said. "But what about Della?"

Luke jerked to his feet, fists clenched. "What about her? You don't have any reason to accuse him. Not really."

"There's the way he was around her," Cash said. "You saw it. And how he kept asking about her afterwards."

"Asking who?" Luke demanded. "He never asked me."

"But then there's what I saw, Luke," Libby said. "Earlier. With the rabbits."

"I explained that to you," Luke said, spinning to face her. "I thought you understood."

"You made a good case," she said. "But so does Cash. I'm just not sure. I mean, Cash would know whether Mike would do something like this. He *is* the sheriff."

"What makes you think that makes him qualified to judge Mike's character?" Luke asked. "He doesn't know him. Not at all." He glared at Cash. "He couldn't. Mike's scared shitless of him. Why is that, Cash? What did you do to him?"

"I didn't do anything to him," Cash said. "Except put on this uniform. Maybe he's got a guilty conscience. And besides, he's the one person in this town that could have poisoned that dog."

That was too much even for Libby. "What do you mean?" she asked. "Nobody saw Mike out here. We don't have any proof he was the one."

"Not yet. But if the state confirms that it was arsenic poisoning—like Stangerson thinks—I'll pick him up for questioning."

"Why?"

"Do you know what taxidermists use to preserve animal skins?"

"No. What?"

"Arsenic."

"Arsenic," Libby said. "Oh, no."

Luke hissed out an exasperated sigh and headed for the door. "I'm out of here," he said, flailing one hand toward Libby and Cash. "You two can trump up anything you want on our poor disturbed neighbor. I don't want any part of it. No part of it at all."

He stomped out, letting the screen door slam behind him.

Chapter 24

Too close to two men in one night, Libby thought, as the sheriff sat down in Luke's chair and took her hand in both of his. She tried to tug herself loose, but he pulled it toward him, eyeing her cuts and scrapes.

"What have you been doing, Libby? Were you and Luke outside?"

She remembered her appearance—the twigs in her hair, the scratches on her skin—and blushed. "No, I was in the woods. By myself. Then Luke came over."

"I think something was going on when I came in."

"Not really. Well, almost. But no."

He sat back. "Good," he said. "Luke's a good guy, but he's not for you, Libby. Still living with his parents, pinning all his hopes on that ranch, when ranching's not a viable way of life anymore… he's not a good prospect."

She pulled her hand away. "I'm not looking for a prospect, Cash. I'm looking for a friend, and Luke's a good one. So is David, as a matter of fact. And they don't go butting into my love life, like some people I know." She stood up and busied herself with the few remaining dishes, clattering them into the sink and squirting them with a shot of Palmolive.

"Who said anything about your love life?"

"You did. Talking about 'prospects.' You sound like my mother." She turned on the hot water.

Suddenly, Cash was behind her, his hands on her shoulders. She twisted a dishrag into a glass, scrubbing hard, and took a step back, hoping to push him away, but he was solid as a wall at her back.

"I'm not your mother," he said softly, his breath hot in her ear. The proof of his statement was pressing into the small of her back, making her very aware of her unfinished business with Luke. He gently turned her shoulders until she faced him, her back pressed against the sink, her front pressed against—well, you know. She clutched the edge of the sink behind her with her wet, soapy hands.

"I want to take care of you, Libby," he said. He was breathing heavily, his hands holding her shoulders a little too firmly.

Libby ducked her head, glancing left and right. No escape.

"Cash, no," she said. "I told you, I can take care of myself."

He stepped back, but dropped his hands to hers, prying them away from the counter and clasping them in a fervent grip. Dishwater and soap bubbles dribbled to the floor as he struggled for words. "Libby, you're wrong," he said. "You're out here all alone, with nobody to protect you. What if Crazy Mike comes back? What if those vagrants show up? What if Luke gets the wrong idea? There's nobody here to protect you."

She shook the bubbles from her hands and turned back to her dishes. "I don't need protecting, Cash," she said. "Especially not from Luke. If anything, he protects me more than you do."

Even as she said it, she wondered if it was true. How well could Luke protect her when he believed the man

who had come to her house and threatened her was some overgrown teddy bear?

Cash got quiet. Very quiet. His silence lasted a beat too long, so Libby turned to see what was wrong. His face was flushed from some inner tension, and he was breathing hard as if trying to gain control. Obviously, the guy had a jealous streak.

"You'd better go, Cash," she said warily.

"I'll go. But I'll be watching out for you. And if something happens, I'm the one who'll be there to help you."

"I know, Cash," she said, placating him. "I know you will. And I appreciate it, I really do. I just need to be on my own right now."

"That's what you think," he said grimly, and stalked out the door.

Chapter 25

THE HOUSE WAS QUIET—TOO QUIET. LIBBY HAD MOVED to Lackaduck for the quiet country life, but sometimes she missed the city—and this was one of those times. All she could think about was her change purse in Mike's drawer, that crayon heart on the calendar. She needed distraction.

She needed company, and maybe a drink. Maybe two.

Throwing on a sparkly top and some jeans, she ran a brush through her hair. She was just admiring her tidy self in the mirror when the phone rang. The dogs scampered into the room, barking, and frolicked around her legs, hampering her rush to the phone. She picked it up on the seventh ring.

"Libby? Mary McCarthy. I hope it's not too late to call."

"Oh, no. Not at all."

"I have the numbers for those two girls. Della's friends." She rattled them off, and Libby jotted them down on the wipe-off board she'd hung near the back door.

"So have you found anything?" Mary's voice sounded doubtful, but there was an optimistic upturn at the end that made Libby wish she had something to offer.

"Not really," Libby said. She paused, wondering how to get the information she needed without giving too much away. "I just have a couple of questions. First, what might have been in Della's purse? In case I find anything."

"Well, she always had gum. Trident sugarless, usually. And she had a little hairbrush, and makeup—she usually used Cover Girl."

"What about a wallet? Or a change purse?"

"Yes, she had a set I gave her. A wallet, a little change purse with a gold clasp, and an address book. Blue leather."

Blue leather. A sick feeling surged in Libby's stomach.

"Why?" Mary asked. "Did you find a purse?"

Libby kept her tone light, but it was an effort. "No, I just thought that was the kind of thing that… that might be likely to turn up, that's all. Oh, and when was her birthday?"

"July seventeenth," Mary said.

"Okay. Thanks. I'll be in touch."

Libby hung up and leaned against the wall, waiting for a dizzy spell to pass. She pictured her own change purse, nestled in Mike's drawer right beside Della's, and remembered the crayon heart scrawled on the calendar. In her mind, the heart seemed to pulse, a danger signal.

Now she really needed a drink.

There was a pool tournament in progress when she got to the Roundup, and the place was packed. Smoke hung in the air above the pool tables, drifting in the dim light while a posse of cowboys smacked the balls around. Crystal was behind the bar, her hands busy mixing drinks, her eyes shining as she flirted with a tall cowboy in a black Stetson. The various conversations in the room blended into a muffled hum punctuated by the alternating cheers and groans of the pool players.

Libby shouldered her way up to the bar and ordered

a vodka tonic, then snagged one of the last empty barstools and downed the drink in record time. She wasn't sure what had gotten into her, but she felt like throwing caution to the Wyoming winds and enjoying herself. Somehow, the vision of her change purse, right there beside Della's like they belonged together, made her uncomfortably conscious of her own mortality.

"Hey." Cash was approaching, two drinks in his hands. One of them looked suspiciously like another vodka tonic.

Damn. She'd been worried she'd run into Crazy Mike, or maybe Luke, who was probably still mad at her. It hadn't occurred to her she'd have to fend off the sheriff.

Cash handed her the drink, then settled onto the stool beside her and gave her a smile that was probably meant to be seductive, but came off simply smug. "I got those test results," he said. "Positive for arsenic."

She wobbled a little on her stool, and it wasn't just the vodka. Facts were starting to come together, and they all pointed in the same direction: straight toward the guy who'd stolen her change purse and kept it like a souvenir.

"So did you talk to him?"

"Not yet."

"But you said you'd call him in for questioning."

"I was jumping the gun, Libby. I'm sorry."

"So Luke was right?"

"Luke's always right," said a voice behind her. "Didn't you know that?"

It was Luke, standing so close behind her she could smell the scent of starch and fabric softener wafting from his shirt. It reminded her of clean sheets. She

shook that connection out of her head. She and Luke and clean sheets would probably never meet. The last time she'd seen him, he'd stormed out of her house, furious because she was siding with Cash against his friend Mike, and now she was with Cash again. And much as she wanted to believe Luke, she was even more certain now that Crazy Mike had something to do with Della's disappearance.

She wished she had a "Team Luke" T-shirt. She didn't know how else to let him know she was on his side in all the ways that counted.

"Hi," she said, feeling awkward.

"Hi." His smile was easy, friendly. "Want a drink?"

She smiled back. "Got one," she said, lofting the one Cash had brought, then stared in wonder at the half-melted ice cubes rattling in the remaining half inch of booze. She really was in a dangerous mood.

"I guess I could use another one, though," she said. "Maybe just a 7-Up."

Luke stepped closer to the bar and set one hand on the counter, waiting for Crystal to finish flirting with her cowboy. His other hand was still on Libby's shoulder. He smiled down at her, and it was the smile of a man who didn't hold a grudge. They both held the gaze a beat too long, and she had an almost overwhelming urge to lean back against him, rest her head on his chest, and heave out a huge sigh of relief.

Cash glowered from the stool beside her, then waved toward Crystal, who had her hand on the cowboy's arm now, and was earnestly explaining something to him.

"Yo, Crystal," he yelled. "Over here!"

A shadow of annoyance crossed Crystal's face, but

she'd put her dimples back on by the time she made it to the end of the bar. "What'll it be, Sheriff?"

"Bud Light for me and a vodka tonic for the lady." He turned to Libby. "See? Some of us around here know how to get things done."

Luke made a faint gagging noise and felt Libby lean into him, stifling a giggle as Crystal handed her yet another tall drink. She'd wanted a 7-Up, but Cash had obviously missed that part. The sheriff got things done all right, Luke thought. Too bad they were all the wrong things.

"Busy tonight," Cash said, oblivious to his own cluelessness. "Everybody's here."

"I don't see Mike," Libby said.

"Don't you worry about him, now." Cash inched closer to her, tossing Luke a dirty look. "You're with me. He won't bother you."

Luke scowled. She wasn't with Cash. She'd come in by herself. He'd seen her arrive, and he'd struggled like a salmon striving for the spawning grounds to make it through the crowd to her side. Cash had beaten him to that barstool, but that didn't mean he was a better fish, or a stronger one. It just meant he'd hit a more favorable current.

"I'm just surprised Mike's not here," Libby said. She tossed her hair. "I'm not worried. I'm not scared of him or anything."

"Well, good," Luke said. "'Cause there he is."

Mike shoved through the swinging door labeled "Bulls." He looked worn out, and Luke wondered how long he'd been up the night before. His hand was

bandaged with an old rag. Blood had seeped through around the thumb, and the knuckles were gray with dirt.

He caught sight of Luke and started to make his way through the crowd, his smile widening when he saw Libby.

"Libby," he said. "And Luke. Luke and Libby." He giggled, the high-pitched chortle oddly mismatched to his hulking frame. He was making slow but steady progress through the crowd until he stopped suddenly about ten feet away. His smile flickered and died. "No, Libby!" he said loudly. "No!" He turned abruptly and headed the other way.

Libby turned to Luke and shrugged. "Am I having a bad hair day? Or is it my outfit?"

"Neither one," Cash said. "He's crazy." The sheriff put on his best lawman expression. Luke had seen it before. It made the guy look constipated. "Libby, you need to be careful," the sheriff said. "You know Mike could have poisoned your dog. He might really have it in for you. Why do you insist on getting involved with all these dangerous people? First David, now Crazy Mike—I don't get it."

"I'm a reporter, Cash," Libby said. "I'm just doing my job."

"I've told you everything you need to know about Crazy Mike, Libby. Remember what I told you about his dog?"

"I remember." She toyed with her glass, making damp circles on the bar. "But I wanted to ask him something."

"That's my job," Cash said. "You need to stay away from Mike. Now tell me what you wanted to ask him, and I'll do what needs to be done." He looked

down at her as if she was a fractious but adorable child. "You need to keep your pretty little self out of this kind of trouble."

He poked her nose with his index finger, and Libby looked like she was about to bite it off. Instead, she rose from her stool, probably so Cash couldn't look down on her anymore. Not physically, anyway. He was making it pretty obvious he'd always look down on her when it came to just about everything else. Luke felt like jumping off his stool and doing an end-zone victory dance.

"My pretty self isn't in any trouble at all, Cash," she said. She downed the rest of her drink. "Matter of fact, my pretty self is about to solve the case you've been working on for two years. I know where there's evidence that'll just about clinch it." Picking up her purse, she headed for the door.

"Wait a minute." Cash spun his stool and called after her. "You can't tell me that and then just leave!"

"Sure I can, Cash. I'm a very capable woman. I can do whatever I want."

Libby swung through the saloon doors and inhaled a deep dose of cool night air. Luke was right behind her.

"You are, indeed, a very capable woman," he said. "I'm impressed."

"With what?"

"Your stunning ability to put Cash McIntyre in his place," he said. "You have no idea how much I enjoyed that."

She laughed. "What is it with you two, anyway? You're like two dogs fighting over a bone."

He looked down at her, smiling. "Exactly."

"Well, what's the—oh," she said. "I'm not the bone, am I?"

"I wouldn't have put it that way," he said, slinging an arm around her shoulders. "You're more like a really nice squeaky toy."

"Thanks," she said. "I think."

The gravel crunched under their feet as the jukebox music faded and the sounds of the night took over—a lone cricket chirping, the faint whistle of a train in the distance. Libby caught her toe on a rock and stumbled a little. Luke grabbed her arm.

"Whoa," he said. "Careful."

"Sorry." She shook her head. "Don't know what was in that drink. I only had two, or maybe it was three. I'm not sure." She giggled. "I feel like I had six."

"That means Crystal likes you," Luke said. "Say it with Smirnoff—that's her motto."

Libby laughed. "That's nice of her, but I'm not sure I can drive."

"Want me to take you home?

"I guess you'd better. Sorry."

"Oh, don't be," he said. "I'm not."

Libby climbed up into Luke's truck and fastened her seat belt. He swung up beside her and cranked the ignition.

"So," he said. "Where to?"

"Um, home?"

He gave her a sideways glance. "We could always stop somewhere. Remember I told you about Lover's Lane?"

"No," she said reluctantly. "I'd better go home."

"Okay," he said. "I was just kidding, you know. I wouldn't take advantage of you in your inebriated state."

"I am not inebriated!" she protested. "I just felt kind of… funny once we got out to the parking lot, that's all."

The truth was, she'd felt more than funny. Once she and Luke had left the noise of the bar behind, she'd felt dizzy with something much more potent that the drinks. It was desire, pure and simple. It was like that song they played on the radio: *I know who I want to take me home… I know who I want…*

"I could take you on a little tour, though," he said. He looked at her like he wanted to take a very private tour—maybe an in-depth exploration of the terrain under her clothes.

A flutter of arousal stirred inside her. She pictured the two of them in the back of the truck, his hands moving slowly over her body, slipping under her clothes, sliding over her skin.

She glanced back at the bed of the truck. Yup. There was plenty of room back there.

Luke must have mistaken her backward glance for nervousness. "It's okay," he said. His voice sounded forced, almost choked. "Sorry. I'll take you home."

They bounced along in the dark, glancing nervously at each other from time to time, the air in the truck cab seeming to warm and thicken with every mile. Finally, Luke set one hand on her thigh. The warmth of it spread over her body like syrup over hot buttered pancakes.

"Do you still feel funny?" he asked.

She nodded. "A little."

He moved his hand higher on her leg. She cleared her throat. "A lot, now. It's… it's a good kind of funny."

"Yeah," he said. "I feel it too."

His hand stroked her leg, his touch nervous, full of suppressed excitement. "Maybe I shouldn't be driving, either."

"Maybe not," she said in a whisper. "Pull over."

He steered onto the shoulder and stopped the truck, and suddenly she was in his arms. There were no careful kisses this time, no tentative touches. His hands were everywhere, his lips insistent, his body hot and hard. She kissed him back, releasing her own pent up tension in a flood of passion, and he upped the ante even more, pushing her down on the seat, pulling her beneath him, tugging at her T-shirt and ducking his head to mouth her breasts through the thin cotton of her bra. She arched her back to offer herself to him and he pulled the fabric aside with one hand while the other slipped under the waistband of her jeans. She felt herself softening, slickening, warming to his touch as he sucked and licked and fondled and stroked, and she threw her head back and gave herself up to him. What harm could one wild night do? They were both drunk, or at least they could say they were. And she'd wanted this for so long.

"Make love to me," she said. "Please."

Need spiraled through Luke, pushing into his mind, urging him to expose every inch of the woman beneath him, lick and suck and fondle her, everywhere, all at once. He was so lost in desire he almost didn't hear her.

"Please, Luke," she said again. She unsnapped her jeans and wriggled them down her hips to reveal a flowery pair of barely-there panties that clung to the

dampness between her legs. She pressed his hand there and flexed her hips. She was soft, wet, ready, and way more than willing.

He'd always known he'd make love to this woman, but he wanted their first encounter to be different from this. He intended it to be planned, orchestrated, arranged—perfect. But one look at her half-naked body sprawled on the bench seat shattered his self-control into a million pieces. He needed to touch her, to taste her, to set her rocking and moaning and begging for more, to fill her up and empty himself, to leave them both gasping and fighting for breath.

"Make love to me," she said again.

His senses were filled with her—the scent of her perfume blending with the sound of her voice, soft, husky, urging him on. Her secret self was laid out beneath him like a gift, and the look in her eyes begged him to take what he'd wanted from the first time he'd seen her. There was only a shred of cotton between his hand and the heart of her.

A shred of cotton and one last scruple.

He took a deep breath and forced himself back to reality—back to the truck cab, the ancient, stained upholstery, the scarred dashboard.

"Not here," he said. "Let me take you home. And then..."

"No," she said, pulling him toward her, whispering. "If you take me home, I'll think about it too much, and I'll change my mind. I don't want to think about it, Luke. I just want to do it." She tugged his shirt open and let her fingernails rake gently over his chest. "Now," she said. "Please."

He looked down at her, one more time. Maybe he could memorize exactly how she looked in this moment—exactly how it felt to have her under him, naked and willing.

Because it would probably never happen again.

"I'm sorry," he said. "We can't. It's not right."

"What?" She grabbed his collar and pulled his face close to hers. "No. Please, Luke." She flexed her hips into his, the pressure sending a wave of need straight to his core. "Now."

"Libby, no," he said. "We can't do this. If you'd change your mind in the time it takes to get home, you'll change your mind afterwards, too. I don't want to be something you regret."

"I wouldn't… oh." She took a deep breath and let it out. The misty look in her eyes cleared. "Oh," she said again. "Maybe you're right."

"I don't want this to be once and done, Libby. I want it to be…"

What did he want it to be? Forever?

Forever.

But he couldn't say that. Not now. Not here.

She sighed and pulled her clothes back into place, shimmied her jeans up her thighs and over her hips. He looked down at his lap, trying to give her privacy, but his eyes kept sliding her way, watching the magic kingdom shut down for the night.

"It's not that I don't want to," he said. "Okay?"

She stared out the window. "Okay," she said.

But she didn't sound like she meant it. It wasn't okay, and he knew it. It wasn't okay to tell a woman no when she offered herself to you like that. It wasn't okay to

reject a woman who'd already been bashed around by clueless men, damaged and hurt and wounded.

But it wasn't okay to take advantage of a girl who'd had a few too many drinks, either.

What the hell was he supposed to do?

Chapter 26

Libby was up early the next day, chucking feed at the chickens so hard the birds scattered like quail dodging buckshot. She ordered the dogs around like a bad-tempered drill sergeant until Penny herded all her babies under the bed, and scrambled the morning eggs so frantically the froth rivaled a French meringue.

But she still couldn't stop thinking about Luke.

She stabbed the keyboard a while, pounding out a scathing editorial about the romantic cluelessness of the average Wyoming cowboy, then deleted the whole thing and stared out the window a while. When she put her hands back on the keyboard, they seemed to tap the keys of their own accord, and she ended up with a highly imaginative ode to the sexual possibilities offered by the cozy crew-cab of the all-American Dodge Ram. The piece was more than inspired. It even rhymed, but its how-do-I-love-thee tone hardly suited the subject matter.

Of course, she had to delete that one too. She was a journalist, not a poet, and a journalist needed hard evidence to back up her stories. *Write what you know*, her teachers had said. And she didn't know a damn thing about making love in a pickup truck. Her attempt at researching the subject had ended in abject, miserable, humiliating failure.

What she really needed was a nap. She'd slept in, snoozing off the effects of those ill-advised vodka tonics,

but she still felt like she'd celebrated Mardi Gras on the Fourth of July at Disneyland every night for a week. Too bad she didn't have any beads to show for it.

She'd certainly earned them.

She threw herself facedown on the sofa and closed her eyes, drifting into slumberland—but there he was, waiting patiently for her at the doorway to her subconscious: Luke. His face. His lips. His eyes, catching the glint of the dashboard light. Her body under his, silvered by moonlight, soothed by the soft trill of crickets and the whispering encouragement of the wind in the sagebrush, seduced by the sensation of his rough rancher's hands on her skin. She couldn't forget that feeling.

She never would.

She turned over and glanced at the clock. It was well past suppertime. Maybe she should go into town. Fill herself up with some new experiences to replace the ones that had shanghaied her memory and hijacked her hormones.

Tossing her bag over her shoulder, she revved up the Ranger and rushed downtown, slamming the sidewalks of Lackaduck with her bootheels, searching for some sign of a story that would fill up some column inches and keep her mind off the night before. But the streets were vacant as a John Ford film set before the cowboys came to town. The only activity was a trio of out-of-towners slurping ice cream outside the mini-mart and Josie lounging by the front door of Chez Joe's, one hip cocked, a cigarette at her lips.

And the only story left was Della's.

"Libby," the waitress said, releasing a stream of blue smoke. "No date tonight?"

"Nope," Libby said. She leaned up against the diner window and crossed her arms over her chest. "I'm never dating again."

"Wow." Josie looked concerned. "What happened?"

"Nothing." It was true. Sad, but true.

"You sure?"

"Positive." Libby flipped her hair out of her face and changed the subject. "Hey, how old are you?"

Josie looked puzzled. "Twenty-two," she said.

"Good. Listen, I need to talk to you. If you'll meet me out at the Roundup later, I'll buy you a few drinks."

"You're not going lesbian, are you?"

"No. I could probably mess up a relationship with either sex at this point. I'm an equal-opportunity disaster."

"Oh. Well, I might not be the best source if you're looking for dating advice."

Libby laughed. "I'm thinking the best advice is just to cut out the whole mess. Go it on my own, and concentrate on doing some good in the world. That's why I wanted to talk to you about Della."

There was a long silence as Josie took a deep, slow breath. "Della? You're a reporter, right? You're doing a story on what happened?"

"That's right. I thought maybe you could help."

"I don't know anything."

"I realize that. But you knew her. I just want you to tell me what she was like."

"I'll be glad to. That's how we keep our friends alive when they're gone—by telling other people about them, remembering them. I'll meet you there at ten, okay? I need to fix my hair."

"Great." Libby nodded, eager to see what Josie's hair

would look like after a few hours of primping. She was halfway home when it hit her.

Why was Josie so certain Della was "gone?"

~

Josie walked into the Roundup at ten on the dot, and every head turned. She'd obviously spent the entire two hours on her hair. It rose regally above her head like the crest of some great bird, maroon spikes stretching a good eight inches to the ceiling. The amazing thing was, she managed to look beautiful in spite of her extreme hairstyle. She'd ringed her eyes in dark kohl, bringing out their pale gray color and emphasizing her perfect skin.

"Yo, Josie," a deep male voice intoned from somewhere in the back of the room.

"Josie. Hey." Another admirer made his presence known.

"Jo-*zeeee*!" That voice Libby knew. It was David. He lunged through the crowd and enveloped Josie in an enormous hug.

"Hey," she said, surprised but obviously pleased at the welcome.

"Holy cow, you're at the Roundup. She's at the Roundup, everybody!" David said loudly. He looked her up and down. "And you look fantastic. Great outfit. Great." She wore a delicate, gauzy flapper dress that hung limply off one shoulder and swept down into a ruffled skirt decorated with stiff netting. A selection of chains, large and small, draped her waist, and a spiked dog collar encircled her neck. She had a ring on almost every finger—big, glitzy rings sporting massive fake

diamonds. She looked like a page out of some cutting-edge fashion magazine.

"How come you're here?" David asked, taking both her hands in his and gazing adoringly into her eyes. "You never come here."

"I came to see Libby," she said shyly. Bold as she seemed, she was clearly overwhelmed by the attention.

"Score! Libby! She's my friend too!" David led her to Libby's table and pulled out a stool. The tables were high, and he hiked Josie into her seat, almost flinging the poor girl across the room in his enthusiasm.

Josie took his hand. "Sit with us, David. Libby wants to hear about Della."

"Can't. Gotta make bar food. You want nachos, don't you, Josie?"

"I sure do."

"And a dry martini? Straight up, with a twist of lemon, not lime?" He winked. Libby had never seen him so happy, not even with the puppies.

"Perfect," Josie said. "And something for Libby."

"Just a Coke," Libby ordered. She was working, after all. And besides, you never knew when your neighbor might show up and hijack your libido.

She and Josie watched David make his way through the crowd. "He likes you," Libby said, stating the obvious.

"I like him," Josie said. "But he wants more than I do. I'm not ready to settle down. David has a biological clock like a woman's. He wants to have babies." She sighed. "Maybe someday."

"You make a nice couple," Libby said. "He's a good person, isn't he?"

"The best," Josie said. "So what did you want to know about Della?"

"Just what she was like. What her friends were like, what she did for fun. Stuff like that. But tell me about yourself first. I hardly know you. What's your last name?"

"Wales."

"You're kidding, right?"

"Why would I kid about something like that? My parents were Frank and Lorna Wales. They named me Josie. Dad was a Clint Eastwood buff. At first, I hated it. But now I kind of like it. Clint's cool, after all, even if he is old. And I like the outlaw part."

"The Outlaw Josie Wales," Libby said.

"That's me!"

"Are your folks here in Lackaduck?"

"No, they live over in Lusk. Hicksville. They've lived there all their lives. I swear they've been dating since the fourth grade, or maybe even kindergarten. I grew up there, but I was determined to get out. Got all the way to Lackaduck, but now I'm stuck."

"Why?"

"I don't know. I like it here. I like my job, and David's here, and it's safe. I went to Denver a couple times. Thought I'd love it there, but I was scared."

"All the crime? The noise?"

"No, not that. I liked that, in a way. It was just that there were so many people like me there. I was afraid I'd get lost in the crowd. Here, I stand out. Everybody knows who Josie is."

That was an understatement. Half the crowd was watching her in fascination—the male half. She was like a brilliant quetzal touching down in a barnyard. In spite

of her extreme hair and makeup, it was obvious Josie was the prettiest girl in town.

"You know, you've made a good decision," Libby said. "I lived in Atlanta for a long time. I wanted the bright lights, the big city, all that. But here I am in Lackaduck, too."

"You started a farm, right?"

Libby laughed. "A ranch. I'm told you have to call it a ranch out here."

Josie rolled her eyes. "Oh, yeah, a ranch. Next you'll be wearing a cowboy hat and shouting 'yee-haw.'"

"Could happen. Anyway, tell me about Della."

Josie bit her lip, staring down at the table. David trotted over with their drinks and a huge plate of nachos. He started to say something, then saw Josie's face. "You're talking about Della?" he asked Libby.

"Yeah. I think so."

"Don't rush her," he said, and walked back to the kitchen at a slower pace, pausing twice to watch Josie with a worried look on his face.

Josie lifted her head and looked at her drink. "No olive," she said. "Twist of lemon. That's what I like about David. Everywhere you go, they put olives in these. He always remembers how I like it." She took a generous sip and held the glass up, admiring it like a work of art.

"What did Della like to drink?" Libby thought maybe a direct question would help the girl get started.

"Anything she could get!" Josie rippled out a high-pitched giggle, suddenly animated. "She was underage, you know. We both were, but she was two years younger than me. And she looked it! Nobody would serve her.

She was the kind of girl who'll be getting carded when she's forty, she looked so young." She stopped suddenly, realizing what she'd said. "She'll never get to forty, though."

"Why are you so sure?" Libby asked. "Couldn't she have run away or something? What makes you so sure she's gone?"

Josie shook her head slowly. "She would never just run away. She had too many people who loved her, and she loved them too, like anything. Especially her mom. She always felt bad about the things she did, that they would hurt her mom. She never wanted her mom to know."

"What things?"

"Oh, you know. Girl stuff. Getting drunk and sleeping around. Della really liked to party, and she liked to fool around with guys. A lot. She was really beautiful, but it seemed like she needed guys to tell her that. She was always flaunting what she had, fishing for those looks you get. You know, it feels good when a guy gets all googly-eyed over you. But that doesn't mean you have to sleep with him."

"Did she have a relationship with anyone here?"

"I think so. There were a couple cowboys we met at the rodeo over in Burns. She had the trailer rockin' with one of those guys, and I couldn't really blame her—he was real cute. But they didn't have to be. Cute, I mean. She'd pretty much do it with anyone who asked."

"But she was so pretty. Why would she do that?"

Josie shrugged. "I don't know. It was like she had to prove she could have anybody. There was somebody else here in Lackaduck too, but she wouldn't say who. Just that he was a stud."

"You didn't have any idea who it was?"

"Not at all. I think David might know. He kept warning her, telling her she had bad taste in boyfriends. But he wouldn't tell me who."

Libby thought about Mrs. McCarthy, home alone with her sick husband, missing the daughter she thought she knew.

"How long did you know Della?" It seemed like a lot of information for a short acquaintance.

"I met her at Lackaduck Days years ago, when we were just kids. She used to come down here with her Arabs, and then with Skydancer." She looked dreamy for a moment. "That was one beautiful horse. He turned heads even more than she did. They were some pair."

"Did you show horses too?"

Josie shook her head. "I had sheep." Smiling, the girl reached into the vinyl clutch she'd brought along and drew out a stack of snapshots. "I thought you might want to see these," she said, handing them over.

The first photo was of two young women standing in front of a carnival ride. One Libby recognized as Della. The other was apparently Josie, though she was hardly recognizable. Her hair was long and straight, and her happy smile revealed a mouthful of braces. The only thing Libby recognized was those pale gray eyes, clear and bright.

The next picture was of Josie alone. She was standing in a fairground arena, leading a black-faced white sheep before a panel of judges.

"Nice sheep," Libby said dubiously.

"As sheep go," Josie said. "Check out the next picture. That's Skydancer."

The photo was a professional shot of a beautiful bay horse standing perfectly squared against a blue sky. The horse was breathtaking, with a finely arched neck, his tail carried high and proud. Libby didn't know much about horses, but she could see he was a beauty.

"Della was paying for college with his stud fees," Josie said. "He was amazing."

The next picture was a wallet-sized portrait, a print of the studio shot of Della Libby had seen on the Internet. On the back, round girlish handwriting spelled out "Friends 4ever! Luv, Della." Josie picked it up and her eyes brimmed with tears. "She was so cool, Libby. We really hit it off during Lackaduck Days, and we emailed and text-messaged all the time after that." She heaved a heavy sigh. "Friends forever." She traced the letters with one finger, then looked up at Libby. "You should talk to Larissa. Talk to Brandy. Maybe they know something." She slumped. "All I know is that I miss her."

"Well, I feel like I know her a little better now," Libby said. "Thanks."

The truth was, Josie had given her a whole new picture of Della McCarthy—one Libby didn't think she'd be sharing with the girl's mother.

Chapter 27

When Luke drove up to the house the next day, Libby was sitting on the porch swing with her arms folded, staring at the warped floorboards. He could swear he saw a wisp of smoke coming out of her ears.

Uh-oh. He'd figured after a good night's sleep she'd see things his way. In fact, he'd thought she might even be grateful. After all, he could have taken advantage of her. He'd thought maybe she'd thank him. Maybe she'd even decide that she still wanted to—well, probably not. But you never know.

All he knew was that he wanted her worse than ever. And if she was mad at him, and she didn't want him around, he was going to have a hell of a time dealing with it.

He took a deep breath. "What's the matter?"

He paused at the bottom of the steps. Either she was mad, or she was going to cry. He wasn't going up there if she was going to cry.

"My truck," she said.

He blew out a sigh of relief. "You're mad at your truck?"

She nodded, her lower lip thrust out in a pout. "I want to go to Billings and talk to one of Della's friends, and my truck says 'Evil Bitch' on it and I can't drive it on the interstate that way."

"Hmm." Luke stepped up onto the porch, moving cautiously, as if he was approaching a pawing, head-tossing

rodeo bull. "That's a problem, all right." He lowered himself onto the porch swing and set it to rocking, just a little. Maybe that would be soothing. Maybe it would calm her down.

"Stupid truck," she said. "Stupid vandals."

"Yeah," he said. "Stupid."

They rocked a while, and Luke wondered if there was smoke coming out of his own ears, because he had an idea that was burning up his synapses and scorching his cerebellum. It would solve Libby's problem, and it would solve one of his problems too.

It was a double-decker problem solver.

"You could take my truck," he said.

"I could?" She turned to look at him, her lips parted, her eyes wide and glistening like she might cry any minute.

"Well, you don't have to," he said. He didn't think the truck was that bad. Sure, it was kind of odd-looking, with parts from four or five other trucks all bolted on where he'd smashed it up, but it was colorful. He liked to think it was kind of like a paint horse. Multicolored. Flashy.

"That would be so—so great," she said. She sniffed, and he edged away. If it was great, why was she getting so teary? Women were weird.

Weird, but nice. They smelled good, or at least Libby did, and they felt good too, when they let you touch them. He wasn't sure Libby would ever let him touch her again, but it was worth a try, especially since she was looking at him like he'd offered her a Lamborghini instead of a piebald Dodge that had been totaled three times. He shifted a little closer and put his left arm into position across the back of the

porch swing. It was a stealth move he'd mastered in high school.

"Well, it's settled then," he said. "You can take my truck. See? Problem solved." He let his hand drop slowly down the back of the swing until it curved around her waist. She'd been sitting on the porch a while, and her black T-shirt was warm from the sun. He was itching to move his hand, just a little, to trace the tuck of her waist, the slope of her hip. That was his favorite part of a woman—that sweet, soft curve.

But he didn't do it. He didn't move. He needed a signal from her, and he wasn't getting it. Romancing a woman was a lot like taming a horse—it was all about give and take, and you couldn't take 'til she gave.

"Why are you so nice to me?" she asked. She relaxed, her body softening, and leaned her head on his shoulder.

Bingo, he thought.

All systems *go.*

"Luke?" she said as his hand edged into place.

Oh, yeah. She'd asked a question. Why was he so nice to her?

Mostly, it was because she was a good person, and because he admired her for setting out on her own, for being smart and independent and spunky. And because she was nice to him, and nice to his parents. Because she had a sense of humor and a knack for seeing the best in people like Mike, despite Cash's efforts to poison her mind.

But right now, it was because she was pretty and she smelled good and because her skin was so soft under his hand, and because that curve was perfect and she was letting him touch it, and because her skin was so smooth right there where the slope of her hip met the

swell of her tummy and disappeared into her jeans, and because he liked the way she caught her breath when he brought his hand up and buried his fingers in her hair, and because…

"Uh-oh," she said.

"What?"

"You're going to kiss me again." She wiggled away from him. "You're doing that an awful lot."

"You like it."

"I—well, yeah, sometimes, but it's not a good idea, Luke."

"Why not?"

"Because we're friends. And having sex with your friends is a bad idea."

He slumped back on the swing. "Shoot. How 'bout if I make you mad, and we stop being friends?"

She slapped him, just a little, and he grinned. "Can't blame a guy for trying."

"Yes, I can," she said. "But if you let me use your truck, I'll forgive you."

"If you let me kiss you, I'll let you use my truck."

She put a finger to her chin and looked up at the sky, pantomiming deep thought. "Hmm," she said. "Maybe my friend Cash will let me use his truck."

Luke groaned. "You win," he said. "When are you going?"

"I was hoping to leave tomorrow," she said. "I finished up all my work early so I can go. It's just for the day."

"Okay," he said. "I'll bring the truck by in the morning." They talked a little longer, until he was sure she felt better, and then he headed back home. Once he took the curve at the end of Libby's driveway, he pounded

both hands on the steering wheel and did an improvised seated happy dance right there in the cab of the truck.

Tomorrow was going to be a good day.

Sunday morning dawned clear, blue, and cool—perfect for a road trip. David volunteered to stay at Lackaduck Farm while Libby was gone, so he'd get a break from his cramped apartment over the bar and the puppies would get some time with their favorite uncle.

Luke pulled in at seven, just like he'd promised, and tooted the horn.

"Hey," Libby said. "Thanks so much."

"You're welcome," he said. "Climb in."

"Okay." She opened the driver's side door and looked at him.

"You want to drive?" he asked.

"I wasn't planning on pushing your truck to Billings," she said.

"Yeah, but I thought I'd drive. At least for the first half, and then we can switch."

"You thought… *no,*" she said. "You thought *wrong*. I'm driving. *Alone*. I'm driving you home, and then I'm driving your truck to Billings. That was the deal. Getting in a pickup truck with you is nothing but trouble."

He grinned. "I thought you kinda liked it."

She didn't say a word, but the look she gave him—brows lowered, eyes flaming—was eloquent enough that she didn't have to.

He pulled his hat down low over his eyes and propped one arm on the steering wheel. Looking out the

windshield, avoiding her eyes, he said. "I thought I'd go along. Make sure the truck runs okay."

"No," she said again.

"Look, it's a seven-hour drive," he said. "And Betsy can be difficult."

"Betsy?"

He patted the dashboard. "The truck. See? I have to come along. You don't even know her name."

She stood in the driveway, staring at him, her fists on her hips. She'd dressed up a little for the trip, in a Western shirt with snaps and a pair of slim-fit Wranglers. Her cowboy boots had been a little too shiny when she'd first arrived, but now they were suitably scuffed and dusty. She'd look just right in the truck beside him, if he could just gentle her down and get her to stop looking at him with that killer glint in her eyes. He gave her his best smile. Reluctantly, she smiled back.

"Oh, all right. I guess I could use some company." She shook her head.. "Why can't I say no to you?"

"You can't say no to me?" His smile widened. "Hmm. So do you want to..."

"No," she said. "Hey, how 'bout that? Guess I'm learning."

She whistled, and Ivan rounded the corner of the house. Dropping the dented tailgate, she stood back as the big dog vaulted into the truck bed.

"Ivan's coming?" Luke asked.

She nodded, tugging the seat belt around her waist and settling in. Ivan thrust his head through the sliding rear window of the cab and slapped his tongue over the side of Luke's face. It was like being smacked with a

wet pound of bacon. Luke reached up and wiped off the slime.

"Oh, look," Libby said. "He remembers you."

The rain started before they'd even made it to Chugwater.

"Pull over," Libby said. "Ivan's getting soaked."

Luke glanced up at the rearview mirror and saw the dog huddled miserably in the truck bed. Real ranch dogs loved riding in the back of a pickup, no matter what the weather, but Ivan was becoming less and less of a real dog. Luke suspected Libby let him sleep with her on the bed, and she was always petting him, stroking him, whispering sweet nothings into his cockeyed ears.

Lucky dog.

Sighing, he pulled over onto the shoulder. Libby hopped out of the car and clucked her tongue, and the dog set his paws on the side of the truck bed and flopped over the side like a trout flipping out of a bucket. After stopping to relieve himself against a mile marker, he hoisted himself up into the cab with an assist from Libby, who grunted as she lifted his hindquarters, then hopped in behind him and slammed the door.

"Hi, buddy," Luke said warily.

Ivan lifted one front paw and presented it for shaking. When Luke didn't take it, he pawed the air, slapping the shift knob and throwing the truck into gear. The truck lunged forward, burped, and stalled.

"Yikes," Luke said. "Can't *you* sit in the middle?"

"He'll be fine," Libby said. "He's just saying hi."

Ivan grinned and panted. A string of drool drained off his tongue and left a damp spot on Luke's jeans.

"Let me rephrase that," Luke said. "You *are* sitting in the middle. He's drooling, he's wet, and he stinks. If you sit in the middle, he'll only smell up one side of the truck."

"Yeah," Libby said. "My side."

She had to admit that the odor rising from the dog's damp pelt as the truck's heater warmed the cab was pretty powerful. "Come on, bud," she said, moving toward him and patting the passenger seat. "Get over."

The dog lumbered across her lap and sat upright with his hind legs splayed wide and his belly pooched out, gazing happily out the window like an old man on a bus trip to Branson.

"I don't think this'll work," Libby said, nudging her knee against the gear shift. "My legs are too long."

"No such thing."

"You won't be able to shift."

Luke reached down and eased her knee aside so she straddled the shifter. "There," he said. "That'll work fine." He thumbed toward Ivan, who was decorating the passenger side window with wet noseprints and streaks of slobber. "And you're a lot less likely to drool on me than that guy."

Libby's mind flicked back to their Thursday night interlude in the pickup truck. Luke might be wrong about the drooling. She kept remembering the feeling of his hands on her skin, his weight on her body, and this ride wasn't helping her forget. The truck cab was barely big enough for the three of them, and his leg was pressed hard against her thigh. When he pushed the clutch to the floor and yanked the gear shift into

second, his hand veered perilously close to her danger zone.

"See? Fine," he said.

She sucked in her breath and glanced at his face, just inches away.

It would be all right, she told herself. The trip was mostly highway driving. The truck would be in fifth most of the time, not second. Luke might touch her knee, but she could deal with that.

She rummaged in her purse and dug out a CD, sliding it into the player. Soon Chrissie Hynde was telling them all about the brass in her pocket and how special she was. It was a seven-hour drive and it was the only music Libby had with her, so Chrissie's pockets were going to be mighty heavy by the time they got to Billings.

It was a good thing the music was there to fill the silence that stretched between them. She'd never been so close to Luke for so long, and she was uncomfortably conscious of his warm thigh pressing into her own, the nearness of his face to hers, the hand he rested casually on the gear shift between her legs.

At least he was trying to behave. That hand stayed on the gearshift a whole hour before it drifted over and rested on her thigh. She tensed and he lifted his hand, flashing her a questioning glance, and the place his hand had been suddenly felt unbearably cold. She slid her eyes sideways and quirked him a nervous smile and the hand settled back into place.

For some reason, that touch felt as intimate as a kiss—partly because she'd invited it with her smile, giving tacit permission for a gesture that felt somehow proprietary. She'd seen couples driving through

Lackaduck this way, their silhouettes almost a Western cliché—the cowboy-hatted driver with one hand on the wheel, his tagalong sweetheart snuggled up next to him in the center of the bench seat, big hair brushing his square shoulders.

But it felt right. Easy. For the rest of the trip, she remembered what it felt like to be half of a couple, and she didn't mind a bit.

Eastern Montana looks a lot like Wyoming—flat and barren, with vast pastures of golden grass and gray-green sage broken by occasional dry stream beds and rocky outcroppings. The sky is broad and deep, colored a rich, glowing blue that stretches unclouded to the horizon, where you can just make out the purple shadows of distant mountains.

Billings isn't the prettiest town in Montana, but it's probably the busiest. The highway into town passes several oil refineries, then carries new arrivals into the seedy south side of town. Boarded up sandstone buildings from the 1800s prove the town's historic pedigree, but they're surrounded by cracked sidewalks, storefront soup kitchens, and pawn shops advertising guns and jewelry.

"Larissa lives up on the Rims," Libby said, "but Larissa married some stockbroker or something. They have a big fancy place that looks out over the whole city."

They left the South Side and cruised down a wide thoroughfare bordered by fast-food joints and quick-lube stations. Beyond the business district, they turned north into a residential area that worked its way

steadily uphill toward the rocky cliffs that bordered the edge of town.

Larissa had a big fancy house, all right—a glass and cedar castle that rose from a broad terrace of rock that overlooked the city. They sat out on the deck, a redwood refuge that offered a gorgeous view of the city spread out below. Lights winked on one by one as night settled over the valley.

Larissa was lovely and obviously older than her friends. Her long Scandinavian face was framed with straight blond hair, cut shoulder length. A wide, sensuous mouth balanced large blue eyes and high cheekbones. Fixing an appraising stare on first Libby, then Luke, she lit a long thin cigarette and let loose a long curl of smoke.

"My one concession to girlish folly," she said. "I started when I was fourteen. Never have managed to quit. It's too good a prop." She inhaled again, then released another stream of smoke. She looked like Marlene Dietrich, like a jaded movie star mourning her youth. Which was odd, since she was maybe twenty-seven at most. "What do you want to know about Della?"

"Whatever you think might help," Libby said. "Especially her love life, I guess. Did she have a boyfriend, somebody she was seeing?"

"Probably." Larissa sat back on the porch swing and swung gently forward and back. "But Della always had secrets. Especially from me. She didn't want me to know what was going on in her life, because she knew I'd tell her what I thought, and she didn't want to hear it." She stopped her swinging to lean forward and stub out her cigarette. "Della made a lot of bad decisions."

"She was young, though," Luke said. He was leaning forward in one of Larissa's padded patio chairs, his elbows resting on his knees, his hands clasped. "Young people make mistakes. It's part of growing up."

"I know. I'm not criticizing her. I'm sorry it sounds that way." Their hostess shook her head sadly. "She was a wonderful person, more alive than any of us—you know what I mean? But somehow, she managed to grow up with zero survival skills." She lit another cigarette and blew out a long stream of smoke. "She came from a family that loved her unconditionally. All her life, she could do no wrong."

"That's how you're supposed to love your kids," Luke murmured. Libby smiled. He was right. If she ever had kids… but she probably never would. With her track record, marriage would be disaster, and she sure wasn't up for the single mom experience.

"Yeah, it's great, until they enter the big wide world where nobody's looking out for them," Larissa said. "Nobody's protecting you in the real world. Look what happened to Della."

"How did you meet her?" Libby asked.

"We were horse show buddies. I was the one who found Cielo for her."

"Cielo?"

"Skydancer," Josie said. "Cielo Bailando was his Spanish name. He was a Paso Fino." She sighed. "He was beautiful. She'd seen my Paso, and she loved him. Had to have one."

"You don't see many Pasos in Western riding," Luke said.

"You don't, but you should," Larissa said. "They're agile and trainable. And such a pleasure to ride." She

looked over at Libby. "They're gaited horses, with a smooth, fast walk. 'Gaited' means they move their legs differently from other horses."

"It's like they dance," Luke said.

Larissa nodded. "My husband calls my Paso gelding 'Twinkle-toes.' But he's nothing compared to Skydancer." She shook her head. "I wish I could have bought that horse myself, but I couldn't afford him. Neither could Della's parents, but they'd promised her a stallion, and she worked on them day and night to buy her a Paso stud. They finally relented. I think they always did. Della always got what she wanted."

"So you told her about Skydancer?"

"Her father came to me for help at a show in Arizona. There was an auction, and he and I traipsed all through the grounds, looking for Della's surprise birthday pony." She flexed her lips disapprovingly. "Once he saw Skydancer, it was all over. The horse went for over twenty thousand dollars, but somehow Mr. McCarthy bought him."

Libby gasped. "He was a schoolteacher. So was his wife, so they had two incomes, but still..." No wonder Mrs. McCarthy couldn't pay for nursing care. They'd probably mortgaged their home to buy that horse.

"I know. I couldn't believe he did it. He just waited until the last bid was in. The auctioneer said "going, going..." Everybody thought it was over, and then Mr. McCarthy threw his hand in the air. Let me tell you, there were some really pissed-off breeders leaving the auction that night. He paid an outrageous amount for that stallion."

"Was it a mistake?"

"I thought so at the time, but no. Skydancer won some major ribbons, and his stud fees went through the roof." A touch of bitterness crept into her tone. "My guy looked like dog meat beside that horse."

"Where is he now?"

"Skydancer? I don't know, and that's kind of strange. I tried to find out from Della's mom, but all she'd say was that she'd had to sell the horse. She said the buyer didn't want to be identified. Since then, no new Skydancer offspring have showed up. I can't believe someone's not out there marketing that horse."

She sighed. "And I really can't believe Della's gone. It's that stupid sheriff's fault." She stared down at her lap. "He wouldn't take us seriously. Said she'd probably gone off with some guy. We had to wait 'til she was missing forty-eight hours before he'd file a report." She laughed mirthlessly. "I really tore into that guy." She smiled ruefully. "I was right and he was wrong. I'll bet he still regrets losing that forty-eight hours. If he'd started looking for her then, he might have found her by now."

Chapter 28

THEY'D COME TO BILLINGS TO FIND OUT ABOUT DELLA, but once Larissa got onto the subject of riding, she was tougher to turn than a runaway racehorse. She seemed to regard Luke as a kindred soul and insisted the three of them stay to dinner so they could compare notes on training methods. Larissa's rich husband had turned out to be as boring as his job in the financial sector, and the conversation had mostly bounced between Larissa and Luke.

"Well, you were a big hit," Libby said to him as they left.

"You jealous?" he asked hopefully.

"More like bored," she said, rolling her eyes. "Horses, horses, horses. The woman never got out of the horse-crazy tween stage."

"Sorry," he said. "Me neither, but don't worry. I'm not Larissa-crazy."

"No?"

"No." He smiled down at her and took her hand as they headed for the pickup, but she slipped out of his grip. This was getting too comfortable. He was starting to take her touch for granted, and that meant he thought they were moving beyond friendship to something deeper. It was time to draw the line. Friends might sit comfortably together in close quarters, like a truck cab, especially if they were pressed together by a gigantic

smelly dog who took up two thirds of the seat, but they didn't hold hands.

The sky had shifted from baby blue to purplish gray while they ate. The late afternoon sun was low in the sky, casting an eerie glow over the cliffs that rimmed the north edge of the city.

Luke climbed behind the steering wheel and ducked his head, peering up at the sky. "Looks nasty," he said. "You might get to see one of those summer hailstorms."

"You think?" She winced as a streak of lightning slashed a jagged white line across the darkening sky. Ivan whimpered and scooched closer to Libby.

"Maybe." He grinned. "You scared of thunderstorms?"

"No," she said. "I like them."

He looked disappointed, and they cruised a while in silence. The road seemed longer heading home, maybe because they were sick and tired of how special Chrissie was. Ivan sighed and laid down on the seat, his massive head and front paws draped over Libby's lap and part of Luke's. They were almost to Kaycee, the midpoint of the trip, when rain started to fall, big fat drops splatting like bugs on the windshield.

"Yup," Luke said. "Here it comes."

"Here what... never mind." Libby watched as a barrage of tiny white snowballs pummeled the truck, bouncing on the hood, pinging off the windshield. In less than a minute, they'd grown almost to the size of golf balls, and it sounded like someone was throwing rocks at the truck.

Lots of rocks.

"Okay. I'm scared of *this*," Libby said.

So was Ivan. The dog plastered himself against her, shivers thrumming through his body.

"It's okay, buddy," she said, stroking his head.

Luke slowed the truck to a crawl. "I have to pull off." He was crouched over the wheel, his knuckles white as he steered through the slush of fallen hailstones burying the road.

"There are lights up ahead," Libby said, pointing. Luke tapped the brakes and the truck skewed slightly sideways, sliding onto the shoulder. Squinting through the windshield, he turned off the road into a parking lot, where a red neon arrow pointed to a low, slant-roofed building. "Sleepaway Inn," read the sign above it.

"That's an inn?" Libby said. "Looks more like a barn."

Luke nodded. The building's gray clapboard side was lined with ten salmon-colored doors, each with a corresponding window hung with crooked Venetian blinds. Black animal silhouettes—an antelope, a grizzly bear, an elk—were stenciled on each door in black spray paint, apparently in an effort to add local flavor. Libby thought the building had plenty of flavor without the silhouettes. The silhouettes made it look like a sheep shack that had been tagged with black spray paint by a wildlife-obsessed street gang.

Luke pulled under an overhang in front of the motel office, an A-frame structure at the far end of the building. The hammering of the hail suddenly ceased.

"Guess we'll wait it out," he said in the sudden silence.

"Guess so." Libby stroked Ivan's rich red fur, watching hailstones bounce on the pavement. It looked like it was raining ping-pong balls. Luke closed his eyes and settled back against the headrest. "Might as well take a nap," he said.

Libby tilted her head back and thunked the gun rack in the back window. "Ow," she said. "Why does every cowboy have to have a gun mounted back there?"

"Tradition," Luke said. "Besides, you never know when you might need it." He shifted sideways, angling himself against his window, and patted his shoulder. "Here. Sit back. I promise I'll be good."

She knew he'd be good. He'd be very, very good. That was the problem. She gave him a long look.

"I mean I'll behave," he said. He blinked, looking up at her from under heavy lids. He practically radiated sincerity, which made her all the more suspicious—but her back ached from the long ride and her eyes were burning from staring into the storm. Shifting to one side, she rested her head against his chest.

"Ow," he said. "My arm." He wriggled it out from under her and draped it over her waist. "Sorry," he said. "There's nowhere else to put it."

Ivan struggled to turn around. It was actually a fairly roomy cab, but having Ivan inside made it feel tiny. He finally made himself comfortable by sprawling across Libby's lap, pinning Luke's arm beneath him.

That would put a stop to any monkey business, she thought. Pinned under the dog, his arm would probably fall asleep. He'd be helpless.

Hmm. Helpless.

She shook that thought away and stroked Ivan's furry head. The dog might be scared of thunderstorms, but he could still protect her when it came to the important stuff.

She closed her eyes and laid her head on Luke's shirt-front, riding the rise and fall of his chest as his breathing slowed. She shouldn't be here with Luke, shouldn't be

resting her head against him, not even with the dog to protect her. It was too much like cuddling, and for her, cuddling was gateway sex.

It always led to the hard stuff.

But she needed sleep, dammit. In a matter of seconds, she wouldn't even be conscious—so it wasn't like she could *enjoy* the cuddling. Besides, stuff that happened in your sleep didn't count, which was a good thing considering those dreams she'd been having. All the things she stopped Luke from doing in their waking life went unchecked in her dreams, and moved along to their inevitable conclusion.

She was just drifting into one of her favorite scenarios, the dream enhanced by Luke's nearness, when something rapped on Luke's window and Ivan lurched upright, letting out a loud bark. A wizened face was pressed against the glass. Luke opened one eye and peered at it, his mouth still slack from sleep.

"Can't sleep here," the face mouthed.

Luke sat up and cranked down the window. An old man stood beside the car, scowling. "Can't sleep here," he repeated.

"We're just waiting out the storm," Luke said. He rubbed the arm that had been pinned under the dog. When he let go of it, it flopped onto Libby's lap.

"Sorry," he said. "It fell asleep." He picked up the dead arm with his left hand and set it in his own lap. Ivan looked down at it and barked.

The old man turned and hobbled back into the office without a word. Luke sighed and rolled up the window. He lifted the arm up and propped it on the back of the seat, and Libby slumped against him again. They were

just drifting off to sleep when a gnarled fist hit the window right beside Luke's head. Luke's arm flopped off the back of the seat and thumped Libby in the ribs.

"Sorry," he said again, rolling down the window. "It's like a zombie arm."

"Jackalope room," the old man said, holding up a plastic key fob decorated with a jackalope silhouette. "Down at the end. That'll be thirty dollars."

"No," Libby said. "No way. Not the Jackalope room." She practically had post-traumatic shock when it came to jackalopes.

The old guy dug in his pocket and pulled out a key. He grinned slyly. "Bunny room, then. Might be more appropriate for you young folks."

"We're not bunnies," Libby said. "We're nothing like bunnies. And we're not staying. Just let us sit here 'til the storm's over, okay?"

The hotel proprietor pointed toward the sign. "See what that there says?" he asked shrilly. "Sleepaway *Inn.* Not 'Sleepaway *Out In the Parking Lot.*' 'Sleepaway *Inn.*'" He set his fists on his hips and stared Luke down, bushy brows lowering over his rheumy eyes. "This here's a business, not a campsite by the side of the road."

"It's hard to tell," Luke muttered, but he pulled a wad of cash out of his back pocket and handed the guy a ten and a twenty. Cranking the key in the ignition, he backed the truck out from under the awning, leaving their host clutching the money, a pile of hailstones gathering at his feet.

As soon as they moved out from under the protection of the roof, the hammering started up again. The wind had picked up, and the snowballs were being

hurled against the truck windows with shattering force. Ivan shoved his nose between Libby and the seat. Then he tried to wriggle his whole body in behind her.

"No," she said. He nudged her again and she slid forward, her knees hitting the dashboard. Shifting sideways, she looked out at the hail. "The poor dog. And your poor truck," she said.

"I know." Luke made a tragic face. "And it was in mint condition when we started out."

She laughed.

"Maybe we should try the Bunny room," he said.

"Let's call it the Rodent room." Libby figured they should probably remove the inevitable associations conjured up by bunnies. She knew what bunnies did, and a motel room was the perfect place to emulate them. Rodents did the same thing, she supposed, but at least they lacked the Playboy connotations.

"Seriously, we might be safer there," he said.

Safer from what, Libby wondered. She'd be safer from the hail, sure, but she could feel other dangers simmering in the cab of the truck.

"Maybe we should get two rooms," she said.

"We won't be here long. These storms usually blow over fast," Luke said. "We can watch a little TV or something. We paid for it, and it's better than sitting out here. My legs are getting cramped."

He backed the truck up, then turned it parallel to the building, ignoring the white painted parking lines and bumping the left tires up onto the sidewalk so there were only a few feet of open air between the truck and the door to the room. The hammering of the hail faded

under the shelter of the slanted eave. Keeping his head down, he hopped out of the truck and poked the key into the knob under the rabbit silhouette.

"Wait there," he said as Libby scooted into the driver's seat. Dashing into the room, he came back with a pillow. "Hold this over your head."

She felt ridiculous, but a couple of hailstones thumped the pillow as she ran inside and she was glad they hadn't rapped her on the skull. "Ivan, come," she called, turning around. The dog flattened himself on the seat, doing his best bearskin rug imitation. She ran back into the hail, balancing the pillow on her head with one hand, grabbed his collar, and pulled.

There was a slight ripping sound, but no movement. His claws were digging into the upholstery.

"Ivan's scared," she said. "Can you get him to come inside?"

Luke tried the collar too. No dice. It was like the animal was nailed down.

Leaning into the car, Luke scooped his hands under Ivan's belly and hoisted him out of the seat. He grunted as he staggered inside and deposited 140 pounds of cowering canine on the carpet just inside the room.

"Stay," he said.

Ivan furrowed his brow and collapsed on the rug.

"He's a big sissy," Libby said.

"I'll take him for a day or two when we get home," Luke said. "He needs bomb-proofing."

"Bomb-proofing?"

"We do it with horses—subject them to the things that scare them a little at a time, until they get used to it and lose their fear," he said.

"Sounds good," Libby said. "Maybe you could throw golf balls at him."

Luke paced through the room, opening drawers in the laminated bureau, sliding open the closet door. "Score," he said, pulling out a pair of extra pillows and a blanket. "All the comforts of home." He plumped up the pillows and set them on top of the two already on the bed, then set the folded blanket on top. Toeing off his boots, he grabbed the TV remote and lounged against the make-shift backrest.

"Come on." He patted the bed beside him. "What do you want to watch?"

"I don't care," Libby said. If she was sharing a bed with Luke, it wouldn't matter what was on TV. She wouldn't know what she was watching anyway. She'd be too conscious of his body beside her. She'd be too busy remembering how much she'd wanted him that night in the truck, how hard and urgently her own body had responded.

"Tell me when you want me to stop," he said, flicking through the channels. He wasn't watching the screen; he was watching her. And despite the innocence of what he was actually doing, his expression said very clearly he was thinking of something else.

Stop, she thought. *Stop looking at me like that. Stop making me want to jump your bones. Just stop.*

Chapter 29

SHE PERCHED STIFFLY ON THE SIDE OF THE BED, concentrating on the television, watching the screen flip from football to *Law & Order* to a black-and-white Western.

"There," she said. "Stop there."

"Randolph Scott," Luke said. "My hero." He settled back against the stacked pillows and laced his fingers behind his head. Libby looked down at the long length of his body and edged a little closer. At least he had those wandering hands under control.

She faked rapt involvement in Randolph Scott's efforts to clean up the outlaw element in his frontier town, but she wasn't catching much of the dialogue. She was far too aware of Luke stretched out beside her.

She was tired, though. She closed her eyes, just for a minute, turning away from Luke so her hands couldn't reach out for him in her sleep. The dialogue from the television gradually devolved into incomprehensible mush as the world drifted away.

She woke to near-darkness. Luke had turned the television off, and the only light was coming from the bathroom, where he'd turned on the light and pulled the door nearly closed. She could hear rain battering the tin roof over their heads; not hail, but an awful lot of rain. Luke must have decided to stay.

Evidently, he'd also decided to keep her warm. His

body was curled around hers, and his arm clasped her waist. His breath warmed the back of her neck, riffling the fine hairs spilling from her sloppy French twist. She turned over slowly, being careful not to wake him. His face was relaxed in sleep, those surprisingly tender lips slightly parted, his lashes dark against his cheek, his face innocent as a child's except for the stubble shadowing his jaw. She lifted a finger and tentatively stroked it across his jawline, feeling the roughness of his beard. His eyes flicked open.

"Hey," he said. His sleepy smile was sweet and seductive. She pulled her hand back, hesitating.

"It's okay," he said. He brought his hand up and mirrored her touch, but slower, stroking her cheek, then moving down the side of her neck, leaving a trail of flickering nerve endings in his wake.

"I was watching you sleep earlier," he whispered. "You're beautiful, you know that?"

She shook her head, looking away, and he tilted her chin up with one finger, forcing her to look at him, scanning her eyes with his own. "You're beautiful," he said again. "I should tell you that every day, every time I see you. Until you believe me." He stroked a finger along her jawline. "And then I should tell you some more."

She shuttered her lashes, avoiding his eyes.

"Hey, you know what?" he asked.

She was almost afraid to ask. "What?"

"This motel is in the Twilight Zone."

She giggled a little too loud, relieved to return to a safe subject. "I thought maybe it was in a fairy tale. I think that old guy is the troll under the bridge."

"No, really. I'm serious. It's in an alternate

dimension." He turned onto his stomach and propped himself up on his elbows to look down at her. "Nothing that happens here has anything to do with the real world. It doesn't count. When we get back home, it'll be like a dream. Like it never happened."

"Really," she said.

"Really." He bent his head and kissed her softly, his lips just brushing hers. "It's just this once, Libby. Just this once. And we never have to talk about it, or think about it, again."

He slid his fingers into her hair and stroked them out, spreading it across the pillow. She reached up and stopped him.

He squeezed her hand. "You're scared, aren't you?"

She bit her lip and nodded.

"You can decide," he said. "I stopped us last time because we weren't thinking clearly. But it's up to you this time. Entirely up to you."

He stroked her hair again, and she scanned his face, thinking. She could trust him, right? He was a man who kept his promises.

He really was.

"Maybe you need bomb-proofing," he whispered. "You know, like the dog. I could introduce you to all the things that scare you real slow. Real easy." He swept back her hair again, and this time she didn't stop him. "Until you got used to it."

She'd never get used to this. Her nerve endings were crackling like radio static.

"What scares you?" he whispered. "Does this?" He kissed her, reaching down as she started to respond and cupping her breast with one hand. "This?" His

thumb flicked lightly over the tip, teasing, stroking. "Or maybe..." He squeezed gently, once, twice. "This?"

"That," she whispered, and he did it again. "Oh, that."

She wasn't afraid. Not really. Not with Luke. She trusted him.

The thought surprised her, but it was true, gloriously, miraculously true.

She lifted her arms and clasped his neck, pulling him down for another kiss, and then another, each more urgent than the last as she released her inhibitions and let herself go, moving her hands down his body, stroking his back and pulling his hips into hers, cupping that tight denim-sheathed butt just the way she did in her dreams, lifting her hips to rub against him, feeling his response hard against her.

"Libby." He let out a shaky sigh and pulled away, looking down at her while he twirled a lock of her hair in his fingers, his eyes exploring hers, searching her feelings. She met his eyes boldly.

"That worked," she said. "I'm not scared anymore."

"You're a fast learner."

"You're a good teacher."

She smiled and he kissed her again, long and hard. He wasn't holding back now, and she returned his passion with all the feelings she'd been holding in the past few weeks. Rolling over, he pulled her with him until she reared above him, straddling his hips. Looking down at him, she felt gloriously strong, totally in control, and she rocked against him, watching his face, reveling in her power as his eyes closed and he breathed in short, sharp gasps.

He slid his hands up under her T-shirt. Her bra was

nothing, thin and elastic, and if he hadn't already realized how much she wanted him, he knew now. He sat up so she faced him, sitting in his lap, and hiked the shirt up and off in one easy motion.

He stopped, just for a heartbeat, and scanned her face, seeking permission, and she felt her passion rise and deepen, grateful for his tenderness, amazed at his self-control. What was left of her own flew away the moment he lowered his head to her breast. She arched her back, pushing against the sweet tugging tension of his mouth, asking for more, and he gave it to her, using his hands, his mouth, his passion to drive her wild with want. She clawed at the flimsy elastic, tearing the bra from her body and tossing it onto the floor as he cupped her head and tilted her back onto the bed.

She writhed and twisted beneath him, needing more, more, more. She reached down and clawed at his belt, tugging at the buckle. He pulled her hands away and lifted them above her head, holding her captive.

"Take your time," he said. "We have all night." He shifted both her hands to one of his and used the other to stroke the tender skin just above the waist of her jeans. His fingers were gentle, barely touching, and she felt a flood of lust fill her to overflowing. She started to lift her hips, asking for more, but he shushed her and kept his touch light.

"All night," he repeated. "Go slow. Give me time to touch you."

His fingers danced over her skin, drifting from breast to belly and back, then skimming down over her jeans, touching, teasing, all the while watching her response, his eyes intense as she writhed under his touch. She

closed her eyes. His touch thrilled her, but the naked emotion in his gaze was too much. She knew what she was seeing, knew what he was feeling, but she refused to name it, even to herself. He couldn't feel that way about her. Not now. Not yet.

Her heart wasn't ready.

But her body was. She closed her eyes and concentrated on the feel of his fingers dancing over her skin, and felt her body ripple like light on running water, shimmering at his touch. He moved his hand between her legs and she lifted her hips again, pressing herself against him, partly to intensify the feeling, partly to control it as it raged through her like a fire on an oil slick, burning up what little sense she had left. All she could think about was Luke—his hands, his body, his mouth, his eyes. All she wanted was Luke.

"Wait," she said. She shifted and struggled against him, pushing him away while she still could. He pulled back, his eyes puzzled.

"My turn," she said, straddling him again, pushing him down on the bed. Clutching his collar in both hands, she ripped it open, the snaps on his shirt flicking open one by one to reveal the hard, square planes of his chest, the dark hair flecking his tanned skin.

He groaned as she opened the clasp of his belt and unsnapped his jeans, rubbing the palm of her hand against him, making him gasp as she released him and shimmied the jeans down his hips, gasping herself as his boxers snagged and followed her hands. She reached up to his shoulders and ran her hands slowly down his body, savoring the heat of his muscles, pausing to run her fingertips over his chest, smoothing her hands down

the soft skin at his sides. She was almost to her goal when he sat up again, holding her against his chest, gasping a faint protest into her ear before his tongue flicked out and set to driving her crazy all over again, licking and probing, the dampness intensifying the sweet cool sensation of his breath on her skin.

Now it was his hands at work, tugging on her belt, pushing her clothes away, sliding under the soft cotton of her panties. He paused, again looking in her eyes, asking permission before he moved his fingers down to stroke her. She was so slick, so ready, that one quick pulse of her hips slid him inside her, and once she started she couldn't stop. She tossed her head back, closing her eyes so all she could know was the river of pleasure flowing from his touch. Her eyes were still closed when he lowered himself over her and she felt a new pleasure pushing against her, into her, and the waves of ecstasy lifted and broke, then lifted again, higher, impossibly higher, and she rode them until they flung her back on the mattress like a leaf tossed by a storm.

As the ripples slowed, she opened her eyes to watch him. Every muscle in his body was straining against his skin, taut and full. His eyes met hers, and for once she could meet his gaze and let him see her feelings. She couldn't have hidden them if she'd wanted to, and she felt more naked now than she had when he'd stripped her clothes away, more vulnerable than when he'd touched her and tasted her. But she wanted him to see, just this once, how much she wanted him.

How much she needed him.

It was the look in her eyes that pushed Luke over the edge. Not her touch, not her warmth, not even her body, wet and welcoming. It was her gaze—honest and open, offering a heat that matched his own. It was a look that was full of possibilities, full of promises. If she could only trust him, they'd be a pair for the rest of their lives. Finishing each others' sentences. Sharing each others' thoughts.

But now that he had her trust, he wondered if he could live up to it. He felt like he was barely human at this moment—just a tangled Neanderthal nest of nerves and sensation poised at the edge of a high cliff, his mind clawing to pull his body back from the edge, his body intent on hurling itself over. He willed himself to stay with her, to stay present, to hold off the inevitable leap, but his body won. He clung to her gaze, willed her to stay with him as everything in his being flowed into her. Overwhelmed, overcome, he arched his back, threw his head back, and closed his eyes, losing her, losing himself, in the sheer bliss of release.

When he opened his eyes again, she held his gaze for one more precious second before she caught herself and shifted her eyes away, glancing around the room like a panicked animal.

She was still scared.

But like a horse taking one step toward him, then two, then three, she'd fought past her first fears and worked her way toward the trust he was looking for.

The nagging grind of a particularly insistent cricket woke Libby at dawn. The room was dark, but slits of daylight gleamed from the overlapping blinds, giving

the room a faint, silvery glow. She opened her eyes and lay still, gradually moving toward consciousness.

As she wended her way out of her dreams and into real life, the edges of reality seemed to blur. Could she really be cupped in Luke's embrace, nestled naked against him, a cheap velour blanket draped over her hips and his? She closed her eyes again. Maybe this wasn't a reality she wanted to face.

She closed her eyes so she could think things through and come to a rational decision about how to proceed, but her memories of the night before were clear and bright, vivid as psychedelic posters under black light. She saw Luke as he'd been the night before and felt the world spin into a new and crazy orbit. She remembered how he'd paused and checked her face at every step, making sure she was ready, making sure she was willing. He'd been tender, careful, caring—perfect.

He loved her. And he would never hurt her.

She was sure of that. The sun was rising in the East, morning had broken as it would every day, and Luke would never hurt her. All facts, all equally certain.

All equally miraculous.

Energized, she slipped her feet out from under the blanket and sat up on the side of the bed. She found her panties dangling from the lamp, her shirt tossed over a chair. Humming softly, she slipped them on and set about searching for her jeans. Ivan waited anxiously by the door, his brown eyes desperate.

"I'll take you out in a minute, buddy," she whispered. "Hold on."

She found her jeans and wriggled into them, then opened the door and followed Ivan across the parking lot.

"You just wait," she told him as he scouted out the perfect pooping place. "That bomb-proofing business? It really works." She kicked a pebble and watched it bounce across the parking lot. "You're going to end up really liking thunderstorms. You're going to wish it could storm every day."

Luke lifted his head and peered around the room.

She was gone.

Hopefully she hadn't left him here and taken the truck.

Not that he'd blame her if she had. He'd sworn to himself he'd wait until she was ready, but last night, the temptation had been too much for him. He'd taken advantage of the situation, telling her it was just this once. Convincing her they were in the Twilight Zone, outside real life. Promising her it wouldn't matter in the morning.

But it did matter—more than he'd ever believed possible. Making love to Libby had changed him forever. Whatever it meant to her, it wasn't something he could forget. He'd never be able to look at her again without seeing her as she'd been last night.

But she didn't have to know that.

He'd promised her it wouldn't matter. He'd told her they'd never have to talk about it, or think about it, ever again.

And he was a man who kept his promises.

Chapter 30

LUKE HAD EVERYTHING PACKED UP AND READY TO GO by the time Libby got back from walking Ivan. He'd even made the bed, smoothing the rumpled sheets, erasing every sign of the night before. The weather had cleared overnight, and Ivan was back in the truck bed. She wouldn't even have to sit in the middle. He was sure that would be a relief.

"Ready?" He flashed her a smile—a friendly smile, not a seductive one, and he was careful not to look her in the eyes.

Don't think about last night, he told himself. *Just pretend it didn't happen. You promised. You promised.*

Libby looked puzzled. She'd probably expected him to jump her again the minute she walked in the room. No way. He was on his best behavior.

"Come on," he said. "Let's get out of here." He was sure she didn't want to spend another minute in that hotel room. They needed to get on the road. Get back to reality, where she could feel safe.

She climbed into the cab of the truck and he flicked on the radio. It was hard to talk, and the music would fill the silence while they both worked their way out of the Twilight Zone. She glanced at him a couple times, as if she was about to say something, but he didn't encourage her. He'd promised her they wouldn't talk.

The trip back seemed to take forever. The two of them stared straight out through the windshield, pretending to listen to the music. He wished he could think of something to say—something harmless, innocuous. But everything he thought of seemed loaded with innuendo. He couldn't so much as talk about the wind without thinking of how her breath had felt on his skin. He couldn't comment on the sunlight bronzing the prairie with gold and silver without thinking about how her skin had glowed under his touch. He couldn't even mention how smoothly the truck was running without thinking of the sweet, soft sounds she'd made when they'd made love.

Maybe if they talked about someone else it would break the ice. He searched his brain for some innocent topic. There'd been something he wanted to ask her last time he was at her house. What had it been? He drove on, thinking. Oh, yeah.

"Hey, do you know Brandy?" he asked. "I saw her number on your message board."

"Brandy?" Libby squinted, as if she could barely remember the name. "Oh. No," she said. "It's just that I need to talk to her about Della. Probably this weekend. Why? You know her?"

Luke nodded. "A little. She used to come into town a lot, hang out. She's a fun girl."

Libby narrowed her eyes. "How much fun was she?"

"Not that kind of fun," he said. "She was just… nice."

She nodded as if she understood, but he wondered what she was really thinking. She probably figured he'd taken Brandy to the Twilight Zone, along with half the other women in town.

She probably figured he did that kind of thing all the time.

She had no idea what it had meant to him.

Libby jumped out of the truck the minute it pulled into Lackaduck Farm and mumbled an embarrassed good-bye. She really didn't know what to say. She'd looked forward to the ride home, to sitting close and holding hands, but he hadn't even looked at her.

She'd thought the aftermath of their lovemaking would be different. She'd thought he was a man who kept his promises, and surely the tenderness of his love-making had been a promise in itself. She'd trusted him, given in to that promise, and for a little while she thought she'd finally found the place where she belonged, the place she'd been running toward—but in the clear light of day, Luke had taken her straight back to where she'd started, and left her there.

Alone.

She leaned over the tailgate and gave Ivan a fare-well hug before sending him off to be bomb-proofed, squelching a stab of envy. She could use another bomb-proofing session herself—although the process had been so successful, she probably didn't need it. She wouldn't have even flinched if Luke had jumped out of the truck and taken her breath away with a pas-sionate good-bye kiss. It wouldn't have scared her at all if he'd carried her tote bag inside and set it in her bedroom, then coerced her into a repeat of the night before. She'd overcome all her fears—but apparently she'd overcome them for nothing.

She waved good-bye as he pulled away with a jaunty toot of the horn.

David ran to greet her, a boisterous herd of puppies tumbling in his wake.

"What do you think?" He gestured enthusiastically toward the little structure that stood beside the barn in an overgrown paddock. It had been transformed from a sad, gray, broken-down shack into a sparkling white stable with dark green trim and tiny, green-painted shutters. It was adorable.

"Wow," she said, shoving Luke out of her thoughts and scanning the revamped outbuilding. "You've been busy. Now I need a pony."

"It was fun. I like to putter around and fix stuff." He met her eyes guiltily. "I gotta warn you about the dogs, though" he said. "Discipline went out the window while you were gone. They're spoiled rotten now."

"Let me guess." Libby pointed an accusing finger. "You let them sleep with you, didn't you?"

He hung his head. "They seemed so sad. They really wanted to come up on the bed. Rooster cried, and I was afraid he might be sick again."

She rolled her eyes. "It's okay. I just appreciate you taking care of them. Any calls?"

"You bet! Most of them from the sheriff."

"What did he want?"

"Wouldn't say. But he wanted it awfully bad." David smiled archly as he shrugged into his denim jacket.

"Yeah, well, he's not getting it."

"You have to call him back, though. I promised. If you don't, he'll think I forgot to tell you."

"All right," Libby said. "You don't need trouble with the sheriff, do you? I'll call him."

"Or not," David said. He jerked his head toward the road and she saw the town's lone cruiser making its way toward them, bouncing over the rocky road. She sighed. An encounter with Cash was the last thing she needed right now.

"You okay on your own with him?" David asked. "I'll stay if you want."

"No," she said. "You go ahead."

She didn't have to tell him twice. Hopping on his bike, he pushed off and pedaled past the cruiser with a casual wave.

She headed inside. She wasn't going to stand there waiting for Cash. He'd think he was welcome, and he wasn't. The guy was a jerk, and she wanted nothing more to do with him.

She tossed her bag on the bed, then returned to the kitchen just as the sheriff tapped on the door. She opened it, but she didn't step aside to let him in.

"I've been trying to get hold of you," he said. "I wanted to apologize."

"No need," Libby said. She started to swing the door closed, but he propped his boot against it to hold it open.

"I'm sorry for how I treated you the other night," he said, as if she hadn't even spoken. "I should have had more respect for what you do. I'm just not used to women like you, Libby. Most of the women I know *do* need protecting. I don't mean to make excuses, though. I wasn't treating you as an equal, and I should have."

She could tell he'd rehearsed his apology. He sounded like a high school jock trying out for the class play.

"You're more than an equal, Libby." He was talking fast, anxious to get to the end of his self-assigned script. "You've gone after this case, and I think you've uncovered things I never knew about, even though I've been investigating for two years. I want you to know that I do respect you, and I'd like to work together on this thing. Maybe, between the two of us, we can come up with an answer."

"Whatever," she said. She started to close the door, but his foot was a maddeningly effective doorstop.

"Can I come in? Can we talk it over?" He took a deep breath. "Look, I know I stepped over the line in other ways too," he said. "I just—I lost control the other night after our meeting. I can't tell you how sorry I am about that. How ashamed. I'm not the kind of guy that forces himself on a girl. I promise, I won't so much as touch you."

She hesitated. If she could re-establish a good relationship with Cash—a *professional* relationship—he might give her some useful information. And it sounded like he was finally willing to talk about Della McCarthy. Willing to share what he knew.

"I know you're not interested in me. Not—that way," he said. "And I'm sorry I didn't pick up on that sooner." He lifted both hands in the air. "I'll lay off. Really, I will. To be honest, I just don't get turned down very often." He grinned. "You're probably good for me. Knocking me down a peg or two. I think I needed it."

She had to laugh.

"Okay." She stepped aside to let him in. "Long as you understand that."

He settled into a chair at the kitchen table and an awkward silence settled between them. "So what's your next move on the Della thing?" he finally asked. "How can I help?"

"Well, I went to Billings and talked to Larissa," she said. "Next comes Brandy."

"Della's other friend?"

"Yeah. Larissa said Della didn't share her secrets with her. It sounds like she was too judgmental to inspire confidence. But I think Brandy was different."

"That's putting it mildly." He grinned.

"What do you mean?"

"She's different, all right. From what I've heard, Brandy marches to her own drum, and it's got a pretty crazy beat. Listen, you mind if I come along?"

Her mind flashed back to the trip to Billings with Luke—the forced intimacy of the truck cab, the trip through the hailstorm, the night in the Sleepaway Inn. She wasn't about to risk that kind of situation with Cash, no matter what kind of promises he made.

"I'm okay on my own," she said.

"It's not a long drive. And I can fill you in on some details on the way down," he said. "Some stuff I didn't release to the papers."

He'd found her tipping point. Putting up with Cash for a few hours was a small price to pay for exclusive information. And Cheyenne was less than an hour away.

She'd go, she decided. It would be fine.

She'd be perfectly safe.

Chapter 31

Libby puttered around the kitchen until almost midnight. The busy work kept her mind off Luke and what had happened the night before. It also helped her forget what *hadn't* happened this morning—how he hadn't kissed her. Hadn't touched her. How he'd acted like they were nothing but road trip buddies, and completely ignored the tremors that had rocked them the night before.

She felt like she'd survived an earthquake that had shaken her world to its core, then woken up to find everything back in its place, broken crockery miraculously returned whole to its cupboards, collapsed walls rebuilt as if they'd never fallen.

But they *had* fallen. And deep inside, they were riddled with cracks. She'd have to work twice as hard now to keep them standing.

She finally decided she was tired enough to sleep. She was worried Luke would play a starring role in her dreams, but the puppies weren't going to allow her to have any kind of dreams at all. She'd herded them into their crate beside the bed, like usual, but they were used to sleeping with David and they weren't about to settle down until she gave in and let them join her.

She wasn't giving in. After all, they weren't her dogs for good. She was going to find homes for them one of

these days, and they'd settle in with their new owners much more easily if they learned to behave themselves. She chided them when they whimpered, then decided even that was probably making it worse; dogs are gratified by any response at all, even an angry one. So she tried ignoring them, but that was impossible. Five weeping, whimpering puppies and a mother dog who howls like a coyote were hard to ignore. She got up and pulled on her bathrobe.

"Come on, guys," she said sternly. "You're sleeping in the barn."

They bounced happily out the door, convinced they were going on a late-night family adventure. Libby was sure it was a rude shock for them when she pulled the barn door shut and went back to bed.

She slid herself under the still-warm blankets, congratulating herself on ensuring a good night's sleep. Opening one eye, she checked the glowing numbers on her digital alarm clock. Two a.m. She turned over and snuggled her head into the pillow. She'd get six hours of sleep if she was lucky.

Half an hour later, the howling started up again, accompanied by staccato barks from Penny. Libby punched her pillow and swore. David had really spoiled those puppies. It could take weeks to break them of their bad habits. She could hear Penny flinging herself against the barn door as the puppies swung into a rousing choral number. Libby jammed the pillow over her head and prayed for silence.

A loud bang made her throw the pillow aside and sit up. That hadn't come from the barn. It sounded like it came from the kitchen. There was a deep moan, then a shuffling noise that seemed to come from the front hall. Someone or something was in her house.

Hiding under the covers and hoping the boogeyman went away was one option, but she needed to find out what was making all that racket. After all, there might be a perfectly reasonable explanation. Maybe Luke had seen her car and dropped Ivan off. Or maybe a bear had gotten into the house. The high plains of Wyoming didn't seem like a likely place to find bears, but you never knew. The news was full of stories of wild animals invading towns and cities. It was also full of stories about lone women being murdered in their beds, but Libby didn't want to think about that.

Could bears climb stairs? She'd heard somewhere that cows couldn't. If it was a bear, maybe it couldn't get to her. Maybe she was safest staying where she was.

Still, she'd better be ready. She grabbed her flashlight and swung her legs out of bed. The flashlight was huge—a heavy sheath packed with four D batteries that would knock an intruder clear to Colorado if she hit him right. She floundered into her bathrobe and slid her feet into her bunny slippers. Bare feet somehow make you feel vulnerable, and she needed all the courage she could muster. Even pink bunny courage was better than nothing.

"Ow! Damn!" Whatever was downstairs was no bear. It wasn't Ivan, either, unless hanging out with Luke had driven him to swearing.

Cocking the flashlight like a Louisville slugger, Libby crept toward the head of the stairs and peered down into the dimness. A dark shadow shuffled across the hall.

"I know you're here," whispered a strangely familiar voice in a menacing sing-song. "Come out, come out, wherever you are!"

Libby ducked back into the bedroom, her heart thrashing like a grounded trout. Whoever was down there sounded completely insane. She suddenly regretted her single-minded pursuit of Della's case. Obviously, whoever had caused her disappearance was in Libby's house, ready to put a stop to her investigation.

Her mind was spinning fast and getting nowhere. The phone was in the kitchen, beyond the hall where the intruder was stumbling through the darkness. Her cell phone was in her purse, and her purse was in the kitchen too. She could scream, but no one would hear her. She was more than half a mile from Luke's house, and he was her only neighbor.

She pressed her back against the wall and glanced around the room. The windows were all firmly sealed with four generations of white enamel paint. She'd have to make it down the stairs and out the front door.

The dogs' barking arced into a dramatic crescendo, drowning out the creaking boards as she crept down the stairs. They covered the sounds of the intruder too, but she was pretty sure he'd moved on to the living room. Maybe she could make it across the hall. She paused at the foot of the stairs, squinting into the darkness.

There was heavy thud in the living room. It sounded like furniture overturning—the sofa, maybe, or her reading chair. Glass shattered next, as her uninvited visitor knocked over the floor lamp.

"Ow! Ow-oooo!"

Her heart fluttered up into her throat as she recognized the last line of Crazy Mike's rabbit puppet show. There was an insane taxidermist in her house, and he was looking for her. She took a deep breath and made a rush

for the door, then turned the knob and pulled. Nothing. The door wouldn't budge. As she flailed at the deadbolt, Mike rushed across the room and flung himself at her.

"Oh, no you don't!" he shouted, his high-pitched voice rising with excitement. "You're not getting away. I'm going to catch you, and everyone will know. Everyone will know what you're really like!"

He slammed into her with a lineman's tackle, knocking the flashlight out of her hands and throwing both of them to the floor. His arms were wrapped around her legs. She struggled to free herself, trying to kick him in the face, and flailed her arms in a desperate imitation of a snow angel. The heavy metal flashlight rolled away from the tips of her fingers.

"No you don't!" he squeaked. He reached up and grabbed her right arm, twisting it behind her. For a second, his grip on her legs loosened and she kicked out fiercely, slamming her foot into the door. Then the pain in her shoulder immobilized her. She wanted to scream, but fear had taken her breath away, and she could only whimper.

"Go ahead, cry, asshole," yelled her assailant. "You'll have plenty to cry about when everyone finds out you were here. Everyone's going to know you were sneaking around. Everyone's going to know you're a bad guy. A bad, bad guy."

"You… bad guy," Libby said hoarsely, her voice muffled by the doormat. He was on top of her, pinning her to the floor. "You…"

"Libby!" he bellowed in her ear. Now her head hurt too. "Call somebody, Libby! I got him, right here! He was in your house, Libby! I got him!"

She lifted her head from the damp doormat.

"I *am* Libby!" she spluttered. "What are you doing?"

"Libby?" He released the pressure on her arm and she sat up. "Libby?"

"Yes, Libby!" she shouted, rising to her knees. "Libby, Libby, Libby! Who the hell did you think I was?" She reached up and hit the light switch.

"Oh my God," Mike groaned, covering his face with his hands. "Oh my God. I'm so sorry, Libby. He got away. I thought you were him."

She stood unsteadily, rubbing her sore arm. Crazy Mike crouched on the floor, rocking back and forth, moaning.

"Who got away? What on earth were you thinking?" She could hardly resist the urge to slap him. Every ounce of adrenaline in her body was flooding her veins, and her fear was gone.

"I thought you were the sheriff, Libby," he said. "I'm sorry. I thought you were him, sneaking around your house. I knew he was here. I wasn't going to let him hurt you."

"He *was* here, Mike, but he went home. And he didn't hurt me. He's the sheriff, remember? You're the one who hurt me. And now I'm going to call him, and he's going to come and get you."

The big man burst into tears. "Please don't, Libby. Please." He grabbed the hem of her robe. "Please don't call him! You don't know what he'll do. You don't understand!"

Libby kicked his hands away and headed for the phone in the kitchen. She'd just started to dial when she heard the door slam.

Crazy Mike was gone.

Chapter 32

The red and blue lights of Cash's cruiser splashed the ceiling and walls as he and his deputies surveyed Libby's demolished living room. The victim herself hunched in a spindly dinette chair, wrapped in a blanket. Cash barked orders while one of the deputies snapped photos of the overturned furniture and broken lamp.

Satisfied they were recording the evidence correctly, he strode over to the table and stood in front of Libby. "Are you all right?" he asked.

"I can't stop shaking," she said. "I'm so cold."

"You're in shock, and no wonder," he growled. "You're lucky to be alive. Who knows what was going through that lunatic's head when he snuck in here and attacked you?"

"He said he thought I was you. He had some crazy idea you were in the house, and he was looking for you. He thought you were going to hurt me."

Libby looked up at Cash, her eyes glistening with tears. He frowned. He'd had enough of Crazy Mike. More than enough. He'd find him, and he'd make him pay for this.

Libby shuddered, and he realized she thought his scowl was meant for her. Clearing his expression, he knelt down and took her hand. He'd promised not to touch her just hours before, but all the rules had changed now.

"I'd never hurt you, Libby. He's crazy. You know that."

"I'm just so scared," she said.

Finally. She'd been so sure she could handle this situation on her own. Now maybe she'd admit he was right. He reached out to stroke her hair, but she ducked her head. He wasn't sure if she was trying to avoid his touch, or if she was just so frightened she didn't know what she was doing. There was only one way to find out, but that would have to wait. Once this was over, she'd be grateful to him for rescuing her, and she'd probably want to thank him with something more than words.

His stomach clenched with excitement at the thought. He clasped his hands to keep from touching her again.

"We'll find him, and we'll lock him up," he said. "You'll never have to worry about him again." He turned to go.

"You're not leaving, are you?"

He sighed. "I had to call Luke. He's on his way over. I can't stay, Libby." He dropped his tone to a whisper. "No matter how much I want to."

He circled her shoulders with one arm. She felt awfully stiff—almost rigid in his embrace. Maybe she was a little bit of a prude. Needed to loosen up a little.

Or maybe she was just scared.

"But Luke doesn't realize Crazy Mike's dangerous," she said. "If he comes back…"

"He won't," Cash said. "I'll see to that." He felt a thrill of triumph. Luke wasn't her savior anymore. That was his job. And once he found Crazy Mike, he'd have the job for good. "I wish I could stay, but I'll be back, okay? As soon as we get him, I'll be back."

~

Luke climbed out of the pickup and stared at Libby's house. The blue and red lights of two police cars strobed across the worn clapboards, and every light was blazing. He felt his stomach twist with shame. He shouldn't have left her alone.

He shouldn't have left her at all.

What happened between them in Kaycee had been too important to ignore. He'd said that stupid stuff about the Twilight Zone—about pretending that night had never happened—and it had eased her fears about sleeping with him.

Why hadn't he been man enough to put the same effort into soothing her fears afterward?

They belonged together. That was a fact, sure as horses ate hay. Why hadn't he found a way to help her deal with it?

Instead he'd taken the easy way out. Hightailed it home. And almost gotten his arm caught in the baler because he wasn't paying attention to what he was doing. All he could think about was Libby. Libby, naked in his arms. Libby, her back arched, her eyes closed in ecstasy. Libby, looking up at him, open, trusting. Libby waving as he drove away, looking solitary and forlorn as she turned and walked toward her tiny house, alone and vulnerable in the wide, vacant landscape.

How could he have driven away from that scene? Why hadn't he turned around and gone back, taken her in his arms, and sworn to stay with her forever?

He took the porch steps two at a time as Ivan vaulted out of the truck bed. A deputy opened the front door

and nodded to him as the dog trotted past, intent on his mistress.

"Rawlins is here, boss," the deputy called. "Okay if we go join the search?"

"Sure. I'll be right with you."

"And hey, there's some kind of weird animal out here," the deputy said. "Looks like a buzzard or something. Keeps rushing the cruisers, pecking at the tires. You want me to shoot it?"

"No!" Luke turned in time to see Wild Thing dart under one of the police cars. "That's her pet. Well, sort of."

"Pretty weird pet," the deputy muttered. "Thing looks like some kind of mutant."

Cash was kneeling beside Libby, his hand on the back of the chair where she crouched with a blanket clenched in both hands. Luke resisted the impulse to push the sheriff away and take his place. Instead, he shoved his hands in his pockets and nodded to Libby.

Nodded.

What an idiot.

Last night he'd been making her writhe and moan, and now all he could do was nod like a casual acquaintance.

Meanwhile, Ivan trotted up and laid his head in her lap, looking up at her with an expression of absolute adoration. She buried her fingers in the fur at the ruff of the dog's neck and bent down to rest her cheek on his head.

The dog knew more about women than he did.

Pathetic.

Cash hiked up his gun belt and scooped his hat off the table. "You might need to take her to the hospital," he said to Luke. "He roughed her up pretty bad, and she's in shock."

"No," Libby said. "I'm all right."

"She probably won't go," Cash said. "Maybe some tea..."

"I'm all over it." Luke sat down beside her and waved Cash away. "You guys go ahead."

They'd go ahead, all right. They'd go ahead and solve the problem, find Mike and make Libby feel safe. Meanwhile, he'd make her a cup of tea.

He might as well put on a frilly apron and give himself a perm.

The rattle of a teacup teetering on a saucer preceded Luke up the stairs the next morning. Setting the cup on Libby's nightstand, he sat down on the edge of the bed. Rotgut was curled up on her pillow, his damp nose pressed against her neck. The rest of the puppies lay scattered across the comforter.

"No," Libby mumbled. "No dogs in the bed." Sitting up, she ran her fingers through her hair and squinted at Luke while she rubbed her shoulder. A dark purple bruise marked the fair skin of her upper arm. "Dang," she said, and fell back onto the pillow. "So much for my peaceful life in the country."

"You okay?" Luke asked.

"Yeah." She didn't sound sure. She ran a hand through her hair again. Her curls seemed to have multiplied overnight and taken on a life of their own. Luke reached out to adjust a particularly rebellious ringlet, then jerked his hand back. He'd seen something pass between her and the sheriff the night before—something that seemed almost intimate. He wasn't sure what was

going on, but it was starting to look to him like a relationship under construction.

He couldn't blame her. He'd seduced her in that motel room, convinced her it was safe to let him in, and she'd opened herself up, just like he'd hoped—and then he'd walked away and left the door unguarded.

"Did they get him?" she asked.

It took him a minute to figure out who she was talking about. He'd been up all night, standing guard in the kitchen, but all he'd thought about, all night long, was the mistakes he'd made. He'd started to see himself as the villain, and forgotten there was another bad guy here—one who had actually attacked her physically. He'd only attacked her trust, her confidence, and her self-esteem.

The tussle with Mike on the doormat was nothing compared to that.

"I don't think they got Mike," he said. "Cash would have let us know."

"What am I going to do if they don't catch him?"

"Maybe you could get David to stay in your spare room," he said. "Just for a while, until you feel safe again. Or maybe the sheriff can provide a car to watch the house." He sighed. "I'd offer to stay, but I don't think I'm welcome."

Libby stared at him. "Of course you're welcome. Don't say that."

He sighed. "Oh, I know you wouldn't throw me out. But judging from the look I saw between you and Cash last night, your new boyfriend wouldn't be comfortable with me here."

"He's not my boyfriend," she protested.

"Yes he is," Luke said. "Definitely."

"No." Her brows lowered. "He'd like to be, but he's not."

Luke knew better. Even now, sitting there with him right beside her, she kept glancing out the window, no doubt watching for an approaching cruiser.

Boys are stupid. Libby had learned that essential fact of life in first grade, and nothing had happened since to disprove the theory. And now, the living, breathing embodiment of clueless masculinity was sitting right in front of her.

How could Luke think she'd have anything to do with Cash McIntyre? Sure, she'd let him stand a little too close after she was attacked by a raving lunatic—but that didn't mean she was going to let the guy move in.

She swung out from under the covers and perched on the edge of the bed, clasping her arms around her midriff, and tried to see things from his point of view, but all she could see was her own disillusionment.

That night in the motel had been magical. She'd never let herself go like that—never trusted anyone enough to ask for what she wanted and take what she needed.

But maybe Luke didn't know that. Maybe he thought she was Floozy Suzy all the time.

Great. She'd had the best sex of her life with the only man she'd ever… trusted, and all it had done was convince him she was a slut. Either that, or it just hadn't been good enough for a repeat performance. Either way she was—well, not screwed. Just out of luck.

"I'd better get going," he said.

She reached out impulsively and clutched his hand. "No," she said.

"No?" He looked surprised. "You want me to stay?"

"Would you?" She lowered her eyes and plucked at the fringe on the edge of the blanket. The poor guy had probably stayed up all night, and now she was asking for more—but she couldn't bear the idea of being alone with Crazy Mike on the loose.

"I'll make you breakfast," she said.

They headed down to the kitchen, Libby limping a little where she'd twisted her ankle the night before. She busied herself whipping up omelets, while Luke grated cheese and chopped up a tomato. He was quiet the whole time, and she chafed at the awkwardness that had grown between them overnight like a mysterious and impenetrable hedge. Was it his suspicion about the sheriff? Or was it just the fact that they'd gotten to know each other a little too well in that motel room?

Luke was scooping up his first forkful of omelet when his cell phone rang.

"Luke?" It was his dad. "I think you'd better come home, son."

That couldn't be good news. "Is Mom okay?"

"She's okay. She's just... well, you'd better come see for yourself."

"Dad, I need to be here. I'm worried about Libby. I told you, Mike..."

"I think this was Mike's next stop, son. You need to come home."

Panic clawed at Luke's chest. What the hell had Mike done to his mother? He clicked the phone shut and clenched his jaw. First Libby, now his mom. Mike had better hope Luke didn't run across him on the way home.

"I have to go," he said. "Something with my mom."

"Is she okay?"

Amazing, he thought. Her attacker might return any moment, and she was worried about his mother.

"Dad says she's okay. He didn't really explain, but he sounded upset." He didn't want to tell her Mike had been to his house. He didn't want to bring up Mike at all. If she could push the attack out of her mind, maybe she'd be okay until he got back.

Unless Mike turned up.

"Do you want to come with?"

"No. Cash should be back soon." She smiled. It was a good effort, but it trembled at the edges. "I'll be fine."

Everything looked normal as the ranch came into view. His mother was sitting on the porch, rocking in the swing. It always warmed his heart to see her there after a long, dusty summer day, her tiny, child-like figure swaying in the white wicker swing. Sometimes she'd have lemonade for him, or iced tea. Somehow, the mist that had taken over her memory parted when it came to sipping tall, cool drinks on the front porch together after a hard day's work. He liked to think it was an indication of how important those times were to her—how much she, too, loved the rhythm of ranch life.

"Ma," he said, mounting the porch. "Did you—*what* did you *do*?"

His mother smiled, a broad, beaming grin that lit up her face. Well, at least she was happy—though he

couldn't say the same for himself. Everyone wants a cool mom, but Luke had his limits, and a mom with a Mohawk was way beyond them.

"You like it?" She nodded her head right, then left, simpering like a fashion model. "Stephanie did it. I said I wanted something edgy, and boy, did she deliver."

"Well, you got that right," he said. "But Mom, Stephanie's in Chicago. Who did this to you?"

She stopped posturing and looked up at him, her eyes filling. He felt like a heel. She had few enough pleasures in life. If she wanted to think she was ready to strut the catwalk in her new 'do, who was he to tell her different?

But he needed to know who'd done this. Someone had come to his house while he was away and turned his mother into Travis Barker.

The question was, who?

"Mom, who cut your hair?" he asked. Sometimes, if you kept asking a question, she eventually hit on a real answer.

"Don't you like it?" Her lower lip trembled. "I'm an old lady, honey. I don't get many opportunities in life. But this shows my true nature."

"Your…" Where had he heard those words before? Her true nature…

Shoot. Libby's interview with Mike. Mike had been talking about the muskrat—how it would never have a chance to become a dancer, but that was *its true nature*.

He smacked his forehead. "Was Mike here?"

"Your friend from school," she said, nodding. "I didn't know he'd become a beautician."

Luke pictured Mike standing over his mother, wielding the scissors while he interpreted her "true nature."

At least he hadn't stuffed and mounted her.

That wasn't as funny as it would have been a week ago. Mike had attacked Libby, after all. Really attacked her. Luke had seen the bruises himself—and no matter what weird disconnect had taken over Mike's mind at the time of the attack, that was not okay. The man was a menace.

And a fugitive.

He knelt by his mother's side, taking her hand.

"It looks great, Mom," he said. "I think he went a little too far with the gel, but it's really—um—different." He took a deep breath. "Now, is Mike still here?"

"Oh, no." She shook her head, the spikes bobbing like a rooster's comb. "He had to go. Said he needed to find you."

"Me?" Luke took off his hat and ran a hand through his hair. That didn't seem to stimulate his brain into any useful activity, so he did it again. "Why was he looking for me?"

"He needs a place to stay. I told him it was just fine for him to stay here, but he seemed nervous. Said he had to talk to you first. But you were always such good friends." She gave him a piercing stare that took him straight back to his childhood, when she monitored his schoolyard relationships and offered advice on everything from girls to bullies. "Did you two have an argument? I don't see why he would even ask, you boys were such good friends."

Luke remembered Mike's guileless delight at seeing him at Libby's interview, his enthusiastic rendition of the secret handshake they'd invented in sixth grade, his simple recounting of his weird artistic vision.

Then he remembered the bruises on Libby's arms, the way she'd trembled, hunched in the chair, after the attack.

"Yeah, Mom," he said. "We had a fight."

It disturbed him that Mike had shown up the one day Mom was home alone—the one day his dad wasn't there to protect her. It disturbed him even more to think of those sharp scissors being wielded by a man who had already attacked one of the women Luke loved.

Loved?

Yeah, loved. Seeing Libby the morning after the attack, her hair tousled from sleep, so alone and vulnerable in her bed, had made him realize his feelings were more than lust, more than friendly affection.

He was in love.

He stood up, waving away the dizziness that had taken over with the realization of just how strong his feelings were for Libby. He had serious business to take care of, here. Family business. Someday, maybe Libby would be a part of that. He hoped so. He felt a surge of happiness at the idea of Libby being here, waiting for him at the end of the day, or, better yet, working beside him.

He'd always been content with his life. Always felt he was right where he belonged, doing what he was born to do. But lately, it felt like something was missing. And now he knew what it was.

It was Libby. Libby Brown—or maybe Libby Rawlins.

The realization slammed into him like a gust of Wyoming wind—the kind that whirled up from nowhere when you least expected it. The kind that slammed into you and nearly knocked you down. He half expected his hat to blow off.

"So what did you fight about, son?"

He gave her a blank stare. "What did who fight about?"

Things were pretty bad when his memory was worse than his mom's.

"You and Mike," she said.

"Mike's got some problems, Mom," he said. "If he comes back, you need to use the cell phone. Do you have it?"

She rummaged in the pocket of her sweatsuit and flourished a small silver phone.

"You need to call me if he comes back, okay? Call me right away. I have to go find Libby. I—I have to talk to her."

"It's about time," She made a shooing motion with both hands. "You go get her, son. Go get her."

Chapter 33

LIBBY DONNED HER OLDEST CUTOFFS, STUFFED HER hair up into a ball cap, and grabbed a pitchfork. She'd lose herself in work—any work, whether it needed doing or not. Hard, physical work would fill her mind, pushing out last night's attack, Crazy Mike, and, most of all, Luke.

Fortunately, chickens grow up fast and make a God-awful mess doing it. She'd owned her new charges all of a month, and they'd already transformed their stall in the barn into a revolting mass of guano. It was time for them to graduate to the henhouse.

She trucked across the lawn with long, determined strides, wielding the pitchfork like a weapon, but playing Wonder Woman couldn't erase last night's helplessness from her mind. She couldn't forget how scared she'd been, knowing there was an intruder in the house, or how vulnerable she was out on the plains all by herself. If Mike had wanted to kill her, she'd be dead. End of story.

But did Mike really want to hurt her? What exactly was going on in that mixed-up mind of his? He hadn't been after her. He'd thought she was Cash.

So what would make him think Cash was sneaking around her house at night? And why would he think he had to protect her from the town sheriff, of all people? Maybe he really was crazy—but there had to be a reason

why his twisted mind would settle on an officer of the law as someone to be feared.

She'd have to ask Cash about his run-ins with Crazy Mike. She knew he'd found the little dog dead in the woods, and she knew he'd had to calm Mike down on a couple of occasions at the Roundup. But maybe there was more.

And if Crazy Mike was responsible for Della's disappearance, maybe there was a lot more. Guilt and fear can scramble a sane mind; no doubt they could really do a number on somebody like Crazy Mike.

She glanced around the barnyard. Crazy Mike could be holed up in any one of the rickety outbuildings. He could be crouching behind the stack of hay bales beside the barn. He could be ducked down beside the rusty tractor that was permanently parked by the paddock.

He could be anywhere. Waiting. Watching her.

She heaved a sigh of relief when the cruiser finally pulled into the driveway. Maybe Cash had good news.

"Find him?" she called.

Cash hauled himself out of the cruiser and slumped against it, resting his arms on the roof. "Nope," he said. His uniform, usually so crisp and neat, was wrinkled and dirty. Stubble stood out on his chin and cheeks, and dark pouches hung under his red-rimmed eyes. He looked battered and exhausted.

"We've been out all night," he said, his shoulders slumped in defeat. "No sign of him anywhere."

"Where could he have gone?" she asked.

"You have to remember who he is, Libby. His dad was obsessed with hunting and woodcraft, and he taught Crazy Mike everything he knew. That boy's

done nothing but tramp the land for most of his life. He knows how to stalk every kind of animal without being detected, and trust me, most animals are a lot more attuned to a man's presence in the wild than any of my deputies could hope to be."

"So he's out there somewhere."

"Yup. We checked out his house, and there's no sign he's been back. We did find some interesting things in his workshop, though."

"The nail polish, and the hairbrush? The little purse?"

His eyes widened. "How do you know about those?"

Libby gave herself a mental slap and fooled with the wire on a hay bale to avoid his gaze. "My chickens... I need to get this henhouse ready." Her back was to the sheriff, but she could feel his hard look.

"How do you know about the stuff in his workshop, Libby?"

She turned and faced him. "I was in there. I checked it out."

"When?"

"Remember the day Rooster was poisoned? The night you came out to the farm?"

"Yeah. You were here with Luke. I definitely remember. Oh, shit. I thought you'd been out in the woods. You had leaves and twigs in your hair. I figured you guys had been getting it on in the great outdoors."

"Well, we weren't. I told you we weren't. I was out at Mike's place. I was looking for evidence, and I found it."

"Libby, that's crazy. I know you don't like to hear this, but you're taking risks you don't need to take."

"I'm taking risks I choose to take, Cash," she said. "You told me you'd pick up Mike if the toxicology

tests were positive for arsenic, and then you never did. I had to take matters into my own hands. I know it was dangerous, but it was worth it." She couldn't resist a triumphant grin. "Found it a week before you did."

"And did what with it? Libby, what you did wasn't detective work. It was breaking and entering." He paced the length of the chicken house, his hands knotted behind his back. "Did you touch anything?" he asked. "Because I've got three men over there now dusting for fingerprints, and it won't be a good thing if yours turn up all over that stuff." He slumped against the wall. "I finally got a good reason to get a search warrant for that place, and it turns out you've been there and fouled up the evidence. You need to stop interfering in this investigation."

"Whatever, Cash," she said coldly. "I'm sorry if you feel I'm interfering."

"Why are you mad at me? Can't you see my point of view?" He turned away and resumed his pacing. "The evidence in that drawer could go a long way toward solving Della's disappearance. There's nothing more important to me than proving Crazy Mike killed Della—nothing. I've been trying to tie things together for over two years, and now I've finally got what I need and it turns out you knew about it all along." He stopped in front of her and spread his hands. "Why didn't you tell me?"

"I just... couldn't." She stared intently at her left foot as she traced elaborate patterns in the dust of the driveway. The truth was, she'd realized she couldn't take her information to the sheriff. She had taken unnecessary risks, with her safety and with the evidence. Her anger deflated like a punctured balloon.

"Okay," he said. "You realize this could be a problem,

right? I mean, a good defense attorney could argue that you planted the evidence to set Mike up."

"Cash, I'm sorry." She took a deep breath. She hated apologizing. Now Cash would have the upper hand. "I guess I didn't think things through well enough to realize I might screw up your case."

"It's okay." He nodded, but his eyes were stern. "But you really need to leave this to me. You're a journalist, not a detective. You're free to follow along and write about the investigation, but it's not your job to go looking for clues yourself, okay? You just let me lead the way."

He looked down at her, and for a minute she was afraid he was going to poke her "pretty little nose" again. He didn't, but his tone of voice was so condescending she wanted to poke his—with her fist.

"I'll tell you what," he said. "I'll still let you come along when I go see Brandy tomorrow, okay?"

She clenched her teeth and took a deep breath. The guy was an ass. She knew that. She'd known it from the first time she'd met him. She ought to just back off, let him go to Cheyenne on his own. Chances were, Brandy didn't have any information to offer anyway.

But what if she did? Libby had found more evidence in two weeks than Cash had found in two years. If he went on his own, Cash might miss something important.

She'd have to go. She'd put up with him one last time.

"Okay," she said. "Tomorrow."

Chapter 34

POWERED BY SHERIFF-INSPIRED FURY, IT TOOK LIBBY less than an hour to finish her chicken coop revamp. She swept the worn floorboards, then hosed them down and let them dry in the sun. She tossed forkfuls of bright new straw under the roosts. It was hardly good agrarian economy to use that much straw for a few chickens, but it made the place look more like a Fisher Price farm. She spread a few handfuls of feed in the yard, then released the chicks into their pen and sat down in the open doorway of Lackaduck's finest henhouse.

She hadn't talked to Mary in over a week. Flipping her cell phone open, she dialed and got an answer on the second ring.

"Libby! I was just thinking about you. Did you get to visit Della's friends?"

"One of them. Luke and I went up to Billings to visit Larissa on Wednesday."

"Did she help?"

"Not really. She mostly wanted to talk about Skydancer."

Mrs. McCarthy sighed. "Still horse crazy."

"Whatever happened to that horse, Mary? Larissa said nobody's seen any Skydancer offspring in years."

"I don't know."

"You sold him, right? Who bought him?"

"I don't know. The buyer used an agent, so I never found out who it was."

"An agent?"

"It's apparently not uncommon among the top breeders to use a confidential agent to purchase stock. If one breeder wants a particular horse, he doesn't want anyone else to know what he's up to. I guess the name of the customer could be used to jack the price up by starting a bidding war. It's a competitive profession."

"Why didn't you send the horse to auction? Or advertise him?"

"He'd lost condition so badly without Della to exercise him. We couldn't bear to part with him at first. Selling him felt like giving up on our daughter, so he just stayed out there in the barn. He'd gotten really difficult to care for. My husband used to go out there and feed him, even try to brush him a little, but he was bitten several times. Kicked, too. Finally, one day, the horse knocked him down and just about stomped him to death in the stall. Sometimes I think that's what led to John's stroke. Then this agent showed up, and he offered us a really good price. We decided to take it." She caught her breath. "The day they took Skydancer away was the first time I faced the fact that Della was really and truly gone."

Libby paused, giving Mary time to collect herself, unable to imagine the grief she'd suffered.

"Mary, who was the agent? I'd like to follow up on this, find out who ended up with the horse."

"Honestly, Libby, I don't know."

"The man paid you a lot of money. There must be a record of his name somewhere."

"He paid us in cash. We never reported it, and we didn't keep any records. The taxes would have taken so much of it, and John was already sick by then."

There it was—another dead end. "It probably doesn't matter," Libby said. "Maybe something happened to the horse—he had an accident or got sick."

She looked up at the sound of an approaching vehicle. It was Luke's piebald truck, bouncing up her driveway, rattling and clanging at every pothole. He pulled up across from the chicken house and stepped out. He'd changed his clothes and showered, but he must have rushed the job, because his hair was still tousled, as if he'd toweled it dry and called it good.

Tousled suited him.

"Thanks, Mary. I've got to go," she said. "I'll be in touch." She clicked the phone shut.

"Is your mom okay?"

"She's fine." Luke didn't seem willing to elaborate. They sat in silence a while, watching the chickens scratch in the grass. Luke kept taking deep breaths, as if he was about to say something, but nothing came out.

"What?" Libby finally said.

He squeezed his eyes shut tight, as if he was in pain, then opened them and met hers. "I lied to you, Libby. I'm sorry."

Oh, great. Here it came. Just in case ignoring her hadn't done the trick, he was going to put his feelings—or lack of them—into words. Confirmation that once again, she'd fallen for the wrong man.

"I told you that night at the Sleepaway wouldn't matter," he said, staring off across the yard. "I told you it wouldn't count." He took a deep breath. "I told you

we'd never have to talk about it, or think about it, again. I promised, and I try to keep my promises. I really do."

She nodded, her face impassive.

"But I think about it all the time," he said. He plucked a blade of grass and shredded it, his hands shaking. "I can't think about anything else. I'm trying, but I can't. That Twilight Zone thing? It's not working." He sighed, staring down at his boots. "That night at the Sleepaway wasn't in another dimension. It was real." He lowered his voice. "It was just about the realest thing that ever happened to me."

She lowered her eyes, looking down at the shredded blade of grass he'd tossed on the ground. That night had meant something to him too. He'd felt the connection between them, sensed the treasure they'd found. He'd only turned away because he'd told her he would.

Because he'd promised.

And he'd kept his promise—as long as he could stand to.

"I know I promised I'd never mention it again. But I feel like I'm lying to you, pretending it didn't matter. I have to tell you the truth." He sighed. "I'm an idiot," he said. "I thought we could just be together once—just get over each other, you know? But it made it worse. Or, not worse. I mean better. It made it real." He took a deep breath. "Libby, I'm sorry. I'm in love with you. I can't help it."

"I can't help it either," she said. She turned and faced him. "And I don't want to."

"You can't… you…"

She'd sworn she'd never say those words to a man again. She'd sworn she'd never make herself that vulnerable. But Luke was giving her everything, all of himself, without holding back, and he deserved the truth.

"I love you too," she said.

He gasped and pulled her into his arms, curling his fingers in her hair, kissing her with a passion he must have been holding inside for the past two days, holding her as if he was scared she'd bolt if he let her loose. This was the real Luke, uncut and unedited, giving her everything he had to offer. A matching heat spread through her body like a spark running up a fuse, and she kissed him back with equal fervor, telling him with her lips and her body what she'd never been bold enough to put into words. His hands moved down her back and he eased her into the fragrant straw.

Good thing she'd just cleaned the chicken house.

"Now you'll have straw in your hair," he murmured. His lips moved down her neck as he fumbled with the buttons on her shirt. She ran her fingers through his hair, pulling him closer.

"Libby," he murmured. She felt a delicious sense of helplessness as her back arched against his body. She was tired of fighting. So tired. For once in her life, surrender was coming easy.

Trust was coming easy.

"Can we go inside?" she whispered.

He nodded and she struggled to stand, but he swept her up in his arms and carried her Rhett Butler-style across the yard and into the house.

"Frankly, Scarlett," he said as he swung her through the doorway, "I give a damn." He grinned. "Matter of fact, I give a whole lot of damns."

They were almost to the sofa when a barrage of barks sounded from behind the house. Luke set her down on the cushions and paused, listening.

"What was that?"

"Who knows?" Libby grabbed his hand. "And who cares? They bark at everything. Don't worry about it."

"It could be Mike." He pulled his hand away. "I'd better check."

He strode out the front door. Libby followed him partway, but her legs were so wobbly she had to sit down on the front steps. Good thing she didn't have nearby neighbors. Her shirt was half-unbuttoned, and she had no doubt her hair had progressed beyond tousled to tangled.

Wild Thing strutted out of the shrubbery and crossed the lawn, her head jutting comically with every mincing step. Spotting Libby, she let out a shocked squawk and ran behind the henhouse, useless wings flapping noisily.

Libby ran her fingers through her hair and came up with a handful of straw.

"So I'm a little bit of a mess," she said to the chicken. "What else is new?"

Chapter 35

Luke headed back around the house, hoping Libby's mood hadn't changed. The dogs had been barking at a tumbleweed; there was no Crazy Mike lurking in the sagebrush, no truck vandal plotting nefarious deeds in the outhouse.

She was waiting for him on the front step, with straw in her hair and her shirt half-undone. Luke thought he'd never seen anything more beautiful. If he'd been willing to share, he'd have taken her picture and pasted it up on a billboard, just to show the world what he'd found.

But Libby probably wouldn't be too crazy about that idea.

"Come here," he said, reaching a hand down to help her up. Wordlessly, he led her through the kitchen, up the stairs, and into the bedroom. It was late afternoon, and the sun slanting through the windows tinted everything with warm sunset colors, bringing out hints of pink and gold in the tender skin that sloped into Libby's half-bared cleavage, tempting him to touch. She sat on the side of the bed and he slid her shirt from her shoulders, kissing each fresh swath of her skin as it was uncovered, inch by inch. When he finally peeled the shirt away altogether, he pushed her back onto the frilly pillows she kept at the head of the bed. She looked even more beautiful in that golden light than she had on the steps—if that was even possible.

"This is right," he said. "This is how I wanted it to be." He brushed his lips over hers and smoothed his fingers over her skin, stroking carefully, almost experimentally, dipping into the hollow of her throat, tracing the curve of her hip, teasing the tips of her breasts. She sighed and surged under his hands like a warm tide rising to meet him. When he palmed her breasts, she closed her eyes and tilted her head back, giving herself up to him, and he moved his palms in careful circles, feeling her nipples rise and tighten. He undid the clasp between her breasts and lifted the filmy fabric away, then resumed his ministrations, alternating light, teasing touches with firmer ones that soothed and slowed the tingling needs he'd created.

He ran his finger across her belly, tracing the waistline of her shorts. His hand slipped easily under the denim, under the elastic of her panties, and he watched her face as his fingers neared her center, then moved away, then slipped downward again. Her eyes were closed, her lips parted as if she was shutting out everything but the feel of him, and she looked so lovely he felt an actual pain in his heart, a yearning so strong it actually ached.

Libby closed her eyes and set herself adrift. Even in the most passionate throes of lovemaking, she'd always anchored herself to some solid reality. Even at the Sleepaway Inn, there'd been a part of her held carefully in reserve. She'd always believed that giving all of herself would somehow diminish her, weaken her.

But giving herself to Luke was different. She'd

watched him, and tested him, and chosen to trust him—and in trusting him, she'd finally trusted herself.

She reached for him and he closed his eyes, his breath slowing as if her touch was some kind of miracle to be treasured and memorized. Tracing the side of his face, the angle of his jaw, she let her fingers wander and play, working her way down to his chest, tracing the rippled muscles of his stomach, teasing the swell of his erection until he pulled her up from the pillows and kissed her breathless.

His lips moved down her neck, down her body, skimming over her skin, tasting the faint sheen of perspiration that highlighted her curves. He opened the clasp of her cutoffs and inched them down her hips, continuing his slow exploration.

She wrapped her legs around him and felt his need press against her, the denim coarse against her slippery flesh. Sucking in a quick breath, she pulled his fly open and took him in her hand, then lifted herself above him and slowly eased him inside.

He rocked her against him, moving inside her, and every cell in her body awoke. She'd never given away so much of herself, yet she'd never felt more complete. She had everything she'd ever needed, but she kept on reaching for more, tensing to take everything he had to offer.

When the tension broke, she crested on a wave of release, feeling all the joy and elation she'd expected, but also a heady sense of power and invincibility that lifted her higher still. Union with Luke made her something more than herself, something bigger and stronger and better. She tensed one last time and felt

him strain with her, and then their eyes met and they fell apart together.

—∾—

He was watching her when she woke.

"I can't wait for tomorrow," he murmured. "And the next day, and the next."

She sat up and stretched. "Actually, tomorrow kind of sucks," she said. "I have to go to Cheyenne with Cash."

"You *have* to?"

She nodded. "It's for Mary. For Della. I have to do it."

"I know," he said. "But do you have to do it with *him*?"

"Yes," she said. "I think I do. If there's ever another crime in Lackaduck—and I hope there's not, but it could happen—I need to have a decent rapport with the sheriff." She sighed. "I don't want to do it either, but I'm trying to think of it as an investment in the future. It's just one day, Luke. Just one." She smiled. "We've got dozens. Hundreds. The rest of our lives."

"I don't suppose it would help any if I came along," he said.

"Not really," she said. "The whole squeaky-toy thing makes it hard for me to get my job done."

"Good point," he said. "But maybe I could get some extra squeaking in once you're back."

"Absolutely," she said. "I'll be saving all my squeaks for you."

Chapter 36

LIBBY REALLY NEEDED TO GET HER TRUCK FIXED. SHE didn't mind driving it around Lackaduck, but she could hardly argue when Cash insisted they should drive his pristine F-250 to Cheyenne and leave the Bitchmobile parked in his driveway.

Unfortunately, playing passenger only emphasized the sidekick role Cash had forced her into. He expounded on investigative technique for most of the drive, but at least he kept his hands on the wheel and his eyes on the road. He even dropped a few tidbits about the Della McCarthy case while they followed Brandy's vague and roundabout directions to a gorgeous brick Victorian that had been chopped up into tiny apartments. Climbing the narrow attic steps, they tapped on the topmost door and heard a crash, then a thump before the door flew open.

"Sorry," their hostess said. "I tripped."

Plump and pretty, she boasted a lush cascade of spiraling blond curls and blue eyes that glowed with good humor, but it was lucky she had good looks and a nice personality, because housekeeping was definitely not her strong suit. It was no wonder she'd tripped. A threadbare sofa piled with cast-off clothing was angled across the room, fronted by a cheap chrome-and-glass coffee table loaded with empty beer cans and pizza boxes that spilled off onto the floor. Shania Twain belted out a girl-power anthem from a portable stereo, and CDs littered the

floor. Libby noticed the Indigo Girls, the Dixie Chicks, and Melissa Etheridge, plus some more Shania. Either Brandy was the strong, independent type, or she was overcompensating with music.

"This is the living room," their hostess said, gesturing around the tiny space. "My kitchen's over here."

The kitchen was about the size of a walk-in closet, and was furnished with a miniature stove, a dorm refrigerator, and a rickety table and chairs. In front of a tiny window, a chipped porcelain sink was piled high with dirty dishes and smudged glassware. "I don't cook much, so it's okay it's so small. My bedroom's the real showplace," she bragged, leading them to a larger room decorated entirely in pink. Flicking on the light, she revealed a huge four-poster draped with an absurd pink fur blanket that appeared to have a brutal case of mange. Clothes littered this room too, and Libby tried not to notice the pink plastic handcuffs that dangled from one of the bedposts.

Cash noticed, though. "This looks like the rumpus room," he said, smiling wickedly.

Brandy smiled back, a predatory gleam lighting her eyes. Shania might have told her she didn't need a man in her life, but she obviously wouldn't mind sampling a few along the way.

"That's one way of putting it," she purred. "I have parties. You'll have to come sometime."

The Buffalo Bar & Grill was just around the corner from Brandy's apartment, so they opted for lunch there. She assured them the food was great.

"And I know the bartender," she added. "So our drinks will be good and strong."

Libby started to protest that it was too early to drink, but Cash silenced her with a quick look. Right. Ply the witness with drink, and you'll get more information.

Dim lights and a dense haze of cigarette smoke almost obliterated the Buffalo's decor, which consisted mostly of old black-and-white rodeo photos, mounted in cheap dime-store frames that hung in random groupings around the seating area. Behind the bar, two battered bridles were draped strategically over a kitschy painting of a reclining nude.

"Breakfast for me," Brandy said as she settled into a dark wooden booth. "I just got up."

Libby stole a surreptitious glance at her watch. One o'clock.

Cash motioned for Libby to sit, then slid in beside her. Brandy immediately shifted to the outside end of her bench, directly across from the sheriff.

They placed their order with a frowsy waitress who had all the personality of a mannequin. Brandy ordered eggs Benedict with asparagus spears and a Bloody Mary, double tall, while Libby opted for a burger with extra pickles and a Coke. Brandy raised her eyebrows when Cash ordered a sirloin steak, rare, and a beer.

"Man food. Goodness. What is it you do up there in Lackaduck again?"

"I'm the sheriff." Cash couldn't help accompanying this line with a self-conscious hitch of his belt, despite the fact he'd locked his gun in the truck.

"Oh, I remember," Brandy said. "You were sheriff before, weren't you? When Della... you know."

"Been a while now," Cash said.

Brandy listened wide-eyed to a few Lackaduck law enforcement stories while they waited for their meals. Cash's ego was growing dangerously bloated under her lash-fluttering adoration by the time the waitress returned, a tray teetering on her upraised hand. Libby's burger was accompanied by a massive mound of steak fries, as was Cash's enormous slab of beef. Brandy's entree looked a lot healthier—two poached eggs draped in gleaming yellow hollandaise trembling delicately atop a neat row of asparagus spears.

"I'm in criminal justice too," Brandy announced. She stabbed an asparagus spear with her fork and lifted it to her mouth, licking a drop of creamy sauce from the tip and nipping off the bud. Somehow, she managed to make eating vegetables look incredibly suggestive. "Probation and parole. Well, I was, anyway."

"Not anymore?" Cash asked.

Brandy turned to Libby. "I like the bad boys, you know?" she said. "And the bad boys like me. That job was like being a kid in a candy store."

Cash snorted, then faked a cough to cover it up. "Couldn't keep your hands off the merchandise?"

"That's right." Brandy said. "I was spending too much time with a two-time offender."

"Not good," said Cash.

"Not only that, but I was two-timing the two-timer with a first-timer."

"Sounds like you had a problem managing your timers," Cash cracked.

"You could put it that way. But I was really good at multi-tasking."

"Anyway, we wanted to talk to you about Della," Libby said.

Brandy's eyes widened. "Oh, I know," she said. "But I can't."

"What do you mean, you can't?" Libby was mentally tallying the lunch bill, and cursing herself for falling for Brandy's free lunch scam.

"I was threatened." Brandy's eyes gleamed, and her voice rose with excitement. "I got a phone call last night."

"What do you mean, threatened?" Cash leaned forward and gave Brandy his best tough-guy squint. He was channeling Dirty Harry again.

Brandy's voice dropped a couple octaves as she rasped, "Keep your mouth shut about your girlfriend. Unless you want to end up like she is."

"You're kidding. When was this?" Libby asked.

"That's the weird part. It was just last night. Kind of late. So it's like whoever it was knew you were coming." Her eyes were wide with excitement. "Do you think it was the killer?"

"Maybe." Cash sat back, his fingers steepled under his chin. He was in detective mode now.

Libby remembered scrawling the number on her wipe-off board. When was that? Who could have seen it? Crazy Mike? Maybe. David? Possibly. But she hadn't written down Brandy's name—just the phone number. It was doubtful either man would make the connection.

And besides, Mike and David didn't know she was here. They'd have no reason to make the threat.

"What did the caller sound like?" the sheriff asked.

"Like someone disguising his voice," Brandy

answered. "Like on TV, when they put a hankie over the phone. All mechanical, like."

"Mechanical?"

"Yeah. You know, no inflection. Like a machine."

No inflection. "Brandy, could it have been someone, um, challenged?" Libby asked.

"Challenged? You mean, like that taxidermy guy?"

"You remember him?"

"Yeah. He was funny, I thought. And he thought Della was a goddess." She thought a minute, nibbling her thumbnail. "That's weird. I would never have thought it was him. He seemed like the gentle giant type, you know? I'd have thought he'd be more likely to protect Della than hurt her."

"That's what I thought too," Libby said. "Until the other night, when he broke into my house and attacked me."

Brandy's eyes widened. "You're kidding!"

"No, she's serious," Cash broke in. "Everybody thinks this guy's a real sweetheart, but he really loses it when things don't go his way."

"So when he doesn't get what he wants..." Brandy was getting the picture.

"Exactly. But keep your mouth zipped, Brandy," Cash warned, looking her straight in the eyes. "Don't tell anyone."

Brandy slanted her eyes toward Libby and mimed a little shiver. Then she looked up at the sheriff, meeting his eyes with a flirtatious flutter of her lashes. "Anything you say, Sheriff. Anything you say." She nipped at another asparagus bud. "And besides, I don't know anything. I mean, I know some of what went on up there. But nothing that really matters."

"Like what?" Libby probed. "What went on up there?"

Brandy glanced over at Cash and toyed with her fork, scraping pools of hollandaise sauce into swirling designs. “I shouldn’t be here,” she said. “That phone call… I shouldn’t have come.”

“Tell me.” said Cash. “I need to know. Don’t let his threats scare you.” He was staring intensely into Brandy’s eyes. “I’m here, and I’ll take care of it. I’m real good at taking care of things.”

“Wow,” Brandy simpered. “I just bet you are. You can take care of me anytime. But I can’t help being afraid.” She fluttered her eyelashes at Cash. “Still, if you’ll promise to protect me…”

Cash relaxed suddenly, his intense manner gone. “I’ll do all I can,” he promised.

“Cash is right,” Libby said, trying to keep the conversation on track. The looks Brandy was giving the sheriff were obviously shorting out the man’s brain, and no wonder. It wouldn’t have surprised Libby if the girl had wrestled the sheriff under the table and had her way with him down there on the floor. She was either desperate or oversexed. Maybe both.

“The caller probably knows you’re here,” she said. “He probably figures you told us already. So you might as well spill the beans.”

“’Cause I’m dead anyway? Right. Okay.” Brandy took a deep breath. “Della was seeing a couple guys up in Lackaduck.”

“Seeing?” Libby asked.

“Sleeping with them.”

“Who?” Cash was giving Brandy that intense stare again. She shrugged and gave him an innocent flutter of her lashes.

"You honestly don't know, do you?" he said, easing back in his seat.

"I'm not sure." Brandy quirked a catty little grin and took a sip of her drink. "I know she was really into one of your ranchers up there. She was always going on about his cute butt and his pretty green eyes. I got the impression she spent a lot of time with him."

Libby only knew one rancher in Lackaduck who fit that description. Cash caught on too. "Luke Rawlins," he said. "Had to be Luke Rawlins."

Licking the hollandaise-coated tip of another asparagus spear, Brandy nodded. "Yup. Luke Rawlins," she said. "Della was always going to his place while she was working for the vet. Supposedly she was helping him with sick cattle or something." She giggled. "Yeah, right."

Cash flashed Libby a smug look. "Funny, he never mentioned that. Now why would he keep that a secret?"

Libby sipped her drink, feigning nonchalance and praying no one would notice how much her hands were shaking. Luke and Della? Luke *knew* Della? They'd been friends? *More* than friends?

He hadn't said a word about it. Cash's question rang in her head over and over—*Why would he keep that a secret? Why?*

She gulped down a slug of coke but a heated flush rose to her face anyway, making her feel sick and sweaty. The soda went down the wrong way and left her spluttering and coughing.

"Restroom," she croaked. "Be right back."

"You all right?" Cash asked as he stood to let her pass.

"Fine. Went down the wrong way." She hacked a little more as she staggered off to the ladies' room, doubled over and gasping.

She stumbled into the handicapped stall and fell on her knees, burying her face in her hands. Luke knew Della. Maybe too well.

That was bad enough. But there was more. Luke had seen the number on the wipe-off board. He'd recognized it—even asked about it. And he was the only person who knew she and Cash were heading to Cheyenne. She'd told him last night—the night the call was made.

Libby's mind scrambled backward, reviewing every contact she'd had with her neighbor. She remembered the folder full of articles he'd brought to her house. There was no way he could have put that much information together in a single morning. No way. Libby remembered how he'd avoided her eyes when she questioned him about it.

He'd been lying. She'd thought so then, and she knew it now.

That's why he'd defended Crazy Mike so passionately. She'd admired the way he stood up for his friend, even though it seemed kind of over-the-top.

But of course it was. He knew Mike hadn't hurt Della. He knew Mike was innocent.

Because he was the one who'd done it.

Maybe it had been an accident. Maybe there were some kind of extenuating circumstances. But Luke was involved in Della's disappearance.

Why else would he hide their relationship? Why else would he make that call?

Chapter 37

Libby tasted pickles at the back of her throat and struggled to keep her lunch where it belonged. She was kneeling by the handicapped toilet, clutching the stainless steel armrests and spitting into the bowl, when she heard the restroom door swing open.

"You okay?" Brandy's face appeared upside-down under the stall door, her curls almost brushing the tiled floor.

"Fine," Libby gurgled, and spit again.

"Sure you are." Brandy said. "You want to talk about it?"

"Just feel sick," Libby said. "All of a sudden."

"Funny," Brandy mused. "It came on right when I mentioned Della's dreamboy. You got it bad, don't you?"

"No," Libby said. "It's just that we're friends. Or at least I thought we were. He—I trusted him." She felt her stomach surge and leaned over the bowl again. "And I think the meat's bad here. Really feel sick."

"More like lovesick," Brandy said.

Libby gagged once, then felt the nausea subside. "No." She stood up, tottered a little, then backed away from the toilet and out of the stall. Feeling a little dizzy, she hoisted herself up beside Brandy on the counter. "It's just—I'm always wrong about men. Always." She wiped her clammy forehead with the back of her hand.

Brandy fished a Kleenex out of her purse and handed it over. "Well, if it makes you feel any better, I'm not sure anything really happened between them," she said as Libby dabbed at the back of her neck. "She liked him, but she said either he was a saint, or he was gay. She just couldn't get a rise out of him, if you know what I mean."

"Really?" Libby's head cleared as if she'd sniffed a shot of ammonia.

"Yeah. She said he was a little slow on the uptake."

"No, he's not." The words were out before Libby could think them through, and she could feel herself flushing again. Brandy grinned and popped her hand in the air for a high five. Libby slapped it halfheartedly.

"Taking Lackaduck by storm, aren't you?" she said. "That sheriff's wishing it was him."

"No," Libby said. "He's just a friend. Not even that, really." She levered herself off the counter and onto her rubbery legs. Brandy tucked a hand under her elbow.

"Take your time," she said. "Take it easy."

Libby splashed her face with cold water and dabbed on a touch of makeup—mostly blush, to make up for her ghastly paleness. Once she'd run a brush through her hair, she felt well enough to make it back to the table on her own.

"You okay?" Cash stood to let her back into the booth.

"Fine," Libby said. "Guess that was too many pickles."

"Right. So, where were we?" he mused. "Oh, yeah. We were at the part where Luke Rawlins turned out to be a lying scumbag." His eyes were fixed on Libby as he said it, and she nodded.

"I suppose," she said. "But Brandy says nothing happened between them. I think Della was too young for

Luke to… well, you know." She was doing her best to convince herself that Luke was innocent, but the images flashing across her mental movie screen said otherwise. She saw the folder, bulging with clippings. The phone number scrawled on the wipe-off board. Luke's face, alive with passion as he defended Crazy Mike.

"She was way too young," Brandy said. "But there was somebody else that didn't care about that. Mr. Second Choice, she called him." She reached over and stole a French fry from Cash's plate and Libby noticed that his face had darkened with anger. What a jerk. It was just a French fry.

"I don't know who it was," Brandy continued. "She hinted around that it was somebody important—rich, maybe. And it was a man, she said. Not some dumb boy our age." She shrugged. "Whoever it was, she was seeing him for a long time."

"How long?" Libby asked. Della hadn't spent much time in Lackaduck, but two weeks might spell long-term relationship to someone like Brandy.

"Years. From the first time she came to Lackaduck," Brandy said. "I think it was serious, in a weird sort of way. She said he even came up to Sheridan to see her sometimes. It was a big secret."

Libby finally realized what Brandy was saying. Glancing at Cash's stricken face, she saw that he got it too. Della had met someone the first time she came to Lackaduck—when she was fifteen. And somehow, the relationship was still going on when she disappeared.

Libby had been almost sure that Crazy Mike was responsible for Della's disappearance. The strange scene at his workshop, the things in his treasure drawer, his

fear of the sheriff—it all added up. But if what Brandy said was true, someone else might have been involved too—someone who'd seduced a fifteen-year-old girl and carried on a secret relationship with her for three years.

And no matter what Brandy said, there was a good chance that person was Luke. Maybe Della had been protecting him when she'd told Brandy nothing happened between them.

"It was serious?" Cash asked. He looked pale. Libby felt a stab of sympathy. Della was underage when the affair began. And it happened on Cash's watch. Libby knew he took his duty to "serve and protect" seriously. And she was sure he was thinking he'd failed to protect Della.

"I think the guy was older," Brandy said tentatively. "Della made a big deal out of it, like they were star-crossed lovers or something. It drove Larissa crazy. She was really worried about it."

"She should have been," Cash said.

"I don't know, really." Brandy waved her hand carelessly. "Della could be a bit of a drama queen. I don't think she was, like, in love with the guy or anything."

Cash shook his head sadly. "No telling how the guy felt, though," he mumbled. "Judging from what we're piecing together here, I think maybe he was serious about her."

"Too serious," Libby said.

"Dead serious," said Brandy. She tried for a theatrical shiver, but somehow it came off as more of a jiggle. She glanced down at the sparkly watch on her wrist. "Hey, I have to go." She eyed Cash like he was yet another asparagus spear. "Could somebody walk me back to my apartment? I'm a little scared."

"I'll walk you back," Libby said, springing from her seat. "Cash, I'll meet you at the truck."

"Whoa," Brandy breathed as she and Libby waited for a break in traffic. "No offense, but I was kind of hoping your sheriff would walk me back. He's really something."

"I thought you went for the bad boys, Brandy."

"I do." A car horn sounded and Brandy waggled a fluttery finger wave at a black Trans Am that was jacked up on super-wide tires. "Bad boys all the way."

"But Cash is one of the good guys. He's not your type."

"Oh, yes he is," she said, suddenly serious. "Trust me, Libby. He's a bad boy. My radar's never wrong. Have you noticed the way he looks at you? Gives me the shivers—the good shivers. He may be the sheriff, but he's dangerous."

"You think?" Libby pictured Cash's square jaw, his bedroom eyes. Brandy was right. He didn't look like a sheriff; he looked like an outlaw. There was definitely a "bad boy" vibe there.

"Oh, yeah," Brandy said. "Definitely dangerous. You ever get tired of that one, you let me know. He's just my type. And I get the impression you might want to move on to that rancher guy."

"Cash is all yours if you want him." Libby kicked a pebble into the gutter. "And forget the rancher. Luke's a lying scumbag."

"He told you he didn't know Della?" she asked.

"No," Libby said. "He never actually said that. It's more a sin of omission. He knew I was looking into

Della's disappearance, but he never told me he even knew her. Why would he keep that a secret?"

"Well, maybe you ought to find out. Maybe she pushed him too hard. She could come on awfully strong with guys. Or maybe there was an accident out there on that lonesome ranch of his."

Libby glanced over at her as the traffic pulled to a stop and they hit the crosswalk. "Were you ever there? At his ranch?"

"Nope," she said. "I met him, but I never dated him. He was cute, but if I had to choose, I'd go for the sheriff," she said. "Much more interesting. I'd say he's capable of just about anything."

"I know. Sometimes that worries me. He gets so intense."

"Well, don't be scared, silly." Brandy nudged Libby and winked. "He'd never hurt you."

Chapter 38

By the time Libby got back to the truck, Cash was in the driver's seat, tapping a restless boot on the floorboards. He couldn't believe she'd taken off with Brandy like that. He had things to say, and he had a feeling she might not be ready to listen. Well, he'd have her to himself for the drive home, and she'd have to hear him out whether she wanted to or not.

It was funny. Most women pressured a guy for commitment long before he was ready, but Libby seemed to actually shy away from it. She'd been hurt, Cash knew.

It wasn't him. It was her.

Libby hoisted herself into the truck and fastened her seat belt.

"So, you were a big hit with Brandy," she said. She upped her voice into Brandy's flirty register and fanned her face with one hand. "My goodness, Sheriff."

"Hey, can I help it women swoon over me wherever I go?"

"Don't let it swell your head, buddy. Brandy swoons over all the boys."

"The bad boys."

"Yeah, well, she says you're one of 'em. Even if you are the sheriff. So look out. I'm onto you."

"She said that?" He couldn't help sitting up a little straighter, smiling a little broader. "She thought I was hot, didn't she?"

"She said lots of things, Cash." Libby laughed, remembering the conversation. "Remember, though, she's a multi-tasker."

"Isn't that another word for slut?" Cash asked.

"She's a nice slut, though."

He remembered Brandy's blond curls, her curvy figure, and most of all, those handcuffs.

Those handcuffs were intriguing.

"The hooker with the heart of gold. A Western staple," he said. "Like Miss Kitty in *Gunsmoke*."

"That's one way of looking at it. Although I wouldn't call her a hooker."

"Nope. Just a slut."

"Cute, though," she said.

She was right. Brandy had the kind of body every man wanted—big-busted and slim-hipped, and, most important, ready for action. He'd thought about taking her up on her offer to attend one of her parties. He'd make it a private party—just her, him, and those handcuffs. He shook his head. That wasn't the kind of woman he wanted. She might get his motor revved up, but she wouldn't keep it running.

Libby would, though.

"I'm sorry Luke disappointed you," he said.

She shrugged. "Hopefully that's all he did." She took a deep breath, and he wondered what was coming next. She looked down at her hands, then out the window—everywhere but at him. It seemed like she was trying to make up her mind about something.

"What's the matter, Libby?" He gentled his tone. "Tell me."

She inhaled again, then finally looked him in the eye. "Luke saw Brandy's number on my wipe-off board at

home, and he recognized it," she said. "I didn't have her name written down; just the number."

"You think he was the caller?"

"He could have been." She swiped at her eyes, but not before he'd caught the shine of a tear tracing the curve of her cheek.

"You know, this takes me in a completely new direction," Cash said. "I'll ask him a few questions." He patted her leg. "See? You've given me a new lead."

"Great." Swallowing hard, she looked out the window at the fallow fields and pastures hurtling past. The highway was practically empty. There weren't many reasons to travel over the barren, stony landscape between Lackaduck and Cheyenne, so they shared the road with a few tractor-trailers and a motley assortment of pickup trucks, all of them driven by men in cowboy hats.

"How 'bout a book on tape?" Cash asked. He gestured toward the stereo. "I listen to them all the time on the road. This one's pretty good."

"What is it?"

"Anne Rule," he said. "True crime stuff."

"She's great," Libby said. She sounded happier. "The best. Sometimes I think about writing one of those books myself."

"Did you ever hear how she got started?"

Libby nodded. "*The Stranger Beside Me.* She worked with Ted Bundy and wrote her first book about him. It was a huge hit, and her career took off." She twirled a strand of hair thoughtfully and stared out the window. "She found herself right in the middle of the story. Dumb luck."

"Not so lucky for all those pretty dark-haired girls he killed," Cash reminded her. "But maybe you're

lucky too. Maybe this thing about Della would make a good book."

"Not really," she said. "Ted Bundy was attractive and intelligent. That's what made it such a good story. Our story's probably about a lonely, unhappy, mentally handicapped man who apparently went berserk one time and killed a teenaged girl. I'm not sure people want to read about that."

"Maybe. But it might be about an attractive, intelligent cowboy who killed a teenaged girl." He glanced over at her hands, knotted tightly in her lap, and saw the knuckles whiten. "The Cowboy Killer. And if he was working together with the mentally handicapped man—if both of them were in on it? Wow. That would be a bestseller."

Libby swallowed hard. "Geez, Cash, thanks. Now I'll be scared to go home."

"That might not be such a bad thing," he said. He offered himself a silent congratulations on steering the conversation right where it needed to go. "You really ought to just stay at my place. I want you to feel safe."

"I'm safe," she protested. "I've got Ivan. I'll just pick up my truck and go, okay? I have work to do."

She was one stubborn lady. It was going to take more than a suggestion to change her mind.

Chapter 39

Libby had planned to pick up her truck and go straight home to avoid spending too much time with Cash—but when she saw the graceful mares and their foals milling around in the paddock she couldn't help pausing to watch. As she approached the fence, one of the foals wobbled toward her on his slender legs. Inching toward her, he flared his nostrils, extending his neck until his muzzle was just inches from her hand. Then he snorted and dodged away, dashing across the paddock with his tiny hooves flashing.

"Look at him prance," she said.

"That's the thing about Quantum's foals," Cash said. "They can really move. And look at the head and tail carriage. They look great in the ring, I can tell you. Want to see the barn? Quantum's in there. My stallion."

She hesitated. It couldn't hurt to look at the stallion. She was getting more and more interested in horses. Luke must be contagious.

She'd just check him out for a minute. Then she'd go straight home.

Cash's barn had two sections—a large area for the cattle and a stable section for the horses. They entered the stables by a separate door that opened into a long hallway paved with bricks. On one side was a single door labeled "Private"; on the other side was a row of seven spacious box stalls, each heaped with clean straw

bedding over a rubber mat to protect the horses' feet from the hard concrete floor. At the end of the walkway was an enormous support post that led up past the hayloft to the roof of the barn, where streaks of sunlight peeped through the shingled roof.

"What's in here?" Libby rattled the locked door on the left.

"Tack room," Cash said shortly. "Nothing much. Some more ribbons and stuff, and my saddles and supplies."

Libby figured the room must be messy, since Cash didn't want her to see it. She turned and looked down the alleyway at the big support post. There was a ladder up one side, almost blocking access to the rest of the barn.

"You'd better hope you never have a fire in here."

"No kidding. That would be a bad thing," Cash said, as if she'd stated the obvious.

"No, I mean the way the barn's laid out. If the horses got going the wrong way in a fire, they'd come up against this post. They won't go backwards in a fire, so they'd never get out."

"They can get around it." He demonstrated by squeezing through the gap, then back on the other side. "It's tight, but it's not like I'm keeping Clydesdales in here. Actually, it works out fine. The opening provides cross-ventilation, but it's too small for the cattle to get through."

He led Libby to a box stall and swung open the top half of the door. "This is the guy, here. Daddy to all those foals out there."

Libby peered in, expecting to see a showy chestnut like the foal, but the horse that swung its head around and nickered wasn't nearly as impressive as his offspring. She didn't know much about horses, but Quantum didn't

look like a winner to her. His color was a muddy brown, and his legs seemed too short for his height.

"Nice," she said, cautiously.

"Not really," Cash said with a short laugh. "He doesn't look like much. But he's from awesome bloodlines, and I knew he'd breed me winners." He grinned. "Everybody laughed when I bought him, said I didn't know what I was doing. But I proved 'em wrong. I mean, you saw those foals out there."

Libby reached up and stroked the stallion's neck. "He's sweet," she said. "I thought stallions were mean."

"Not this one." Cash turned and started down the aisle. "Great temperament."

Libby lagged behind, petting the horse. He sure didn't look like a pricey foundation stallion, but what did she know? She was stroking his nose when she heard a rustling noise in the straw. Quantum shifted nervously as a skittering shadow crossed the back of the stall.

"Hey, Cash," she called out. "There's a mouse in here." Quantum was jigging in place now, and his eyes rolled nervously as another, larger shadow bolted under his feet. "A rat!" she screeched. "Cash!"

"I know," he said. "I bought this place seven years ago, and you should have seen it. The stalls were knee-deep in manure, and there were old grain sacks everywhere. That's why I got the Bobcat—to clear out the mess." He gestured toward the barnyard, where a tiny white bulldozer with a cab barely big enough to hold a driver was parked in the sunshine.

"Oh, that's the thing you guys use for that square dance thing," Libby exclaimed. She went over and checked out the little machine. "It's cute!"

"It's a great toy, and it cleaned out the barn in no time. I've done everything else I can think of to cut down on the pest population, but this place is still infested with rats and mice like you wouldn't believe. It drives the horses crazy."

"You need Jack Russells," Libby said. "You make fun of my dogs, but they'd have this place cleaned out like that." She snapped her fingers.

"You think?"

"I know," she said, an idea forming in her head. "You should let my little Verminators pay you a visit. They'd get rid of your problem in no time."

"So those little sissy dogs can make themselves useful, huh?" Cash looked thoughtful. "Maybe you should bring them over sometime." He turned to face her. "I'm going to a law enforcement conference in Rock Springs tomorrow, but maybe Wednesday?"

"I don't know, Cash," she said. He was doing it again—gathering up the reins, pulling them tight, trying to steer her his way. He stepped closer—too close. She was practically backed up against the wall. He set his hands against the wall beside her shoulders.

Damn. She was trapped. And now he was going to kiss her.

Or at least he was going to try. She turned her head and started to duck away under his arm.

"Hey, come on," he said. He grabbed her shoulders and pressed her against the wall, grinding his hips into hers. She felt him twitch against her belly, and a bolt of revulsion and panic shot through her, making her dizzy and sick. She tried to squirm away, but he was too big. Too strong.

"No," she said. She writhed against him, trying to break away, but the motion only seemed to excite him. He crushed her breast under one hand as he moved the other to the waist of her jeans and fumbled with the buckle on her belt.

"No!" Reflexively, she jerked her knee up hard, hitting him in the crotch, and twisted away. Without stopping to see if she'd hurt him, she ran for the door, fastening her jeans with shaking hands and tugging her shirt back into place. She slammed the barn door behind her, then ran across the yard and jumped into her truck, locking the doors as soon as she was safe inside. Resting her head on the steering wheel, she tried to stop shaking, wondering if she'd be able to drive.

The barn door swung open. Cash's silhouette filled the doorway. He was hunched over, obviously in pain, but his clenched fists hung at his sides, ready for action.

"Hey," he called. "Wait a minute!"

Shaking or not, she had to get out of there. Cranking the key in the ignition, she gunned the accelerator and reeled out of the driveway.

Chapter 40

Libby knew something was wrong the minute she pulled into her driveway. Light beamed from every window, and an eerie silence hung over the house. Ivan wasn't in his usual spot on the front step, and there was no sign of the puppies. Normally, there would be a chorus of yelps and barks the minute she pulled in.

"Penny?" she called. No answer. Something was definitely wrong.

It had to be Crazy Mike. He was back. He'd killed her dogs, and he was waiting in there for her. She turned off the engine, shut off the headlights, and sat frozen in the truck, wondering what to do next.

She reached into her purse and fished around for her cell phone. She could call her home number and see if anybody answered. She ran her hand through her jumbled belongings—wallet, checkbook, spare keys. No cell phone. She cursed herself silently. She must have left her phone in the house when she'd left for Cash's place earlier that day.

She clicked off the dome light and eased the car door open, sliding out of the seat. Her feet hit the gravel driveway with a crunch that seemed loud enough to wake the whole state. She didn't dare shut the car door—it would explode like a gunshot in the quiet Wyoming night. Stealthily, she crept up to the house, placing each foot carefully, testing her footing before she shifted her

weight. Walk like an Indian, she thought. Be quiet, be quiet. She was almost to the house when she felt something poke her in the butt.

"No!" She whirled and kicked out, banging her ankle against a rock-hard skull covered with fur. Ivan. Playfully, he jumped up and knocked her down on the grass.

"Shhhh." She grabbed his collar and hugged him hard. "What's up, boy?" she whispered. "Where are the puppies? Who's in there?" The big dog licked her face and flailed at her chest with his paw. So much for canine intelligence. A killer was in there waiting for her, and Ivan wanted to shake hands. He'd probably shown Crazy Mike right to the door.

"Staaay," she hissed, forcing him into a sit. "Wait." Knees bent, she crab-walked over to the side of the house, where a dim radiance fanned out from the living room window. She plastered herself against the side of the house and peered through a break in the curtains.

She was right. Someone was in there. She could just see the end of the sofa and one side of the coffee table. An empty beer bottle stood on the table, and Penny lay on the floor. She looked dead, or maybe drugged, her head lolling, her feet in the air. There was a puppy beside her, lying on his side. The intruder lay on the sofa, but all Libby could see from her vantage point was a pair of cowboy boots, caked with mud, crossed on the armrest. Damn. He was going to ruin her furniture before he killed her.

She crouched beside the house and thought. She needed a plan. She couldn't go back for Cash now. She'd have to shut the door to the pickup and start the engine, and that would alert her uninvited guest to her

presence. He'd be gone before she got back, and they'd lose him again. Cash would be furious.

There was a can of mace in her glove compartment. The boots hadn't moved, so her quarry was probably asleep. Either that, or he was watching and listening. She'd have to be careful. Hopefully, she could sneak in the back door and disable him before he realized she was there.

Getting back to the car seemed to take hours. The mace canister was right where she always kept it. Shoving it in her back pocket, she bent almost double and ran around to the back of the house.

She was worried about jingling her keys, but she didn't need them. The door was unlocked, and swung inward without a sound. She held the mace in front of her at arm's length, imitating the FBI agents she'd seen in movies, swinging from wall to wall with smooth, sudden moves. She needed to get through the kitchen. That would get her around to the back of the sofa, so she could take her quarry by surprise.

The kitchen was a mess. Someone had helped themselves to popcorn, of all things. A torn microwave popcorn bag lay on the counter, spewing unpopped kernels. Three empty beer bottles sat in the sink. The cookie jar where she kept the dogs' treats was open and half empty. That explained how he'd silenced her puppies. Tears sprang to her eyes as she thought of Penny and her babies, how excited they must have been to see someone, anyone; how they'd probably sat up and begged on their hind legs for poisoned milk bones.

They should have been begging for their lives, she thought grimly.

A noise behind her made her spin, aiming the mace toward a skittering, scratching sound. It was Rooster, running into the kitchen. She almost cried out, but she caught herself and grabbed him, lifting him against her chest. He trembled, then heaved the contents of his stomach all over her good shirt. Popcorn. And beer. Ever since the arsenic incident, he threw up even more than Rotgut. The poison probably never had a chance to enter his system. Clutching the puppy to her chest, she edged into the doorway, peering into the living room.

There was someone on the sofa, but it wasn't Crazy Mike.

Chapter 41

It was Luke.

A half-finished bowl of popcorn was propped between his legs, and his head was thrown back on a pile of pillows. A faint snore rose from his open mouth, and he had a sleeping puppy cradled in one arm.

He sure didn't look like a serial killer. Libby dodged back into the kitchen to collect her thoughts.

Should she tell him the game was up, or play dumb? If she played dumb, he'd probably try to kiss her again. Incredibly, despite all she'd learned from Brandy, she felt a wave of anticipation at the thought. She had to remind herself that this wasn't the boy next door anymore. This was the Killer Cowboy, subject of her upcoming bestseller. A single man over thirty who lived with his mother. He had known the missing girl and kept their relationship a secret. He had collected news stories about the crime the way some guys collect baseball cards, and he'd recognized Brandy's number just hours before the girl got a mysterious threatening phone call—a phone call that concerned an interview only he knew was going to happen. He'd defended Crazy Mike passionately even though local law enforcement was certain the taxidermist was guilty.

Of course, local law enforcement was Cash McIntyre, and he had his own issues—but still, there was probably enough circumstantial evidence on Luke to merit a search warrant. Maybe even an arrest.

So why couldn't she believe he was guilty?

Because.

Because somewhere deep inside her, the sight of him ignited a spark of love that stubbornly, stupidly refused to die. If Luke really was the Killer Cowboy, she wasn't the intrepid reporter who uncovered his dastardly deeds. She was his next victim, lured to her doom by his good looks and charm.

Unless she killed him first, for making a muddy mess of the only decent piece of furniture she owned. In her scrambled mental state, the fact that his muddy boots had soiled the fragile upholstery of her antique sofa suddenly enraged her beyond reason.

Swearing, she threw the mace container at him. It bounced off his chest, releasing a puff of spray, and hit the floor. Penny raised her head groggily, blinking, annoyed at this interruption to her beauty sleep.

"Hey!" Luke spluttered, coughing. The mace hadn't hit him full in the face, but the chemical traces in the air were enough to make him choke. His eyes watering, he peered over the back of the sofa and saw Libby standing in the doorway.

"Nice," he said, still coughing. "You sure know how to wake a guy up." He squinted at his watch. "It's late," he said accusingly.

"I know. What are you doing here?" she asked.

Uh-oh. He knew that tone. It meant he was in trouble.

It wasn't fair. She was the one who should be in trouble. He understood she'd had to go to Cheyenne with the sheriff, but did that really take all day and half

the night? She'd said she might be late for the puppies' dinnertime, but it was nearly nine.

"I was watching your dogs," he said. "You told me to."

"I told you to check on them and feed them," she said, "I didn't tell you to stay here, and I certainly didn't tell you to mess up my kitchen, eat my food, drink my beer, and get mud all over my furniture."

"I was waiting up for you. I wanted to make sure you got home okay."

"What are you now, my dad?"

"No." Hardly. The way he felt about her would be totally inappropriate if he were her dad. "But if I was, I'd be awfully upset with you. It's late."

"I—I was busy."

"Where? Doing what?"

"At—at Cash's house."

He swallowed a half dozen questions—*What were you doing there? Did anything happen between the two of you? Why didn't you hurry home to me?* But he didn't ask any of them. She trusted him, and he'd have to trust her. But it still hurt to think of her spending time with Cash McIntyre.

He sat up, setting the puppy on a pillow, and began brushing dried mud off the sofa with tense, vicious motions. "It's a good thing I stayed," he said. "Your dogs do have to go out once in a while, you know. Ivan's out there now. You would have come home to a worse mess than mud on the sofa, Libby."

"Hey, things got—complicated. I couldn't help it."

He squinted at her. His eyes were still unfocused and sleepy, but even through his blurred vision, she looked unhappy, and there was something on the front

of her shirt. It looked like she'd been puked on, but he wasn't about to say anything about it. You couldn't tell a woman her shirt looked like vomit. With his luck, some decorative chunky substance had come into fashion while he wasn't looking, and she'd be all insulted.

"Is everything okay?" he asked. "You look upset."

"I'm fine," she said, but she wouldn't meet his eyes.

"Things go all right with the sheriff?" he asked.

"Fine," she said.

"Whatever." She obviously wasn't about to tell him what had happened, but judging from her tone, things weren't looking good for the sheriff.

Good.

He picked up the sleeping puppy and cradled it against his chest. "We watched an old movie and had popcorn. Did you know your dogs like beer?" He nudged Penny with his foot and she popped up onto her back legs to beg, then swayed and fell over. She'd been doing that all night. "Penny drinks it right out of the bottle. It's cute." A piece of mystery matter fell off the front of her shirt, hitting the floor with a damp plop. Definitely vomit. "Hey, what happened to your shirt?"

"Rooster happened," Libby said. "He can't eat popcorn, Luke. And he can't drink beer, for heaven's sake. He spits up everything." She waved the little dog in his face. Rooster burped.

"Yikes." Luke mumbled. "Not on me, buddy. Save that for your mom."

Libby scooped up the beer bottles and headed for the kitchen. "Men," she said. "Idiots."

"Does that include the sheriff?" Luke tried to wipe

the sarcastic edge from his voice, but it was obvious how he felt. "What did you guys do all day, anyway?"

"Like I told you, we went to see your friend Brandy," Libby said snidely. "You were right. She's quite a gal."

"Yeah, she is," he said. "A little wild, but she's got a good heart. Not my type, though."

"Really?"

"Really."

"So." She narrowed her eyes like a CIA interrogator. "Was Della your type?"

"Della?" Where had that come from? He scratched his head. "No. Why would you ask me that?"

"Oh, no reason," she said. "We just unearthed some interesting information today, that's all." She fixed her eyes on him. "Like the fact that you had a relationship with Della."

That woke him up.

"I didn't have a relationship with Della," he said, jumping up and following her into the kitchen.

"That's not what I heard." She folded her arms across her chest and leaned against the counter. "I heard she was over at your place all the time. Helping you with your sick cattle, supposedly. I'm sure that was a lot of fun."

"Oh, it was a blast, Libby." Luke set the popcorn bowl on the counter and rolled his eyes. "There's nothing like having an oversexed teenager throw herself at you every time you turn around. I never responded, Libby. Not in any way. Hell, I finally had to call Ron Stangerson and tell him to keep her away from me. The girl had a problem, that's all."

Libby wanted to believe Luke. And his description of Della was right in line with what she'd heard from everyone else. Josie had told her about the hookups with the rodeo cowboys, and the vet had even mentioned a customer who complained about Della's advances. Apparently, Luke was that customer.

"So why didn't you tell me about it?" she asked. "Why did you keep it a secret?"

She stood back and folded her arms, tapping her foot while she waited for his answer. Not that it mattered. There was no answer in the world that would make this okay. No good reason for him to leave out the crucial detail that oh, yeah, he'd actually spent a lot of time with the missing girl. Alone. In his barn. Just him and the oversexed teenager, communing with the horses and cows.

She'd been a fool to believe in Luke Rawlins. Even if he wasn't a murderer, he was a liar, just like Bill Cooperman. Whenever she'd complained about her boss, Bill had been basking in recollections of their sneaky little get-togethers; and while she was searching clues to Della's disappearance, Luke was probably lost in memories of holding hands with the girl over the deworming guns.

"I don't know," Luke said, scuffing the floor with the toe of his boot like a guilty schoolboy. "I didn't want to say anything bad about her, you know?" He lifted his eyes to Libby's. "She's missing. Something bad happened to her. No matter how much of a tease she was, it wasn't her fault."

"Of course not."

"But if I talked about how she was, some people would blame her for what happened. You know, some people say a girl's asking for it just because she needs men to like her."

Libby stopped tapping her foot. His logic made sense. Maybe he really had been protecting Della with his silence—not himself.

Maybe he was a good guy after all.

Yeah, right. And the Easter Bunny and Santa were on their way to shower her with pixie dust. She tossed her hair and turned away, pretending to be absorbed in plumping the pillows on the sofa. Luke had kept the relationship secret, and even if it was entirely innocent, that secrecy made him unworthy of her trust. That was the bottom line, and nothing could change it.

"Besides, I was embarrassed," he said. "What would you have thought of me if I'd told you some pretty sixteen-year-old was hot for me? You would have thought I was some kind of delusional pedophile or something."

He had a point there, but she wasn't about to admit it. Besides, there was the phone call.

"So why did you call her?"

"Call who?" He looked genuinely puzzled.

"Brandy. Why did you call her and tell her not to talk about Della?"

"I didn't. I don't know what you're talking about," he said.

"Well, you saw her number on my board, and you recognized it," she said. "And you were the only one who knew we were going."

"Really? Nobody else knew?"

She shook her head.

"Cash didn't tell anybody?"

He had a point there. Maybe Cash had said something—to one of his deputies, or a friend. She slumped her shoulders, the fight flowing out of her, relief flooding in. It might not have been Luke. It might have been somebody else.

He might be telling the truth about the phone call. But still, he'd hidden his relationship with Della. He hadn't been honest with her.

She couldn't let this go. She couldn't give him her trust.

"Well, Cash will be asking you some questions about her," she said. "He was really surprised to hear she'd spent so much time at your place."

"I don't know why," Luke said. "It's not like he didn't know."

Libby shook her head. "He had no idea."

"That's not true," Luke said. "He's lying."

Libby threw her hands in the air and spun away from him. "Of course he is. That's what men do. They lie. Look, just get out, okay? I've had enough. I don't know what ever made me think you might be any different from the rest."

"I'm not lying, Libby."

"Not now," she said. "But you did. And you will."

"I never told you I didn't know her, Libby. I didn't lie. I just—I just didn't tell you, that's all."

"Well, that's enough," Libby said. "Remember that first promise you made me?"

He looked confused.

"The one where you said you'd give me background on the case?"

He nodded.

"Well, you brought me those clippings, the stuff everybody knew, right out of the paper, but you didn't tell me you knew her. You didn't tell me she'd hit on you, or whatever it is you're claiming. That's background, Luke. That's what I needed. You broke your promise."

He sighed. "Okay. I see your point. But can we get over this?" He stepped toward her with slow, cautious moves, as if she was a fractious pony he didn't want to spook. "What we have—we'll never find it again. Not with anyone else."

She shook her head and folded her arms over her chest.

"Are you telling me yesterday didn't mean anything to you? Are you going to let something like that go because I forgot to mention one little thing?"

"It's not a little thing, Luke." She folded her arms over her chest. "Not little at all. So just go, okay? Go."

He looked at her a long time, as if he was searching her eyes for forgiveness. She stared back, cold and hard, and told herself she was glad when he finally walked out without a word.

Chapter 42

MORNING CAME WAY TOO SOON. LIBBY HAD SPENT THE night tossing and turning, wondering if Luke was telling the truth about Della.

Slipping out of her T-shirt and into the shower, she wondered why it mattered so much. Even if Luke's story was true, he'd kept important information from her. He'd known Della—known her well—and he'd never told her. That was a deal-breaker, right? So why did she care what his reasons were?

She cranked the water on, closed her eyes, and let the spray spatter her face. Why did she care? Because—because she loved him.

And being Libby Brown, the inimitable, idiotic Libby Brown, she'd forgive him.

This relationship was following all her old patterns. It felt like she was walking down an old familiar road, enjoying all the lovely landmarks along the way even though she knew the journey ended in a heaving swamp of gurgling misery. She always gave her heart too soon, and once given it was gone—gone for good, for better or for worse. And with the guys she picked, it was always for worse.

Look at Cash. She'd known better than to date him, of course, and he'd never held a shred of her heart, but she'd been fool enough to follow him into his barn last night—and he'd reminded her, very effectively, that men were not to be trusted. Cranking the shower up as

hot as it would go, she lathered up a loofah and scrubbed away the soiled feeling that lingered from his touch.

Don't think about it, she told herself. Think about something else. The baby horses. She remembered the friendly one dashing across the paddock, his hooves flashing in the sun. He moved so fast, so gracefully. It was like ballet. Like…

Like twinkle-toes.

Larissa's description of Paso Fino's came back to her in a rush. *"Gaited" means they move their legs differently from other horses,* she'd said. *My husband calls my Paso gelding "Twinkle-toes."*

Maybe the foal had Paso blood in him. She was no expert, but she'd never seen a horse move like that.

And Quantum clearly was no Paso Fino. Matter of fact, Quantum wasn't much of anything. She remembered the stallion's bullet-shaped head, his concave neck, his short legs. The foal had looked like a much better horse, even to her untrained eyes.

She remembered what Cash had said. *Everybody laughed when I bought him, said I didn't know what I was doing. But I knew he'd breed me winners.*

What if Quantum wasn't a winner? What if Cash had been wrong? Would a guy like him admit his mistake, laugh about it, tell his buddies they were right?

Never. Not with an ego like his.

She slipped into shorts and a T-shirt, then tossed Luke's jacket over her shoulders. Sitting down at the kitchen table, she powered up her laptop. A few pokes at the Internet brought up a video of a Paso Fino exhibition, showing the unique Paso gait.

It matched the foal's exactly.

She felt a jolt of recognition, followed by a weird mixture of triumph and fear. Triumph that she'd caught Cash in a lie and fear of what that realization meant. She hopped up and paced the kitchen. Ivan watched her like a spectator at a tennis match, his eyes following her from one end of the room to the other.

"What do you think, buddy?" she said to him. "Does the sheriff have a secret?"

He had a secret, all right. The secret was that he'd damn near raped her. She couldn't do anything about that. Without a witness, or some kind of proof, she'd never be able to expose him for what he really was.

But if he'd done something else… something worse…

"Maybe I should go out there," she said, still talking to the dog. "Do him a big favor, and let the Verminators clean out that barn. He's at that law enforcement thing—he'll be gone all day." She tapped her chin with one finger. "All day. I'd have plenty of time to check a few things out."

She turned to Penny, who was lounging on the sofa. "What do you think, girl? Wanna catch some mice?"

Penny leapt off the sofa and ran to her, jumping up and down, reacting to the excitement in her voice.

Ivan strolled up behind them and whined. She'd feel safer if she took him along, but someone had to guard the home front. Crazy Mike was still on the loose, and she didn't want to come home to find the guy hiding under her bed or crouching in her closet.

"No, boy," she said. "You have to stay. You have to be the watchdog. Sorry, old buddy." He hung his head and shambled off, lowering himself onto the worn floorboards with a sigh and a sorrowful glance her way.

The phone rang, and the dogs joined in, barking along. Libby hollered at them to quit and picked it up.

"Hey," said Luke's voice.

"Hey," she said. She didn't know what else to say. The issue with Cash's horses had pushed the argument with Luke far into the background. Somehow, what Luke had done seemed far less earthshaking in the light of today's discoveries.

He cleared his throat. "I called—I don't know why I called, except you're mad at me and I'm miserable and…" There was a long silence. "And I love you. And I want a second chance."

She sighed. What could she say?

"I should have told you about Della. But when we first started talking about her, I didn't know you that well. I just knew you wanted to do a story on her, and I was afraid if you knew how she was, you'd put it in the paper or something. And then by the time I knew you wouldn't do that, it was too late. I couldn't find a way to bring it up. I know I should have. I know I messed up. Let me make it up to you. Full disclosure, okay? From now on."

It all made sense. She could see why he'd hidden Della's promiscuity in the first place, and she could see how hard it would have been to bring it up later.

"We'll work it out, Luke," she said. "Just give me a little time."

"Okay," he said. "How 'bout an hour? I miss you like crazy."

His voice was low and husky. It sent a thrill ricocheting through her body, lighting up every place he'd touched, reminding her of just how good his hands felt, his lips, his…

"Maybe later," she said. "I'm busy this morning."

"What are you doing?"

She didn't want to tell him she was going to Cash's, but what if he found out? Wouldn't that be just as bad as him keeping his… *acquaintance* with Della a secret? He'd promised full disclosure. It was only fair for her to do the same.

"I'm going to Cash's," she said. "He's not home, so don't worry. I saw something over there yesterday, and I want to check it out."

"Can I come along?"

"No."

She had to do this on her own. Cash had taken advantage of her—of her weakness as a woman. She needed to prove she was stronger. She needed to bring him down herself.

"Are you sure it's a good idea? Last night when you got back, you looked… upset."

"Luke, you know how your dad watches your mom? How he lets her do what she wants, make her own mistakes, live her own life? I was so impressed by that—by how much he loves her, respects her, even through her illness. I need you to be like that for me today. Let me do this on my own, okay? If you love me, let me do what I need to do."

"This is serious, isn't it?" he said. "What's going on, Libby?"

"I'll tell you later," she said. "I'll call you as soon as I get back. I promise."

He was quiet for a beat too long, but when his voice came back over the line it was sure and steady. "Okay," he said. "How about this? If I don't hear from you by noon, I'll come out and check on you."

"Okay," she said. She'd be home well before noon. What she was looking for was too big to miss, and it wouldn't take the dogs long to make mincemeat of the rodent population.

Clicking the phone shut, she slipped into Luke's jacket and piled the puppies into the truck. It was a gorgeous day, with a light breeze that carried the scent of damp earth and freshly mown grass across the plains. She checked the rearview mirror and smiled to see the puppies running from one side of the bed to the other, sniffing the air in ecstasy, yapping at trees and bushes and telephone poles.

Everything was quiet at Cash's place. Libby opened the Ranger's tailgate and let the puppies tumble out of the truck. With Penny leading the way, they raced in circles for a while, then took off for the barn that stood beside Cash's double-wide. She watched them go, marveling at how big the pups had gotten. They were nearly the size of their mother. She'd about given up on finding homes for them, although they were still adorable. She'd see how they performed as Verminators. That might be the key to talking some local ranchers into giving her babies a home.

Cautiously, she entered the barn, glancing at her watch. 10:45. She had well over an hour before Luke would start worrying. That should give her plenty of time to poke around. Plenty of time to find the horse she suspected was siring those beautiful foals.

Meanwhile, the dogs were dashing back and forth, yipping with excitement. It was clear the rats wouldn't be underfoot for long. Penny was obviously an experienced ratter, and went after every rustle in the straw

with gusto, and the puppies' instincts kicked in right away. They weren't as efficient as their mother, but she saw Rooster shaking a rat almost as big as he was, and Rocket tossing a dead mouse in the air. It was brutal, but the rodents had to go and the dogs were making short work of it.

She glanced out the window. Quantum was in the paddock, bucking and kicking up his heels, flaunting his raging testosterone. The mares were in the pasture, grazing peacefully, ignoring the stumpy stallion's histrionics. As she watched, she heard whinnying from somewhere behind her. She strained to hear as the horse whinnied again. The sound was muffled, as if the horse making it was in a separate room.

The tack room.

Cash hadn't wanted her to go in there. Maybe this was the reason why.

Libby's heart thumped as she rattled the handle on the rustic double door. It was locked, top and bottom. She could hear heavy hooves hitting the walls of the locked room, and the whinnying rose to a panicked scream.

"Hold on, baby," she said soothingly. "Hold on."

She ran over and grabbed a ring of keys that hung beside the barn door. The horse was still screaming and kicking, and her hands trembled as she tried each one in the lock.

None of the keys worked. She glanced around, looking for more keys. There was a metal first aid box nailed to the wall by the tack room door. Maybe the horse was sick. Or maybe Cash was drugging it to keep it quiet. She opened the box and looked inside. Bandages, alcohol, syringes, and bottles of medication were laid out in

neat rows. On top of the rolled bandages was a key. She turned and slid it into the padlock.

"Easy, baby," she muttered.

The key turned easily, and she eased the door open. "Okay, baby, it's okay," she purred, trying to sound relaxed. Peering into the dimness, she saw a tall, dark horse backed into the far corner of the room, pawing the straw. As soon as he saw her, he jerked his head back and screamed, eyes rolling, and lifted his front hooves to strike. She pushed the door shut and held it, her heart pounding. It was dark in there, but from what little she could see, the stall was filthy and the horse was insane. Why would Cash have this animal in his barn? She edged the door open again. The horse had calmed down a little, and stood trembling in the manure-caked straw.

"Hey," Libby said, gently. "Hey, boy." She stretched a hand cautiously toward his head. "Easy," she said softly. He turned to the left, and Libby saw a flash of white on his hip. She jerked her hand back, and the horse reared up again, spinning away from her. But she'd seen it.

That white spot was shaped just like a map of Texas.

Libby slammed the door and leaned against the rough wood paneling, her heart throbbing, her chest constricting until she could barely breathe.

Skydancer. It had to be Skydancer. Cash had the horse. He was the secret buyer. It wasn't Quantum that was breeding those mares. It was Skydancer.

Della's horse.

But why would Cash hide the horse, instead of just showing him? Why would he lie?

Libby sat in the dusty straw for a long time, thinking

hard and listening to the big horse shifting in his stall. He finally calmed down a little, so she tossed in some hay, replaced the padlock, and stepped out of the barn into the sunshine.

She headed to the field behind the barn, where the ranch's original homestead stood baking in the hot sun. She needed to know if Skydancer was the only secret Cash was hiding. He might be able to explain the presence of the horse, but she had a sick feeling that there might be more.

The dogs were busy attacking a pile of manure-caked straw that was stacked against the barn's rear wall. Penny was in front, the hair on her back raised in a ridge along her spine, her ears laid back, teeth bared. The puppies were ranged behind her. Once in a while, one would dart forward toward the mound, then yip and run back, while Penny continued a low, steady growl.

"Get 'em, guys," Libby said. The manure pile was probably a regular rodent condominium. It would keep them busy while she checked out the old house.

The abandoned homestead was old fashioned and picturesque, but it needed an awful lot of work. The porch roof sagged over broken pillars, and the windows hung crooked in their frames. Libby stepped up onto the porch and peered into the dark interior. An old wood-burning stove took up most of the far wall, along with an ancient refrigerator. A crowd of mismatched kitchen chairs cluttered the room, along with two battered wooden tables.

She moved around to the back of the house and peeked through another window. A white canopy bed with frilly lace hangings dominated this room, and an old-fashioned dresser with an oval mirror stood against

the far wall. Tiny glass horses bucked and reared in front of the mirror, and pictures of horses hung on the walls. The whole room was covered with a thin coat of dust. Libby wondered if Cash had a daughter he hadn't told her about. Maybe he'd been married before, she mused. This was clearly a room designed especially for a young girl. A horse-crazy teenager.

Like Della.

She framed her eyes with her hands to block out the sunlight and looked a little closer, then wished she hadn't.

There was a pair of handcuffs hanging from the bedpost.

Chapter 43

Libby stared at the handcuffs, so out of place among all the trappings of girlhood, and the sick feeling in her stomach intensified. She needed to go home. The scene in that bedroom told her everything she needed to know about Cash and his secrets.

She remembered their meeting with Brandy. He'd looked so threatening, so intense. "I'm really good at taking care of things," he'd said. He was warning her. He was Della's secret lover—and he was afraid Brandy knew.

Everything began to fall into place. The way he stared at Libby, looking almost angry. The way he fell silent when Josie called her a "commitmentphobe." The way he insisted he needed to be with her all the time, to protect her. His hostile attitude toward Luke. The man was obsessive—first about Della, now about her. Everything else was a cover-up—a thin fabric of lies to conceal his real nature.

Brandy was right. He really was one of the bad guys.

She glanced at her watch. 11:45. She had just enough time to get home before Luke started worrying.

"Come on, dogs," she called. "Time to go." The tall grass rustled behind her as she turned away from the window. She blinked in the bright sun, squinting up at a looming silhouette. For half a second, she thought it was Luke. Then she took in the size of it, the breadth of the shoulders. It was Cash.

"Libby," he said. He reached out and grabbed her arm.

"Cash." The sight of him made her dizzy, and her heart fluttered high in her chest, stealing her breath. "You're home early." She tried to smile, but he must have realized from her expression that she'd seen the room.

That she knew.

"I can explain this," he said, squeezing her arm.

"You don't have to." She shook her arm free, and he let it go, dropping his arms to his sides but keeping them bowed and stiff, like a gunfighter ready to draw. She scanned his hips and shoulders, checking for the bulk of a holster. As far as she could tell he was unarmed. "That was Della's room, wasn't it? Where is she, Cash? What happened?"

"I don't know," he said, shaking his head. "Honestly, Libby, I don't know. She just never came back. I don't know why. I loved her."

His voice broke on the last sentence. As far as Libby could tell, he was telling the truth. "That's sick, Cash," she said. "She was a child."

"She was seventeen," he said. "Old enough."

"Not according to the law."

"She was a woman, Libby, I swear." He shook her arm roughly, as if he could force her to understand. "As much as you are. It was her that made it happen, not me. I wasn't looking for trouble. I wouldn't have touched her. But she kept rubbing up against me, touching me, looking at me that way. I couldn't help it. And then—it got to be so special. I loved her."

He nodded toward the room. "I fixed this up for—for visits." Libby felt her stomach clench tight as a fist. "I set it up with all the things she liked—to make her

feel at home when we were together. To show her—I don't know." He slumped his shoulders and unclenched his hands, looking away. "It didn't work anyway. She stopped coming. We only used it a couple times." He lifted his head and gave her a pleading look. "You won't tell, will you?"

Sickened as she was by Cash's admission, Libby was even more repelled by his suggestion that she become a co-conspirator in his secret life.

"I have to tell, Cash," she said.

He lowered his head, and when he looked up again, his face was contorted with anger. Looking at him now, she wondered how she'd thought him attractive that first night at the Roundup. The angular jut of his cheekbones, the sharp-cut line of his jaw, the unearthly blue of his eyes—every facet of his appearance seemed frightening now as his mood shifted in a half-second from repentant to furious. He grabbed her arms, roughly this time, and almost jerked her off her feet as he shoved her against the wall of the house.

"I didn't kill her," he said. "I had an affair with her, but I didn't kill her."

She wanted to believe him. Could he be telling the truth? Maybe he'd really loved Della. Maybe it was like he said—she'd just stopped coming.

"Nobody will believe you," he said, giving her another shake. "And who are you going to tell? The state cops? They're all my friends, Libby. They're not going to listen to you."

She didn't say a word—just nodded toward the window and the room beyond it.

"That'll be gone," he said. "By the time anyone gets

here, there won't be a shred of evidence left. You've got nothing, Libby." He moved closer, pressing up against her. She could smell his desperation as he clutched her arms tighter, his fists shaking. Blood rushed to his face and a sheen of sweat broke out on his brow and cheeks.

"You've got worse than nothing," he said. His voice was hoarse and thick. "You've got me to deal with. Who knows you're here?" He shook her twice, hard. "Does anybody know?" He shook her, knocking the back of her head against the wall of the old house. His fists clenched tighter around her arms, almost lifting her off the ground as he stared into her eyes with frightening intensity.

"Luke knows," she said. "He'll be here any minute. You'd better let me go."

Cash glanced wildly right and left, then grabbed her arm and hauled her away from the house. Dammit, why had she spilled the beans about Luke? All he had going for him was surprise. He had no idea what he was walking into.

Dragging her into the barn, Cash fumbled with the padlock on the tack room door. The horse screamed as he flung it open and shoved her inside.

"Wait there," he said. "I'll take care of you later."

Chapter 44

Libby cowered in the hay as Skydancer reared and let out another panicked shriek. Great. If the sheriff didn't get around to killing her, the horse probably would. There was no sound from outside. What had happened to her dogs? She strained her ears, trying to hear what was going on outside, but the room was paneled, and apparently insulated. She remembered how muffled Skydancer's whinnies had been. No one would hear her if she screamed. And for all she knew, Cash was out there killing her dogs one by one. She stifled a sob.

The horse had stopped screaming, but his eyes were rolling crazily, and his face was pulled taut by a distorted grimace that made every vein stand out.

"Skydancer," she said softly. "It's all right, Skydancer." She tried to remember the Spanish name Larissa had mentioned. "Cielo?"

He calmed a little. She tried to remember how you were supposed to approach a frightened horse, what you were supposed to do, but all she could remember was how to hypnotize a chicken, and that probably wouldn't work. Skydancer might have lost his mind, but he was still probably smarter than a chicken.

"Look, baby, I won't hurt you. And if we ever get out of here, I'll introduce you to a friend of mine." She remembered Luke's soothing touch, his caring gaze. He'd calmed her own fears; she had no doubt he could

do the same for this frightened, damaged horse. "He'll fix you right up."

She sat up and pulled Luke's jacket off her shoulders, then rolled it into a ball and rested her head on the worn corduroy. It smelled faintly of woodsmoke and leather, with a hint of horse. The scent stirred up her memory, bringing a series of images to the surface—Luke stacking hay, Luke lying on her sofa asleep, Luke standing beside her, drying dishes as she washed them. Luke bringing her tea the morning after Crazy Mike's attack. Luke touching her hair, tucking a flyaway strand behind her ear. Luke kissing her, holding her.

She glanced at her watch. It was almost noon. She pictured Luke pulling into Cash's driveway; Cash running out of the house, gun raised; the windshield of Luke's truck exploding in a spider web of cracks around a jagged bullet-hole.

And she saw her life stretching out in front of her, empty as the barren plains outside the barn.

She had to do something. She couldn't just lie here and let Luke walk into a trap. Standing up, she shrugged into Luke's jacket. A bulletproof vest might have been a better choice, but the jacket would have to do.

She closed her eyes, trying to remember the hasp that held the tack room door closed. It had been old, and it hung crooked.

Maybe she could break it. She glanced around the room, searching for a tool. A crowbar would have been nice, but all she could find was a shovel. She snatched it up and shoved the blade between the door and the jamb.

Skydancer snorted and jerked his head back, then let out a panicked neigh and extended his neck toward her,

teeth snapping inches from her sleeve. Instinctively, she spun and he stumbled backward, his eyes on the blade of the shovel as it swung toward him. She hadn't meant to scare him, dammit. She just needed him to stay back.

"Just let me get out of here, baby," she whispered. "I'll come back for you, I promise."

She wedged the shovel blade in the door again and shoved the handle hard. The top of the door popped open and slammed against the wall. Skydancer flattened himself against the far wall, ears back, trembling, and she vaulted over the lower half of the door.

She was free. Now what? She edged along the barn wall, making for the door. Maybe Luke was here. Maybe it was going to be okay.

Or maybe Cash had already gunned him down.

She stepped out of the barn, half-expecting a scene out of the Charlie Manson playbook—bodies and blood strewn around the landscape, bloating and baking under the sun. But the place was eerily quiet. Luke's truck wasn't there, and Cash's cruiser was gone.

Gone? Where would he go? Maybe he was trying to cut Luke off. Or maybe he'd gone off to hide the evidence somewhere off the property.

She stepped out into the sunlight, the gravel crunching underfoot sounding like fireworks to her hyper-alert senses.

"Hello?" Her voice came out in a shattered croak. She tried again. "Penny?"

She took one step away from the barn, then two, walking like a cat in wet grass, mincing over the lawn

to the old house behind the barn and peering into the window of Della's room. Cash hadn't actually removed anything but the handcuffs, but the room looked utterly different—and totally unlike an actual room. It looked more like the rest of the house—like a storage area, with the bed and dresser shoved up against the wall, the pictures removed from the walls and piled on the floor. If she'd seen the room she was looking at now, she never would have suspected its true use.

A sharp bark sounded from behind the barn. She glanced around the corner and there was Rotgut, covered in cow shit. He was beyond hearing her, but he wasn't dead like she'd feared. Instead, he was still feverishly digging at the manure pile with the blind concentration Jack Russells bring to everything they do.

"Come on, Rotty," she called, her voice quavering. At least she had one dog left. "Time to go." She strode briskly toward her truck, hoping he'd follow, but he barely lifted his head from the hole where his frantic paws were tossing up a cloud of flaked manure.

Libby walked over to pick up the dog, intending to carry his struggling body back to the truck, but she caught a glint of sunlight sparking off something where he'd been digging.

"What did you find, buddy?" Her stomach clenched with dread. "Come on. Just leave it."

The dog ignored her, paws scrambling, dirt flying. She watched, frozen in fear and fascination, as he uncovered his treasure. Then he yipped once and disappeared into the ground as it gave way beneath him.

Libby knelt and shoveled dirt away with her hands, uncovering the hole he'd fallen through, her stomach

heaving in anticipation of what she'd find. The hole was about two feet long and a foot wide, and it opened into a cavernous underground space. She reached in and grabbed the dog, hauling him out by the scruff of his neck. Then she braced herself and looked inside.

It was a car. She'd uncovered the open sunroof, which let in just enough light so she could make out the compost-heaped seats and the steering wheel. She peered inside. There was nothing in there but a couple of beer cans and some fast-food wrappers. A graduation tassel hung from the rearview mirror.

This had to be Della's car. Buried under the manure pile at Cash's house.

Libby straightened, her mind scrambling, readjusting to the sure knowledge that Cash had, in fact, killed Della.

He must have. He had Della's horse. He'd hidden her car. And that room…

She didn't know why he hadn't killed Libby herself yet. Maybe she'd just gotten lucky, but she didn't expect that luck to hold out for long. "Come on," she whispered to Rotgut.

Maybe she could get away. Or maybe Luke would finally get here.

She hoped Cash hadn't intercepted him somehow.

She'd barely taken one step toward freedom when she heard the sound of an engine roaring up the driveway, then cutting off. Gravel crunched in the driveway.

Someone was coming. Please, please, let it be Luke, she thought. Please.

A car door slammed and someone swore in a low, angry voice.

It wasn't Luke.

Chapter 45

CASH STEPPED AROUND THE CORNER, HIS FACE SET IN A tense scowl. Rotgut ran at him, barking, and Cash kicked him out of the way. The little dog hightailed it around the side of the barn, yelping with pain.

"Having an interesting time, Libby?" he asked. Casually, he leaned against the corner of the barn. This time he was armed. He pulled his sidearm from the holster and eyed her through the sights. "Got the case cracked now, don't you?"

"No, Cash," she stammered. "I know it looks bad, but I figure you've got an explanation. I mean, you didn't want anyone to know the car was here. That's okay. You probably found her, didn't you? You knew she was dead, and you didn't want to tell her mother, right? Or something like that. There are lots of reasons for the car to be here, Cash."

"No, there's only one reason, and you know what it is," Cash said grimly. "What are we going to do here, Libby?"

He was going to shoot her. That much was obvious—unless she could think of something to say—something that would make him give up. Something that would speak to his good side. He had to have a good side, didn't he? Doesn't everyone?

Her mind dashed through every true crime book she'd ever read, looking for a way out of this situation. Murderers had big egos, didn't they? Maybe she could

convince Cash she was in love with him. Too much in love to tell. The idea made her sick, but it was worth a try.

"It's okay, Cash. I won't tell," she said. "I understand."

"Sure you do," he said roughly. "You don't understand, Libby. The only thing you understand is that damned career of yours. You'd be the big hero, wouldn't you, if you found Della? The big investigative reporter who made a fool of the town sheriff. Well, that's never going to happen. Not in my town."

Stepping forward, he raised the gun and cocked it. Libby grabbed a shovel that was slanted into the dung heap and swung it at him, but he grabbed it with one hand and wrenched it away, spinning it and slamming the blade against the side of her head. She barely had time to see the rusty metal coming toward her before the whole world exploded in a flash of pain. *You really do see stars when somebody hits you on the head*, she thought. *Green ones, and purple*. Her legs collapsed beneath her.

When she came to, Cash was bending over her. She started to reach for him to pull herself up, then thought better of it. If he thought she was unconscious, or even dead, he'd be more careless. Maybe he'd slip up and she could get away.

She visualized herself as a sack of sand and went limp as he lifted her, letting her mouth hang open. She even drooled a little bit. Usually she drooled for a different reason around men, and she faked something other than unconsciousness once in a while, but this had turned into a different kind of relationship. He swung her over his shoulder—it was all she could do not to yelp—and carried her over to the dung heap.

He was going to put her in the car.

Every nightmare she'd ever had about being buried alive ran through her head as Cash stuffed her through the sunroof and sat her in the passenger seat.

She heard a hard click as he cocked the gun. Carefully, she cracked one eye open. All she could see was the dashboard of Della's car, the graduation tassel swaying gently.

She willed her body limp and collapsed sideways, letting her head loll to one side so she could peek up at Cash looming above her, the black hole of the gun barrel staring straight at her like a flat, lifeless eye. She tensed, weighing her options.

She didn't have any.

She was trapped like a gopher in a hole.

"Shit," Cash said. He lowered the gun, then slid it back into the holster.

"Sorry, Libby," he muttered as he turned away.

She figured that was about all she was going to see of Cash's good side.

Next thing Libby knew, it was raining compost. She concentrated hard on lying still as the stinking dirt showered down on her. He was going to bury her in cow manure. Could anything be worse? She started hoping he'd change his mind and shoot her after all.

"This isn't going to work," Cash mumbled, and tossed the shovel aside. She heard him walk away, and used the opportunity to shift her position. Where was he going? Did she have time to run? She bent her legs and crouched, ready to spring. In the distance, she heard an engine start. He really was crazy. Or stupid. Or maybe he thought she was dead.

In any case, he was leaving.

Libby moved over to the center console, pulling herself up so she could peek out of her intended grave. She must have looked like a prairie dog, poking her head out of the ground and swiveling in all directions. Just when she thought the coast was clear, just as she was getting ready to climb out, the engine noise got louder and Cash careened around the side of the barn in the Bobcat. Heading for the dung heap, he lowered the scoop and charged.

Strategy be damned. Libby was getting out of there.

She sprang upward, banging her knee on the sunroof as she vaulted out of the car. Stumbling, she ran across the barnyard. Cash and the Bobcat were between her and the truck, so she headed for the barn. Maybe he wouldn't see her. Maybe she could get out the other side.

She yanked the door shut behind her, but she slammed it too hard. It bounced open as Cash spun the Bobcat, raised the scoop, and sped inside. The machine raked against the side wall, yanking the bottom of the tack room door off its hinges. Great. If Cash didn't kill her, Skydancer would.

The stallion bounded out the door, screaming in fear as the Bobcat ground to a halt. The engine groaned and roared, struggling to climb the wreckage of the tack room door as the big horse skittered and slid on the brick floor, desperate for a way out.

Libby was trapped. One way was the Bobcat, with Cash swearing and red-faced at the wheel. The other way was Skydancer, his eyes rolling crazily. It wasn't much of a choice. She turned and grabbed the horse's mane, swinging herself against his side, struggling to scramble on board. He was slick with sweat, but she

managed to hang on, half-sitting, half-lying on the stallion's back.

The big horse reared and spun, heading for the center pole. Libby tried to flatten herself against his flanks, but it was no use. The opening was just too small. As Skydancer bolted for freedom, she hit the pole hard and slid to the ground.

The roar of an angry engine filled the barn as Cash freed the Bobcat from the rubble of the tack room door and floored it, careening down the alley straight toward her. Ten seconds and he'd be on her. She wasn't sure what he planned to do, but she wasn't about to lie there and find out.

She grabbed a rung of the hayloft ladder and hauled herself to her feet. The barn seemed to revolve around her with the pole as its axis, spinning until she couldn't see straight. All she could do was stagger around the pole to the other side. She couldn't escape—but at least she wouldn't be crushed to death by the Bobcat.

Cash would have to kill her some other way.

The pole shuddered as the machine slammed into it at top speed. She heard Cash curse as he jumped out of the cockpit and ran to her side.

She braced herself for the shot.

Chapter 46

Libby woke up with her head in Cash's lap. She didn't even try to move.

She'd given up. She didn't care what happened to her anymore. Her vision was foggy, her ankle hurt, she was scraped and bruised all over, and she knew it was just a matter of time before Cash put her out of her misery.

Good. The sooner the better.

"Wake up, Libby," Cash was saying. "Wake up." He was slapping her cheek with one hand while the other supported her head. She thought about faking unconsciousness again, but it was too much work.

"I'm awake. Stop it." She swiped at him, trying to make him stop smacking her.

"Sorry." He started stroking her hair as he rocked from side to side. "Sorry about everything, Libby. I was hoping we could be together, you know? I was hoping you'd help me forget."

"Yeah, right." She tried to laugh, but it came out more of a groan. "I thought you were one of the good guys, Cash." Everything got blurry again, but this time it was tears.

"I am," he said, rubbing her arm and looking her in the eyes. He obviously believed what he was saying. "I am. She was the bad one, Libby. You don't know what she was like."

Now she had to laugh. "Who, Della?" she asked incredulously. "A seventeen-year-old girl was the bad one? No, Cash. It was you."

"You have to understand, Libby. She was evil."

His voice seemed to fade into the distance, and darkness was closing in on her. She let her head drop, but he slapped her awake. Hard.

"Listen to me, Libby," he said, and slapped her again. She struggled to open her eyes and focus. "She was evil, but I didn't kill her."

"You didn't?"

He shook his head. "No. We were just playing a game. I thought I'd teach her a lesson. Make her miss me, you know—so she'd want me more. I only left her for a little while. I was going to come back."

"You were playing a game?" Libby wished she could take the question back as soon as it left her lips. She didn't want to know what kind of games Cash had played with his teenaged victim.

Because whatever Cash believed, a seventeen-year-old girl was not evil. A seventeen-year-old girl sleeping with a man like Cash was a victim.

"You saw the handcuffs," he said. "She liked me to…"

"No." Libby's voice was weirdly loud in the quiet barn. "Don't tell me about it."

"But I have to, Libby. So you understand. So you know I didn't kill her. I just left her there, just for a little while."

Libby closed her eyes tight against the image of Della handcuffed and helpless, alone in that room.

"Crazy Mike found her, Libby. It was terrible."

"Crazy—no," Libby said. "No."

"He found her, and he broke her neck. Kind of like that little dog he had. It was terrible."

"No," she said again. It was all she could manage.

"See, she'd made him mad once before. He'd tried to hug her or something, and she pushed him away."

Libby remembered Mike with his grisly jackrabbit puppets and nodded. The motion made her head ache, as if parts of her brain had broken off and were bashing around inside her skull, but she waited for the pain to stop and thought about what he'd said. It didn't make sense.

"But why didn't you arrest him, then? Why didn't you report it?"

"Because then they'd know," he said. "They'd know about me. About Della. So I hid her. And I scared him so he'd never tell and he'd never do it again."

Things were getting hazy again.

"Him? Who?" she asked.

She couldn't remember what they were talking about.

Smack. Cash hit her again, harder this time. "Wake up, Libby," he said. "I'm trying to tell you. It wasn't me. It was Mike."

"I'm awake. I am," she mumbled. "Tell me." She tried to nod, but it made everything go black again. She knew he'd hit her again if she passed out, but she just wanted to rest, to sink into darkness. Just for a minute.

"You're not listening, Libby," he said. His tone was darker now. "I'm going to have to end this."

"No." She tried to lift her head, but he pushed her off into the straw and stood up.

"I thought I could explain this to you, but you won't listen," he said sternly. He stood over her, drawing the

gun from its leather sheath and pointing it at her head. "It's over, Libby."

"No," she said again, but she really didn't care. Everything was fading out again. She heard a soft click as he cocked the gun. There was a loud bang, unbelievably loud, like the world exploding all around her, but no pain.

No bullet.

How could he miss? She'd fallen back into the straw when the gun went off, and she laid there, trying to figure out why she wasn't dead. Maybe she could fake it again, she thought. She wanted to open her eyes, to see what he was doing, but she kept them shut. Maybe he'd think he'd killed her. Maybe he'd go away. Maybe she was going to live after all.

But she heard the click of the pistol and knew there was no hope. Everything went black as the gun roared again.

Chapter 47

Libby woke to something wet on her face and a horrible smell like dead fish. Someone was slapping her face again, with something damp this time, and she groaned. Not Cash. Not again. She opened her eyes, and Rotgut was standing over her, licking her face and breathing his horrible doggy breath into her face.

"Rotgut?" Maybe Cash had killed her dog, too, and they were in heaven. She'd always wondered if you got to see your pets again in the next world. Surely dogs would have better breath in heaven, though. She tried to sit up, and a sharp ache pierced her temple.

Nope. This definitely was not heaven.

"Libby!" She turned her head and saw someone standing over her in the dim light.

"Cash?"

"No, Libby, it's me. Mike. Mike Cresswell."

She tried to turn over and realized Cash was beside her, lying on his back. His eyes were wide and unseeing, and a thin rivulet of blood trailed from his ear, staining the straw.

"Mike?" Libby stared up at him through the haze, remembering Cash's story. Mike had killed Della. That was why he'd been so angry when she was asking questions. That's why he'd gotten so upset in the bar. He'd killed Della, and now he was going to kill her.

"I found you," Mike said. "I found your dogs. Well,

kind of they found me. All but that one." He nodded toward Rotgut and she shuddered, wondering if he'd killed the rest of them yet.

As her eyes grew accustomed to the dimness, she saw he had a gun—a shotgun, like the one Luke kept in his truck. He was holding it loosely under one arm, his finger on the trigger, his other hand supporting the barrel and aiming it directly at her. She closed her eyes against the weird fairy fireworks dancing in the air and waited for the blast that would kill her.

Her life didn't flash before her eyes, like all the old stories say. Instead, an endless parade of regrets marched through her mind. She remembered that first night in Lackaduck, when she'd looked out at the desolate prairie and realized nobody would miss her if she were lifted out of the world, murdered or abducted. That had changed now. Mrs. McCarthy would miss her. And Crystal, and Josie. David would miss her too. And Luke.

Luke would definitely miss her.

She'd miss them too. Because of them, she was starting to feel like she'd found the place where she belonged. But she'd never told any of them what they meant to her.

She kept her eyes closed, feeling tears hot against her eyelids, but she still sensed it when the room suddenly darkened even more. Something was cutting off the light that angled through the open door. She opened her eyes and saw another silhouette looming behind Mike.

It was Luke—unmistakably Luke, with his long legs and battered hat. He didn't stand in that doorway long. He couldn't have. It was a minute, maybe even less. But

in that short time, Libby's whole world rearranged itself around a single fact.

She loved him.

Loved him.

She'd wanted men before, even needed them—but Luke, she loved. She'd said it, and she'd meant it, but she hadn't realized what it meant until now.

And when Crazy Mike turned, swinging the barrel of the gun toward the doorway, she realized she wasn't ready to give up after all.

She clenched her teeth against the pain of the bright light shimmering around her field of vision and struggled to hold on to consciousness. Bracing one foot against the post, she gathered every ounce of strength she had and kicked out hard, grabbing for Mike's boot with both hands. She clutched it and twisted, clenching her teeth, and an arrow of pain shot through her head and exploded as Mike fell to the floor and a final gunshot shattered the twilight.

"Libby! Libby! You awake?"

Would people ever stop hitting her? She'd had about all she could take. She flapped her hand in the direction of the voice, trying to slap it away, and somebody grabbed her hand. She cracked her eyes open, then closed them again. The light was too bright.

"Libby?"

Why couldn't everybody just leave her alone? She thought death would be lonesome and dark, but apparently not. Apparently dead people were subject to all the same aggravations as live people. Cautiously, she turned her head and cracked her eyes open again.

Luke. It was Luke. He was sitting beside her, holding her hand. She opened her eyes a little wider. Things were coming into focus. He was smiling. He looked beautiful. Sensationally beautiful. Like an angel. A halo of flickering light surrounded his head.

Crazy Mike must have killed them both.

"Are we dead?" she asked.

He laughed. "No. Not quite. Cash is, though, and you hit your head pretty hard. You really should wear a helmet when you ride a crazed Paso Fino into a support post."

She tried to sit up. "I can't move my legs," she said, panicked.

"You're covered with dogs," Luke said.

She looked down and saw the puppies draped over her legs and feet. She was on her own sofa, safe at home. The dogs were on the sofa and all was right with the world. Mostly.

"They look all fuzzy," she said. "I mean, more than usual. And they all have halos. That can't *possibly* be right."

"That's the concussion," he said. "You're going to be okay, though. How do you feel?"

She looked up at him and the flood of feelings that had washed over her when he'd walked into the barn swept through her again. Judging from the look on his face, he was feeling the same way. She squeezed his hand and sighed.

"Are you okay?" he asked gently.

She nodded. Everything hurt, but she was alive. That was way more than she'd expected earlier in the afternoon.

"How 'bout you?"

"I'm fine," he said. "It's you I'm worried about."

"You should be," she said. "You need me."

"You're right. I do," he said. "What made you see the light?"

Libby leaned back against the pillows, struggling to focus her eyes and trying to figure out where her gunshot wounds were. She must have hit her head really hard. She couldn't even tell where she'd been shot.

"You need me to look out for you," she said. "Like back at the barn." She dredged up a grin from somewhere deep inside. "I saved your butt."

He gave her a blank look, and she wondered if she'd let his good looks distract her from a less-than-stellar brain.

"Mike was going to shoot you, Luke," she explained.

"Oh," Luke said. He looked down at his hands with a tight little smile, as if he was suppressing laughter. "Yeah. Uh, thanks."

She nodded graciously, but her moment was cut short when the door swung open. Two of the puppies sat up and barked.

"Oh, and look," Luke said. "Here he is now."

Crazy Mike stood in the doorway, all two-hundred-odd pounds of him, blushing like a May queen behind a bouquet of daisies.

Chapter 48

"It's okay, Libby." Luke pulled away the pillow she'd clapped over her face at the sight of Mike in the doorway. "He's on our side. He was there with me," he said. "He's my backup."

"Your wingman," Mike said.

"Right." Mike laid the flowers on the end table and went through his complicated handshake with Luke as Libby looked from one to the other, her eyes wide, her mouth opening and closing like a gasping goldfish. She finally managed to croak out a few words.

"So you're telling me…"

"It was Mike who shot Cash, Libby," Luke said.

"After Cash shot me?"

Luke shook his head. "He didn't shoot you, hon. He never got the chance."

"I saved you, Libby," Mike said cheerfully.

"What?" Nothing was making any sense.

"It's true," Luke said. "Those gunshots were Mike's. He got Cash just as he was about to pull the trigger on you."

"But—but you disappeared," Libby said to Mike. "After you, um, broke into my house."

"I was hiding," Mike said. "In the woods, out behind Cash's place." He hung his head. "I'm sorry I scared you, Libby. But I was so afraid the sheriff would hurt you. That's why I guarded you."

"That's why you were in my house."

"That's right. I thought he was there. And, I don't know, I'd been thinking about it a whole lot, and Luke says sometimes I go overboard about stuff. I thought he was there, and I knew, I just knew he was going to hurt you. So I came in and I was waiting for him. Then when you came up behind me, I thought you were him." He sighed. "Luke says I gotta lay off the Mickey Spillane. He says it's going to my head."

"But how did you know Cash was a bad guy?" Libby asked.

"I knew about him and Della," Mike said. "I told him I was going to tell. So he killed my little dog, my Barney, and he said he'd kill me too if I told."

"Oh, Mike. He told me *you* killed the dog," Libby said. "But he couldn't have killed you."

Mike stared down at the floor. "He killed Barney. And he could have put me in jail. He did, once, to show me what it was like. I didn't like it in jail, Libby. I didn't want to go back. So I couldn't tell. Then he poisoned your dog. The puppy."

She couldn't bear to tell Mike she'd thought he was responsible for that too. But he knew.

"He tried to make you think I did it. He took my stuff, the stuff in the bottle, so you'd think it was me."

She remembered how quickly Cash laid the blame for Rooster's poisoning with Mike. He'd promised to pick up Mike for questioning if the toxicology tests said arsenic. But he never did.

"*Nothing's more important to me than proving Crazy Mike killed Della,*" he'd said. "*Nothing.*"

No wonder. If he "proved" Mike killed Della, no

one would ever uncover his secret. Everyone would stop looking.

Even Libby.

"So when I saw the dogs running loose, I could tell something wasn't right. And I grabbed my gun and I came in and I shot him." He grinned. "Those little dogs saved you."

"No, Mike. You did," she said, dredging up a faint smile. "You're the good guy," she told him. "Just like in your books. You're the one who rescued the dame."

"I know," he said, squirming with pleasure. "So are you going to write about it? In the paper? With my picture?"

She smiled. "I sure am," she said. "I think *The Holler* might sell a lot of papers that day."

"Heck, you should write a book," Luke said.

"I should," she said. "I could."

"You have all the stories," Mike said. "From my folder. I kept all the stories about Della."

Libby looked over at Luke. "That explains it," she said. "It was Mike's folder."

Mike nodded enthusiastically. "Luke said we shouldn't tell it was mine. He said you'd think I was ob… obstressed. But it'll help you write the book."

A surge of excitement surfaced from Libby's drugged lethargy, leaving her dizzy and weak. "I was right in the middle of the story," she said.

"You sure were." The light went out of Luke's eyes. "But that never should have happened. I should have followed my instincts. I should have warned you about Cash."

"And said what? That the guy gave you the creeps and you didn't know why?" Libby shrugged, then

winced as a jolt of pain zipped up her arm. "I wouldn't have listened."

She looked up at a rap on the door frame to see David framed in the doorway. "You would have listened to me," he said. Josie stood beside him, her gray eyes solemn. "Because I knew."

"You knew Cash killed Della?" she said. "And you didn't tell?"

First excitement, now anger. Her head was spinning, and the concussion was the least of her problems.

David ducked his head, and Josie put her arm around his shoulders and gave him a quick squeeze. The chef breathed deep, then released his confession in a rush of words.

"I knew she'd, um, spent time with him. I didn't realize how long it went on, though. I told her to stay away from him." He sat down, hands shaking slightly. "I thought she ended it. She told me she wouldn't see him again. She promised."

"Della was a good friend," Josie said. "But she liked to keep secrets. Even from the people who cared about her."

"When she disappeared, I tried to tell myself it couldn't have been him," David continued. "I thought she'd kept her promise. I wanted to believe her." He hung his head. "And I sure didn't want to go up against the sheriff. I knew he'd find a way to get me if I told. I'd end up back in prison, Libby." He slumped his shoulders. "If I'd known what would happen, I'd have told, and to heck with the consequences. You have to believe me, Libby. I'd have gone back gladly if I'd known it would save Della."

"It's not your fault, David," Libby said, reaching for his hand. He squeezed hers, and she squeezed back. "She

made her own choices." She smiled, trying to lighten the mood. "Women just don't listen."

"You can say that again," Luke said.

Mike was standing awkwardly by the door, shifting from one foot to the other. "I gotta go," he said. "Stuff to do at home."

"Well, thanks, Mike." The words sounded weak after all that had happened, but they were the best Libby could do. "Thanks so much."

He waved away her gratitude and grinned. "Okay."

"Come see me again."

"I will."

"Mike." Luke's voice was low and stern. "Didn't you forget something?"

Mike hung his head and nodded. Digging in his back pocket, he pulled out Libby's change purse. "I'm sorry," he said. "I—I don't know why I do it. I just like to have stuff—you know, from people I like. So I can kind of be with them. When I get lonesome." He glanced over at Luke. "I'm going to stop doing it, though. It's kind of crazy, I guess. That's what Luke says."

Libby took the coin purse from his outstretched hand. "It's okay, Mike. I understand."

And she did. She knew about being lonesome. She looked down at the puppies lying across her lap and remembered how they'd helped ease the isolation when she'd first come to Lackaduck. Hoisting Rooster up into the air, she gave him a quick kiss on the nose, then handed him to Mike.

"Here," she said. "He's yours, Mike. That way you won't be so lonesome anymore, and you won't have to take stuff."

She'd expected Mike to grab the puppy and run, but he actually recoiled. Maybe she'd misjudged him. Maybe he didn't want another dog after what had happened to Barney.

"Aren't you afraid I'll hurt him?" he asked.

Libby shook her head. "I know you'll take good care of him."

"Wow." Mike reached out and gently took the dog, then stared down at the little animal as if he'd been given a Fabergé egg or an honorary degree from Harvard. "Thank you." He clasped the puppy gently to his chest and his voice dropped to a whisper. "I love him already." He shuffled out of the room, his broad shoulders hunched, his head bowed over his new best friend.

"We're out of here too." David patted her leg. "We just—I needed to see you were okay. And we wanted to tell you, Josie and me—we're—we're good. We're together."

Josie smiled, and for a moment Libby remembered the snapshot of the teenaged Josie Wales grinning through her braces, sunny and confident, her whole life in front of her.

"Life's too short, you know? Too short to put things off." Josie took a deep breath, and her voice barely shook as she said, "Della taught me that."

Libby watched the two of them leave, feeling very, very small. "I was so wrong about everything," she said.

"You couldn't help it." Luke patted her hand. "You had Cash around, filling your mind with garbage, telling you lies."

"I didn't have to believe him."

Penny jumped up onto the sofa and wriggled her way between them. They sat quietly, stroking her soft fur.

"That was a good thing you did for Rooster," Luke said. "And for Mike. But I wonder how the rest of the dogs will be with the horse."

"Horse?"

He grinned. "According to Ron Stangerson, you have a very delicate, um, backside, or something like that."

"What? Oh, yeah. I told him I wanted a Paso Fino."

"Well, now you've got one."

Libby snapped upright, ignoring the pain in her head. "What?"

"Skydancer needed a home, so he and Glenda trucked him over here. He's out in that little stable David fixed up for you. He's calmed down a lot, but he's still scared to go outside. Cash kept him hidden so long he's scared of the sky. He let me touch him today, though."

Libby felt tears burn behind her eyes. "Will he be okay?"

Luke nodded. "It's going to take some time, but yeah. He'll learn to trust people again."

Libby remembered the desperate, panicked animal racing through Cash's barn, slick with sweat, crazed with terror. "I don't know how to help him," she whispered.

"He'll be fine," Luke said. "You two can heal together." He stroked his fingers through her hair. "You'll help each other, and I'll help you both."

Libby nodded, picturing Skydancer pacing her paddock, his hooves flashing in that unique, twinkle-toed gait. She imagined riding him, gliding across the endless plains outside her window, getting to know where the birds nested, learning the placement of every rock and tree. Maybe then the land would really belong to her, and more important, she'd belong to the land.

She must have dozed off, because when she opened her eyes, the sky outside the window was dark. Luke was still beside her, though, slouched on the sofa fast asleep, with her hand still clasped in his, her legs draped over his lap.

"Luke?" she said softly.

He opened his eyes and gave her a gentle smile, and love hit her with a blow that almost knocked her off the couch.

"Did they find her? Della?"

He nodded.

"Does Mrs. McCarthy know?"

He nodded, his expression sobering. "The state troopers told her."

Libby edged closer to him and rested her head on his shoulder.

"At least she can stop looking now," he said. "Stop looking, and start grieving. At least she has closure."

Libby felt tears burning behind her eyes. Could there ever really be closure? For Mary? For herself?

Maybe. She felt like she'd laid a ghost to rest. A ghost that had haunted her, and Mary, and the entire town of Lackaduck.

Libby knew Della now. She wasn't the perfect pretty teen she'd conjured from her portrait on the web. She was a girl, almost a woman, flawed and foolish as Libby herself, who'd chosen the wrong man and suffered worse consequences than anyone ever deserves.

Libby could identify with that. But the hurt she'd suffered was a hurt that would heal.

Chapter 49

"So," Luke said. "David and Josie are together. Are we…?"

Libby looked up at the ceiling in mock contemplation. "I don't know. Will you wear the chaps?"

Luke nodded.

"To bed?"

He grinned. "You want me to put them on now?"

"Not necessary," she said. "Not necessary at all." She pulled him down beside her, wrapping her arms around his neck, and kissed him.

And kissed him some more. He returned the kiss, gently and tenderly, stroking her sore ribs, handling her with all the care he could, but she pressed hard against him, arching her back. He'd planned to take care of her, to help her rest, but now she was all fired up. Resting seemed to be the last thing on her mind.

"Don't you have a headache?" he asked.

"I suddenly feel a lot better," Libby said. "We ranch women are resilient."

Wow. Maybe he'd get lucky after all.

But he was already lucky. Lucky she'd come to Lackaduck in the first place. Lucky to be here beside her. Lucky to have her in his life.

"We should get married," he said.

"Whoa." Libby pulled away. "You're moving a little fast here."

"We cowboys are like that," he said. "We rope 'em and tie 'em in 12.5 seconds."

"The roping and tying might be interesting," she said. "But I was hoping things would take a little longer."

"I was talking about baby cows," he said. "With women, I like to take my time." A mischievous glint lit his eyes. "But I'll bet I can get you to moo."

"Is that a dare?"

"No. It's a promise. And I always keep my promises."

"I know you do," Libby said. "I know."

She rested her head on his shoulder, and suddenly the mood in the room changed as surely as if the lights had dimmed and "Sea of Love" had swelled from the stereo. He kissed her, sweetly and slowly, taking his time. All the desperation of their previous encounters was gone. The last time he'd kissed her, he'd thought they might never touch again. This time, he knew it was forever. It was a keeper kiss—long, luscious, and so precious he swore he'd hold it in his mind forever.

"You should be in bed," he murmured when the kiss broke. "*We* should be in bed."

"I don't know." She gave him her most seductive smile. "I was thinking we'd christen the sofa. It's French Victorian Baroque Provincial, you know."

"And that means…"

"That means we could do it all four ways. That kiss was the French part."

He glanced nervously over his shoulder at the carvings on the sofa's high back. "I don't know. Victorian—that doesn't sound too exciting."

"Hey, you don't know how wild those repressed

women could get. You snap off those corsets and there was no stopping them."

"No?"

"No."

"Show me." He tugged at her T-shirt, feeling a shiver skitter over her skin. He slipped his hands beneath the soft fabric and cupped her breasts.

She moaned.

"That was a moo," he whispered.

Libby moaned again, just to prove it wasn't.

He took her hand and tried to tug her off the sofa. She made a little mew of protest. Cows, kittens—she was a regular barnyard festival. If the chicken thing didn't work out, she could always get a job with Looney Tunes.

"We're fine right here," she said, tugging at his shirt. She hooked a finger inside the waistband of his jeans. "Come on," she whispered.

"I can't," he said. "Not on the sofa."

"You *can't*?" She scooted back on the cushions. "What do you have against my sofa?"

"It's *them*," he said, pointing to the carved cherubs on the back. "It's like having babies watch us. It's wrong, somehow. And besides, they're flailing around with that ribbon thing. It's like they're going to swoop down and capture me or something."

"Hmm," she said. "You're worried about being captured by babies. Sounds like a commitment issue to me."

"Not a chance," he said. His face grew serious. "I'm yours, and you know it. Always."

"Always?"

"Always. Babies, whatever. Heck, we've already got puppies."

We, she thought. He'd said *we*. What other man would be willing to take on the Terrors? He was committed, all right. Or at least, he should be.

To an institution.

Luke bent down and wrapped one arm around Libby's shoulders while he tucked the other one under her knees and hoisted her up against his chest. He kissed her all the way to the bedroom, and then he laid her on the bed and kissed her some more, moving his hands over her body, stroking and smoothing, touching and teasing.

He looked down at her face, feeling helpless and powerful all at once, possessed and possessive, and caught his breath, stunned by the look she gave him. It was as open and soft as her body had ever been. It offered him everything, her thoughts, her feelings, her life—her trust. He'd never realized how wounded she'd been until he saw her healed, never realized how much hurt she'd held inside until she finally let it go.

"Make love to me," she said. "It's not the concussion, I swear. I know exactly what I'm doing." She tugged at his shirt, releasing the snaps one by one. As they opened, she recited, "I, Libby Brown..." *snap...* "do solemnly swear..." *snap...* "that I am of sound mind and body..." *snap...* "especially body..." *snap...*

He fell back on the bed, trying to laugh, but he could barely breathe. Every ounce of him was focused on her—on her body, her heart, her sweet soul. He wanted

to know her, see her, love her. Especially love her. And he wanted to do it right.

She looked up at him, open, trusting, and more than ready. She was finally his.

And he was hers. All hers.

"Luke," she said. "I have to tell you something."

He swallowed a hot bolt of panic. There was something wrong. She was already married. She'd discovered she was a lesbian. She was in love with David. Or maybe Ivan.

Whatever it was, he'd have to hear it. And then they'd talk about it, and together they'd work it out. They could do anything together.

He took a deep breath. "What?" he asked.

A slow smile spread across her face and a wicked glint lit her eyes.

"Moo," she said.

Luke held Libby close, his eyes sleepy and satisfied. "Every night," he said. "Imagine this every night."

It was a tempting notion, but Libby knew she wasn't like this every night. The day had charged her up, pumping her full of adrenaline and endorphins and whatever other chemicals make every light brighter, every sound sharper, every taste sweeter, and every nerve more sensitive.

What would it really be like, having Luke with her every day? Would they get used to each other? Would they take each other for granted?

"I don't know about this marriage thing," she said. "I mean, I'd come in from a hard day with the chickens,

and you'd be all worn out from chasing cows around, or whatever it is you do all day…"

"Cattle," he said. "I work cattle. And train horses."

"Oh, yeah. Cattle. But anyway, you'd be all worn out from that, and maybe we'd just kind of grunt at each other like old people and turn over and go to sleep."

"Oh, there'd be grunting, all right. But for all the right reasons. I mean, look at us now. You're tired from solving a two-year-old murder and fighting off a killer, and I'm tired from worrying about you. And in spite of all that, we both managed to work up a little Wild West rodeo action. And I'll bet you're ready for another go-round."

He shouldn't have reminded her of what her day had been like. All those energizing chemicals blew out of her system like air from a punctured balloon. Suddenly, she felt exhausted.

"I don't know, Luke," she said. "I'm pretty tired. Maybe I should just go to bed."

"Okay," he said.

She sat up. "Okay?"

He was giving up way too easily. Didn't he realize she wanted to be coaxed? He was so good at everything else, she'd figured his coaxing would be world-class.

"Yeah. We should just go to bed," he said.

"We? You're staying?"

He nodded. "Every time I leave you alone, you get attacked by somebody—Crazy Mike, the sheriff, those bikers from the bar… I figure you could use a break."

She sighed. "You got that right."

She hadn't thought about the other side of marriage. If you were married, sleeping together wasn't just sex. It

was lying side by side, cuddling, snuggling. It wouldn't just be exciting and alluring and knock-your-socks-off sexy—it would be *nice*. It would be like washing the dishes together. Like cooking dinner. Like stacking hay together in the barn.

It would be a good life, shared.

She crawled under the covers and curled up on her side. Luke spooned his body around hers, and she was so tired she didn't even think about what the next day would bring, or the next month, or the next year. She just knew he was Luke, and he was hers, and having him there made her feel safe and warm and wanted.

She closed her eyes. It was over. She knew who the bad guy was. More important, she knew who the good guys were, and one of them—the best of them—was lying there beside her, keeping her safe.

She'd survived her broken heart. She'd moved halfway across the country, made a home in an empty landscape, forged friendships with total strangers. And somewhere in all that, she'd found the place where she belonged.

"You okay?" Luke asked.

Libby took a quick inventory. Her arm hurt, her ankle throbbed, and her head still ached a little. Cash was dead, her effort to live an independent life was an utter failure, and she was sure her hair was an unprecedented mess.

But Luke was there, and he was holding her close.

"I'm fine," she said, and for the first time in forever, she meant it. "I'm fine as long as you're here."

THE END

Acknowledgments

Writing acknowledgments is kind of like composing an Oscar speech: you may never need it, but you'd better be ready just in case you ever get lucky. So hold the music—I've been working on this since I was ten years old, and it's going to take a while.

Luke and Libby would still be locked in my laptop were it not for my supportive friends. Hugs and true gratitude to Vanessa and Troy Keiper, Laura Macomber, Gail Brown, and Mel Schwartz. And to Jeff Brown, my first and best writing buddy, special thanks for tolerating my self-obsessed monologues every day at work and always being so generous with your support. You know you're next! I'm forever grateful to the Cheyenne Area Writers' Group: Jeana Byrne, Mary Gilgannon, Heather Jensen, Liz Roadifer, and Mike Shay, for talking me through the tough times, and to Rocky Mountain Fiction Writers, whose conferences gave me my start. Ten truckloads of gourmet chocolate would not be enough to repay the dedication of the amazing Elaine English, my agent, friend, and hand-holder-in-chief, who took a chance on a new writer and never, never, never gave up.

And of course, I'd like to thank my Academy—the amazing women of Sourcebooks, including my talented and patient editor Deb Werksman, the inspirational Dominique Raccah, the hard-working Danielle Jackson,

and the oh-so-cool sorority of Casablanca authors. Thanks for giving me a part in your show!

I'm eternally grateful to Scott McCauley for guiding me through the technological universe; to Alycia Fleury, for inspiring me with her beautiful family; and to Brian Davis, for adding what was missing in my life. They say you can choose your friends but not your family; I've been lucky enough to pick both.

But most of all, thanks to Scrape McCauley, all-around champion boyfriend, who never stopped believing in me even when I doubted myself. No romance writer could invent a hero as generous and supportive as you, and no reader would ever believe a girl could be so lucky.

About the Author

Joanne Kennedy lives in Cheyenne, Wyoming, with two dogs and a retired fighter pilot.

The dogs are relatively well-behaved.

For more from Joanne Kennedy,
read on for an excerpt from

One Fine COWBOY

Coming in Fall 2010 from Sourcebooks Casablanca

Chapter 1

THE COWBOY BOOT WAS THE MOST PATHETIC PIECE OF footwear Charlie had ever seen. Upended on a fencepost, it was dried out and sun-baked into dog-bone quality rawhide. She glanced down at the directions in the dude ranch brochure.

After pavement ends, go 1.6 miles and turn right. Boot on fencepost points toward ranch.

The boot's drooping toe pointed straight down toward the ground. Evidently, Latigo Ranch was located somewhere in the vicinity of hell.

No surprise there.

Still, the boot was a welcome sight, signaling the last leg of the weird Western treasure hunt laid out in the brochure, and putting Charlie one step closer to getting done with this cowboy nonsense and going home to New Jersey where she belonged. Back to New Brunswick, with its crowded streets and endless pavement; its nonstop soundtrack of whining sirens; its Grease Trucks and commuter buses. Back to the smog-smudged brick of New Jersey and the slightly metallic, smoky scent of home.

Wyoming, on the other hand, smelled disturbingly organic, like sagebrush and cowflops, and offered nothing but endless expanses of featureless prairie with a few twisted pines wringing a scant living out of the rocky ground. If this was home on the range, the deer and the

antelope were evidently taking the summer off. She hadn't seen so much as a prairie dog at play since she'd crossed the Nebraska border.

Cranking the steering wheel to the right, Charlie let her back end spin up a plume of dust, then winced as the Celica jerked to a halt. Hauling on the emergency break and flinging open the door, she stomped around to the front of the car to watch the right front tire hiss out its life in a deep, jagged pothole.

She pulled in a long breath and let it out slow. She could handle this.

Reaching below the dash, she popped the hood latch, then hauled the jack out from under the front seat. Setting it just behind the rapidly expiring tire, she set the handle and started cranking, ignoring the itch that prickled between her shoulder blades as the sun leached sweat from her skin. The car rose, then rose some more. Then it shifted sideways, groaned like a tipping cow, and slammed back onto the ground, its wounded tire splayed at a hideously unnatural angle.

This was no ordinary flat tire.

Charlie knelt in the dust, staring at the crippled car. What now? She was in the middle of nowhere, with a screwdriver, a roll of duct tape, and a 1978 Celica hatchback that looked as if euthanasia would be the only humane solution.

She pressed the heels of her hands into her eye sockets to push back the tears. She wasn't scared. She really wasn't. That couldn't be her heart pounding. Couldn't be. It was… it was…

Hoofbeats.

Hoofbeats, drumming the road behind her. She

turned to see a Stetson-topped silhouette approaching, dark against the setting sun. Lurching to her feet, she fell back against the car as a horse and rider skidded to a stop six feet away, gravel pinging off the car's rear bumper.

The sun kept the horseman's features in shadow, but Charlie could see he was long-boned and rangy, with pale eyes glimmering under a battered gray hat. She could almost hear the eerie whistle of a spaghetti Western soundtrack emanating from the rocky landscape behind him. She'd have been scared except one corner of his thin lips kept twitching, threatening to break into a smile as he looked her up and down.

It had to be her outfit. Saddle Up Western Wear called it "Dude Couture," but she was starting to think "Dude Torture" would be more appropriate. The boots were so high-heeled and pointy-toed she could barely drive in them, let alone walk, and she was tempted to follow local tradition and upend them on a fencepost for buzzard bait. Then there was the elaborately fringed jacket and the look-at-me-I'm-a-cowgirl shirt with its oversized silver buttons. She cursed the perky Saddle Up salesgirl for the fourteenth time that day and straightened up, squaring her shoulders.

"Whoa," the rider said, shifting his weight as the horse danced in place. "Easy there, Honey."

"I'm not your honey." She tossed her head and her dark hair flared up like a firecracker, then settled back into its customary spiky shag. The horse pranced backward a few steps, then stilled, twitching with restless energy.

"I know. Easy, Honey," the rider repeated, patting

the horse's neck. "Tupelo Honey. That's her name," he explained.

"Oh." Charlie looked up at the animal's rolling eyes and flaring nostrils and blushed for the first time in fifteen years. "I thought you meant me."

"Nope. The horse. So you might want to calm down. You're making her nervous, and she's liable to toss me again." Honey pitched her head up, prancing nervously in place as he eased back on the reins. "It's her first time."

"Her first time," Charlie repeated blankly.

"First time under saddle," he said. "Doing just fine, too." He bent down to fondle the horse's mane. "Doing just dandy," he crooned softly.

Charlie watched him rotate his fingers in tiny circles, rubbing the horse's copper-colored pelt. Honey's long-lashed eyes drifted shut as she heaved a hard sigh and loosened her muscles, cocking one hind leg.

"Niiiice," the rider purred. Charlie felt like she'd interrupted an intimate encounter.

"Sorry." Dammit, she was blushing again. "I'm trying to get to Latigo Ranch. My car broke down." She gestured toward the crippled Celica.

"Latigo? You're already there," he said. He swung one arm in a slow half-circle to encompass the surrounding landscape. "This is it. You a friend of Sandi's or something?"

"A customer," she said. Sandi Givens was listed as "your hostess" in the glossy dude ranch brochure that lay on the Celica's front seat.

He straightened in the saddle and widened his eyes. "You came all this way for Mary Kay?"

"Mary Kay?" Charlie shook her head. "No way. They

do animal testing. I came out here to do some research on horse whispering." She attempted a smile. "I'm a grad student. Psychology."

The rider bunched the reins in his fist and backed the horse a step or two. The horse moved cautiously, one foot at a time, nodding her head and laying back her ears. "Well, Sandi could sure use a shrink, but she's not home. And don't let her tell you she knows anything about horses. Whispering or otherwise."

Charlie shrugged. "Well, duh. She's just the hostess."

"Hostess of what?"

"The dude ranch. I'm going to a Nate Shawcross clinic."

The cowboy narrowed his eyes. With his battered hat and the two-day growth of stubble on his chin, he bore an uncanny resemblance to the young Clint Eastwood. That eerie, fluttering whistle pierced her subconscious again.

"Nate Shawcross doesn't do clinics," he said.

"Yes, he does. I have a reservation." She set her fists on her hips and squared her shoulders. "Is there some kind of problem?"

"Kind of." He leaned forward and pointed a thumb at his own chest. "Because I'm Nate Shawcross, and I don't know a damned thing about any clinic."

Charlie stood stunned, her mouth hanging open. "But… but I'm Charlie Banks. From Rutgers. I came all the way from New Jersey. My boss sent a deposit."

"To Sandi, I guess," he said. He looked down and fiddled with the reins. When he lifted his head, a muscle in his jaw was pulsing and his gray eyes glistened. He swallowed and looked back down at his hands. "Sandi's

my girlfriend," he finally said. "She up and left a week ago. Went to Denver. I guess that makes her my ex-girlfriend." He shook his head, still looking down at the reins. "Sorry. She didn't tell me anything about this."

"I'm supposed to stay here for three weeks," Charlie sputtered. "And my boss expects me to come back with enough notes for a paper. There's a conference..." She shook her head and blinked fast, pushing back tears. "I got lost, and now the car's broken down and..." A single tear welled up in one eye and she flicked it away, praying he hadn't seen it. She was angry, not scared, but she always cried when she was mad. And the madder she got, the harder she cried. It made her look weak, and she didn't want to look weak in front of this stupid cowboy.

Because that's what he was—a cowboy. No matter what the brochure said about "horse whisperers," the man in front of her was a cowboy.

And she didn't like cowboys.

She'd tried to explain that to Sadie Tate, but Sadie really didn't care what Charlie liked.

Three days earlier, Charlie had parked her butt in an orange vinyl chair and devoted a solid half-hour to convincing Sadie Tate that the trip to Latigo Ranch was a bad idea.

The orange chair was part of the psychology department's sixties vibe—a decorating concept as attractive and up-to-date as Sadie herself. The woman looked like an advertisement for "What Not to Wear" in her shapeless grey sweater and high-water pants.

"So you want me to spend the summer on a dude

ranch, harassing innocent animals with a bunch of cowboys." Charlie grimaced. "Please. I'm begging you. Don't make me do this."

"But it's perfect." Sadie's nasal voice meshed perfectly with her appearance. "You love animals. And this is valuable field research." She pushed her heavy glasses up the long slope of her nose and glanced down at the research proposal on her desk. "You'll be assessing the parallels between the training techniques of Western livestock managers and the non-verbal cues with which humans communicate their wants and needs."

Charlie snorted. "You can't fool me with your academic double-talk, Tate. I know what a Western Livestock Manager is. It's a *cowboy*." She shoved the glossy brochure under Sadie's nose, tapping one crimson fingernail on a color photo of a man in Wrangler jeans and a Stetson. "I'm a PETA member in good standing, Sadie. That's "People for the Ethical Treatment of Animals." I won't 'bust a bronc,' and I don't want to deal with anyone who does." She sighed. "Can't we just experiment on a few more freshmen instead?"

"Times have changed, Charlie," Sadie said, dismissing her last question with an imperious wave of her hand. "They're not called 'cowboys' any more. They're called 'horse whisperers.' They use non-verbal cues to communicate with another species. They soothe them and gain their confidence by mimicking the body language the animals use to communicate with their own kind. It's exactly the sort of thing we need to understand."

Charlie sighed. Her summer was ruined, but she'd stand on her head and whistle Dixie for Sadie Tate if she had to. Sadie was the only professor who'd been

interested when Charlie shopped around for grad schools. The others figured out that her choice of psychology as a field of study was an afterthought. She'd majored in biology with an eye toward veterinary school, but she'd never make it with her mediocre grades. She'd spent too much time at PETA protests and not enough at her desk.

At least a degree in psychology would lead to some kind of meaningful work. No way was Charlie going to end up like her mother, sacrificing her life to making a living in a succession of dead-end jobs. Waitress. Receptionist. Hostess.

Mom.

Charlie knew her mother loved her, but being saddled with single motherhood at seventeen had been the equivalent of a life sentence to New Jersey's minimum wage Gulag. Mona Banks could have escaped, but she'd saved every penny she earned for Charlie's education. That's why she was still waitressing herself half to death on the night shift at the All-American Diner, still pushing her only daughter to succeed at something, anything. *There'll be time enough for fun later, after you get your education,* she said. *Make some sacrifices.*

But cowboys?

That was going too far.

"Do you realize what you're asking me to do?" Charlie demanded. "You're asking me to spend half my summer with men who make their living subjugating helpless animals. Men who think getting ground into the dirt by angry bulls is the ultimate proof of manhood. Who swagger around in chaps and cowboy hats, chewing tobacco and looking for 'buckle bunnies'."

"Exactly," Sadie said. "I'm glad you have such an accurate grasp of the concept. Your flight leaves in three days."

"Flight?" Charlie blanched. "Oh, God, Sadie. Don't make me fly. I hate flying. Can I drive? Please, let me drive. I'll take my own car."

Sadie smiled and slit her eyes like a satisfied cat. "Why, certainly, Charlie. I'm so glad you've agreed to go."

Charlie cursed herself silently. She'd fallen right into Sadie's trap.

"But you'll need to leave tomorrow since you're driving," Sadie said. "It's at least a two-day trip, and I arranged for you to arrive early in order to receive some individual instruction."

Individual instruction? That meant Charlie would be on her own—all alone with a cowboy who would no doubt try to tell her what to do. She pointed a finger at Sadie and took a deep breath, preparing to plunge into verbal battle.

Sadie stared back, calm as a Buddha, and Charlie felt her anger fade into hopelessness.

"I need to pack," she mumbled, and slouched out of the office.

Reaching the doorway, she turned. "But if they abuse their horses, I'll…"

"You'll observe and report," Sadie said, raising her eyebrows and stabbing the air with a ball-point pen. "As a student of psychology, you will maintain an objective perspective and will eschew any personal involvement with your subjects."

"Yeah, that's just what I was about to say," Charlie muttered.

"Good." Sadie shoved the pen behind her ear and nodded sharply. "I'm glad we understand each other."

Charlie's mother tossed a plastic-wrapped package into Charlie's suitcase.

"Here," she said. "I got you these."

Charlie scanned the model on the cover. "Mom, these are granny panties," she said. "Yuck." She flipped through her underwear drawer and pulled out a pair of polka-dotted hi-cuts and a matching bra. "I wear pretty stuff."

Her mom flipped her waist-length gray hair over her shoulder and peered into the drawer, picking through the satin and lace pretties. Pulling out a flimsy scrap of lace, she held it at arms' length and eyed it as if she'd found the decaying corpse of a dead trout.

"What is *this*?"

"A thong," Charlie said, snatching it out of her hand. "It's so you don't get panty lines." She tossed it into the suitcase, but her mom immediately snatched it out and flipped it back into the drawer.

"Don't you have any *regular* underwear?"

"This *is* regular," Charlie said, holding up a scanty bikini panty with lace panels in the side. "I like pretty things, Mom. It's not a big deal."

"How do you expect to be taken seriously in your career when you dress like that?"

"I'm not going around in my underwear, Mom," Charlie said, rolling her eyes. "It just makes me feel good to be pretty underneath, you know? And I'll be wearing jeans and stuff the whole time. I need a little pick-me-up."

"Just don't let anyone *else* pick you up," her mother said.

"They're cowboys, Mom," Charlie said. "I told you. I'm not going to fall for some dumb bronco buster."

"I didn't think I'd fall for a football jock, either." Her mom sat down on the side of the bed. "But it happened. And you know what it got me."

Charlie sighed. What the football jock "got" her mother was Charlie herself. Then he moved away a year later, never to be heard from again. Charlie barely even knew what her father looked like. If she passed him on the street, she'd probably walk on by—and he'd probably run away. He'd never paid a dime in child support.

"Just don't get involved with anybody until you finish your education."

Charlie sighed. "I know."

"Because men are different. They can just walk away, even from their own child." She slipped the panty package back into the suitcase. "Men don't love like we do. Just remember that."

Charlie sighed. "Maybe they're not all like that," she said. "Maybe there are a few good ones out there."

"Maybe," her mom said. "But it's not worth the risk. Not for you. Not now."

She set her hands on Charlie's shoulders and looked her daughter in the eye. Charlie looked up at the ceiling and offered a quick prayer for patience, then met her mother's gaze.

"What's The Plan?" her mother asked.

It was their own private catechism, and Charlie had the answers down pat.

"Get my degree."

"And after that?"

Charlie sighed. "Get meaningful work. Work that fulfills me. Work that helps people."

"Right." Charlie's mother patted her shoulders twice and beamed at her. "Just keep your eyes on the prize, and you'll be fine."

"Okay," Charlie said.

"And keep everyone else's eyes off your underwear."

"No problem." Charlie grinned. "They're cowboys. I'm not interested, and anyway, I've heard they only have eyes for sheep."

Available September 2010

By Carolyn Brown

Beau hasn't got a lick of sense when it comes to women

Everything hunky rancher "Lucky" Beau Luckadeau touches turns to gold—except relationships. Spitfire Milli Torres can mend a fence, pull a calf, or shoot a rattlesnake between the eyes. When Milli shows up to help out at the Lazy Z ranch, she's horrified to find that Beau's her nearest neighbor—the very man she'd hoped never to lay eyes on again. If Beau ever figures out what really happened on that steamy Louisiana night when they first met, there'll be the devil to pay…

Praise for Carolyn Brown:

"Engaging characters, humorous situations, and a bumpy romance… Carolyn Brown will keep you reading until the very last page." —Romantic Times

"Carolyn Brown's rollicking sense of humor asserts itself on every page." —Scribes World

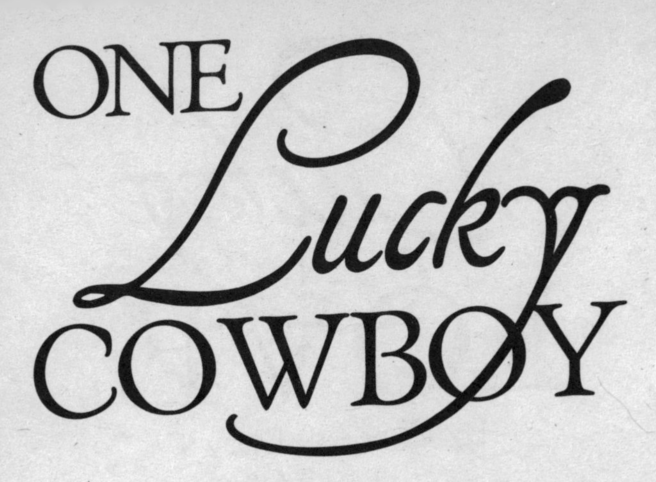

By Carolyn Brown

No big blond cowboy is going to intimidate this spitfire!

If Slade Luckadeau thinks he can run Jane Day off his ranch, he's got cow chips for brains. She's winning every argument, and he's running out of fights to pick. But when trouble with a capital "T" threatens Jane *and* the Double L Ranch, suddenly it's Slade's heart that's in the most danger of all.

Praise for *Lucky in Love*:

"I enjoyed this book so much that I plan to rope myself some more of Carolyn Brown and her books. Lucky in Love *is a must read!"* —Cheryl's Book Nook

"This is one of those rare books where every person in it comes alive... as they share wit, wisdom and love." —The Romance Studio

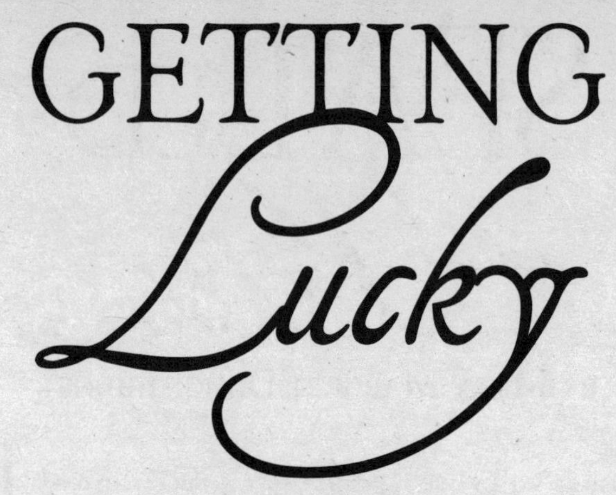

BY CAROLYN BROWN

Griffin Luckadeau is one stubborn cowboy…

And Julie Donovan is one hotheaded schoolteacher who doesn't let anybody push her around. When Griffin thinks his new neighbor is scheming to steal his ranch out from under him, he's more than willing to cross horns. Their look-alike daughters may be best friends, but until these two Texas hotheads admit it's fate that brought them together, running from the inevitable is only going to bring them a double dose of miserable…

Praise for Carolyn Brown:

"A delight to read." —Booklist

"Engaging characters, humorous situations, and a bumpy romance… Carolyn Brown will keep you reading until the very last page." —Romantic Times

"Carolyn Brown's rollicking sense of humor asserts itself on every page." —Scribes World

SEALED *with a Kiss*

BY MARY MARGRET DAUGHTRIDGE

THERE'S ONLY ONE THING HE CAN'T HANDLE, AND ONE WOMAN WHO CAN HELP HIM...

Jax Graham is a rough, tough Navy SEAL, but when it comes to taking care of his four-year-old son after his ex-wife dies, he's completely clueless. Family therapist Pickett Sessoms can help, but only if he'll let her.

When Jax and his little boy get trapped by a hurricane, Picket takes them in against her better judgment. When the situation turns deadly, Pickett discovers what it means to be a SEAL, and Jax discovers that even a hero needs help sometimes.

"A heart-touching story that will keep you smiling and cheering for the characters clear through to the happy ending." —Romantic Times

"A well-written romance...simultaneously tender and sensuous." —Booklist

SEALED *with a* *Promise*

BY MARY MARGRET DAUGHTRIDGE

NAVY SEAL CALEB DELAUDE IS AS DEADLY AS HE IS CHARMING.

Professor Emmie Caddington's quiet intelligence and quirky personality intrigue him. When he discovers that her personal connections can get him close to the man he's vowed to kill, will their budding relationship be nothing more than a means to revenge…or is she the key to his salvation?

Praise for *SEALed with a Kiss*:

"This story delivers in a huge way." —Romantic Times

"A wonderful story that will have readers experiencing a whirlwind of emotions and culminating with an awesome scene that will have your pulse pounding." —Romance Junkies

"What an incredibly powerful book! I laughed and sniffled, was turned on and turned inside out." —Queue My Review

Romeo, Romeo

BY ROBIN KAYE

Rosalie Ronaldi doesn't have a domestic bone in her body...

All she cares about is her career, so she survives on take-out and dirty martinis, keeps her shoes under the dining room table, her bras on the shower curtain rod, and her clothes on the couch.

Nick Romeo is every woman's fantasy—tall, dark, handsome, rich, really good in bed, AND he loves to cook and clean...

He says he wants an independent woman, but when he meets Rosalie, all he wants to do is take care of her. Before long, he's cleaned up her apartment, stocked her refrigerator, and adopted her dog.

So what's the problem? Just a little matter of mistaken identity, corporate theft, a hidden past in juvenile detention, and one big nosy Italian family too close for comfort...

"Kaye's debut is a delightfully fun, witty romance, making her a writer to watch." —*Booklist*

978-1-4022-1339-7 • $6.99 U.S. / $8.99 CAN

Too Hot to Handle

BY ROBIN KAYE

He sure would love to have a woman to take care of…

To Dr. Mike Flynn, there's nothing like housework to help a guy relax, while artist Annabelle Ronaldi doesn't have a domestic bone in her body.

When they meet at her sister's wedding, Mike is sure this is the woman he wants to take care of forever. While Mike sets to work wooing Annabelle, she becomes determined to sniff out the truth of the convoluted family secret that's threatening to turn both their lives upside down.

PRAISE FOR *TOO HOT TO HANDLE*:

"Entertaining, funny, and steaming hot." —*Book Loons*

"A sensational story that sizzles with sex appeal." —*The Long and Short of It*

"Witty and enchanting." —*Love Romance Passion*

"From the brilliant first chapter until the heartwarming finale, I was hooked!" —*Crave More Romance*

Breakfast in Bed

BY ROBIN KAYE

He'd be Mr. Perfect, if he wasn't a perfect mess...

Rich Ronaldi is *almost* the complete package—smart, sexy, great job—but his girlfriend dumps him for being such a slob, and Rich swears he'll learn to cook and clean to win her back. Becca Larson is more than willing to help him master the domestic arts, but she'll be damned if she'll do it so he can start cooking in another woman's kitchen—or bedroom...

PRAISE FOR ROBIN KAYE:

"Robin Kaye has proved herself a master of romantic comedy," —*Armchair Interviews*

"Ms. Kaye has style—it's easy, it's fun, and it has every–thing that you need to get caught up in a wonderful romance." —*Erotic Horizon*

"A fresh and fun voice in romantic comedy." —*All About Romance*

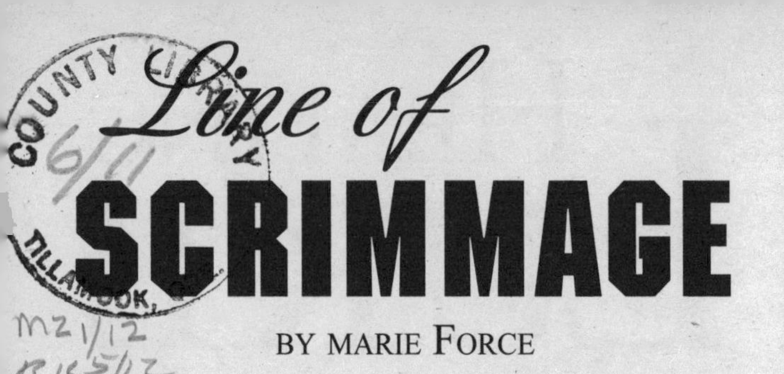

BY MARIE FORCE

SHE'S GIVEN UP ON HIM AND MOVED ON...

Susannah finally has peace, calm, a sedate life, and a no-surprises man. Marriage to football superstar Ryan Sanderson was a whirlwind, but Susanna got sick of playing second fiddle to his team. With their divorce just a few weeks away, she's already planning her wedding with her new fiancé.

HE'S FINALLY FIGURED OUT WHAT'S REALLY IMPORTANT TO HIM. IF ONLY IT'S NOT TOO LATE...

Ryan has just ten days to convince his soon-to-be-ex-wife to give him a second chance. His career is at its pinnacle, but in the year of their separation, Ryan's come to realize it doesn't mean anything without Susannah...

978-1-4022-1424-0 • $6.99 U.S. / $8.99 CAN

Healing Luke

BY Beth Cornelison

She can't escape her past...

Occupational therapist Abby Stanford is on vacation alone, her self-confidence shattered by her fiancé's betrayal. Romance is the last thing on Abby's mind—until she meets the brooding and enigmatic Luke…

He won't face his future…

Scarred by a horrific accident, former heartthrob Luke Morgan is certain his best days are behind him. Abby knows how to help him recover, but for Luke his powerful attraction to her only serves as a harsh reminder of the man he used to be. Abby is Luke's first glimmer of hope since the accident, but can she heal his heart before Luke breaks hers?

"Beth Cornelison writes intriguing, emotionally charged stories that will keep you turning the pages straight through to the end. Fabulous entertainment!" —Susan Wiggs

"Healing Luke *is a breath of fresh air for romance fans... a stirring novel and a five star read!"*
—Crave More Romance